ROCKINGHORSE

Also by Yoram Kaniuk

Adam Resurrected
The Acrophile
Himmo, King of Jerusalem

ROCKINGHORSE

YORAM KANIUK

Translated from the Hebrew
by Richard Flantz

Harper & Row, Publishers
New York, Hagerstown, San Francisco, London

This work was first published in Israel under the title of Sus^cets.

FIRST EDITION

Designed by Janice Stern

Library of Congress Cataloging in Publication Data

Kaniuk, Yoram.
  Rockinghorse.
  Translation of Sus^cets.
  I. Title.
PZ4.K165Ro   [PJ5054.K326]   892.4'3'6   76–5546
ISBN 0–06–012245–5

77 78 79 80 81 10 9 8 7 6 5 4 3 2 1

To my daughters

Writing is but a guided dream.

BORGES

First Make thy Will.

ANON., OPENING OF "OFFICIAL
GUIDE TO VOYAGERS TO THE
NEW WORLD" IN THE LATE
SIXTEENTH CENTURY

The English translation of the Hebrew
word *sussetz* is "rockinghorse."

1

I'm not sure I even wanted to come back to Tel Aviv. There were plenty of reasons not to. People laughed, asked for what. My doubts left me on boarding the ship and sailing the ruffled sea in the wake of a hurricane. The spume left behind by that savage eruption was sudden, the ship swayed. Homeward bound, I thought. People off to places they came from, to places they're going to. Water to water. Dust to blue mountains on some invisible horizon. I fell to drowsing, and so knew that days were passing, and nights into nights. Arriving, a city bowed at me. This was after days at sea.

Before this was New York. So I was going. For what? Mira asked me to take my daughter to school. Get acquainted with the teacher. Naomi was in first grade, it was the end of the first term. Mira said, I've had this splitting headache all morning, whenever I shut my eyes I see fire. What she thought was: The walk to the school, and sitting in Naomi's classroom, ought to cool him down a bit. The fury seeping through me those days. Months now I'd been tearing canvases, smashing frames, yelling, cursing myself, the world, guilty, not guilty. Refusing to see people. Banging down the phone on Mr. Zwiegel, who rang every morning at exactly ten-thirty, I set my watch by his call. Take the receiver out of Mira's hands and say, or yell, sometimes: I'm all washed up, Zwiegel, if I had anything in me before, there's nothing now.

1

A gentle soul, Mr. Zwiegel. He lets me yell myself out into the phone and then he says: You're impetuous, Aminadav, you're hot-tempered. Come over to the gallery, we'll have coffee, and talk. Stop acting like a child. Don't you see what a beautiful day it is out? And I say: Dreary skies, clouds obscuring the face of the heart, ugly as all hell, Zwiegel. I breathe the charming smile on his lips, the coffee he drank that morning, the soft-boiled egg, three minutes, eaten with a pink plastic spoon, the smell of fresh printers' ink on the invitations for the next grand opening. The city that hangs for him from his roof. He sees pigeons and spires and towers and doesn't see ecological holocaust or population explosion. I feel sick and bang down the phone. Every morning at exactly ten-thirty.

Sometimes the sky really is blue like Mr. Zwiegel. Especially in the fall, two months ago, but mostly in your musings. Two months ago, for his sixtieth birthday, I bought him the collected works of Thomas Mann, soft-cover, twenty-two dollars.

He sat and read to me from Lotte in Weimar. How Charlotte Kestner came to Weimar to fish up her youth from an image of so romantic a story. Unbearable, I said to Zwiegel, though I liked it, but inside me a demon of hostility already nestled. And he was a kind of posture of a man, like straw on the back of a soft chair, reminding me of Father, with Goethe. I felt like kicking anyone from Goethe's climate. But I have nothing to say to him. He wants me to come. We'll have coffee and *kuchen*, I'll bring pictures, we'll hang them, for whom, for what? We'll frame them, and we'll stand looking at the wall and argue where to hang the tree, where the woman. I bang the phone down on the base. Mr. Zwiegel's traveled with me a long way, the reward could have come, I was told by a collector named Dr. Sheffey. What dreadful days. And the pain, dripping like nectar. I have nothing to bring. I don't want coffee and *kuchen*. I want to rip things, and lie in bed, wrap myself up in myself, and cry. The sweet joy of defeat. And these tears from deep inside me, tears my father never cried when he smashed his violin and waited for me in every corner with his sweet smile and gentle manner and said: Why don't you smash your violin, Aminadav? Meaning the painting I thought I had in me. From Tel Aviv he wrote me nine words every week: Shalom Aminadav, how are you, I'm well, Love, Father. Every week. Ten years. Perhaps he had held me too close.

That morning I didn't get out of bed. Bundled up under the blue woolen blankets, I waited for Mr. Zwiegel's call. He rang, I set my watch. After that there was the taste of Mira in the blankets her mother had secretly given us. I insulted Mira. I told her that she'd started living through me and that I was washed up, disintegrated, only a shadow. That I'd disappointed her. Banalities. I could have, or not, but I'd given in, the surrender was right here inside me. Why don't you stroke the vanquished hero. They've all betrayed me, Mira, I said to her, and was able to feel absolute contempt and absolute pity for myself and to be a corner of the man I once, like many others, wanted to be. There's no one to stand by me, I said to her. Everything's ruined, you can start picking up the fragments. My voice was melodramatic during the sharp moments. When I was young I went to the beach after my first sea voyage, and stood watching the salt beating at the walls of the esplanade in rain-lashed Tel Aviv, and I said to myself: Always be yourself. So Socratic. The sea answered me with the roar of an eruption and I had this intense thought that I was one against the sea, or the astonishing sunset, or the mighty forces which are also God in disguise, or not in disguise.

She didn't take up the challenge. She put on a kettle, made tea, dressed Naomi and took her to school. She came back and sat on the edge of the bed. To look at the lover of her youth. The shame of it. Spouting bitterness at her. She didn't see my life as a failure, and was willing to enlighten me with exhilarating calm this wintry morning.

Across the street: closed windows. The roof of the house opposite swarms with pigeons, like the view from Mr. Zwiegel's window. A faded flag drooping from a window with a torn blind. Eyes peeping out at the street below. I hear the slam of brakes and know the light has turned red. Sometimes I think that if someone gets killed at those stupid traffic lights down there, it'll be a kind of recompense for me. I imagine my death, and someone demonstrating it. She doesn't understand why I don't smile or laugh. It

3

isn't all over, this isn't the end, she says. She doesn't know what to say and keeps making up things from The New York Times Book Review. She finds summaries of plots, great melodramas in so many hundred words, and they're all just like my story. So she says. Trying to find hackneyed words for the difficult quivering, seeping things. Run away perhaps, and then stand there like a fart, knowing from here there can be no more flight. Yes, to flee. Mira doesn't understand why flee.

In the afternoon I took my daughter to Riverside Drive to buy The New York Times. I hadn't bought it in the morning, I'd been in blankets and Mira had taken Naomi to school. I got up, and Naomi's eyes glittered. Mounted on my shoulders in a red snow-suit, her face lashed by the wind. The street snow-covered, a fierce wind from the river. Like a canyon rimmed with big houses. My daughter growling like a bear. I kicked at a snowball that was turning black. An old man, very tall, with flushed cheeks, was shoveling snow outside 410 West. He asked if I had a light. Then he stopped shoveling and leaned his spade against the wall. He blew into his hands and vapor curled from his mouth. I gave Naomi the Zippo. Mounted on my back like a horseman in red, growling like a bear, she lit the old man's cigarette. The man smiled at her, twisted up his face and went moo. He thinks I'm a cow, said my daughter, I'm not a cow. He didn't know who Naomi was, she looked like a doll, growling like a bear, his eyes red with whiskey, his mouth small and narrow, thinking a girl-doll was a cow. He didn't know how cute and how clever, in the first grade, reads Dr. Seuss, knows addition and subtraction and already possesses, I know this with no great joy, the sad wisdom of orphans. She could easily become cruel, or overmerciful, looking for a wall to lean on, pushing through the world as if it were a corridor. A black dog, with cropped hair, sniffed at my shoes and attached himself to me. I shooed him away. My daughter wanted to get down, she pressed me with her legs and said, Daddy, really Daddy, to be his, she said she wanted to, but I couldn't adopt a lover.

My daughter cried. We came home with The New York Times, glowing from the razor-sharp wind that came from the river. Mira refused to reopen our discussion about the essence of failure, and closeted herself in the kitchen. She was making ravioli, to a recipe she'd got from Mrs. Hershaw on the seventh floor. Her husband had never been found. All that mourning there. Mira sat up days and nights, in vigil, and said he'd come back. They brought in a fortuneteller who said she clearly saw Mrs. Hershaw's husband walking somewhere in vague spaces, heading homeward, but he never arrived even though they paid her by the hour. Naomi so lovely on the carpet with teddy bears in the dim twilit apartment. Mrs. Hershaw's windows were shuttered, the tea that had been drunk up there, the dreadful things she'd said about life. There, in the dread of those who never return. The smell of ravioli filled the apartment. Naomi, among the teddy bears on the carpet, reading Dr. Seuss. And laughing. A sound like bells.

I left the house and went to the bank on the corner of Eighty-sixth and Broadway. To draw out my savings. I hoped the dog wouldn't run after me. I saw him a way off wagging his tail in the snow. To be an abandoned dog in winter, in the snow, like Mr. Hershaw. Does he like it. While she watched me from her shabby window as if her man was coming home, the one who never returned. I escaped her and the dog behind buildings, and it was cold. Delancey Street was swarming with people. Colors sharp this fierce winter's day. Signs in Hebrew and Yiddish. A market that might have been a consolation to me on other days of homesickness, or a coming out from within yourself and back in again. I bought a small gas range, with three burners, a pressure cooker, a car and a toaster. I can't stand toast and Coca-Cola. I also bought an automatic can opener you affix to a wall, I bought a white Ford, a 1962 model with push-button windows. I asked to have it all sent to the Zion, sailing tomorrow at dawn. I liked the Ford. The lighter still worked, what did I know about cars, the man had said, Look, even the lighter works. I bought a ticket for the passage. They said it was too late to send and buy things. I said it's winter and all that, and how many people were sailing anyway, and why not. They said well all right. Second-class, make it fast. Have the car packed too. A short man helped me. His eyes were like the things twisting inside me: things dark, maybe dead.

5

He said he'd lived in Israel, but he had fled the place. A long time ago. Austerity, everyone ate shoes and shoelaces, and he had no shoes to eat. Dov Yoseph's time. No homeland. No language to speak. Dreaming about something that no longer exists. Ah, in Vilna there had been things. What do you know about it. A Kant and Hegel circle. One thing after another. Among the Hebrew and Yiddish signs. He also said, Here's Avraham Avivi, electric goods. A Yemenite from Tel Aviv, made a match with a fat American woman, certificates and citizenship of the U.S.A of America. Examinations with a lawyer who wrote the answers on his fingernails, who were the first presidents and what was the tea party. Now he sells things with Israeli voltage. Two hundred and twenty volts. And television sets with European bands. Why don't you buy a set, you know you're allowed to bring one in. Thanks a lot. What would I do with it. I'll see things live. I want to bury myself. Do you have holy soil. He didn't. The man with the broken heart who helped me said that no one returns to Israel except the beaten, the escapers. Not him. He'll die forsaken in streets of snow. He knew he'll always be what his father was. The chutzpah of it, creating a state for Jews where you eat shoelaces. I said to him, Everything's different now, my mother wrote me. The newspapers say so. He didn't believe. He said, This stove's good business. And the toaster. I hate toast, I said, and thought how I loved Mr. Zwiegel with his blue sky and his beautiful day Aminadav, come over to the gallery, we'll hang paintings and have coffee and *kuchen.* The man paid for everything, packed everything. I gave him my money as if it were somebody else's.

At the consulate they were polite as usual. The girl behind the counter was ugly, from need of having her problems solved. She took her time filling in my forms, asked embarrassing questions. She smiled when I said I was married and had a daughter. As if to say: They're all alike. She might have agreed to embrace this failure that I was, as if I deserved it. She signed the forms and the consul came in with a pipe and a smile and asked, Why, Mr. Sussetz. I told him that as a consul he should be wishing me bon voyage instead of asking why. If there's one thing I detest more than myself, it's consuls. Once I came here for an Independence

Day party. Consuls with names out of a biblical zoo, whispering dirty jokes in German and drinking Israeli wine. I told them what I thought of them. The miserable girl licked an envelope, put the papers inside, and I was filed away like any dog in this city.

The snow was pent up inside the heavy clouds now. Not falling. Black sky. Evening. Glorious lights like Christmas with sacred clowns with white beards and red clothes, to distribute dreams to children awaiting salvation from chimneys. Music and cabs bringing the city's elect to restaurants with year-old frozen steaks hanging from hooks. Houses, one rising over the other in a kind of frenzy. Drunk on the light. The subway below emitting heat through gratings in the streets. Smoke mounting from the frozen earth. High buildings above me all the time. The German of consuls in my ears because of a girl licking an envelope. Thinking: Samson in a Brooks Brothers suit speaking about Israel's Far Eastern policy on Taiwan, the China Straits and Guam. Should we support Guam or Upper Volta. Tomorrow at the U.N. conference on algae he'll rebut an attack by three scientists from Uganda who are working for the Soviets. The worries they have. My godfather was Chaim Nachman Bialik. Do I fuck in anapestic pentameter. They'll rebut Sir Alec Irving, the shrewd antagonist from Great Britain. Two Jewish women from Hadassah, wearing hats with fruits and vegetables on their brims, will sit in the gallery clapping hands in turn.

I walked through the streets I've loved. The black snow lay like bored dogs. Some stranger I didn't know, in my body, had bought a white '62–model Ford with a lighter that still worked, a boat ticket, and had fixed a passport, as if it were important and could earn me a place on some shelf. I heard my voice speaking to the ugly girl or to the cardboard consul, Mr. Tamir, or Alon, or Shamir, with a German accent, Goethe's works in his inside pocket and the Bible in his shorts for quoting a verse from the Psalms in minced speech. She spoke to me, someone else answered. I didn't know if I was fleeing to. Or from. Why was I going. I wanted to lay myself down on an operating table, on my back, neon light glaring above me. The surgeon is me. With a knife in his hand. He who is I sees my insides which are mine.

In the evening I went to Naomi's school. Arrows hanging in the long narrow corridor, leading to Grade 1B. Not looking to either side, a lone father, something embarrassing about this, going into the classroom, forcing my body into a seat. Tomorrow I'm sailing away in a ship. There'll be sea. There won't be teachers wife daughter. All the things that there won't be tomorrow. I walk over to a little chair. Sit and stare at the walls decorated with children's drawings. Around me a lot of chattering women in hats. Drawings in crayon, chalk, pencil. Charts. Sentences in large capitals, MOMMY DADDY I LOVE MOMMY (DADDY) MY COUNTRY 'TIS OF THEE IN GOD WE TRUST. I look at a chart with names on it. Forty columns. The children's names in blue and red. Naomi is listed in the last bench, second row, right-hand seat. I look at my knees. In blue corduroy trousers. I'm sitting in Naomi's seat. What she has the power to do to me. To plant me on her seat. Her little ass rubs against this wood. Five hours a day. With lunch and recesses, and the boys looking at her. She will be a woman who has fixed me in her seat.

The bespectacled teacher rescued me from my thoughts. She had a suddenly sexy body with big spectacles. She spoke to us. Her voice was soft, and grating too. Precise, slow, stressing each syllable. I know the voices of nursery teachers and schoolteachers. No signs of feeling, only punctuation signs. Grammar instead of life. She'll tell a story about knives and forks. Her face is really small, with a snub nose. Her glasses are too big. Her body doesn't belong with her face, her glasses, her toothpaste voice. She too is out of place. Despite the stresses and the phony voice. That was how I wanted it. A girl from the Ziegfeld Follies. She put on big glasses and smeared her vocal cords with Colgate toothpaste with extra chlorophyll. She plays the part of a schoolteacher in an MGM movie. The lion roars and she bursts out of the cake, puts on her glasses, and speaks to people about the responsibilities of parents. Soon she'll start dancing and her clothes will drop from her one by one, apart from a shimmering little triangle between her legs, which she'll leave there, and sing Diamonds are a girl's best friend. The mothers listen longingly. I read their dreams. Let my son be Einstein or John Wayne. The future is written on the

8

walls, MY COUNTRY 'TIS OF THEE. Grandsons with houses on Long Island. The old bones will live again.

If you knew Susie like I know Susie, oh, oh . . . That way it'll all be natural. Outside the snow's piling up by the sidewalks. Inside it's hot. The teacher's speaking. The teacher didn't strip. She didn't sing. She spoke about our little darlings.

Her voice had no warmth, and was equally distant from everyone there. It turned an audience of mothers (and one father) into a single body. Maybe because she spoke like a professional radio announcer. She spoke of the teaching method she used. Soon, she said, they would be moving on from the Cuisenaire rods to concrete numbers. We, the parents, would have to be prepared to answer questions on arithmetic, spelling and grammar. The apple can fall far from the tree, laziness is a psychic condition, not a physical one, resulting from too much permissiveness. She looked so distressed, so tired after her long journey into the night, by neon light, to face these painted mothers, that perhaps she said this last sentence absent-mindedly.

I filled my pipe, lit it, broke the match into my hand so as not to dirty the floor, and for the first time in two months I think I smiled. Perhaps my lips encompassing the pipe recalled youthful days in the Ziegfeld Follies. White slavery and all that. Girls from the South sold into sex slavery. I read about it in a girlie magazine. Our looks crossed. Her glasses glinted in the deathly neon. In her eyes, through the lenses of her glasses, in the enlarged pupils, I saw a plea.

I considered the plea soberly. Now there was nothing to lose. I considered the plea with an interest that did not lack warmth or pity, I wondered at the distinction I'd made suddenly, or not so suddenly, between a plea as despairing and a plea as an aesthetic entity. Then I thought for a moment how beautiful Goya's execution picture is. And then the mothers got up, each one in turn, approached my teacher, and spoke with her in whispers. They wanted intimate details, classroom secrets. They wanted to know who their kids were, what they were. At home the cord's been cut. The distressed bowed backs bending toward her: Our kids come home, don't tell us who they are.

I know Naomi, my daughter. I want to talk to her about her youth in the Ziegfeld Follies, a Rolls-Royce at the stage door. To speak with her about a stage flooded with lights, eighty wondrous breasts bouncing in the glittering trousers of diamond and whiskey dealers. She looks at me. The question mark I was, with the pipe sending up smoke rings like an Indian seeking peace, thinking of Goya's Execution. I wanted to touch her. I didn't know if we'd be able to discuss the plea as a formal reality or as a human yearning, perhaps even a tragic one. I thought: What can you expect. I extinguished my eyes, took the pipe out of my mouth and started walking toward the door.

Her face repressed fury. Had I dealt her a blow. I went back to my place and waited.

We remain alone. To speak about Naomi. She says things and I nod. In my mouth the pipe looks like the tail of Mickey Mouse in the cartoons. She said Naomi's clever, catches on quickly. Arithmetic. Reads well. Writing. Neat. Making progress in all her studies. I recalled things that are said. Beautiful city, or long street. Man is a social animal, or Who doesn't seek love? They used to tell me: You're a "talented" painter, this picture you've painted, it's something. What's "something"? Nothing. But then she said, in the empty classroom: Sometimes I think Naomi wants something that isn't clear to her. . . . She gets up without permission, walks to the door, stops, looks at the other children, hesitates, and goes back to her seat. Perhaps she wants to be somewhere else and here at one and the same time. And she has a strong personality.

Who doesn't want to, I said. Don't you?

What?

Want to be somewhere else and/or be somewhere else and here at one and the same time.

What kind of a question is that? she tried in precise English. The teacher from the Ziegfeld Follies. To preserve a last vestige of pretense. I didn't have the time (sailing tomorrow) or the *largeur* to play the game according to the rules, of I'm a Taurus and you're an Aquarius, I'm looking for an address so why not, and a hand fumbling inside the blouse to feel her pulse and gauge

10

the response and then shift toward the breast. I said to her that what we have is family, and we're all we have left, and to be somewhere else is always better. And then I added hastily, without giving her time to say anything: Tomorrow Naomi's going to be fatherless and that's the meaning of the sadness.

I didn't say she was sad, she said.

Shall I dance for you, baby? Tomorrow I'm leaving and the sadness will only grow, I said to my teacher with the huge glasses. The teacher's a woman. We'll dance pressed together in a whisper. Trapped in the bitter beam of light from the deathly neon. We're huge in this room to which arrows lead. I knew that what was before me was real, just as sometimes the sun really shines when Mr. Zwiegel calls and says the sun's shining.

We extinguished the light and went out. Wind from the river. A watchman wearing a pistol smiled and growled a greeting. He's waited a long time among the arrows. To close the gate behind us with heavy locks. To put out the lights as if it were the end of the world. We went to a bar and grill and she ordered sherry. I ordered Jack Daniel's without ice, double. She took off her glasses and became soft, maybe bewildered, she spoke about her coat, saying how nice it was. The bar and grill, the people, the drinks, she didn't understand any of it. What's sherry? A wine, a liqueur? She cooks with sherry. Chicken. With potatoes, too. She spoke about her mother. Without glasses. Maybe because before I'd said that all we had was us. She told me she had a Siamese cat called Sam. I said, Naomi has a cat too, and we talked about cats and if you can domesticate them and how fickle they are, ungrateful and hard. She said they're fascinating and stealthy. She said that at Bonwit Teller you can get Japanese lampshades designed by Noguchi, made of rice paper and soft steel hoops. I told her that in Tiberias, where my mother was born, the bride price for a woman like her was a camel with two humps. She wanted to know where you sit on a camel with two humps. I drew it for her on the white paper that covered the table. We ate roast beef with Worcestershire sauce, cucumber salad with vinegar and sugar, and we drank Beaujolais. The waiter placed things on the table as if that was how it was supposed to be. He wasn't playing any games. I said something about the waiter to the teacher, whose name was Peggy. She recalled that she'd once eaten in a French restaurant where there were charming, mustachioed waiters who smelled of eau de Cologne. Once she'd been to Paris. They'd thought she was sexy, she said.

On the TV screen next to the wall a war was being fought soundlessly. Only the barman, in a green vest, wiped glasses and watched. Smoke rose. To my eyes came tears of the many months during which I'd been dying slowly, and she didn't see. I asked her to put on her glasses. I wanted a teacher, not a Ziegfeld girl. Her silk blouse touched her breasts with a fluttering gentleness. We ate mousse fine as silk.

She said she didn't have a dog. Her mother is scared of dogs. They mess up the house, her mother says. I listen and don't listen. My hand inside the blouse. Stirring up everything. I think: Mira, one woman I loved. She says, They dirty the seat covers and you have to take them down to the street three times a day to do their things.

We went up to the apartment from the cab. Her mother in the next room wanted to know what time it was, and afterward, after she knew, she said something grim about life. My teacher went to her mother's room. I opened a yellow cabinet and found a bottle of Cutty Sark. I drank straight from the bottle. I took off my shoes. The carpet was soft and thick and my feet sank into it. I want to ravish the carpet. A savageness welled up in me for all the years I hadn't seen straight. Tomorrow I flee or die. Tears jeweling in my daughter's eyes in a black dress with straps, holding an eyeless teddy bear, crying for her father, my orphan, knowing that her father has entered the circle of eternity, the perpetual cycle of life.

Above the cabinet hung a cross and on it, crucified and tortured with nails, the beautiful God of the sadists. With holes in his hands and blood that looked real sticking to the beam. Above the cross my teacher had hung a Shield of David made from animal bones, I don't know which animal. Above the Shield of David stood a small statuette of Buddha, serene and rotund. Puffed-out cheeks, smiling to himself. Arrogant and humble in the glory of his serenity. To the left of these things, by the window, under a portrait of my teacher, a Yale football pennant. The friends she has. Under this, a candle with a plastic flame. A green curtain and a chair with two lions' heads on its back, one of them broken. Everything brushed and shining. A dread lurking in the room; to be polished night and day.

My teacher came back in a pink robe, her marvelous body touching the robe in all the unexpected places. She brought raisins. Sam wailed by the door and came in. He rubbed up against my legs and waddled off to the kitchen. Someone threw an empty beer can down the staircase. The sound of it falling echoed like a burst of automatic fire inside a tin pipe. Then a piano started playing with a blast of sound. If you knew Susie like I know Susie, oh, oh . . . and Alexander's Ragtime Band. The mother yelled from the next room in a strangled spaghetti voice, If O'Leary doesn't stop, I'll call the police! I thought: Now she'll start stripping to the rhythm, but she walked to the kitchen, fed Sam and went to her mother's room. She came back with a box of chocolates. Later she moved out from under me and said, It must have been hard, I always cry when I shouldn't.

I stroked her long hair, which had slipped free of its pins, and I said it had been very nice. We ate sardines out of a can, with our hands, like they were alive. We devoured them and she said, Take me.

Where to? To where I'm going? Into myself? She didn't answer and we listened to music on the radio. The announcer whispered in a deep voice that came from inside our bones. We were together. She inside me. The broadcaster spoke to us; a storm outside, my dears. What's nicer than to lie in a warm bed, with or without. To bundle up if necessary . . . To listen to soft music and drink Rheingold beer . . . Your quiet, regular breathing reaches me here . . . It's warm here. I listen to the hum of things, between your words. My dears. I know, Oh. Henry called New York Bagdad on the subway. The things that hum below. Inside you all. From you to me, from me to you. Listening . . . Knowing a kind of sorrow without name, inside houses. I want to whisper to you, to you and you, yes, don't worry dear, be brave, you're richer than Rockefeller because you've got everything you need and he doesn't. Zsa Zsa Gabor needs you, you don't need her. O'Neill said that man's born broken. He lives by mending. The grace of God is glue. See yourselves in those secret inner mirrors, shhh. . . .

Peggy laughed in a wild voice, her white teeth gleaming in the neon light winking, outside, over the Brown Inc. record store. Then she said, in a sudden sadness: I have him every night. I know his voice by heart. He has dimples in his voice. Must be very handsome, elegant and modest. Who are you handsome for, you, fleeing from me. She didn't put a question mark at the end of the sentence and the radio played Making Whoopee, with Gerry Mulligan. Something's wrong, I thought. Why the sadness. The world's still yours, at your age to fear this way. To hide in houses. To listen to a prick perfumed with eau de Cologne on the radio. That body of yours, a moral mistake. Her grand sadness depressed me. In a little village she'd have been raped six times, and smiled. My mother has Mongolian features. There was a pogrom. Peggy the sexy teacher with big glasses gobbling sardines. The gift I was to her. Cheating on Mira, one woman I'd loved. The closeness to the announcer arouses an inexplicable jealousy. He was speaking to her. Why did I listen. It was like eavesdropping. To speak to a million women with a phallic voice isn't easy, I know. And so I could go back to pitying myself. Standing on the bridge, waiting for whom for whom for whom. For a word. A code. Who who who. I'd burned the pictures that were me. Destroyed the fury in me. That too is happiness. She sensed, or didn't. Her mother yelled: Bring me a hot-water bottle and a sandwich. I finished another quarter of the Cutty Sark bottle and left. My father broke a violin and opened a frame shop in Tel Aviv, near Jaffa, among the citrus orchards. The first Hebrew city. He framed Ensor, Chagall and Gottlieb for Mr. Dizengoff, the mayor, who wanted to erect a museum on the sands. It's a little shop, my father's. The corner of Nahlat Binyamin and Ahad Ha'am. The best in the city. Now he's probably reading Goethe by lamplight. Who cares. Writes me nine words, ten years, Sha-

14

lom Aminadav, how are you, I'm well, Love, Father. He embellishes the fetters artists place around their suffering.

In the cab I sprawled out, and it was cold. My hands trembled until the car heater started humming. The driver asked in what accent I spoke. Icelandic, I said. He asked if I had any stamps. I recalled my little girlfriend in Naples who'd traveled to all the places on the stamps, with a new hat for each trip. Peggy had said that my Naomi wants to be in two different places at the same time. It'd become an obsession, this thing of two places. My father in Goethe's country and in his frame shop. His nine-word love. Stifling. The beauty of the sabra hedges, somewhere near Gedera. I told the nagging driver, I don't have any stamps but I'll send you some. Read the name on the back of the seat, he said, and passed me a pen. I wrote in my notebook: Chaim Glickstein, 505 Kings, Queens, New York, N.Y. He asked, How do you say I love you in Icelandic. I said, Yo ho ho. He wrote it down word for word and repeated it slowly, learning it by heart, Yo ho ho. I corrected him, Yoho-o ho, short at the end. I repeat. Not yoho-o ho, yo ho-o-o ho. It comes out something like air rushing out of a bursting tire. He notes down phonetic remarks. For my son, he apologized, he's interested in countries.

What street am I in. Maybe a different one. They look so alike. Sober-eyed, or lying in Icelandic. Who here doesn't want to travel. The driver's son. My teacher. In class or out of class. The city's empty. Only a few cars at the red light. The snow whips down and doesn't thicken. It's mixed with strong rain. Behind the lenses of my teacher's glasses there were two Aminadavs. Behind her, a cabinet and on it a bottle of Cutty Sark. Who have I been with. The driver's teeth are yellow with nicotine.

We talked about lung cancer. His fear of it makes him smoke more. Chaim Glickstein 505 Kings Street Queens I didn't ask which entrance.

Skip. Mira's at the door, in spite of the fierce cold. In tight jeans that give her a slinking beauty, like a rare fish. Her hair's tied back. Her eyes cold. Where did you get to? After the meeting I got lost. I met a hungry Santa Claus. I fed him.

What did he eat?

Roast beef, cucumber salad with vinegar and sugar, sardines out of a can. He drank sherry.

What happened to the whiskey?

Her bitterness, her love that she even hated, no denying it, she's so transparent, Mira. I could have touched the aching spot. It was late. Everything was piled up in me, layer upon layer. Tomorrow, on the sea, vanishing on her horizon. Mira. The beautiful Mira of the toilet bowl in the most sumptuous bathroom in the Western world. How I loved this awful and marvelous face. This body that had slept beside me ten years. And Naomi, who had come out of us because we'd planned her like architects. We said she'd be beautiful, with dark eyes and brown hair. She'd be like this or like this, and she was. The cabdriver Yo ho ho. What am I doing. Cry. Ask forgiveness. The one woman I've loved. Whom am I cheating on. I never know how to love. I try and I fail. I entered into women and waited. It didn't come. I used to think: See, there's always something wrong. Something wakes up after a day or two and vanishes. The glare of it. Something pale, stifling inside a room. No way out. Running away. Torrentuous love letters and confessions. My mother's of Russian extraction, pogrommed. Love letters and the next day wanting them back. And talking all night. Selling everything precious, in words, like a junk dealer. The shame of it. Looking for a way out, not to hurt, not myself either. Always exposed to all the injuries. Those streets. Dimly lit apartments. Dark rooms and they come out downstairs and say something. They laugh at you. Or cry about themselves. You do too. You go to a movie. That too. You smoke together. You drink whiskey, wine, maybe coffee. Percolated, early in the morning. With warm rolls she brings up from downstairs. With double beds, narrow beds, walls of all colors to get up to in the morning.

Describing a future that won't come to be. Once there was a little bed in a room. A kind of cot. We said she and I. Her name might have been Patricia. This is where the kid will live. But there was no kid. Once there was an abortion, with nastiness, a two-hundred-dollar loan, a trip to Pennsylvania, and then gradually not to meet again. And there was a girl who looked like Ava Gardner, in the subway. We said some things. We lived together. She brought a broom and I brought an easel and a book of Paolo Uccello. With the spears in the big painting in the Louvre. Three triptychs. The way she looked at it. She brought me the Japanese Tea Book and the Bhagavad-Gita. We ate organic food in Fifty-seventh Street. And—no. And then came Mira and I didn't look anymore. Like Kant's moral concept, embedded within me. She, with all her mannerisms. I used to call to her in my dreams. I didn't want to marry her because I was afraid that if I married her I'd never be able to marry her again. So we used to get married every morning. Those ceremonies. And in the middle of it came Naomi, like the riddle we'd asked ourselves and the answer was another riddle, and it was nice like that. My godfather once wrote: "They say there is love in the world. Where is my love." On Frances Elliott's toilet bowl. On a day of snow. When I met Mira. And she looked at the wall behind me. Here she is. And this bitterness. What for. And the teacher, Peggy. There was no need, but how things get messed up. What the hell's a hungry Santa Claus. I could have made up something brighter. But I'm so tired. Peggy's still inside me. There's no getting her out. How many people, Mira and I yes, but how many people really touch each other. Now Peggy's smell on my clothes. Mira's miserable, Naomi will cry, tomorrow I'll be at sea. How everything's broken. Mira's robbed me of the fun of failing.

I shouted at her, You're messing me about.

As if it was she.

She never messed me about.

She believed. Why do you wait up, I'm a free man, I went for a walk.

My daughter woke up and came into the room. We were already inside. Marveling at Mira. On the way from the door to the room she didn't forget to put out two empty milk bottles, presence of mind at unhappy moments. Naomi in white pajamas with elephants on them. In her hand a piece of an old ragged diaper, without it she can't fall asleep, the princess. I love to see her two fingers, ring finger and little finger, with what delicacy, my God, they hold the piece of diaper while her eyes slowly close, serenity itself. There is nothing that can depress and exhilarate me all at the one time as much as the sight of a child in pajamas, how fragile and gentle. My daughter's alarmed, and sleepy. My face flushed from the cold, my hair frayed by the wind, frighten her. She wants to grab hold of a safety hook, but I'm not it. I said, I release you both.

Mira didn't understand.

I'm leaving, Mira.

Daddy isn't leaving, said Naomi. Mommy said Daddy isn't leaving. In her voice there was the slightest tone of doubt.

I'm leaving, I said.

My daughter in the pajamas with the elephants. Sweet as a lollipop she cried, No no no. Mommy didn't know, I said. Mira tries to shut me up. Her eyes, cold before, are pleading now. Why, Ami, why hurt her if you want to hurt me? Sometimes I think you enjoy saying awful things.

I don't enjoy it. I told her I was tired, it's been a heavy night. All my life was heavy. The dream I'd had, smashed like my father's violin, the courage he'd had. Naomi in the pajamas with the elephants, Mira seeing a man melting . . .

Mira knows. All my life I've lived in improvised biographies. To be somebody else. To father a different family, to dream in a different language, not to hurt you, Mira, let's be honest, let's not go around in circles. Words I know. It's not you, Mira, not Naomi, it's me. My daughter cries. Don't cry Naomi, I love you. My wife gazes at me, weary-eyed. All night she's waited. I was on top of a teacher, looking for salvation in her tangled hair. The purple prose of her thighs spoke to me. The jokes of between her legs. The abyss in the folds of her belly. That smell. Always cries when she shouldn't. It was nice I said to her. What does that mean, nice. You tried to give her a child, didn't you. She with her diaphragm and I with my stubborn effort to hang on inside her. Not to alarm her too soon. The mast that rose toward her. The flag that saluted it. Loathsome. When there's Mira for a squashed man like me.

I should have been, ought to have been, the dream I dreamed.

She believed so strongly. She appended herself to me. Funny. With an easel. With outdated paintings. The twenty-one Miras on a toilet bowl that I painted. Looks like Giotto in shorts. The day she thought that I was, perhaps, too holy, something that always ached began to laugh.

The night hangs in the room. Canned smoke, stale, stinking. Orange peels. An aging sandwich. Mira's cigarette butts. A cup of coffee with ash inside. The mark of her lips on the rim of the cup. Mira said: You like saying hurtful things, to imagine situations and to take them to extremes. . . . To focus a pain and then stab yourself. Always competing with somebody. By rules. Art by the rules of football. Why don't you understand how stupid that is. Why compete like kids, in kids' games. Only because there's a fashion now and you're not in it. So what. Maybe you will be. And maybe you won't. Bach was, Stendhal. To put this night away with the series of nights that had been. To flee, tomorrow. To search for the dream in the place where it began. In my father's frame shop. This city's finished for me. This life. Love you Mira. Don't know why I have to. Love and run away. God, how beautiful you are, Mira, how human. And you know how to love, I don't. That's the trouble. Not even myself.

Naomi: Mommy said you wouldn't go. She said you'd stay with us. I took her in my arms. Warm, bright eyes. What softness. I said to her, and Mira listened: What are two ounces of misery, how do you measure failure. I stayed the clown, a powerless king. The cat got up off the bed, came up to me, and purred. The things that suddenly make you go soft in the heart. The sight of a trusting cat. A night of snow and wind. Inside it's hot, thank God, the heating's working. Soon the night will go out. The radiator will die down. Then there'll be a wonderful stillness. Like after the smashing of violins. Take this animal, I said. My daughter bent over the cat, picked it up, and hugged it. It's not an animal, she said, it's Kadarlaomer. I yelled at Mira: Say Kadarlaomer! She can't pronounce his name, calls him Cudry. I laughed, Cudry, my sweet little daughter in her pajamas with the elephants cuddling a desperately purring cat. Is desperation a plea or a formal experience. The grief of a little girl. Her father screaming, wild-haired, off to sea tomorrow. Her mother weeping. How such a stable world can be destroyed in a minute.

What does she think, this little sphinx that I designed and is now a human being, keeping things in and speaking to herself in a whisper. I should have asked Peggy, instead of counting the dimples on her amazing back. I didn't ask.

I've bought a boat ticket, I said. In a few hours I'll be sailing. I so wanted things to work. This body to be equivalent to the will. You mistook me. I mistook. There's only one Aminadav, the boy I was before I left everything and started traveling. Before I went away from my own city. From the frame shop. From the gutters of Tel Aviv on weeping winter nights. The boy who dreamed himself. Maybe I'll find him.

Mira's embracing Naomi who's embracing the cat who's embracing with its invisible eyes the most terrible of fathers.

I know it's stupid. Why shouldn't I know. Pointless. Absolutely hopeless. If that sounds pompous, let it. The Aminadav I was can't wait for me because he's traveled all this way with me and he's as crumpled as I am. I, many men, return to be the boy that was. I was endowed with a name. My godfather Bialik came from a poem and left to a poem. A rib on a stick. It was a fragrant spring day. My mother lay in the Freund Hospital in Tel Aviv and waited thirty-eight hours for me. Bialik came and said, just like that, call him Aminadav. When he gets to be a boy call him Ami. And he went off to bring sweet and bitter words to the people of Israel. In a house with a dome among trees. A people from ships. Eating soup with knaidlach. Not me. I don't belong. You gave me a new name, Mira. In Frances Elliott's magnificent bathroom on a cold snowy day. Maybe it was night, who remembers. You were pure, fine, under a hundred veils. The way I knew I'd found my reflection. In you I saw myself. I closed an eye and didn't cry. But things got messed up. I waited for a miracle and it didn't come. Jerome paints Panamanian flags. Who needs twenty-one Miras on a toilet bowl. Outdated paintings.

I'm going back a beaten dog, who's waiting for me.

Naomi said, Daddy, everybody can be in every place.

I thought of what the teacher Peggy had told me about Naomi.

I thought: So that's why you get up and then come back, to be in every place. Naomi cried to me. She came up to me, and stroked my face. She had my face. She said, When I was big, that's what she said, when I was big I had a house with lots of animals in it. Then I was little and I was born to you. You promised me camels from Tiberias. And wolves. You promised you'd take me. If you're going and you're there, when you were a boy, and when you were old too, then don't forget to bring me. You're there with all the ones we've been and when we talked about the house with the animals. And she blushed, the little one. I stroked her. She's so wise.

I said to Naomi, I was at your school, I met your teacher. Peggy.

Peggy. She's very nice.

Mira said, She has a nice body, that's what your father means. Your father likes beautiful women. I sipped some of the wine that was standing on the table. I was so tired. My hands were trembling. From across the city there came a dull roar. Someone had let the air out of the city, tomorrow they'd pump it up again.

Peggy said that she's a smart girl and that—My daughter came up to me. She dropped the cat, who licked itself. Purring at the touch of its tongue. She put her hand on my lips, which held a pipe in honor of her teacher. She can't stand being praised to her face. She's liable to stamp her feet on hearing a compliment. Her eyes fill with tears, she gets frightened, all prickly, and her voice, God, why, gets hoarse. I suggested to her that she leave the room for a while so I could tell Mother. She leaves the room with her face lowered. Trying not to hear in the next room. The stillness of the night carries the sounds of pins dropping. I spoke in a loud voice and she heard without wanting to hear, Peggy said that Naomi's very bright and quick, good at arithmetic and reading, she's doing well in all her studies and every morning she has to be beaten with a whip because laziness is psychological. She came back, covered up, angry-faced at her father, a load of disappointed love. Mira said, The end doesn't fit. I told her that sexy women can be cruel. Mira said, So now she isn't just nice, she's sexy. Naomi dug herself in deeper still. Mira's eyes were dry and crying.

21

I'd never seen dry eyes crying before. The sight of my retreat in a mirror. Soon it'll be sea. I can't burst out into love. What did I have in my life, I said to her. You! And that isn't much. The connections I invent to defeat myself.

Go off for a few days, she said. You need a rest, you're torturing me, Mr. Zwiegel, Naomi. But come back! Don't go home. That isn't fair, Ami. . . .

How hard it is, I know her, to ask like this. I know her pride. To ask. Not fair. Don't go, she said. Where shouldn't I go, Mira.

I look at her. Are we suddenly strangers. Ten years we've lived inside each other. My daughter's crying in her pajamas with the elephants. Take me, Daddy.

You're trying to commit suicide by hitting out at us, said Mira in a slack voice. She's thinking aloud. There are no more words in her. Speak about the weather. In Bonwit Teller you can get Japanese lampshades designed by Noguchi. I wanted to tell her. Soon it'll be morning. Sea. The last months have been hell. Naomi cries with her pug nose and I love her sensuous very secret mouth that curls around what Mira calls the secrets of the mouth, those two creases on either side of the lips. Aminadav, she said, and the words were dry. What a singular thing you're destroying with your own hands. Should I plead? You want to go, go. Come, don't come, now suddenly nothing matters anymore. Now, because I'm hurting, I want to sleep.

I mumbled no no but we both fell asleep standing up. Suddenly in the middle of the war over our lives, we fell asleep. She mumbled out of the doze, What sides? Who isn't on your side? And she also said, You're full of charm and intrigue. I love you because you're you, and anyway, what are you? As if I knew. And she fell asleep again. We stood there, asleep. And she whispered, out of her drowsing. Through your love I've been able to live for the first time in my life. To love the lover himself, immeasurably. A rare thing. And you're stealing . . . you've stolen . . .

What, Ami.

The delight of defeat.

That's melodramatic.

I'm melodramatic, Mira. I always have been. Do you remember the way I sang when you got pregnant?

You always sang. Even when you were child-making without making any children.

Naomi's here.

I forgot. I'm asleep. I'm talking in my sleep.

So am I.

The children we've suddenly become.

The darkness went out outside and a clean blueness burst through the dimness. The snow's stopped falling, I thought in a sudden sadness.

It's not defeat, she said, but go. Go search in Tel Aviv. Maybe in the womb.

The jealousy in her outdated voice. My daughter sitting quite still, afraid. Cuddling Kadarlaomer. Mira hasn't forgiven me the last five months of my stay in the womb that I carry with me.

What else do you have to say, Mira?

How did you dare to bring Sylvia Hennig, that whore from the Cider Bar, to my bed?

I laughed. That's not to the point.

I know, she said, and slid down.

Our eyes are closed. On the floor. Naomi, cuddling the cat, has fallen asleep. I opened my eyes and saw the sweet child sleeping on the carpet. Her skin white and fresh. The pained expression on her face had changed into a serene smile like that of the fat tranquil Buddha on her teacher's wall. Mira opened her eyes as if it was a new day. The light in the window was bluish gray. We gazed at Naomi from either side of the carpet, in disbelief. Is she for real, our eyes asked. I went up to Naomi and picked her up. To throw out her arms and press herself to her father, in her sleep, oh, God, she threw out her arms and embraced me with a terrible warmth. I carried her to her bed. Put her down among the teddy bears, one of them open-mouthed. Her hand, in her sleep, clutched the tattered diaper. I kissed her on her mouth, which was dry and warm. On her eyes, where the tears had dried that she'd wept earlier. I licked them and they weren't salty. I turned off the light and went back to Mira. She was suddenly wide awake with morning. She heated some red wine. It was cold, the heating had stopped. We drank from two large goblets we'd bought together that summer in Fairfield Connecticut. The wind beat at the windows. Mira said that to sail in this weather wouldn't be much fun. I said that the sea calms me. She said she'd pack for me. I nodded and said, I didn't sleep with Sylvia Hennig.

She didn't answer.

I'll come back, Mira. Meanwhile, I have to go.

Yes, I know, she said.

Later, there were five packed suitcases. Something reddish, astonished, replaced the blue outside. Into the suitcases Mira put my things, fragrant Spanish soaps, soft toilet paper, clean towels and powdered tears—a little water and warmth and there'd be instant tears all the time. We talked in whispers, to pass over things that don't matter. We remembered Naomi one month old. In her first pajamas. The first time I changed her diaper, and I was afraid I'd prick her with the big safety pin. How did Mira learn to fasten the pin so dexterously and to change diapers with such devilish speed. The first tooth. It pushed through the skin of her gums and we dabbed it with cognac. I told her about archaeological diggings in Central America where there were pyramids and no one knew if they were built by man or god. We talked about what a light-year is and about how far the stars of Andromeda are from us, and for the first time in a long time we didn't rage, we waited for morning.

We went up to Naomi's bed hand in hand. My throat contracted. I thought: I'm choking again. Mira knows the symptoms and urged me to leave the room. Naomi slept whisperingly and the rustle of her breathing was a music. I took the suitcases and left. It was cold and a strong wind blew from the river. She stood in the kitchen, making breakfast for Naomi. She didn't come out to say goodbye to me. I hailed a cab and stretched out. Until the heat starts hitting you you freeze.

2

I had been a seaman on a small ship that brought immigrants to Israel. There was a hotel in Haifa. It was spacious enough staying there, ten of us, seamen from the Geulah. The State of Israel's first ID cards were being issued and there was a curfew. The radio played marches. Among the ten were Tarzan and Jan-Jan. Tarzan was violently silent and Jan-Jan told jokes.

In a corner I read Kafka's Amerika and above me they played cards. Tarzan went into the lavatory and ripped the toilet bowl out of the concrete. The water leaked through the entire building. There was nothing to do. To sit in a locked room. I tried to interest him in the marvelous chapter about the circus in Oklahoma in Kafka's book, but he was nervous and irritable and paced the floor. We ate dry sandwiches and drank warm beer. Then we became Israelis with ID cards and returned to the ship. We sailed to Naples. My new friends knew there'd been things in the Jerusalem hills and that I'd seen blood sticking to Nahum's face, death was on the electricity poles, in the vultures' beaks, and sticking to me. The sea filled me with a sense of loss and stillness. The propeller fell into the sea near Sicily. We waited for a tug to tow us. We jumped into the sea. There were no fish. The rescue crew brought out a girl who sneaked on board our ship. I didn't see her but I heard them laughing at night in Jan-Jan's room— he was the eldest among us. We got to Naples. Men dreaming of women in pink and purple. We went ashore and there was riot in the streets. People selling cloth made of paper and stealing money from pockets. Fine-looking women sold little girls for a pack of American cigarettes. In niches, in the hard stone walls, madonnas wept. People spoke of a miracle. Fat priests placed alcohol lamps and water bowls behind the madonnas. In a single moment a hundred madonnas had wept in Naples. Women in black fainted on seeing the miracle and spread their arms out like scarecrows. Involved in the system of miracles was inflation. Elections were approaching. In the streets people collected horse dung to warm their shattered houses. Among the rubble of buildings and smashed palaces naked children yelled around bonfires, eating bread. Abandoned forts and palaces. Tarzan and Jan-Jan went to Sixty-Eight with women in pink and purple. They tried to talk me into coming.

I went to a museum. I was young. The war had torn me up. My friend Nahum's brains were still sticking in front of my eyes. The smiling face I'd seen brought down with a grenade. The sea was elusive, and that was better. Saturated with sweet dread. The museum was on a hill you had to climb. Far from the broken things that had been a city. Once Naples had been a fort, and the Goths had guarded it. The Byzantines broke in through the water canal, marvelously entering the city. Belisarius captured it with stratagems. The museum above the city gave me the feeling that if you close your eyes things don't happen. Beautiful frescoes from Pompeii, with marvelous women, like snakes. The statue of Atlas holding the world on his shoulders. Paintings by Titian and Tintoretto. A painting by an Italian artist from Tuscany, I don't remember who, maybe Fra Angelico, that was like an absolute stillness. I was astonished by it after the Ensor and Gottlieb in the Tel Aviv Museum. A guard with a limp, a soldier of the distant days of glory, stumbled after me. We were alone in the huge palace. The halls evoked an echo and an aroma of an erased kingdom and old paintings and the aroma of lacquer and gold that my father sprays on frames to make them look old. The man said he had to lock up. I paid him and he let me feast myself. Until

I felt hungry. I went outside. Naples swam in brilliant twilight. For a moment I was unborn.

A pleasant wind blew and everything floated in the gold pouring from Vesuvius and the setting sun, sticking to the houses below with the most marvelously fine rustle.

A very thin man sold spaghetti from a huge barrel hanging around his neck. I ordered a serving and he asked, in eight languages, with or without. I answered with, in English. He smiled and said, American? I didn't answer. I saw in his eyes: Maybe the Germans are back. He took two bottles from his swollen pockets, brought them to his mouth, emptied a little into his mouth, mixed them with a kind of gargle and I heard a kind of *brrrrrrr* and then he sprayed it onto the spaghetti. He wrapped this in newspaper and took the money. Out of sight I threw the spaghetti into an ornate garbage can made of bronze and decorated with the figures of Daphnis and Chloe, so fine, with a quotation in Latin from an old poem, maybe Ovid, with wreaths crowning the heads of the two darlings. A hundred and fifty thousand children darted out of niches and from branches of trees and fell upon the serving of spaghetti. They tore up the serving and devoured even the newspaper the sauce had moistened. I hurried down, stopped a cab and said in a loud voice, for the man to hear, I wanted to apologize, but how can you, Sixty-Eight, I said like one who knows. The seller of spaghetti smiled. He took one step toward me as if he'd remembered something. But then he stopped and yelled into the empty street: Spaghetti! Spaghetti! The cabdriver told me that it was easy to see that I was young and he bet I had something between my legs. He laughed jerkily and his body shook. Between his gleaming gold teeth I saw a dark gap, so we may read: *How to feed a starving city with gold teeth.*

He stopped laughing and I didn't want to fall into any delusions. I asked his pardon. He didn't understand what I meant and asked why the pardon. Sixty-Eight's a special place, he said, for those who have.

There was a big house there draped in night and a woman came up to the cab that had stopped for a moment, and tried to buy me for her daughter who stood on the corner eating her finger. Little, with a pretty dress, white, with legs like matchsticks and the face of an angel. She's a virgin, said the driver, and waited, respectfully. Priests rode by on bicycles, shouting, Miracle! Miracle! and crossing themselves.

In the vestibule of Sixty-Eight stood a naked woman who circled around on a stool like a piano stool. She circled slowly. Heavily painted. Long lashes, cheeks rouged, mouth red. I saw Nahum's blood on my face. Around her, demobilized soldiers, looking. Dressed in faded garments, with medals like rags, with wounded eyes, with a hard smile, in absolute silence. From time to time one of them suddenly burst out laughing and everyone joined in with him and stopped all at once. When they laughed, their faces were sad. In a heavily carpeted room I saw Jan-Jan, Tarzan, Fat Menahem and Amnon the Dope. Drunk, all of them. On the table stood empty Cinzano bottles and a half-full bottle of brandy. They said, Aminadav's come. Go to a woman.

First time.

He doesn't know what it is.

They didn't laugh. Solidarity, said Tarzan, who'd ripped up the toilet bowl, and laughed.

No one else did.

I was hungry. They gave me a sandwich of long white bread. In my mind's eye I saw the children from the hovels, and, like everyone, I ate. I drank a little brandy. It burned the throat.

They asked the madam for special treatment for me. With the money they had there was no need to ask twice. A woman in purple and pink came up to me. She nimbly grabbed my things and blew wine and cigarettes into my face. Her breasts were in my face. I'd never seen a woman's breasts so close. I tried to explain why I'd come. The woman was beautiful but she frightened me, she was worn, as if all the wars had been waged on her body. Jan-Jan told a story: Once this guy rang on a whorehouse door. He had no arms, no legs, no teeth, no ears, no hair. The madam opened the door and said, What do you want? You have no arms, no legs, no teeth, no ears, no hair. He said, I rang, didn't I?

The little girl in the doorway, the thin one, looks at me and sees the wall behind me. The way Mira'll look at me later in Frances Elliott's magnificent bathroom in New York on a night of terrible snow.

Listening to Jan-Jan's fragmented English, a thin sneer of disgust on her face. I moved toward her and Jan-Jan said, Go with a woman, not with bones!

She looked so much like a girl I loved in third grade, who lived opposite our house in Mendele Street. We sailed in a boat in Ben Yehuda Street, during the big flood. She was a sail and I was an oar. That's what we said. Then she moved to Ramat Gan. That was a long way away. I told Uncle Avner that I love a girl in Ramat Gan. We drove there in his black Ford. I sneaked into the yard and peeped inside. Her father was standing behind her. She was sitting at the piano. Her hair was long and silken. He stroked her hair and she played. Above the piano was a mirror and in it I saw her face, like a white mask. That kind of sadness. The tree creaked and she looked around. I hid. Her father was frightening, in a suit and tie, inside a house with white curtains. And her white face. Suddenly she'd arrived in Naples at a house called Sixty-Eight, with Jan-Jan. Her gaze pierced me. The boy I was, I said love, love. Always looking in the wrong place. The way I laugh at funerals. She stood there, submitting to a sentence. She was neither painted nor impudent. As if waiting only for me. Upstairs in a magnificent chamber there was the charm of antiques. Everything so beautiful and thick. Carpets, furs, a large armchair with silver armrests, paintings of nymphs, heavy curtains. A lamp on a marvelously chiseled wooden stand. The girl is lovely. She looks into my face. She tries to look without seeing. She got undressed. I looked at her boyish body. It seemed to pour out of the thin clothes she wore. Her small breasts stood arched. We measured each other as if we were playing a game. But I was trembling. She said, Don't tremble. I laughed, embarrassed. But when I was inside her, loving her, I didn't laugh and she became serious and whispered something to me in Italian. Who doesn't want a little love. I consoled myself by thinking that she was the girl I knew once, Re'aya was my love's name. And her father stood behind her in a dark suit and wrote stories that no one read. The blanket that had been a shelter became a crumpled thing. And then she asked in a child's voice, shrunken, her arms around her thin knees, whether I had any bus tickets or stamps. I ferreted through my clothes and found two Ma'avir bus tickets and a Drom-Yehuda season ticket, a Hamekasher ticket and a torn Egged ticket.

On a letter from my mother (with an addition by my father: Shalom Aminadav, how are you, I'm well, Love, Father) were two new stamps with drawings of coins from the days of Bar Kochba. She took the tickets and the stamps. The pallor that covered her, everything stilled for a moment, even the flickering of light in the window from the bar opposite. She was bowed over the stamps and the tickets, as if she'd touched some sacred objects. Like the women in the church in Jerusalem kneeling in front of a statue of the crucified one when I went to the Old City with my father. Gently she stroked the tickets and the stamps, barely touching them. I covered the lower half of my body with the blanket that had covered many before me, and their smell was dim now because of the agitated look in her eyes. I lit a cigarette. The smoke rose into the ceiling on which I now clearly saw paintings of faded angels doing the things we had just been doing in bed. I wanted to be that father, the one who writes books no one reads, and to stroke her hair. She handled the stamps as if they were prayer beads, mumbling something I didn't understand. I knew she was sailing off to distant places. Traveling to all places with old tickets. The city rustled outside the window. If this isn't love, there is no love. Madonnas wept in the Street of the Saints. Lights flickered over the bars. Number 16 glowed electric. Two seamen came out of its door and a woman laughed and then there was a terrible noise and a bottle flew out. Children ran about the street collecting dung. A woman raised her skirt and a huge black seaman howled into it and entered her with a savage roar that forced the lampshade off our lamp.

We sneaked outside. We went to the Galeria. I bought her stamps from Ethiopia and the Philippines, bus tickets and a map of Rome. She asked me if I had a sweater. I gave her the sweater. She wrapped it around the stamps and the map of Rome and said,

I don't want them to feel cold. I told her some sea words. Through me she could smell unimaginable distances, mountains of water and breakers, mountains of salt. She said her father had been a fisherman, he'd had his head blown off during a bombing raid, the demobilized soldiers disgusted her, but war, she said, is a huge thing.

Santa Lucia was empty. Everything there glittered in vain. The water was silver by the light of the full moon. Waiters stood in the doorways of classy restaurants, slowly polishing windowpanes.

Beside me, she traveled on a well-wrapped map, to the distant places. Suddenly she was frightened. You'll go away like they all do, though they didn't buy me stamps. The tears that her eyes still kept. Why, I thought, did she ask me of all people.

I said I wouldn't run away. She asked for proof. There was a shoeshine boy in the quiet street. No one in Naples polished his shoes. He was smoking a cigarette butt and looking at his own torn shoes. She stopped next to him and said buy me some shoelaces. I bought. She wove the laces into a long string, tied it around her neck and gave the end to me. Now I'm a dog, she said, and one doesn't run away from dogs. The shoeshine boy laughed and I threw him a coin. She kissed the gleaming sidewalk. Even in my first memories there's a shoeshine boy who smoked a cigarette. When I was two years old, in Jaffa. I went out with my mother to buy cloth. We bought cloth in Bustrus Street. My mother said that in 1918 she'd planted trees in King George Avenue in honor of General Allenby. Girls from the Neveh Tzedek Girls' School stood there singing *Hevenu Shalom Aleichem*. After we'd bought the cloth I got lost. And so, suddenly, I became aware of myself. For the first time. I alone. Jaffa. Sharp, fragrant, twilight. Intoxicatingly colorful. A host of colors. The mosque. Arab men in tarbooshes, Arab women hiding their faces. My first memory is clear and shining. Not a thing missing. Complete, and everything there has a name. All of a sudden I am I. Very alone, in a strange city, crying for my mother, lost.

Big houses around me. Many windows. A shoeshine boy sits on the edge of the sidewalk smoking a cigarette butt. How did I know it was a cigarette butt. I remember the terror. The little boy I was, crying for his mother. Where is she, Mama, Mama. Women with veiled faces swarming over me. I in among their skirts. Between their legs. Bent. They smelled strange. One said, *Adesh umraq, adesh umraq.* I didn't know my name. I didn't know my mother's name. From between their legs I see the eyes of the shoeshine boy. Very light, maybe blue even. How could I know what blue is. In their brightness there was something hollow, startling, opposite the houses with the open windows and the voice of an old man with a creased face selling tamarinds. *Suss! Suss!* cries a man. He's huge. From here. With the face of a robber. I thought: He has blue eyes. Later, at Mrs. Kotzelman's kindergarten the teacher whose name was Mrs. Cukierman tells me that all Arab children have black eyes and I shout, no, no, it isn't true, they have blue eyes and the children laugh at me. The boy sucks happily at his cigarette butt, smiling through broken teeth. His leg bouncing up and down on the sidewalk all the time. A policeman rushed in, in brown high boots. The boots close me in. Mama ma. People whisper. Strange voices. A strange language. I wanted, I cried, Mamamama, they didn't know her name and they found her in that darkness that I was in there. They brought her from out the mystery of the bustling alleyways. Everything clear: the smell of *hel* and *zatar* and strong coffee. The smell of the sea. And the moon rising over the spire of the mosque. A boy mounted on a donkey drinking water from the white trough. A lane. Many shops. Incredible piles of red tomatoes. Fruit. Live fish swimming in a shopwindow. A bleeding cut of meat. A butcher with a mustache standing beside a fat barber, both of them laughing and looking at a woman carrying a basket on her head with large exposed eyes, an impudence. Intense light and the sound of the waves. The moment my mother appears and runs to me with the tears of a frightened mother, the shoeshine boy throws his cigarette butt at a cat ferreting in the garbage. The cat howls and runs off in terror to hide under a cart. The boy on the donkey laughs.

I told my little dog.

Povero, she said.

Who?

That boy, she said. I told her that that was how I discovered cruelty on the first day of my life.

But you were born before that, she said.

True, I said, but I didn't exist before that. His eyes became steel and the cigarette hit the cat. The mother of a boy without a name found her son. Terrible cruelty, I said. My little dog sympathized with me and didn't speak. She said that once, for every trip she'd worn a new hat. Not anymore. There'd been a Norwegian seaman. She'd thought of Norway, and it had been hot.

Cold.

Hot. It was that kind of game, she said, and almost cried.

I said I understood it was a game and then she smiled, appeased, the little dog.

She told me there'd been American sailors. She'd traveled to New Orleans. Once she'd gone to Pompeii with a thin Englishwoman, who was tall and wore a suit like a man's. She'd given her sardines and kissed her on the mouth. She'd given her artificial flowers and told her the names of cities: Manchester, Liverpool. London. France.

That's a country, I said.

She knew, my little dog. But sometimes it's nice to say France, just like that, because it's a place, with stamps, or woods and a forest. Names are a great thing: the Indian Ocean, she said, or Topeka Kansas.

That's a train.

It doesn't matter, she said, tell me names. I said Zikhron Ha'akov, Rosh Pina, Yesud Hama'alah, Hebron, Sussetz.

She said, Sutz-ess.

The bay was still. Thin thin smoke rose from Vesuvius. Water slid onto the esplanade, whispering. We went into a restaurant. Empty. Waiters. They sat us at a table covered with a red tablecloth. In the middle of the room stood a huge table with chipped ice on it, where the best seafoods and marvelous salads glistened. Along an ornamented wall draped with rugs made of fox furs stood tense waiters. An admiral wearing a colored hat came up to us. He motioned with his hand and two waiters gave us a menu and wiped the plates. As we sat down the two waiters held our chairs and moved them. It looked as if no one had dined here for many days. The waiters' eyes. There were so many of them. Deputies and deputies of deputies. All in white tunics. See the black under the collars and the cuffs. Their hands moved all the time. The admiral wore medals and in a corner, beside a table set apart from the other tables, a fat man snored with a cigar in his mouth. I wondered at the rings of thin smoke rising from the sleeping man's cigar. From time to time he opened one eye, smooth and rare, like a green-brown stone, looked at us, and relapsed into his peaceful snoring. Behind the admiral stood two waiters. They were tense and their eyes darted around all the time. All the eyes focused on the table. My girl licked her lips for a moment, tied by a string wreathed of shoelaces. I asked the admiral how much the table cost.

He didn't understand. My girl burst out laughing and as suddenly stopped. The admiral retreated as if smitten, the horrible expression on his face then, and the whisperings started.

He returned to me and stammered, What does the signor ask? I raised my voice and said, How much for everything on the table. Everything, I repeated. This time the fat man woke up. The cigar vanished into his mouth for a moment and reappeared. A conjurer with agate eyes. All of them bowed to him. Waiters retreated to clear a path for him. I said to the admiral, I want to buy everything here. *Comprendo?* A baker in a huge hat and a cook came running out of the kitchen. Everyone whispered. The waiters beside the wall like soldiers. Excited whispers, occasionally glances in my direction. The fat man whispered something in the ear of the admiral, who came up to me and said, The signor asks how much costs the whole table. Yes?

Yes.

He retreated again. Whispers. Wearying deliberations. What am I doing here. My little darling kissed by Englishwomen. They reached some kind of decision. Something was written down on a piece of paper. The fat man passed it to the admiral. The admiral to the baker. The baker to a waiter. The waiter to a boy. The boy came up to me. Trembling all over. His face red. Peeping at my little dog. The boy laid the note on the table. Face down, and retreated. Before reading it, I looked at them. The line of waiters along the wall. All looking at me. Perhaps they wanted to vanish into the wall, but a fox fur is no mirage. The fat man returned to his seat, opened both eyes, took the cigar out of his mouth and waited. On his face was a smile that looked like what you sometimes see on a dead dog. I turned the note over and read: The whole table, signor, cost fifty or forty-five dollars. Maybe?

My little dog was very quiet. Now and then she looked at the waiters who were looking at me. Perhaps this was her greatest hour. Celebrating in a kind of prayer. Holding the stamps and tickets with restrained love. A moment's glory. The question mark at the end of the sentence looks larger and more tremulous than usual.

I took out a fifty-dollar bill and called the admiral. I gave him the bill. He bowed and passed the bill from hand to hand.

Eat, I said.

Silence.

I shouted at them: Eat. Not a move. Later they understood. The way they fell on everything. A prayer that had found its god. Words that had found their reality. The onslaught was fierce. My throat began to pinch. I thought: Why does my throat hurt. I thought I was choking. I touched my little dog and the warmth of her hand, the warmth of her body, was a slight relief. I thought: Here I am dying before their eyes. A dead Santa Claus. A superfluous thing. I thought about myself. Why had I told her about the Arab boy and the cigarette. I remembered that before meeting him I hadn't had any memories. That today I'd known a woman. I'd had girlfriends. We'd sat in Keren Kayemeth Boulevard, feeling up breasts. There'd been Rina Faktorovitz who taught anatomy on the beach, near the Moslem cemetery, near the cave. But I'd been afraid of her. She had a very coarse voice and she said, Aminadav can shove me up the ass too. I didn't want to. Her anatomy was on the other side. My girl taught me the gentleness there is in violence.

Suddenly I knew that I'd remembered a kind of wonderful darkness and that it had been warm for two years before the memory in Jaffa and then I knew that I'd known a kind of serenity inside my mother. How I didn't want to be born, I fought, choking terribly, for thirty-eight hours so as not to come out onto the face of the earth. Vesuvius in the display window that gleamed too much. This marvelous light. The bay. I, with a girl, tied with a string wreathed from shoelaces, with stamps and tickets, with a hot Norway, an Englishwoman and sardines, a kiss on the mouth at Pompeii, with plates that remained on the table when the lava came. The choking was quick and it passed. She asked what happened.

Nothing. I remembered how I was before I was born, I said. She laughed.

Good for you, she said. And perhaps she wasn't referring to the fact that I had fifty dollars. She sat erect. And waited. I told her to eat. She devoured. Oh, how my first woman devoured. Once I saw the way they bring lambs to their mothers. The gate of the pen was opened and the ewes ran to their lambs. The pen resounded *mehhhhh.* Each mother looked for her lamb. She fiercely pushed aside any lamb that wasn't hers. Strange lambs were rejected. Each lamb smelled out its mother, each mother her lamb. And then there was silence. All of them bleated in a huge stillness. All the lambs sucked and all their mothers were calm. The onslaught of the waiters was an eruption. Their eating was a fine stillness. Bottles of wine were brought, and hot dishes from the kitchen. I said to them, In the Belgian Congo they eat people, and they don't invent ghettoes. There's a limit! One of them asked, with a mouth full of crabs, What's a ghetto.

The admiral said, A place for Jews.

They laughed with their mouths full of food, drunk on the delight spreading through them, no no no.

I said, No no no what.

My girl said, What are Jews. What's a ghetto.

I told her. She said, There are stamps.

She showed them the stamps from the Philippines. They kissed her stamps. They stripped her. They put her on the table. They smeared her with sweet cream and licked her. They poured Cinzano over her. They drank her. The fat man got up, took a cut of cold meat, swallowed it as if he had no teeth, lit another cigar and fell asleep again. Rococo for whore and waiters. I go outside. To go. To get away. She's laughing inside. The string's still tied around her neck. I hailed a cab and went back to the ship. Jan-Jan was waiting for me on the gangplank. Where had I disappeared to. I didn't tell him. He said, Aminadav found a consumptive, he fucked bones. I said, Right, and lay down to sleep. I dreamed of *badim badim.* When I was eight we shifted to Qiryat Meir, which was then outside Tel Aviv. My father used to go outside at night to drive jackals away from the garbage cans. A path made of planks led to the quarter. Citrus orchards grew green all around. Gan Hadassah. Insistent fields in that awful winter. Sumeil, an Arab village, and Sharona. A colony of German Templars with real cream and yellow yellow butter and houses like toys. Monsieur Ketzele sold apples on the path. A little man, Monsieur Ketzele. Prayed in a whisper as if he was ashamed. Even before God. His mouth was split. He almost didn't speak, he only mumbled *badim badim.* Cloth cloth, or branches branches, I didn't know, *badim* could mean either. The children hid in the carob tree and yelled, Monsieur Ketzele, robbers! He was hard of hearing. He came out of his hut, chewing salt herring or *halva,* dressed in torn dark brown clothes, his face charred too as if he'd been through all the wars, as if he'd been in the fire, and had bent an ear in an attempt to hear, mumbling *badim badim.* He had no cloth for sale. On the trees there were oranges, not pieces of cloth. At night the children stole apples from him. He didn't hear. He got up in the morning and saw—no apples. In the evening they yelled, robbers, he said *badim badim,* woke up in the morning, no apples. At night the jackals howled. The children of Sharona donned black shirts, held parades, and shouted *Sieg Heil!* The Arabs of Sumeil looked at them with admiration. In the groves of Gan Hadassah they did terrible things to little girls. People said that virgins came out not-virgins from those trees. The stories the children told then. I wanted to save this wrinkled man. He disgusted me. Frightened me. His face was awful and torn. They called him Monsieur Ketzele because maybe he was a sorcerer. I told the children that he was born in Hebron and that one day

37

he'd seen his wife and three children being slaughtered, and since then he'd looked like this.

He's not from Hebron, they said. He's Polish. He snores. A lot of rain fell that winter. Monsieur Ketzele shivered and sold his remaining apples. I had a little pocket money. My father was a meticulous man. Every week he gave me one grush. I went to the Bezalel Market, to an old woman who had known my grandmother, bought apples from her at a discount, and at night I'd sneak them into Monsieur Ketzele's hut. Fear all around, jackals howling, like the land of Canaan where jackals howl. I got drenched to the bone. I sneaked the apples in. He snored, mumbling *badim badim,* who knows why. The children said he smelled of naphthalene, from Poland. He had small eyes, like a mouse, and a harelip. Once he hired a watchman, who caught me. The policemen at the station laughed, what's this, a matter of two shillings at the most. And he cried. Without tears, in a kind of terrible opacity. As if all the forests had been cut down in him at once. The look of hatred he threw at me. I wept into my pillow. At the grocer's they said about my mother: Here's the mother of the *ganev.* The children said nothing, nor did I. Once at school David and a Half said what can you expect from Aminadav now, everyone knows he's a thief, there's proof of it. And they all laughed. To the police station my mother went, as if I didn't exist, and my father mumbled, This is very serious. At night, while he was beating the cans to drive away the jackals, he thought it over and decided to cut down my pocket money.

My uncle Avner from Haifa arrived, took me into the other room, and asked:

Did you steal?

No.

Why didn't you say so?

They didn't ask me.

Who stole?

It doesn't matter.

We went to my school. He looked around and saw David and a Half. He went up to him and said, Is it true that Aminadav's a thief.

Yes.

And he really took apples?

Yes.

Aminadav refuses to talk, said my uncle, but I have proof of something else. Are you willing to talk?

David started crying.

My uncle slapped him across the face. Right away he had the whole list of thieves in his hands.

By the time a furious headmaster reached my scurvy uncle— so he called him to the teachers—by the time he arrived on the run with a sandwich in his mouth and a cup in his hand rattling on a saucer, the confession was complete and the headmaster, who so wanted me to be the thief, was forced to turn pale. They organized a ceremony. The headmaster spoke. I stood there, embarrassed. My mother stood there, proud. Monsieur Ketzele was brought there against his will. He mumbled *badim badim* and refused to offer me his hand in apology.

At night, on my return from the restaurant and my little dog in Naples, I dreamed I was bringing her apples. She wrapped them in her dress and said: *On the branches of trees leaves will grow, and on me nothing will grow.* And then, when I woke up, I knew why Monsieur Ketzele said *badim badim.* The look on his wrinkled face always.

Afterward I didn't want to be a seaman anymore. The sea was shores. The shores were deserted little dogs. There wasn't enough pity in me. I tried to love the little boy I'd been. I went to Paris to learn to paint. In the Beaux Arts we painted Greek statues. In the Grande Chaumière I painted naked women. There was a blond woman who called me *mon loup.* She was married to a Polish nobleman. We drank coffee together at Deux Magots. Then she came to me and asked how one said *mon loup* in Hebrew. To them I was a fake savage. I hated the beautiful city that Paris was. I thought of it as a grand railway station with magnificent conductors, but no trains. I fainted in the street in the snow. No one came up to me. I almost froze. I was wounded from the war in Jerusalem. An old Algerian took me to the Cité. I was advised to go to America. There are good Jews there, and you can have an operation, they said. Otherwise you'll go on fainting in the street and there'll be no one to pick you up. They gave me the name of an excellent teacher called Hans Hofmann. My little dog was my first woman. The saddest of them too, and the most innocent.

From Paris by train to Le Havre. From Le Havre, by an Italian ship, Panamanian flag, to Halifax, carrying German migrants to Alberta. All merry, stuffing down chickens and drinking beer. At night they swarm to the decks. Italian sailors collect them and throw them into cabins that aren't particularly pleasant. The ship, an old party from the thirties, with faded wallpaper and carpets, and a band out of a firemen's ball. The Germans vomit beer into the sea and the sea is calm most of the time. Once sharks appeared. A woman drank, drink for drink, with an Italian sailor, and fainted. In the ship's hospital a priest sat drinking tea, waiting. The band in the clubroom plays a waltz. The captain took off his hat with a wig and someone laughed the way I sometimes laugh at funerals. The woman recovered and the storm began. Because of the rocks they thought the ship would founder. Menacing ice floated on the surface and they said wait, imagine what's below. They said gale force nine, fringe of a hurricane, the ship leaped up and struck dully on the sea. The waves washed the deck and touched the funnel. A German wearing a Russian fur hat said that if there were a Jew on deck they could throw him overboard and the sea would subside. He laughed in alarm at his own voice. The captain cried desperately to the bridge through a pipe which carried stifled wails to the machine room, where usually an officer sat who before the war had been a communist and now wasn't. The German in the fur hat spoke to the Italian wireless officer who refused to speak German and claimed that today everybody spoke English. I broke a beer bottle and approached the German with the broken bottle in my hand. I wasn't particularly angry. His talk about Jews was wasted on me. The moment I came up to him he bent over and started crying. His mouth dribbled spittle and there was fear in his eyes. He crawled up to me and no one present intervened. The Italian smiled, lit a cigarette and trembled with excitement. The German drew nearer. I didn't move from the spot, I wanted to retreat, but I couldn't. Everyone looked at me. The German came too close and saved me, he rubbed up against the bottle and cut himself.

When he saw the blood coming from his hand, he tore his shirt. He wept tears of warm beer.

The Italian laughed a dry laugh like when you rub two stones together. A woman said excitedly, He'll kill him.

A fat man standing to the side shook his head and said sadly, No, he won't kill. And I didn't know which of us he was pitying. He drank beer from a large glass and wiped his mouth on his shirt. The wireless officer cut his cigar even though he could have thrown it into the sea. Fierce waves broke on the deck. The German asked for mercy. I threw the bottle into the sea. A talisman for the fish. I took out a clean handkerchief and offered it to the German. The fat man said in disappointment, I knew, I knew.

You don't know a thing, I said.

German?

I know it, I said.

He looked at me with renewed awe. The German on the deck kissed the handkerchief. I thought he'd clean the blood with it. He raised his bleeding hand to me and the flow of blood nauseated me. He looked at his hand as if it amazed him that he had blood of his own. I went to my cabin and he was pushed along by two Italian sailors. One of them stopped and pissed on the German, who tried to smile at me. I went into my cabin and slammed the door. They thought I'd laugh. I lay on my bed and tried to think. What funny things happen to me. The sea brings me wonders.

I could have got on board and said I'm a Jew. A farmer from Alberta, what do we have in common. Maybe I should've got up on deck and sung Getting to know you, like in The King and I, and saved the little man the shame. I went up on deck and heard whisperings. The German hadn't come back on deck. I read Dostoyevsky's Idiot in an easy chair. Stewards competed with each other to bring me a drink. I had no money. The captain with the wig paid for me. On the last evening I dined at his table. The only one from third class. The band played Viennese waltzes and gaudily made-up women danced with each other. The ship carried on to Halifax. When I went ashore I saw the German waving to me. A steward ran after me with a letter.

Dear Sir! My English is no good. Forgive me. In the war I was in the Wehrmacht. I did no one bad thing to thou. I go to be farmer in Alberta. I am very sorry and ask forgiveness. The blood on the hand is shame to us all.

Respectfully,
Robert Marx

N.B. I am not uneducated, please, I understand to the heart of the esteemed gentleman. Thank you very nice for everything. For the bottle unthrusted into me?

Very respectfully,
Robert Marx

I sailed to New York in a fishing boat. Along the East Coast. The spell of December with trees bare and black. A rugged coast and houses with gleaming roofs. We reached Hoboken New Jersey and there were many ships anchored there. A woman in a red hat waited in line for a bus. Aminadav with a bag. I said I'd come from France and was looking for Eighth Street. She said it was in Greenwich Village. They're all artists there. For twenty cents you can get to any place, she added. She sat down next to me and asked who I was. Try and explain. I showed her a colored drawing of Ashtoreth. The windowpane glinted and beyond it flashed houses, trees and a river. She explained that we were entering

Manhattan and the houses really were suddenly huge, an immense world closing above you. The first sight was unforgettable. Ships in the river. Beside them a train flying. Bridges, and inside the bridges cars charging in all directions and above them a plane preparing to land at La Guardia. They looked so serene through the window. The ships, the plane, the train and the cars. The woman claimed that everything'd work out fine, and vanished. The driver operated the bus door, which emitted a fascinating *ooffffff.* I got off and walked south toward Greenwich Village. From all the shops two songs blared, Somewhere Over the Rainbow and Stormy Weather. I let the world embrace me, caress my face, I smiled and I knew I was home. I thought: The world really is round, and I took an imaginary stone and threw it, and here were the waves, for I was the center of the world, circles going to every place. It was a long walk, I had ten cents left. I drank coffee at an automat and laughed when I saw my reflection in the mirror above. Above the boiling coffee. My tattered bag attracted no attention. Nor did I. Maybe somebody laughed, but there was no malice in it. At Forty-second Street, tired, I sat down on the bag and took a look at my city.

A short man with a cigar came out of the hotel, stopped, and looked at me. He started walking, then came back. He dropped the cigar and wanted to say something. I thought: If he speaks, I'll speak too. He didn't speak and went off again, then came back and stood there. A smile crept over the wrinkles of his eyes. Suddenly he took a coin out of his pocket and threw it to me. I picked up the coin and threw it to him. He threw it to me again and this time the smile was full. I smiled too, and threw the coin to him again. He stopped smiling, puffed at his cigar, coughed and said, *S'zol a riyach in dain taten arayn.*

I smiled. Puzzled, he screwed up his eyes and said, with something like melancholy: Jewboy? I said yessss. Long. Later they made it into a joke in a musical. But nothing was funny in Forty-second Street in the fierce cold with a blue sky as pale as steel and a little man with a cigar who'd thrown me a coin. I felt like a lord. The city whispered to me, I'm yours, Aminadav, my houses, from every window peered my father. With nine words:

44

Shalom Aminadav, how are you, I'm well, Love, Father. Such love.

Where you from? He didn't play at being polite and had a hoarse voice, as if he'd smeared his vocal cords with shoe polish. I told him. He said Ahhhhh. He drew out the Ahhhhhhh so long that I thought he'd choke. He was a strong man, with a round, smooth face. The cigar moved all the time. He invited me to have brunch with him. Me and this bag of mine. The brunch was nice. He asked a lot of questions. I didn't want to give him too many details, but was smart enough to tell him the story about the German in the Russian fur hat and the broken beer bottle. He called the Jews who were sitting around the bar and drinking whiskey. I repeated the story and told them about how the German had said what he'd said and how I'd drawn the beer bottle and threatened him. The German on his knees. The crying. My innocent action, from the movies, became a quick draw, I wanted something and didn't know what I wanted. Maybe I was pleading, something, with my story about the German and the beer bottle. In the new version I was the hero of a Western and I drew. That phrase, and of course I knew that was how it'd be, pleased them. They slapped each other on the back, hard enough to hurt, and said, These Israelis, they'll screw 'em all, the bastards!

My financial situation was discussed extensively and one of them said, Hey, we contribute every year, why not do it direct to a fighter for the honor of Israel? And so I became richer than I'd been. They bought me clothes and a hat. They gave me fifty dollars, cigarettes and razor blades, and left me, very pleased with themselves. The man who smoked the cigar said he was a lawyer specializing in visas and passports and if I ever needed anything he'd help me. Who knows what might happen. He gave me his visiting card. Rothschild & Co., Attorneys. He advised me to take a bus to Greenwich Village but I left him. I kept on walking. The evening was fragrant and descended upon me like a solace one looks for more than one finds. The sky turned red. It was very cold. A wind blew among the buildings, and all the shops played two songs: Somewhere Over the Rainbow and Stormy Weather.

I walked to Hans Hofmann's school on Eighth Street, opposite the drugstore. Hofmann took me up to a room, looked at my paintings for a long while, mumbled something to himself and told me there was nothing I could learn from him. He didn't want me to work in this school, he said. I almost pleaded, but he was decisive: No. Here there's a special atmosphere, a unified one with ups and downs, he said. You're too much of a painter, he said, or not a painter at all.

I went to Mount Sinai Hospital and the head doctor received me graciously. A nurse in green received me after the operation, with chocolate and ice cream. She sat beside me and played with things that had slumbered since Paris. She waited for me in the evening and I told her what I thought about the curves of her body. The sorrow of nurses. Afterward she went to meet her fiancé and I waited for her in bed. She saw me shaving and asked, Why a cutthroat. I told her I was an old-fashioned man. And she said that maybe she'd kill me, and that we were strangers to each other. You kiss strange people, enter strange women, while the closest to you you don't know and you're even afraid to wet your lips with them. I washed dishes in a hotel on Sixth Avenue. People said, with a malice wrapped in affability, that Hofmann had seen terrible things in my paintings. I knew what Hofmann had seen. He'd seen old things. There's nothing funnier than that. He'd seen things that were too real: A room. A window. Ashtoreth. The sacrifice of Isaac. I'd painted them in my little room with a battery radio and a telephone in the corridor, in a coat given me by two poets who had lived upstairs before me and one of whom had died out of unrequited love for himself. My paintings looked as if they were painted on ancient pots.

My house is pressed between other houses and supported by them. Fourteen dollars a month. Four rooms. One room stuck next to the other, like compartments, in the last room an old gas range and a refrigerator. The bath is under the table of the sink. Whenever the subway passes underneath, my home rocks as in prayer. Division Street. Windows covered with old curtains, left by a woman who once lived here. Everyone who has lived here has fled and left some traces. Cushions embroidered with tears, a small guitar on the wall, a decayed pair of pink ballet shoes, books, a broken vase, poems. Each thing saturated with a sorrow they hadn't been able to bear. No one had taken these things. They'd been piled on top of each other. Fourteen dollars a month. Without heating. I ordered a telephone. I had a number of my own. My name was in the phone book. I rang the exchange and asked for the number of Aminadav Sussetz. She looked it up with a pleasant voice and told me. It was lovely to know they knew about me. She said thank you and please as if I were really someone to her. And this was at night. At three in the morning. I wanted to kiss her. I slammed the phone down. Despairing in the midnight of all the people who had ever lived here. On this one bed, on which tragedies I could not imagine had occurred. The houses in the street looked like the faded décor for a play that had vanished from the stage while the audience still waited for the beautiful words, the whispers, the music, the actors, to return.

Opposite my house was an old movie house. Can an old movie house weep. Shops stuck to it on either side. Food shops and sweet shops and clothes shops. A shop for religious books, tefillin, mezuzahs, talithim. Bar mitzvah sets. *Fruchten. Mentelich. Pe'er Toroth. Billig. Koift do un seift gelt. God Bless America. Tzitziyes. Tchiken. Market kusher. Yohrzeit. We are proud to be Americans.*

Next to my house was a shop that sold Hebrew books, with a man in a hat under a lamp hanging on a cord with dead flies stuck to it and an empty can of olive oil from Palestine (Eretz Israel). There are fewer Jews here now, I was told at the grocer's. Mainly Puerto Ricans and Chinese. Chattering in Yiddish. The Jews are frightened, something's pushing them, they're looking for something that others have lost. In my room an old piano stood against the wall. I played it, a dry, frightening creak. Everything was under a layer of thick dust. On the piano was a pile of old yellow Tribunes that crumbled at the touch. They contained interesting reports from our correspondent Karl Marx on the condition of the miners in Liverpool.

On the walls of the movie house pasted notices, torn, flap in the wind. Alan Ladd, the lover from Honolulu. Compost heap of shreds. The African Queen with Katharine Hepburn and Humphrey Bogart, between Charlie Chan Does It Again in an Opium Den in Satan City, Will Cleo Moore Recover? Errol Flynn the glamorous bullfighter, a glass of whiskey! Corrida in Peru! The Murderer from the Panama Canal. Esther Williams will swim into your life, ah, with champagne and Ricardo Montalban and wondrous greetings from golden sewers. Our Esther, Queen. Teacher of mosquitoes, life size. Frankie, oh, Frankie! A girl had written on the notice: I'm crazy about you Frankie! And a boy had written beside this: Frankie, she's crazy about you but she gives it to me, vive la difference. Myrna Loy will captivate you!

An old man was selling *kvas* under Myrna Loy. A girl with bagels on a string. Under I'm crazy about you Frankie. The man from the Hebrew bookshop peeps out. Looking for me. He's always after me. A sad face under a lamp, reading J. L. Gordon.

Bagels a boy said. The Indians on the wall of the movie house are headless. Someone has torn Ava Gardner's eyes. The innocent violence of the forties. Next to the movie house, old and worn, stands a Yiddish theater. Smoke rises, from a chimney. They're cooking charity soup. The poor stand in line. Each with his tin plate and then they'll go and get drunk on Third Avenue. On the theater entrance a poster of the Committee for Sacco and Vanzetti. A general in paper clothes, riding on bandy legs, smoking a cigarette without touching it with his hand. In the yard Mrs. Chan Li sells enemas to Jewish women in colored aprons with kerchiefs around their heads. The general smokes all day. Never moves from here. Winter and summer. Once he climbed into the movie house through a broken window. He slept there. Smiles at me with his broken teeth and horrible black mouth and says, Please mister, please mister. He wants to take my coat, to let me out of a magnificent limousine, maybe a purple Packard. I don't have anywhere to go, General! Only the blind go to the closed theater. Into the yard with the enemas by mistake. The girl dances because of the cold, and throws bagels to the general, pitying him. The toothless general eats, sucks his bagel beside Sacco and Vanzetti, beside the enemas.

In a Chinese restaurant with Neapolitan décor, with Vesuvius painted on the wall and a sweet Capri and a girl sending doves off the bay of the girl I called my little dog, with an erasure containing an advertisement for a Japanese ascetic center, eating a tasty knaidlach soup and hallah like my grandfather used to bake. To the side, in gold letters: With a good word—and a gun —you can get almost anything! The proprietor in an undershirt with long sleeves refuses to accept payment. *Shabbes* today. The next day I came and paid. It was as if he didn't believe, looking from me to the money and back, mumbling. He guessed I was Italian and said *grazie*, which sounded like *toida*. Across the river, near the bridge, flickers an old Coca-Cola sign. On the other side of the river, my side, next to the general and the girl with the bagels, is a relatively new sign, DRINK PEPSI-COLA IT'S MORE RE- FRESHING.

Pepsi and Coca wage war over me, opposite my window, through which New York at night looks like a huge, ever-extend- ing fire. I know there's life behind the stained houses. I don't go very far. I paint my Ashtoreths and wash dishes in a restaurant. Every day up to Sixth Avenue. To embrace huge pots. To feel panic every time a glass broke. Who has the strength. I didn't go very far. In my house, with the old piano, crumbling newspapers, round colored cushions, with all those who ever lived here. To sense them, to touch their pain in these rooms. Sometimes I'd go to the Village to meet my friend Jerome and his wife Stephanie. Then they still lived together and they'd sit together in the bathroom: she shaving her legs and he his beard. I met some painters who laughed because Hans Hofmann had said I was too much of a painter or not a painter at all. I looked for someone who'd know that I existed, through my paintings. There was no one. I met the famous art critic Kurt Singer with an eighteen-year- old girl at whom he already looked as if he'd gladly give her a child. He'd look at me and say, It's really strange, truly strange. Why strange? I drink beer and the courage runs through my veins again.

That you at all, that is . . .

That is, what?

Are present.

Exist?

I didn't say exist, I said are present. There's a difference. Surrender, young sir, feel what the canvas does to a painter's hand. Not what El Greco does to a miserable imitator. I smiled because I didn't have anything to say. After all, who knows better than Kurt Singer. Once we were drunk. He was holding the hand of a girl who'd been in my bed. She wanted to get to know the world and moved to him with the suitcase and easel she'd brought to my apartment. Her name was Natasha even though she wasn't Russian. He sat in the bar opposite me and we drank brandy and I revealed to him that I remembered five months of the nine I'd been in the womb. And Kurt Singer didn't laugh. He looked at me for a long time and never have I seen such an expression of disappointment creeping over any face. Not because I remembered, but because a wonderful memory had been wasted on me. The girl with the easel and the suitcase tended to agree with him even though the night before she'd told me she loved me more than anybody in the world. She didn't believe in the fact that people have souls, so this was a great and exciting compliment. Now she said that she'd always known that nature had wasted a not unattractive face on me. A mediocre body and a startling memory. I was shocked. I thought: Why such piercing jealousy. Since then I don't know what Kurt Singer hates more, my memory or my paintings which look as if they've been painted on pots. Who needs pots in these days of fluorescence.

Then I started working at the Yiddish newspaper. Between the Hebrew bookseller, my paintings in the bitter nights with all those who'd ever lived in my apartment, and the newspaper, nothing remained. At night a man died. It was then I rang the operator to ask if there was an Aminadav Sussetz in New York and she said yes, and gave me the phone number and even my address. That night I really felt easier. Somebody knew I existed. For at the entrance to the newspaper office stood dying men arguing fervently. In another month or two they'd turn into obituaries, or death notices with black frames around them, Yiddish newspaper style. And the more someone insisted on standing at the office entrance the greater grew his chances of turning into a black notice. They argued fervently. No little spit was sprayed on those coming in and going out. But no one seemed to complain. One gets used to everything. Then I also understood that God is not the delightful transparent wings of the butterfly. He's the tormented legs of the worm. At the entrance to the newspaper office tracts and pamphlets were handed out: Zionist and anti-Zionist, Trotskyist and Socialist. They were pale, meticulously dressed, with hats on their heads, trembling, these dying men. I sold one of them a bundle of old Tribunes containing articles by Karl Marx and he kissed my hand. With the money I bought canvas and paints. Men dressed up as reporters, hatless, slip eagerly out of the newspaper office, rush past the dying men, fly off in cabs, yell at the driver, Step on it, to cover bar mitzvah ceremonies in Avenue A. They always look as if they're off to interview the President. They speak of intrigues.

Old typists typed on old typewriters and in the intervals darned socks. I walked from room to room carrying matrices, receiving instructions. Boy come here! Boy come here!

In the entrance hall, next to the switchboard, a woman dressed in black with a waxen face, oh, how beautiful she is, say the old men. She's beautiful as an old book is beautiful. Crystalline, her black clothes suit her. All those days she sat behind a large desk, intently reading death notices while the old men in the entrance grew fewer and fewer.

She goes into the building in the morning, past the dying men, without seeing that they're growing fewer, they all love her so, bring her flowers, dream about her at night, ask me if she wears a black slip and if anyone ever rings her up. They want to know what kind of underpants she wears. How would I know. She takes off her old fur coat every morning, sits down by the desk and reads death notices. After she's read the notices she cuts them out, with what gentleness, she was almost coquettish at that moment, files them, and erases from a thick book with a bordeaux binding and pages rimmed with pure gold. Her hands shake slightly. The names she erased were buried within her as if they were all her lovers. Yet she'd never known what they looked like. She carefully checked if the dead man had left a wife. If a woman, had she left a husband. The children they didn't bother. The lonely husbands who grew fewer and fewer at the entrance to the newspaper office waited for her, trembling in some kind of fever. They got specially dressed up for her. Every day a different tie. They took out of mothballs things the wife had put aside for the grandson's wedding. And they stood outside. In the wind. In the heat. Once there was a heat wave and they fainted. She didn't see. Dead people continued receiving the newspaper after they were dead, and not a few unpleasant incidents ensued. There were sons who received the newspaper for breakfast with their American wife and seemed amazed and wrote furious letters. She read the letters with a smile and on her face was an expression of pity and revenge. Then she filed them away. The file grew and swelled. Later she replaced the file with a tin cabinet that was painted black, and that stood next to the coat hanger. Whenever she went to the cabinet she shook slightly. The letters of complaint were answered in Yiddish. Slowly, slowly, the newspaper yielded to death and stopped arriving.

She didn't like me. I'm using the wrong verb, she detested me. The Hebrew I spoke was a slaughterer's knife to her. She hated the man who sold Hebrew books and me with the same hatred. As if it were I who had slaughtered her subscribers. That was unfair. Her enemy was America, not me. But she chose her enemies with the same noble misery garnished with immeasurable charm with which she cut out the death notices.

As an enemy I was comfortable, young, uncombed, the son of a father who wrote nine-word letters, Mother—pogromic features, like an Italian she said once, perhaps to justify her hostility, taking pleasure in the sight of the stab that I was in her eyes. Carrying matrices and galley proofs to hatless newspapermen. She knew that I knew the letters but didn't understand the language. Once she burst out laughing with a brittle wildness and her mouth contorted and I saw her as she was. A hundred years old, her throat and neck old. Her open mouth was gold teeth and a kind of ancient misery, preserved, age revealed in all its nakedness. What underpants does she wear. Why, she could be your sister and your bride. Her wrinkles were not protected for a moment.

The switchboard operator occasionally exchanged a few words

with me. She tried in vain to find out who I am and why. She has relatives in Haifa. In secret she knew how to say If I forget thee Jerusalem, but her husband is a Trotskyist radical. And she said to me with a smile that was not lacking in malice that the woman in black (she called her by name but I'm not willing to bring it to the verge of my lips) is not willing, so she said, to recognize my existence.

During a lunch break I asked her straight out why she isn't willing to recognize my existence. I remembered Kurt Singer, who said he wasn't willing to believe I was present. Was this an international conspiracy. The fact that she wasn't willing to acknowledge my existence seemed strange to me on the background of erasures of subscribers' names and hatless reporters. I saw a smile of pain curl out from the corners of her mouth. I so loved her pain, I understood it, her eyes looked at me and at the man who sold Hebrew books fortified behind me with three volumes of *Ha-Tekufa* and peered at us as though from here some salvation would come to the table of bargains next to his shop where lay, torn and weary, books by Smolenskin Brenner and Agnon in thin red bindings stained with the marks of public libraries which no one wanted. It was from within me that her pain seemed to well. Her smile began within me. From my heart.

She erased a huge thing in which I had no part. I left her alone. I regretted that I didn't really understand the hatless reporters. Writing alertly, shoving pencils behind their ears, wearing unpressed vests, shouting, typing on old typewriters with cigars in their mouths, looking like carbon copies of Alan Ladd, George Raft or John Garfield. They crumbled before my eyes like the notices on the front of the ruined movie house. The importance they attached to the malicious intrigues of the deputy reception clerk of the sanitary department of Brooklyn Heights, or to the schemes and delaying tactics, hidden from all eyes, of the deputy general registrar in the bailiff's office on Canal Street. It was as if they were playing soundlessly, in a huge hall, some rhapsody for carbon copies of journalistic inventions. They listened attentively to Mr. Yankel, the owner of the small supermarket on the corner of Avenue B and Third Street, next to funny houses with broken roofs, with fat women singers who'd come down in the world and had got stuck here in the Ziegfeld Follies of Third Avenue, opposite a bookstand of the Jehovah's Witnesses. Mr. Yankel made a powerful speech at the wedding of Miss Mabel and the dentist from Chicago and they wrote it up and hinted at its far-reaching political implications. The movement of the stars in the sky was conditioned to no little extent by the number of shopkeepers from Canal Street who went off to seek new pastures in Queens or Long Island. Everything was saturated with signs and secrets. A huge acrostic which they interpreted with open eyes and uncertain hearts.

Except one.

The immense Mr. Herzberg. The man to whom the woman in black smiled, the one she longed for. Whose name her eyes celebrated. A Morse code of blood clots stuck in the heart. Tall, dressed like a baron. In Tel Aviv there'd been a rich man who had a big house with a swimming pool and a private English garden. Gesundheit was his name. We'd stand there and wait, maybe the car would come out. We thought of carriages like Queen Therese's. I thought about Gesundheit. With the English gardens in Little Tel Aviv of carts and watermelons. Watermelons! After *badim badim,* in Ben Yehuda Street. The man in the house of Yiddish was Gesundheit in the desert. Shining shoes. Beautiful shirt. The face of a poet, magnificent white hair. Might be a hundred years old, or forty. Walked as if dancing ballet. To him smiled my lady of the black dresses.

Always evasive. Doing is a private thing. No one sees. Actually he has a hidden room. With a huge filing cabinet, a new typewriter, newspaper clippings. His articles have a rare beauty, they say. Every morning he arrives at nine sharp. Pauses beside the dying men outside, surveys them, like a father inspecting his son before he goes to school. If there really are fathers like that. They smile at him. They joke, despite a certain discomfort. As if they're being inspected not by a father but by God. But God is also the Devil, they said with a smile of clowning, mixed with fear. He enters, accepts as his due the greeting of the woman in black and the list of that night's black frames. He reads the names and sees

54

hearts that have stopped beating, a sorrowful night in a forsaken room. He sees an empty apartment and an old man, a heart beating and stopping. Blood clots stuck in the old sewerage system. Without protest, with no challenging cry. The woman in black smiles and sings to him good morning, how are you today Mr. Herzberg, it's a lovely day or dreadful one today, and what's new. After taking the list that has already been erased from the subscribers' book he goes up in the elevator to his solitary room, opens a drawer in the iron cabinet, ferrets through the files, finds all the details, all those beautiful things that give a man a body, and without an erasure, in clean, pressed writing, without a crossing out or a typing error, he allows the words to write themselves and become an impressive obituary. Every subscriber gets two obituaries. One written, clean and crystalline, and one recited in a dry and personal voice beside the open grave before it is closed up. Mr. Herzberg knows the dead he writes about just as the woman with the black dresses knows the black frames. Several months back Mr. Herzberg celebrated his eightieth birthday. I think, said the switchboard girl, that since I started working here, in August '38, Mr. Herzberg has written a thousand obituaries.

Over the years he'd learned that you can't rely on anyone. The files were classified material. He had the only key. If he dies the writers of obituaries will have no data. He inspects every one. Examines him. Learns him by heart. Who doesn't want a little pity and love on the day he dies. There are obituary writers, said the switchboard girl, who go to the relatives and ask questions. Not Herzberg! His filing system knows everything, he's done their obituaries many years before they die. And people treat themselves with a degree of reverence, for everyone wants to arrive at the cemetery as if he's Albert Einstein or Rabbi Fishman. Mr. Herzberg speaks about the posture of the deceased, about his smile, about his eating habits, about the beautiful things he said at the opening of the Maccabee Conference in Grodno in nineteen thirty-one, in January. . . .

Mr. Herzberg told me that he no longer believes in the power of youth to save life. Do you know, sir, he said, that a young man I knew well forty-seven years ago, when I was thirty-three, died thirty-one years ago and I didn't know what to say about him?

He knows everyone. Every day he stops at the cafeteria in Fourteenth Street. He walks among the tables, embracing future obituaries in crossed glances. He goes to the little park next to Delancey, jots in his notebook the stability of legs, eyebrows concave or convex. Files intimate details with a twinkle. He's never been married. They say that once there was a woman, "modern," handsome, communist, she'd gone to Russia, written letters, asked him to come, and vanished. He took sand and put it in a bottle, as if it were her dust. He buried her in the yard and cried. Since then he hasn't cried. He has excellent quotations. Every morning he reads three newspapers and gleans wise sayings. He loves to say jovial and amusing things about simple deeds, detests generalities, pays the dead true respect and not a grief wrapped in fears and banalities.

Death comes suddenly is his motto. The young men in my department, dispatchers and copyboys, are afraid of him. They sneak off into the lavatory when they see him passing along the corridor with his magnificent carriage and a handkerchief in his top jacket pocket. The day before yesterday he looked at Hershel and yesterday Hershel died. They joked about his interrogating gaze but their eyes didn't laugh. I respected him because of his professionalism, like my lady in black of the death notices. I won't say he isn't frightening. But I think of the woman cutting dead men out of the newspaper with terrible gentleness and I calm down. If he dies, he'll manage to walk to the cemetery, to speak his own obituary, to cover himself with earth and to vanish forever. Once we found ourselves in the elevator, he and I. He pressed the button because he wouldn't let a boy like me take him up for nothing. The elevator stuck between the fourth floor and the fifth. It was hot and the light was on. We rang the emergency bell and someone promised he'd call the technician, who'd gone out to eat lunch. Mr. Herzberg said to me, don't worry, what can there be to be afraid of, he spoke English for my sake, and I knew very well how hard it is for him to say personal things in English. He didn't loosen his tie and I felt I was choking. At first the choking was only a movement of the esophagus muscle. I rubbed my throat and the hawk's eyes rested on my neck. My eyes were open but I was on top of the Jerusalem mountains. A cold wind blew. A tracer bullet lit up the darkness and my friend who was dead beside me. I said to him, Nahum, shoot! He didn't answer. I turned my face and saw his head dropping and then I covered myself in the remains of his brain. Mr. Herzberg examined my face. I wanted to break through the door or the roof. His eyes fixed on me. Measuring me. My throat convulsed again. Someone shouted from below, any minute now, a little patience. He didn't move.

He sweated quietly. Perhaps he was as perturbed as I was and I didn't see. Someone tried to release the elevator, the cable shook, the light went out for a moment and then lit up again. I knew he was inspecting me. After all, death comes suddenly, and youth is no guarantee against death. My throat felt strangled. I'm convulsing. Someone writes my obituary. I wasn't dreaming, for I was with Mr. Herzberg all the time, and I saw his face and his closed mouth. But I traveled out from inside myself. There were three houses there. One of them sprung from a large car. The second's roof was a boat and the third was a flowering garden with tropical plants. Suddenly I knew names that I immediately forgot. We went up the mountain. Then I fell into the valley, like a stone falling from a high place. I couldn't stop and then there was a sudden joy and I said to myself, here I am, dying in Mr. Herzberg's mouth, and what's this sudden joy. And a man whispered to me from inside my brain, a man without any dimensions, big and small at the same time, and said that I wasn't dying. I wasn't being born, and I didn't rejoice. Mr. Herzberg's eyes continued contemplating me. The trip didn't take longer than a minute. For at the moment the choking began, Mr. Herzberg took the hand-kerchief out of his pocket, wiped his forehead, and put it back in the pocket. All this occurred while the handkerchief left the pocket, reached the forehead, wiped the beads of sweat, and returned to the pocket.

I was with my friend. Vultures waited for blood on electricity poles, in marvelous expanses empty of air or wind. I ascended and descended. The houses with the roofs changed in a landscape that was both savage and serene. Something desolate like the face of the moon in a huge telescope. I floated in black expanses, in immeasurable spaces, and so I was able to return to Mr. Herzberg without knowing that I'd been sailing for a billion years in anti-matter that greedily swallows up spaces. Suddenly I was pushed and found myself in a dark, silent cave. My throat pinched. I couldn't breathe. I wanted to get out. To be born or to die. I didn't know which was which. The waiting was long and marvelous. But I wanted to breathe. There were folded legs there waiting for me. And Father with nine loving words. Shalom Aminadav, how are you, I'm well, Love, Father. The marvelous potentiality that I was for myself. I came from out of the obituary to my father and I said something to him. From the black spaces I came into a cave. The houses with the roofs. I was born and I died. Before his eyes. One minute, a wondrous shackling. I dreamed my death and my birth. Five months in the womb. The entry into the womb from the black spaces. The trees. The light coming on and going off. The mechanic who was late in arriving. The cabdriver Yo ho ho. Everything is one thing. And I'm nothing but a single cell trying to conquer a place for itself, to know it exists in spite of everything. The terrible was soft and conciliatory, the conciliation was sharp and violent. I flashed past my entire life. All the Aminadavs I'd been sat in the elevator and laughed. Mother with her Mongolian face. Father smashing violins. Uncles, aunts. *Badim badim.* Oh, God, even Naomi who was yet to be born. Kurt Singer the famous art critic speaking about his own sex life wearing a hat made of newspaper. The people who expect things from you. The women who want you to be someone else. The children who want to grow up. The grownups who want to stay as they are. Mr. Herzberg with the dying men at the entrance to the newspaper office.

My throat was choking and I was pale. I had known a death that went on for too long a time. Coming out to my knees. The doctor, Dr. Freund, waiting for me with scissors. The cutting of the cord and the sucking that awaited me now. And the hair that would grow. People would ask boy or girl. My father would say Aminadav, my mother would say three and a half kilos. Like chicken, by weight. They'd say, a beautiful child. Thirty-eight hours, in Little Tel Aviv, the second of May, the fourth of Iyar 5690. Born: Aminadav Sussetz. In the Freund Hospital. Behind Cinema Eden. And Bialik would come leaning on his stick and say, Call him Aminadav. And here the loss begins. I went out, extinguished, until the moment an Arab boy threw a burning cigarette at a cat. I remember black spaces and afterward a womb, a womb of wombs. Mother. Knees. Doctor. Dr. Freund, arrogant and kind. Mr. Zwiegel from the gallery wants me to hang some new creations. My father wants me to smash my violin. What's to be done, Mr. Herzberg. Has the moment arrived.

He said, what's wrong with you, listen, you're pale. . . .

I said, my throat. He smiled. Did he know. The voices outside grew louder. I returned, with a certain facility, to the stuck elevator. The stink of trapped men's sweat. And meanwhile in his eyes I read the obituary: Young and rebellious . . . darling . . . his language is Hebrew, but his heart beats with the nation's eternal language. . . . The eternity of the language is not measured by its antiquity, by its having been written on ancient pots, but by its vitality, its persistence . . . hundreds of years, thousands, millions of living words, never erased, trying to bring to life a dead past. . . . The present . . . he runs, fleet of foot . . . between compositors and editors . . . carrying proofs in letters he knows and in a language he doesn't know . . . a Jewish tragedy. . . . The nation's love for its destroyers flowing from within him . . . that sadness. His brown eyes. Burning in a two-thousand-year-old Jewish anguish. The touch of his hand on his neck, like silk. Fear of closed places. He died before his time. . . . He has gone from us, a boy. . . .

I thought: From C. N. Bialik who was my godfather to Mr. Herzberg who composed my obituary, and that's it. My mother was a daughter of the Feldman family. A daughter of Bialik's friend Nehemiah Feldman, who, you may have heard Mr. Herzberg, wrote a poem "O my crown, that how much to my friends . . ." My father was from the well-known Sussetz family from the Ukraine. I planned my entry into the world with formulae. I asked myself, Which is more correct, Mr. Herzberg's obituary or the godfatherhood of the knight of Hebrew poetry. Am I a poem by Bialik or an obituary in Yiddish. Now the mechanic comes. The woman in black from the death notices calls to her love through the elevator shaft. She didn't call to me. The light glares. It melts the last of my hope. I yield to the gaze of Mr. Herzberg. A modest smile, ironic and daring. Filling me. Into the black iron cabinet. In the middle of the letter *S.* Aminadav S., Israel. Godfather: Bialik. Was born and died. In between: things. Chokes in elevators. His mother Feldman, Yiddish for man of the field. His father Sussetz, Hebrew for rockinghorse. Framemaker. Smashed a violin. Mongolian faces in the Feldman tribe. The day will come. The cable was released. We were saved. For the time being.

We arrived at the fifth floor. The air blew at me. I almost fainted. He left me without saying goodbye. He just waved his hand.

At the end of the day my lady in black was waiting for me downstairs. Lovely day, isn't it? As if I had an answer. Outside the street was getting darker. Drugstores. The ruined movie house. The theater. The soup kitchen. The old general with no teeth. The girl selling bagels. The seller of Hebrew books, wearing a poet's hat from the thirties, sadly gathered the pamphlets and books from his bargain table outside. He stared at me. As usual. Outside the usual battles raged on: Alka-Seltzer against Bromo-Seltzer, Coca-Cola against Pepsi-Cola. Aspirin against Anacin. Side-curled children against Hebrew books.

The seller of Hebrew books returned to his store. Defeated, under the naked lamp, behind him a can of oil, Shemen, made in Israel, and a collection box of the Jewish National Fund. Reading an old book. The woman in black came out for a breath of air and to wait for Mr. Herzberg. The old men had gone home to sleep or to turn into black frames. Perhaps my lady in black wanted me to kill the seller of Hebrew books. But his subscribers had died long before her subscribers died. How defeated the two of them were this evening. Trotskyists handed out leaflets. Girls from the Salvation Army, wearing purple and red, sang the songs of the Saviour. A Chinese wept in the doorway of the restaurant. A distant America celebrated beyond the houses.

On the day I was born, my father, Naftali Sussetz, stood in the yard of the Freund Hospital in Yehuda Halevy Street in Tel Aviv and waited for me. Beyond the yard, in Cinema Eden, they were showing a talking movie for the first time in the country. The Jazz Singer. "The Mad Singer" in Hebrew. While Al Jolson sang Sonny Boy and rolled his famous eyes I struggled with what I did not know then was Mr. Herzberg's obituary. I did not want to come into a world of professional obituary writers and I made my poor mother suffer. I fought. Thirty-eight hours. The crime was perpetrated, my mother was torn apart with terrible pains, and I was.

4

The choking didn't leave me for many days. One night I couldn't fall asleep. Death crawled toward me. I had an hour or two left. I felt fierce pains in the stomach, in the throat, as if I'd swallowed a huge bone. I went to the city hospital and asked to be examined. The doctor in white with smooth white hands. He examined me with a certain curtness, I sensed something solemn singing in my suffering. The doctor spoke in a professional and compassionate voice. He asked, Where are the pains, in the back? I nodded. In the stomach, here, feel the pressure? Yes. And in the throat and esophagus. I nodded. I'm dying before the eyes of professional players, my lady in black, Mr. Herzberg and now the doctor, who mumbled something. My special pains, the combination of which aroused horror, had a name. I went to the drugstore on the corner of Division Street where the pharmacist called me Aminodev, and asked him if there was a disease by that name. He laughed; during the past year there have been one hundred and two cases of it just on Horatio Street. What do you say, he said, the city's full of terrors. Maybe it's an epidemic. I asked him, and what about the choking, the desperate calls to the telephone operator at night, the fear of elevators, and the awful dread, the death waiting for me on tiptoe. He laughed. Yes, yes, he said, a disease is an objective thing, not a subjective one, as many people erroneously think.

And so I was classified. At night I awoke with fierce pains. A cold and objective sweat covered my body. I couldn't breathe. The darkened room glowed with the Pepsi-Cola sign. I couldn't concentrate on Karl Marx's articles on the conditions of the miners in Liverpool. Farther away the city resounded like the roar of a beast. The red lights, a fire above my house, a godforsaken bridge. A drunk yelling down below, let me in you whore. A spotted cat skipping out of garbage cans outside the movie house. It digs its claws into the tails of the posters. They come loose and start flapping in the wind. Yellow strips of posters, a faded and mosaic picture of strange parts of a painting. The drunk cries, You whore, you whore . . . what if I've had a drink, what's wrong, you think I've been having fun, hell. The shape of a woman in a poster. Leaning forward. Wearing evening dress, with a long train, trailing on the carpet. From among the folds of her dress, from out a dense forest, flows the inscription Spring Is Coming with Walter Pidgeon. A bull butts a train, God, what a sight. My head's heavy. I can't breathe.

At the hospital they'll just send me away. What can I say to them, I've been classified. I look around the room. Cushions. Piano. Call the operator. She says, Aminadav Sussetz, and pronounces the telephone number. And then she'll add, Division Street. She knows. I smiled at her through the telephone cable. She didn't know I was dying and slammed down the phone. I look at my suitcase, into the wicker basket I brought from Paris. A tag, ZIM-Negba. Beside it a Panamanian flag. I remember how once the rain water burned in the heat. It was beautiful in some distant land. Someone once wrote on my bag many years ago, before Nahum died in the Jerusalem hills, I am the splendor, I am the glory, I am the undersigned, Israel Kremer the Fart. And I found a note my mother had written me jubilees ago and for some reason was still among my belongings. "Aminadav my dear, remember what I told you. Don't drink cold water after eating grapes. Brush your teeth in the morning and before going to sleep. And if there's a curfew go into the nearest house. And don't smoke in shelters."

The moon peeps out between fragments of cloud. A heavy, dying man sits in a window. Aminadav Sussetz will not see the morning. All the houses opposite, clowns laughing at my desolation. On a distant radio, among the houses, Sister Rosetta Tharp sings:

> He's so high you can't get over Him,
> He's so low you can't get under Him,
> He's so wide you can't get around Him,
> You must come in through the door!

I fled from her God. The stairs echo. Doors all around me. The Hebrew bookstore's closed. Is he staring at me. Hans Hofmann whispers from inside me: He's too much of a painter or not a painter at all. I walked through the streets as if it was mercy I was seeking. I got to Fifth Avenue. Quiet and empty. The tower of a small church covered with lilac. The shadow of a black bell and a dog barking from inside a house. Slaughterhouse of night.

A policeman swinging a stick in the entrance to the adjacent house. Yawning into a thousand dusty rooms.

Next to the Olivetti agency there's a concrete stand. Attached to it is a typewriter and beside it the inscription: Come and try! The policeman approached me and shoved his gaze onto the weird thing that I was. Did he smell the death. I asked him if it was permitted to write on the typewriter.

No law against it.

So I may?

You a poet or something?

Painter.

Same thing, he said, write. In the middle of the night they come and write, poor bastards, they can't sleep. Suckers. I know the type. I heard his voice and I knew, one more who'd been spewed up. One more person who rings the exchange to ask if he exists somewhere. The representative of the law. New York's Finest. Coca-Cola's pillar of salt.

Johnny Machine-gun wrote poems with a machine gun, he said. His voice was an intimate thing in the night. But I was afraid, I didn't want him to know my plea. In this city you're lost if you've got a plea on your face. Horace would have said:

If you want me to cry, you'll have to be sad first.

Would the policeman cry.

I've got no paper, I said.

That's tough.

But I have to write.

What's it to me.

Give me a break.

Dark intrigues behind them walls is my duty.

Give me a ticket.

I got better things to do.

Give me a ticket.

What for?

So I can write on it, I've got no paper.

I got rotten tickets, he said, and you? All poets have a hole in the head, I got one in the ass. Steal a car, drive a hundred miles an hour—you'll get a ticket.

The last man who'd see me alive, my obituary written in the flickering of distant neon, I don't have the courage to steal, I said.

You need guts to steal! What do poets know. Writing in newspapers . . .

I'm a painter.

Same shit. Guts is like a bridge. Ever seen a bridge? A huge thing. It's got balls. Iron. Not a poem. Shove your poems up your ass.

He grew silent suddenly, his face pensive. He looked at me, humaneness in uniform, a light in his face, I'm a cop, he said, *and I got an ass too.* But it's got to be lawful. Get it, kid? Who are you anyway. A foreigner. Where you from.

Ukraine, I said.

Anticommunist! His voice rose over the opacity of the lonely night. That's what I like, he added. Look at this stick, that's me, a stick's a bridge, with permission, this stick is to steal or the opposite, a bridge isn't a poem.

I'm a painter, I said.

Same shit.

I thought: will my dreams recognize me. A dying man. Will his death recognize his life. Will his dreams know who I am. And he tells me, openly and frankly tells me about his wife. Her name's Doris. And I'd better not get him wrong, Doris is a wonderful woman, but she admires people who get written about in the papers. She sits at the hairdresser's with this thing on her head and reads magazines. Who writes that stuff, people who get written about in the papers write in the papers. Who writes, poets write.

I'm a painter.

Ah. Poets with Doris under that thing on her head, silver-colored, with magazines. They write about O'Callahan. You think I never knew him? We grew up in the same street. He sat in that room with that fat woman and got a chicken's foot stuck in his mouth. The door was locked. The woman couldn't get off her chair 'cause she'd eaten two chickens and had bloated up. The servant yelled. And who was outside? I was outside. I broke down the door. Him with the chicken in his mouth and her with her ass inside the chair. They couldn't get out. And in the magazine Doris reads it says that a cop saved O'Callahan and Mrs. Robin Robin.

Then he took a chair and killed Robin Robin. That was a month afterward. And his face pops up in all the magazines again for Doris with a Thermos on the head, at the hairdresser's. Smiling at me on television and Doris comes home with a million-dollar face and wants me to kill someone for her so's the papers'll write about me. Every morning she asks, Have you killed anyone yet? With the stick, sweetie, with a permit.

Poetic, I said.

Yeah? he said. Who'm I going to kill for her. I caught three fags in the yard at two hundred and thirty Fifth Avenue. One of them's sick in the kidneys. Once I caught a pickpocket. A kid. Chewing gum eyes he had. Tears on his sleeves. His father's somebody's deputy.

There's a disease like that—kleptomania.

Poets know the fucking names for everything.

I'm a painter.

Same shit. They let the kid go. What, wasn't I happy? I was happy. Him and those weeping eyes of his. What can you do.

66

Once it was different. Before the reds took over. Look at the street. Dead. Nothing happening. Alarm bells in every building, and thieves stealing in Harlem.

I told him I'd once seen a robber sleeping in a public park in the Ukraine.

He said that in America it wouldn't happen. Robbers don't sleep in public parks. If they'd only sleep! I said maybe it was because of the exchange rate of the dollar and he tended to accept my view. For a moment America lit up in him: Joe DiMaggio, Teddy Roosevelt, Buffalo Bill, Jane Russell, John Wayne! I thought he'd stand to attention and sing the national anthem. How could I know. I'm sensitive to moments when people sing anthems. Like in cemeteries. I want to cry and I laugh. But he says, here everyone can sleep in the public park, there's enough room.

I said that maybe it was so but that people didn't do it. Anatole France had said that in Paris poor and rich alike can sleep under bridges. My friend was suddenly moved to tears. The things that can happen in this great big world.

I reminded him about the ticket. He gave me two. The street a smudge of lights and shadows. A drunk in a long coat stumbled toward us. He wanted to know where the cemetery is. My friend took his papers, looked through them and told him where he lived. The man mumbled thanks and said, That's where I got to get to. The incredulous gaze he fixed on us. I wanted to give him Mr. Herzberg's address. But I didn't know if he was Jewish. A woman came out of a house and saw Aminadav with a ticket next to the typewriter, in the middle of the empty street, and ran for her life. Francis Mulligan, the policeman, laughed, and I started to write. In the bright light writing at night about my death. He left me, see you, at celebrations and all that. We wished each other nice things. I wanted to tell him to come to my funeral but I took pity on him. I wrote a poem about choking, about a city in which I had no one to telephone some parting words to. I wrote that I'm a little boy drawn in black chalk on a white desert.

Then I put the poem in my pocket and walked through night streets. I saw lighted shopwindows, beautiful shoes, washing machines, toasters, plastic candles and several people who looked foreign. A fever of not-life seeped through. I thought: What's a journey. The word for journey in Greek means a book in Hebrew. In 1929 my father took my mother for a trip to Germany, to meet those who smashed his violin. They slept in a little *pension* in Heidelberg. At night my mother got frightened. My father brought his bed closer. A vase smashed. And he entered. And so I was born nine months later, in Tel Aviv the tragedy I'm testifying about occurred.

I went down to my streets. The signs in Yiddish and Hebrew settled my mind. It was morning. I went upstairs. The janitor let me in and said, ah, working overtime, and chewed salt herring. I wrote a letter. I placed it on the table of the lady in black.

Dear Madam,

I am a footstool for your feet and you are lovelier than hell. I don't know your name but your devotion has conquered my heart. Today you looked at me for the first time (after having refused to recognize my existence all this time), and you wanted to know if it was a lovely day, and I didn't know. Forgive me. Please tell Mr. Kremer in the errand boys' department that I was forced to leave suddenly and that I ask his forgiveness for not handing in an official letter of resignation. If anyone wants to know what has happened to me he can ask Mr. Herzberg who knows everything in advance.

I love you. Because you are beautiful and sad, and I understand sad people. You lack reality in a world of black frames, and that's a huge thing. You are crystal, pure and perhaps even terrible, in a world filled with retreat. You are dry and wonderful inside the sheaf of light that erases dead people in a dead language.

I admire brave soldiers, like you, fighters for a cause that doesn't exist and is therefore so exalted. Soldiers who die on a familiar and official altar seem less brave to me. Once I knew a woman who committed suicide because the curry in India no longer contains the twelve species of curry it once contained. She didn't even especially like curry. That was beautiful, sad and touching. War is something mighty but superfluous, and vice versa. Only the truly superfluous fight just wars. Just wars are those that don't make sense anymore. Your war is hopeless, both qualitatively and formally, because Yiddish will vanish and the dead won't return. The well will be emptied. Your book will be closed and will dry up. The notices will be no more. The children will die in English, or Hebrew. Even my Hebrew is not so great a conquest. A renewal of tribalism is not such a glorious idea in the twentieth century.

We are a sad people, madam, a stubborn people, and, in the final analysis, funny. We wage wars against all the great empires, we're always defeated by them, and we outlive them all.

Yours, Aminadav Sussetz

How can we know what has been when we don't know what will be. Two days after she came out of the hospital my mother went to the famous Mrs. Kantorovitz and asked her to do my horoscope. I'm a Taurus, in the fourth house. My sun is in the third house, next to Gemini. My mother copied the horoscope into a yellow notebook and I used to examine it secretly. I measured my life by that guess. The death creeping up on me arouses memories in me. I've already died twice. When I was four Dr. Fabrikant passed a death sentence on me. She was a doctor famous for her hopeless war against mothers who let their children drink water after eating fruit or vegetables. She asserted—with amazing certainty—that my heart was damaged. I was put in bed. They covered me with five woolen blankets. They put sweaters on me. They sealed the windows. That was when we lived in Mendele Street, near the sea, and Re'aya my beloved sailed in a boat with me. I was dying of lack of air, food and water. I longed for the chill hand of the lady doctor with her diploma. Every few hours she'd come, take off her coat, wash her hands, enter the room and give me an injection. The touch of her hand was refreshing, I wept with the pleasure and dread of it. My nostrils cracked and alarmed. I didn't know what death was, but I'd heard them talking about it in the next room. People sat there waiting for it, mumbling it softly. They sat by the pleasant sea breeze, beside the window, and waved notebooks and books so that there'd be air, they talked about death and about their dying child. Their dying child was me. I saw the thing they were talking about sitting on the big toe of my right foot. I wanted something. I don't remember what. My mother wept for me. I drank her tears thirstily. My father sat with Heine's works and looked for a clever aphorism to put on my gravestone.

The fact that I was saved had an ironic significance. Several toughs wearing black shirts, not particularly ugly, but energetic, had appeared a few months earlier in the clinic of Dr. Hermann Neidler, a friend of my father's, in Berlin, and had destroyed his clinic. They'd stuck yellow Shields of David on Dr. Neidler and his family and had said some especially unpleasant things to him. Dr. Neidler understood the hint, packed his belongings, and together with his wife and two children arrived in Palestine (Eretz Israel). This happened three days before I was about to give up the ghost. Dr. Neidler hurried to our apartment and saw Aminadav dying. He asked if he could examine me and then the reputed lady doctor spoke the famous sentence that is engraved in my memory: "It won't help but it won't hurt either." So much greatness did she possess. Dr. Neidler was a renowned children's doctor and Dr. Fabrikant did not dare offend him, especially on his first day in Eretz Israel. By the look on his face she guessed that he would allow the drinking of water after eating grapes and she knew that the cemeteries would fill with wretched children. But she behaved with forced affability and he thanked her for it.

He came into my room and examined me. He was so meticulous. From my faint I remember a measuring instrument cold to the touch, trained hands, and such gentleness. I wanted to tell him about my silkworms that had become coils and about the death sitting on my big toe. He left the door open. I saw people waving magazines, making wind, whispering. My father found a clever aphorism, his aching face smiling a broken smile. No one will forget the sight. Many days later they would say, that was a year after Dr. Neidler, who was such a delicate person, gave Dr. Fabrikant that awful slap. The anger of the delicate. And poor Dr. Fabrikant was finished. Mother, who had stopped believing in the horoscope and had started believing in Dr. Fabrikant, stopped believing in Dr. Fabrikant and started believing in the horoscope again, was as white as snow. What sweetness there was on her beautiful face. It was Dr. Neidler who told me how my father had broken the violin. He'd left the lady doctor surrounded by frightened screaming women, returned to my room, broken open the windows facing the sea, ordered my father to get up off his Heine and to bring water, aspirin, orange juice and towels. He stripped me of all my Russian clothes, and stood me up in front of the window until I fainted. He asked for a dropper and dripped fluids into me. For hours he stood there, dripping them into me. His face, I remember it as if it were today, was pleasant and solemn. Then he washed me in a lukewarm bath and when I grew stronger he put me in a cold bath and gave me orange juice to drink, and two days later, on the balcony, Aminadav built castles. Three days later he swam in the sea of a May heat wave. Dr. Neidler's children had funny clothes: Trousers with shoulder straps. Tyrolean hats. Striped swimming suits. White skin, faces red as beet root. They laughed about the living dead thing that I was. Neidler's pinkies and his pleasant wife built a castle in the sand. We sprayed wet sand. I called the castle Dr. Fabrikant's grave. He objected. He said you shouldn't make fun of beaten people, and regretted the slap. He wrote her a letter of apology and she didn't answer. She came to my mother in tears and said, He'll let Aminadav drink water after eating fruit. My mother was amazed. What terrible heresy. But my father put his foot on the carpet and said, What Neidler says goes. In Berlin he was the greatest of all children's doctors. Dr. Fabrikant said, And how many died there? And my father said, They live more than here. And my mother went back to the horoscope and read where it said that I'd fall sick at the age of four, there'd be complications, someone would come from across the sea and I'd be saved. The child will suffer greatly, but a miracle will save him. My father said that it wasn't a miracle and people who believe in miracles finish up depending on miracles and thus come to the end of their way. Thus spoke the man who smashed his violin and wrote me nine words, ten years, Love, Father.

The second time I didn't die at all. During the war my parents were informed that I had fallen on the altar of the homeland. They said I'd been a silver platter and all that. A soldier came, stood to attention, trembling. My mother was knitting a sweater for her son, with a zipper, as I'd asked her to before I went to war.

71

In those days a lot of men wore sweaters with zippers at the front.

My mother didn't stop knitting. She read the horoscope. It said that in my eighteenth year I would suffer a severe blow. Maybe a stone. Maybe I'd fall from a roof. Maybe something would hit me. But in some complex arrangement it would turn out that no, and I'd live. It was there in detail and my mother believed. She went on knitting me the sweater even though I was dead. But my father cried. My father cried twice in his life. Once when he smashed his violin and once when he was informed that I'd died in the war. My mother's hair turned white overnight, but she didn't stop knitting. Three days later I appeared at home. My father looked at me with a certain ire. Not of not-love, but of shame. Somewhere in him I'd caused him an unnecessary outburst of emotion. My mother said, I knew you'd come, here's the sweater, but when she tried it on me her hands trembled and there were tears in her eyes.

After that I was wounded but they didn't worry about me, because they didn't know. My death wasn't announced even though I was absent for two days in the Jerusalem hills while I lay with Nahum and the vultures waited for his blood on the electricity poles. After I returned I went to see Nahum's parents, and told them he had died beside me. The grenade had made a mistake, it was meant for me, they said in their hearts, why him and not you. I wanted their pity. I didn't know that in a bereaved home you don't find pity. I wanted them, them of all people, to love me and forgive me. They neither loved nor forgave me, but they didn't hate me. I sat there and drank tea. I pleaded and I was contemptible, in their eyes and in my own.

Outside my window signs like sails. A young woman runs in the street. Soon it'll be morning. Have I died. I have to decide. What do I want. I've left the Yiddish newspaper. What now. Things change. A kitten mews in the doorway of the Hebrew bookstore. Old men hurriedly walk to prayers. Bent over because of the fierce cold. Dressed in black. A glass of milk is put out to the kitten. Someone cares for all that lives, I thought. I took out the poem I'd written on the typewriter on Fifth Avenue and copied it out clean. Here and there I corrected my sufferings. I placed commas and periods in the right places. Between the sighs. Between the frozen tears on the page.

To take my belongings. To say goodbye to all those who have ever lived here. To play on the piano one last time. To say goodbye to the ballet shoes. To the ruined movie house. To the general. To the girl selling bagels. To the old men. To the seller of Hebrew books. To this room. To leave the rent for the landlord. To say goodbye to the cats. To Joseph Cotten. To Al Jolson. To take everything and disappear. There's nothing but the pain of others mixed with your pain. And that's too much. What are Sacco and Vanzetti to me. We're talking about my death, mine. I walked through the morning streets like someone who's been saved. Like one whom girls, perhaps, might love, for what is gentler than the withdrawal that's already at my fingertips.

5

I told Mira, in Frances Elliott's magnificent bathroom, about my trip to the Dead Sea. She said: You wore khaki. Your face was kinda cute. You turned around, you sweetheart, you thought I could see the wall through you!

I loved you. All these years I've loved you.

Mira raised her eyebrows.

And then I said, But how is it possible. You couldn't have been there.

From the day I awoke from the death that waited for me on the big toe of my right foot, things started pulling in some misty direction. In a mist to walk erect and see the life of someone I could have been. Dr. Neidler's children with shoulder straps and Tyrolean hats, real Meccano set and wonderful stamp albums, aroused in me an optimistic anguish. Aminadav was born in Germany, said Aminadav in his heart. And he didn't know how close he'd been to being born in Germany. Like the ironic action of his father, Naftali Sussetz, passionate lover of Goethe. He told the kids in his class that he was born in Germany and they didn't believe him. At nights he practiced saying *hau* when it hurt, instead of *ai,* as those born in Palestine said. He said that his name was Peter. That it had been changed to Aminadav on their arrival in Palestine. They didn't believe. Then he said he'd been born on a ship on the way to Palestine. He so wanted to have been born somewhere else. With leather shoulder straps and a real Meccano set. He could describe Berlin from the book Emil and the Detectives. Little Distang. The good aunt. The streets of the city, and the houses. The house of Father and Mother, logical and cold, pleasant and elusive. The love on separate sides. His parents sleep in separate rooms. They meet at lunch and dinner. Mustn't speak during dinner, says Father. And the silence. Polite living. No one touched anyone. The life Aminadav invented for himself was more stormy, more real, more true. And then he started telling it not only to himself but to others too and was able to start believing in it. He invented a grandmother in Tiberias, seventh generation in Palestine, with an Arab lover near Mount Arbel. Uncle Abner became a fisherman and a hunter. A noble savage. And the uncle convinced the inhabitants of Tiberias that a lion was approaching the town. The people of Tiberias came and demanded that he hunt the lion and he said why should I. They said to him you're the best hunter there is. At night they heard the roaring of the lion. Children couldn't sleep. Women cried to their husbands. And Aminadav's uncle had to go out and hunt the lion he'd made up himself. Did he believe in the lion? He went out to hunt it in complete sincerity. That's what he was like. And he took Aminadav with him. So he'd learn to be a man, he said.

And so how is it possible that Mira, whom I did not create from my imagination, and whom I met on the eighth of January nineteen fifty-eight in Frances Elliott's magnificent bathroom in New York, N.Y., how is it possible that you were there, in the Dead Sea plains, and met me on my way with my Uncle Abner to hunt a lion that never existed. According to Aminadav's story it's clear that he was nine or ten years old at the time. That is, a year before Mira was born. But you were there. And Mira said: You wore khaki. Your face was kinda cute. You turned around, you sweetheart, you thought I could see the wall through you! Uncle Abner and Aminadav were walking in a canyon. They were walking on a narrow ridge above a great abyss. Opposite them rose a wall. Inside the wall they saw a monastery cut into the bared rock. Uncle Abner sat down to rest, closed his eyes and dozed off.

Hawks hovered. An eagle flew by with a flapping of wings. The monastery was decorated with Corinthian pillars, but they were cut into the rock. The entrance to the monastery was dark and in the darkness was a black cave. In the entrance stood a very white nun, dressed in black. A cross of gold danced on her breast. The gold caught in the rays of the blinding sun. Its dancing was a signaling to God. Young and very beautiful against a background of copper mountains. Paths to lead bandits to the mountains of Trans-Jordan. Caravans of salt and spices. Mountains that looked like mysterious cities. And suddenly a startlingly white woman, in a black dress, with a cross, and between you and her an abyss. Grace on a background of cruel desolation. Grace, grace, he said in his heart, this boy Aminadav who I was before I fled from your face, you said, you're Rehab the whore! Lie with eagles and give birth to rocks . . . woman. And sensed a not understood desire. Aminadav yelled: Who are you! Why are you! You didn't answer, Mira. A smile crept across your lips. So close and so distant.

She looked through him and he turned his head to ascertain what she was seeing behind him. Behind him was only the wall of the canyon rising to cliffs inside thin and transparent clouds. And then she laughed with her mouth closed, the terrifying laugh of a she-eagle. She turned around and was swallowed up inside the cave. Aminadav stood there with tears in his eyes. Uncle Abner woke up and said, Why are you crying. He didn't tell him. Abner wanted to go but Aminadav was adamant. He wanted to stay forever. Uncle Abner pulled Aminadav away by force, and Aminadav beat on his uncle's hairy chest and yelled, No no no. Uncle Abner said, Don't cry, boy. And he looked angrily at the monastery, from which the sound of laughter, fine and muted, still seemed to echo. He said, Mad Christian women, what are they doing in the desert, what are they doing, whores, and Aminadav fought her injured cause, and the ridge was narrow and one could fall into the abyss. Uncle Abner knew and slowly drew him after him. Time passed. The monastery is sunken in slumber. Aminadav longing to go back and Uncle Abner pushing. They didn't find a lion. The lion Uncle Abner had made up managed to escape. They went to the Jordan River. There a Greek with a large mustache lived in a kind of house on stilts in the shallow water, among reeds and grasses the like of which he'd never seen before. They bought a hyena skin from him, drank coffee and went on to Jericho. They saw a monk riding to the canyon. He spoke Latin to them and they didn't understand. He let Aminadav ride a little. Aminadav didn't know for whom the monk leading the donkey was crying as he sang his heavy songs. They reached Jericho. Uncle Abner said, Look at the cloak he's got, he's got nothing on under the cloak, whom will he be with at night? Aminadav didn't understand whom he was supposed to be with at night and said nothing. The image of a white woman in black clove to his eyes, and thus Mira was born.

At night we slept at a friend's of Uncle Abner's, Abu-Selim Darwishi. The *khan* owner. Jackals howled. Aminadav thought they were wolves, howling in the empty night of the Jordan rift. Palms rose erect in the darkness. The moon cast a bewitched light on the sea and the mountains of Moab, which looked like x-ray pictures, dark and transparent. Abu-Selim said that two nuns lived there. An old one whom no one's ever seen, and the beautiful young one. They go there and cry to her.

There was a young man in Jericho, Hassan Abaddi was his name. He stood there for days. She didn't come out. They say he howled like a jackal. And she didn't come out. He tried to climb to her. He didn't see the abyss. The demons sealed his eyes. His bones are still down there. There had been others. There's a monk who brings them food. On a donkey. From the monastery next to the Jordan, near the Greek's house. They lower a rope and he sends up food and water. He too, they say, sings songs to her at night. . . . Who knows. The two nuns are silent. They speak with God. In whispers, they say. They say what's inside is skeletons of nuns who've died there, and skulls. Every year, at Easter, a man comes from America. He wears a sombrero, like in Mexico. He goes to the canyon. He stands opposite the monastery and calls to her. And she doesn't come out. They say that once she came out and looked at him, and he cried. Every year he comes and calls to her. And then he comes to me. He finishes a bottle of *zahlawi* and goes to Jerusalem. From there to America with his sombrero.

A handsome man. He comes in a large automobile with a driver. The driver goes and plays cards at the Greek's. Every year he comes.

When I told Mira the story she said: You wore khaki. Your face was kinda cute. You turned around, you sweetheart, you thought I could see the wall through you!

And then I said to her: But it isn't possible. . . .

回回

From Jewish streets of professional mourners I was taken by my friend Jerome. It was he who introduced me to Mr. Zwiegel the gallery owner. It was through him that I went to Frances Elliott's party to meet Mira though I didn't know she'd be there. But why or how I got an invitation to the party I don't know. Maybe because of Kurt. Kurt who hates me for the oppressive memory of the womb. Perhaps he wanted to enjoy a Hebrew clown. One morning I find a gilt envelope in the letter box. And what's inside it. An invitation on paper that looked like toilet paper. Among the good and the beautiful invited to Frances Elliott's seasonal party my name was also included. Very strange, I said to Jerome, who laughed. Go, he said. See who they are. They're not monsters. Push a little. There's a chance. I said nothing. My name was written there in India ink. Not printed. Someone had taken the trouble to write my name. A. Sussetz. It said, on the eighth night of January you are expected at Frances Elliott's, 1093 Fifth Avenue, twenty-first floor. You are to bring: a prick in usable condition, clean underclothes, feet in walking condition, washed if possible, and good will. See you.

I had no good reason to go. Jerome pressed me and I gave in, though not with great effort. I lived on Sixteenth Street and I wanted to forget things about the city I'd left down below, next to the burned-down movie house.

Come, said Jerome. Get to know those who hang in the museums. The beautiful people! You know what a marvelous ass Frances Elliott has. Tell them about the Middle East. About your grandfather's camels. About your grandmother's Arab lover. About the nun from the Dead Sea. It'll make an impression on

78

them. They're mummified and they laugh in convulsions. They'll die of envy. Tell them about the war, they think war's something sexy. Flatter them. Be a savage from the desert for them. Screw their girls. They'll respect that. Be daring and corrupt, keep your naïveté to yourself. Let them discover that it's faked. How they love fake things. They might write that you're something. Perhaps the most daring of the corrupt. They'll fix a label on you. Like the rest of us.

I said to him why me. Hofmann said that I'm too much of a painter or not a painter at all. Kurt Singer knows me. He thinks I hang or should be hanging in the Museum of Natural History.

I paint the banal, I like Cranach, Paolo Uccello. I paint Ashtoreths, false Messiahs, Sabbatai Zevi! I yearn to paint things that touch the compressed mystery of meaning . . . what will that say to them. They want to embrace the conceptions themselves, to express an opinion, objective if possible, about nonexistence. I speak about some possible flower. Even growing on a dunghill. What will that say to them.

And Jerome said, You talk just like them! What's this compressed mystery of meaning. You paint things the way they look to you. You paint things as they are and also what's behind them, and that's beautiful. You engrave humans on canvas and they're humans as well as the humanity they ought to contain. Like the color that's painted on the canvas and the no-color that exists in every color. You live in a mysterious word of legends and demons. Don't talk like them, don't fall into their traps, conquer them from your own stamping ground.

The winter's cold. The New York Times forecasts a storm for four days. The storm has enveloped my city. People float. The gloom there, traveling by bus to Frances Elliott's party. Jerome and I. He with a scarf and coat, I with an orphaned smile for my friend's sake. Smile, he said. I smiled. In my pocket, a recipe for a better world. Who'll listen. The panes are draped in vapor. I blow on the pane and draw a rabbit with my finger. Pretty rabbit. Jerome draws Panamanian flags with a pocketful of coins. In secret he draws Jesus with stones and a tortured face, and hides him. Mr. Barr from the Museum of Modern Art doesn't like figures between January and July. The dizzy pace. People run from galleries to museums and declare revolutions. Everything turns into gold. Painters buy swank cars. Gallery owners discover significances in dark corners. People paint white on white. Houses melt in the compressed air. The bus makes its way with difficulty. The windshield wipers work on and there's no salvation. At Fifty-seventh Street the bus stops. Sorry, boys and girls, says the driver. No further.

Bareheaded into the storm. Cars by the hundreds are stuck in the snowstorm. In front of the Plaza Hotel the fountain is frozen. Beside the fountain carriages stand in the snow. Horses wrapped in blankets emit clouds of vapor into murky lights. The drivers smoke cigarettes in the rear entrance of the hotel. The park is a white and enchanted forest with gray patches. Will a queen draped in furs come out to go by carriage to her palace. A young man wearing a fashionable yellow coat, deerskin gloves and hat leads a terrier wrapped in a blanket. We ask him the time. He took off a glove with deliberate slowness and snow lashed his face. He looked at his watch and then at us and said in a contemptuous voice, William the Conqueror! He put on his glove and turned his face. The terrier, who from the outset had not shown us any particular signs of affection, pulled his master in a kind of grand jeté and the man vanished, a swan in the snow. Jerome shouted after him, Thanks you prick! A carriage driver approached us. Blowing hot air into his hands and laughing wildly. Jerome fumed at his laughter. You underestimate my intelligence, sir, he said. And the driver replied, Go fuck your mother! Thus we made acquaintance with characteristic warmth. I swallowed snow. The driver spread out his arms as if he wanted to embrace somebody. He bowed politely to the keen air. Jerome said, He thinks he's somebody.

Who?

The prick with the terrier. You know why he said William the Conqueror.

No.

He thought I was nobody. That's why he said William the Conqueror. He goes out into the snow to make an impression on his mother. Who does he think he is. I know the type. In enlightened countries with sewerage and all the rest they kill them when they're little. He thought, and Jerome turned to the driver, who hadn't stopped laughing, and says to him; He thought I'm shit, that I'm shit like you! And the driver laughs and puffs into his hands; there's gentleness in him too, I see, Jerome doesn't see a thing.

I know why he said William the Conqueror, said Jerome, his anger increasing, he said William the Conqueror because any intelligent person, and he thought I wasn't, knows that William the Conqueror is ten sixty-six, which means that the time is six minutes after eleven.

Who's the conqueror? The driver asked me if I had a cigarette. I said that for a long time now I don't smoke cigarettes, only a pipe. He said that all the foreigners smoke pipes, and again asked who. Jerome said, Somebody, someone like Teddy Roosevelt, only more. The driver didn't laugh anymore and looked at me with suspicion. Know thy enemy. Far away we saw the man with the deerskin hat, bound to his terrier. He appeared in a sudden beam of light which flooded him as if he was still dancing. The driver said that only a carriage could travel on a night like this, he said it with genuine sorrow. I asked him if he'd sell us the bottle of brandy that was sticking out of his coat pocket. He was pleased to sell it to a foreigner at an exorbitant price. The brandy was cheap bourbon but we didn't complain. At first it burned, but then it was pleasant enough. We rode in a carriage to Frances Elliott's party. The park was all around us and we saw nothing but the ends of his mustache. The blanket the driver gave us gave off a sharp smell of horse piss. Suddenly high, I spoke of Mathias Grünewald and there was no better place in the world in which to speak of Mathias Grünewald. To Jerome, who didn't want to listen to me and was attending to his inner voice which was telling him other things. The driver didn't approve of the style of my speech. He knew I was the enemy and behaved accordingly. What interested Mathias Grünewald, I said to Jerome, was dread and exaltation. . . . He was like the Meister Eckhart, who said that the eye with which he contemplated God was the same eye with which God contemplated him. He painted the glory of the truly lost, the joy of the vanquished, he smashed and desecrated dread and filled it with a scarred exaltation. He expressed the dread of death and life as if it were a psalm. He sang hopeless and joyful hymns to his own funeral. The driver interrupted and said that he bet this Mathias didn't live in New York. I said he didn't. He said that Eisenhower had sold America to the reds, who were jew-niggers. All the reds are jew-niggers, he said. Once the park was a park. The flag's in danger. The winter isn't what it used to be anymore. All because of the jew-niggers. He said the air's changing because of the oxygen breathed out by the jew-niggers. I told him that what he meant was carbon dioxide. He said he didn't care what, but they're ruining the air. Everything's changing because of what the foreigners breathe out. All of them, he said, and looked back at me in an anger that also had in it— despite his efforts—a kind of gentleness. As if he wanted to believe in something but didn't know how. Every four years he comes out of the burrows to vote for Joe McKinley for President, says Jerome. The driver smiles. He says something. The jew-niggers are harnessed to the carriage and he'll lead them all to hell. He starts singing: "Winston tastes good, like a cigarette should, Winston tastes good, like a cigarette would." And thus the winter was protected against the reds. I wanted to tell him that grammatically there was something wrong with the song but he was already singing the Alka-Seltzer anthem with all the right gestures and smiles and I didn't want to interrupt him.

We reached Frances Elliott's house and Aminadav was sad. A jew-nigger foreigner polluting the air. The driver said that further up, in One-hundred-and-twenty-sixth Street, you could fuck nigger chicks standing up, next to the Minton Playhouse. Whatever you like. And a camera for twenty smackers, and trumpets. What they can sell. His hands—I remember—were a peasant's hands. A red face, wind-beaten. He took the money and sat back on his seat erect and called out, Glory to the Kingdom! Glory to the Kingdom! He vanished into the dully lashing snow. There was an imbalance in things and that was why I was able, later, to sit in Frances Elliott's magnificent bathroom on the twenty-first floor and to say things to Mira that I could never say to anyone else and to hear that she was in my invented life.

I thought about this for a whole minute. I thought: here I'm flying toward my birth. My father fathers me in Heidelberg. In a small inn where a bench bears the inscription: Goethe sat here. I knew that the gods of galaxies that are distant from each other don't understand one another. The time dimension doesn't exist, so it's impossible to take aim. All is one and one is all. The houses in the street next to the park were washed in cascades of snow. We fled into the warm like the scarecrows we were. I thought: How do the birds know that a scarecrow's a scarecrow, and then there was the elevator and I pressed a button. Twenty-one floors to get to the apartment. The terrible heat. We peeled off like onions. A blazing palace on the twenty-first floor, Frances Elliott's. People looked queer inside the waves of heat. We walked from room to room. I showed my invitation and huge Frances coiled up to me and said that she hoped I'd have a good time and that I mustn't forget the main thing at the end of the party, and I mustn't leave before that. You, she said to me, are a part of this thing.

I didn't fully understand her. A waiter in a bathing suit without a trace of hair on his body or face, red like a rare sea horse with an expressionless face, offered me a glass of whiskey with ice cubes rattling inside it and Frances turned slightly. When she turned around to go I saw what a wonderful thing were the buttocks of Frances Elliott. I wandered around the rooms, there were too many. I bumped into people who seemed familiar. Jerome had vanished as soon as we came in. Occasionally I see his profile for a moment, and then it vanishes again. The rooms are big, one of them larger than the rest. And empty. Four large barred windows. The room's painted orange diluted with an opaque white, a little rough. In the center of the room stands a large Italian table from the fifteenth century, with ten straight-backed chairs of pure form. Marvelous muteness, monasticism that is sumptuous and humble at once. In the four corners of the room stand four Chinese vases from the Ming dynasty, pale blue with snakes of gold and silver painted on them. An abode of silent stillness. I walked from vase to vase. I looked at the chairs. A yearning rose in me for things I'd never had. I thought of all the beautiful rooms in which I hadn't lived. Of people who'd sat in rooms like these in smoking jackets, or had come and gone out of knights' suits of armor. I thought of Tancred and of Frederick Barbarossa. All 'of us in the room. There was a feeling of splendid loneliness. As if I'd found the resonances of the important things even though the things themselves I didn't know by name. I thought of Godfrey of Bouillon and of the silk-clad maidens of Acre with the vassals of Montfort, Tyre and Sidon. I stood beside one of the vases. In the window there was a storm, on the roofs snow piled up. A wind blew, carrying objects which weren't clear enough. Through the open door I saw people in clouds of vapor. A fine and filtered sound of noise came as from within a stylized hell. I knocked on the vase beside me. The blow gave birth to a startled stillness. An expressionless waiter in a bathing suit came into the room, let out a short scream, ran to me with a glass, and stopped all at once. Someone from distant worlds tried to whisper something to me. The echo struck the huge apartment with amazement. A general astonishment ensued. The echo went from room to room. They tell me that the Chinese heal with needles. Here vocal needles were stuck into people's flesh. I thought: If it were only possible to neutralize the echo of the knock on the vase, that's how I would paint. Without sound. To bring silence into a world. The echo of the echo. Like neon light in a world overilluminated by a mighty sun. The sound, the echo torn from its source, put on a body of its own. And then, from out the delightful meditations of the unrepeatable moment, I saw in the frightening vapor a woman passing by the doorway. There was in her something savage, like anguish that had put on clothes and come out to celebrate. She had the face of all the women I had loved. But I remembered that apart from the girl in the third grade who'd fled to Ramat Gan and played the piano I had loved no more than three women in my life: the nun near the Dead Sea from my invented biography, Pharaoh's daughter in an illustrated Passover Haggadah from Berlin that Dr. Neidler had given me one Seder night, and a beautiful woman named Rivka from one of the volumes of the Chronicles of the House of David. Three women. The three of them prickly candles. Suddenly all three had put on a body and passed in front of the room. All the people returned to their revelries. The echo died as all echoes die when their time comes. The vase was cold. It waited for a more decisive blow. Let it come. The failure of love, I said to myself. The beautiful Rivka from the Chronicles of the House of David used to go down to the well and speak into a little synagogue to serve her God. She loved a prince but didn't want to marry him, because she was a ravished woman and as pure as the sky, and she didn't want to grieve him, lest he should kill himself. Pharaoh's daughter bore an amazing resemblance to her. She was drawn on a page in a Haggadah where you could move the pages and bring Pharaoh's daughter to Moses in the ark and see Moses taken up into her arms and from there to the river and from there to the glory and to Mount Sinai. On the hard winter days when the drainpipes of Tel Aviv wailed, and inside the blankets Aminadav lay with women drawn on old pages, moving and not moving. The failure of love, I said, for that was Mira running through the corridor and she didn't know at all where she was.

6

People hugging and kissing one another. Kurt Singer on a table, a large crowd gathered around him, the table covered with a wax cloth and the prick standing on top of it, lecturing on the sex life of Kurt Singer. He was wearing a baby's diaper fastened with a pink safety pin. White socks on his feet and on his head a hat made out of folded newspaper. A delicate face, and such sensitive hands. His little mouth with curved lips, yellow teeth, some claim his mouth bespeaks decay. From time to time, as he lectures, he points with a delicate finger toward his renowned groin, and Frances Elliott sends kisses in the air toward the desired spot. Frances Elliott's hand reaches forward, her mouth kisses the air, and the kiss is blown through puckered lips and lands directly on the groin. On the face of the most fervent of loving women rests the most apathetic of expressions. I looked for the woman who was Mira and I didn't know who she was. Kurt, with his fine antennae, discovers that I'm looking for someone, his face knows how to fish up the prey that I was.

Kurt declares in a chirruping, slightly nasal voice that women are good only horizontal. Every one of them wants to be stuffed, there are no unstuffable women. There are women who demand guarantees and every man has guarantees in the form of checks or compliments. Famous gallery owners like Kootz, or Sidney

Janis and other enlightened and important people stand there open-mouthed listening to the words of Kurt Singer. I notice the wise men of the Herald Tribune and the Times, Art News and others. Directors of museums in Boston and New York. Dressed in suits. Sidney Janis wears a daring Hawaiian shirt and laughs with his mouth closed. They're hoping that Kurt will announce a new ism. For two months now no new ism has been created, and a sense of helplessness exists, and there's a lack of confidence in the market. Kurt says *bris,* like my grandfather. He speaks about his circumcision. Kurt speaks from the point of view of a social critic: to lie down is to destroy. He said: Words, words. Kill the mosquito and rescue the painting. What for. There's art photography, isn't there. What's stronger than a close-up in a movie. The disgrace of nothingness. The terrible celebration of painting conducted by its merry gravediggers. Maybe he fucks paintings. Who knows. Frames fence in. Once I had a woman, he said, and she had the biggest boat in the world. It was a dream, he said. I went right in with my fist and smashshshsh! Surprise surprise. Inside there was a mirror and whom did I see, I saw myself, not my first, I was waiting for myself there, ah, in that wonderful heat, and off we went. In Kurt's diaper a tent rises now, a geometrical marvel in this hot and vapor-filled room with its waiters without a trace of beard unstintingly handing out glasses of whiskey. And I photographed her in the middle of it, says Kurt. I developed the photographs, he said, and she waited for me. She smoked L&M and listened to Honegger on the record player. I came back and I hung her triangles, blown up, above the bed on a string, with clothespins. And then I got into the boat a second time, and it was even more wonderful. Above me hung the blown-up pictures of her boat, above them a mirror, and her real boat was doubled! With Honegger on the record player and the smoke of L&M. The boats hanging on the string were doubled images. It was as if I was fucking a thousand boats, getting into all of them at once, what a sight. And my *bris* was digging inside the treasure troves of life, finding a fine gentle poetry. The woman listens to Honegger. Smokes L&M. And I travel inside her. We didn't tell each other our names. Endless triangles with a thin serrated stripe like the mouth of a shell. I think, says Kurt, that I traveled into a boat that had no boundaries.

Like Broadway boogie-woogie, I thought. Mondrian and the asceticism of holy forms. And, Kurt says, and then I attained a metaphysical transcendence, something like true religiosity. In his baby's diaper, fastened with a pink safety pin, with an erect cock inside his diaper, telling me about true religiosity with Honegger and L&M. That erection. Mr. Barr furrows his brow. Perhaps the lady with the marvelous triangles is the last word that should be hung in the museum. And I look for Mira, among the giants of art of the Western world, painting (as they know) things that exist unto weariness, as if they don't exist. I thought: Everything's been painted by Paolo Uccelli, Grünewald, Rembrandt, Giotto and Cézanne. And for a moment I was a brother to my father, the breaker of violins. Who buried himself with the Bachs and the Scarlattis, the Monteverdis and the Cimabues and didn't go on. And then I thought: Perhaps today that isn't enough. Perhaps Greco isn't enough for what's going on in this room, for example. And then I understood why I'd been invited to this party. The clowns of the Formica world needed a clown of their own. And their clown would be made of wood. I thought of the line by Alterman that said that man is a riddle that asks riddles, while Kurt speaks about painting with gloves. Emotionalism, he says, we'll leave to Disneyland, painting is a mirror contemplating a mirror contemplating a mirror until reality is no longer real. He emptied half a bottle of J&B into himself and blanched like a clown's mask. I hated his moist eyes and then he said something and two drops of whiskey landed on my face.

I left the large crowd and wandered through the mazes of the apartment. I knew by hearsay that there were twenty-four rooms in Frances Elliott's apartment but I counted fifty. I remember sitting in the Cider Bar with Kurt once. Upstairs there was a little theater and beside it a café called Pandora's Box. Around us were advertisements for cigarettes and plastic underpants. Kurt said, Aminadav's desperately searching for stratagems that have been chewed to death already. I asked, What nucleus that has no actuality at all is capable of destroying an entire city, Kurtis?

You're trying to ask me riddles, he said, with a wicked smile.

No, I'm trying to reach you.

Why?

That's love.

He tried to imagine but he couldn't. A malicious smile on his face. I said, It's a Sufi parable, a parable of Al-Ghazzali the great Moslem mystic, and it means: a tiny flame is capable of burning an entire city. Me too. I'll destroy you. From within you all, I'll come and you won't be.

I didn't know at the time that I wouldn't be able to destroy even myself with a dignity worthy of the name.

Kurt laughed. He has a deeply wrinkled laugh. I told him that he liked robot artists who'd measure the intensity of the passing moment with Geiger counters, and that I detest people who elegantly celebrate extinction. Picasso's a brilliant journalist, I said to him, while Soutine—he's a real painter. Nolde . . . And he said, what would Giotto and Piero della Francesca be painting today?

A woman passes by me. She says, The people in this apartment are multiplying like minks, I do what the minks do, to get some minks. She hung two plastic telephones on her boobs and invited me to dial. There'll be a population explosion here, she said, the lines are all engaged, the traffic is heavy. Museum directors and gallery owners stand in line to dial with one hand in their pockets. I went and met Mira. Sweltering from the heat, isolated from them all. As if there was a kind of partition between her and the world. She looks through me. I turned my face around to see what she was seeing and there was a wall. I stood facing her and my thoughts started racing. I was like the acrobat who catches wooden hoops in a circus at devilish speed. Trapped, and the tempo increasing. I was afraid I'd disintegrate before her eyes; a woman dressed in black slowly drew a black frame around my name. My throat choked. Someone said, A disease is something objective. Mira smiled but not at me. People passed in front of her. I didn't know them anymore. We'll tell a Decameron to each other. Music by Duke Ellington. Clouds of smoke. Whiskey. Waiters without a trace of hair. People peeling. Like onions.

Saxophones and violins by Charlie Parker, Max Roach on drums. This was love.

She's searching in a wall behind me. All real women look for a wall behind you. The pigeons flee from the snow-whipped roofs. The wind threatens. The whiskey spills. A magnificent palace on the twenty-first floor on Park Avenue. Kurt Singer speaking about *bris*. Trembling toward Mira. Is she Pharaoh's daughter. Maybe nesting inside me, hidden inside me, is a sleeping king. Years after that night, Mira said to me, You're spoiled, Aminadav, you're cruel, resigned, self-aggrandizing and ashamed like a king.

I smiled at her. That was the day after Naomi was born.

She said, Yes yes.

You were destined to fail like a king, she said, and afterward she denied that she'd ever said anything about failure. But she said, You're destined to fail like a king! You rule over the fragments of shattered ambition, or the skeletons of a family tree. I said to her, My father was the Caesar of smashed violins, and she didn't laugh. She said, Naomi you'll love always, but me you won't. I'll disintegrate before your eyes and you'll seek new Miras. Swear that you'll always love Naomi, and I swore, shmuck that I was.

Her gaze sees, through me, the wall behind me. Stillness between the musics. Duet for stillness and boiling whiskey. Waiters in bathing suits. With a tray of cheeses.

Toward my bride I went a different man. Very slowly, we went. We talked about Kafka. She with a smile. Everyone's so generous with each other. She said that The Castle's a startling book. I asked her if she had a diaphragm, apart from Kafka, in her purse. I played a game and she adapted herself to its rules. She said yes.

Where do you love in this damn place.

(It wasn't I who spoke, it wasn't she who answered.)

She listens with contempt and dread to the word love. Her face moves in an expression of disgust.

Here you don't love, baby, here you fuck!

I rejoiced at the phony sound that was her voice. The innocence mixed with arrogance. We agreed to meet in ten minutes' time outside the door of the bathroom. Before she went off she asked, What's your name.

Aminadav.

What an awful name.

I could have said Kurt!

Kurt's an ass. She thought for a moment and added, What, Ami—

Nadav.

Aminadav, she repeated, is it really worth your while?

I laughed, to cover my confusion.

Since we've agreed I'll come. Whatever your name.

In the big room in which masses are milling. Kurt is still speaking about the sex life of Kurt Singer. Sarah Vaughan sings from loudspeakers hidden in the walls. Kurt says, Aminadav, his delicate finger pointing at me, paints at an easel! According to the book, the way Doerner says. He paints pickity-peck. Like in the beak of a shitty bird. Messiahs mounted on horses. Everyone laughs. Billie Holiday replaces Sarah Vaughan on the record player. The snow piles up on the windows. Kurt shouts in anger, sadness over the loss of the beautiful things which he too bewails. Horses . . . where do you get horses today. Artificial innocence is deception, is distraction, and what it amounts to is: charlatanry! In heated rooms with electronic elevators, where do the horses come in. Rembrandt painted his own world of Coca-Cola. Frustrated chicks ride horses. Before I knew Frances, she rode horses in the park.

And when Kurt yelled that today one traveled on ultraviolet rays at the speed of thought, I told him how Jerome and I had got to Frances Elliott's party.

I looked for Jerome, so he could testify. But he'd vanished. Mr. Kootz and Mr. Janis are chuckling. I told him that the ultraviolet buses had got stuck in the storm, that New York airport was closed. The radio dies from time to time. Only horses and candles. It's fortunate that Frances has a private generator in her magnificent apartment. Soon it'll go bung too and there'll be a total stoppage of electricity. And then I'll stick my candle into your groin and everyone will see what you've got there under the diaper, a Coca-Cola prick.

The profile of the woman who would be the mother of my daughter appeared for a moment and vanished. I walked through the rooms and asked questions like what's the time and when will all this end. They didn't answer, or they answered with a shrug of the shoulders. They drank whiskey and measured things between their legs. In the future people will sit in electronic houses and paint conceptions and weep tears of cellophane and fuck into huge glass test tubes. They'll invent a theology without God and what's worst of all, without godness, even that which is in a fly. What are the tears of a child, a geometric decoration, Broadway boogie-woogie, black stripes of Franz Kline.

A woman wearing a tunic asked me why I am laughing to myself at a moment when a person as important as Kurt Singer has just insulted me. I told her that I'm his secret brother and no one knows this and it'll be worthwhile to broadcast this bitter truth. She looked at me in belief. I asked the body under the tunic if she by chance knew where the bathroom was in this huge apartment.

There are four, she said, and one for Kurt's exclusive use. They're all magnificent, she said, and they're all being used right now by hot-blooded people. She said that Franz Kline is in right now. John Cage has gone down a bit. Theater doesn't exist. The Reichian therapy thing's been going too long, everyone's sick of it. Things aren't what they used to be. Even Marilyn Monroe isn't what she used to be. She likes to fuck with whispers, on a bearskin rug, singing while she. And that's a moving and a marvelous thing. With the soft music of Count Basie, who's in again. At Frances Elliott's there are always incredible parties.

Season or off-season. Hot-blooded people always have brothers in far-off places, she said. And the police are keeping their eye on the theory of sex on a bear rug by lamplight with soft music. Maybe it's the end of the world. Snow and all that . . . she said. I thought about my Irish friend from Fifth Avenue. Waves of love rose in me. I loved her. All of her. She went from me. She walked off, tapping her heels, seeking people in a place where there were so many humans. Beside one bathroom there was no Mira. I got lost in the maze of rooms. Again I saw the room with the vases. The echo wasn't there. Light filtered in, I don't know from where. Whispers could be heard. Soft music. Two young men embraced each other in a corner and licked each other's dread-stricken faces. African statues stood still and silent in a large empty room. A black maid came out of it in a panic, with big breasts and a torn blouse and crying. Someone thought that. Telephones rang in every corner of the house and no one picked up the receiver. A lone bathroom at the end of a corridor. A sign on it: Strictly private. And in smaller letters: For the sole use of Kurt Singer. I went in, squashed out all the tubes and dirtied the room with toothpaste, shoe polish, cream for electric vibrators, cream for the back and cream for his cock. I left. I met a painter who was hitting his head against the wall and crying out in despair, *Picasso is the Franco of art! Picasso is the Franco of art!*

7

Abandoned in front of the door. Separate from the others. White. In the lamplight that bathed her. And then I approached her.

Don't we know each other?

Two couples standing there laughed. Maybe because of my accent. She turned to me as if groping out of her musing, or her sleeping.

I don't remember. Yes . . . maybe.

If I'm standing here, it means I'm waiting. Why not for you.

There was a Japanese whose wife left him. He went to the beach and raked sand. At night his friends came and said, What are you doing. He said, I'm looking for my wife. They said to him, Why on earth are you looking for her in the sand, and he said to them, She has to be somewhere, why not here.

A nice story.

And a true one.

What's your name.

Aminadav.

Yes.

Sussetz.

Right.

One of the two couples suddenly lost its last trace of patience, darted into the next room and crawled into the space under a table on which sat a roasted porker with burning candles in it for decoration. The bathroom door opened and a couple came out. The couple standing in front of us went in and slammed the door. We remained alone. We spoke about Israel. I told her that I was from Israel, very much so, because she said we were all from Israel. She called Kafka the greatest poet of violence, but said she didn't agree with his view that you have to throw life behind your back in order to gain it.

I told her I was a seaman, on furlough. From time to time she forgot my name. I reminded her with great patience. She said she wouldn't be a homeland for anyone when I said I was looking for a homeland. That depends on your Kafka, I said, and she didn't laugh. I kissed her and she said that if I intended to lay her I'd have to pretend that I was doing it with more emotion. I loved her and she didn't know. She looked at me through her glazed eyes which became denser and darker and said, I say things that not I say. Body speaks and I don't. There's another woman, I hate her, she lives inside me, her hands grope, they don't touch, but they want to touch, I hate her touches, kiss *her!*

I tried to smile. But her face was still dark.

I'm a guest in my body, she said, not by choice. And that's terrible. Like two people kissing on two sides of a windowpane. If you ever meet the woman who lives in me, a woman who's dead, and if you say the key word for God's sake, this body won't be strange and I'll touch someone and something tremendous will happen.

She mused for a moment, switched off and said in a dull voice that seemed to come from far away: But it'll never happen. Her face became ascetic and distant. How apart we were. And then she said, Twenty thousand condemned men and they laugh at my hat. To my great surprise she said, War and Peace, about what people think, don't be surprised, who am I. We have made a date. You and me.

Real. Maybe I should go on playing so you'll believe that that's the truth.

She looked at me, a sharp gaze, a hawk on an electricity pole in the Jerusalem hills, blood blood, examined me for what to me seemed too long a time, and said, Get back!

I'm not ready yet, she said. Not ready. And then in a different voice: *Not with some seaman from Nicaragua.*

And in this way I was able to recognize that she'd come out to me from a painting by Giotto. I closed my eyes hard, I saw stars with eyes closed, I opened them again and she was a Burgundian woman from a painting by Van der Goes. Without the elongated hat. Her face veiling a dense mist.

The couple came out of the bathroom with savage laughter. I'm not sure if they were a man and a woman or a man and a man. One of them said, don't bother turning the rug over. The other side's wetter.

She walked to the pretty toilet seat and sat down crouched. I, she says to herself, I'm outside, I've left myself outside. She's sitting on a terra-cotta toilet seat as if on air. A magnificent bathroom. Reproductions of Rubens, Renoir and Modigliani hanging in gilt frames. Several beautiful icons. Antique cabinets with bottles. A wicker chair, and on it a doll dressed in elegant clothes. A statue of a naked woman, an S.S. officer's hat on her head. Mira on the terra-cotta toilet seat. Above her the window frame. In the window a braked storm. Snow snow. The sky cleared suddenly. The snow stopped. A cold clear moon among clouds flying at dizzying speeds, at changing heights, and then from out of the rays of the startled moon, inside the window, through the gray and astonished dough, the snow started lashing again. Sitting opposite her on the carpet. Squatting. Mira on the terra-cotta toilet seat. A window that's a geometric marvel. Pictures by Rubens and Renoir. A cabinet. Her bowed face. Her skin's too white. Pale, her dress is too green. The wall's pink. The gold on the frames. The silver paint on the water faucet. The many-colored carpet. The face from out of a painting by Giotto. The mist from Van der Goes. I saw a picture that had a bitter and conciliatory face. The echo came to rest in her face. Same echo that had broken from the vase.

Tell. Don't let silence waste this marvelous sight. I'm trying, I'm in love, all the women have come and met in you, romance is an outdated thing. Come and let's talk straight. I tell her about my girl in Naples. I tell the story at length, of my first woman, facing my first love. Mira had a clear view of my shoelaces. When my girl said, you'll leave me like all the others, I saw my reflection twice in Mira's eyes which until then had been so dead. I told her how my mother knitted a sweater for her son, with a zipper, and they told her I'd died for the homeland and my mother believed in Mrs. Kantorovitz's horoscope and didn't stop knitting.

What parents you had, that you returned to them alive after the war . . .

Like all parents. Were they deceived?

I ask a question and you answer with a question.

They were deceived.

All of us are deceived. But there's compensation. For example, you can put on masks and be somebody else.

I returned alive, I said as if I hadn't heard.

How do you return. First you have to come out from somewhere. And then return. After all, you're an artist or something.

A sailor.

And an artist.

Something like that. I said to her, After the war I kept quiet. Who could talk then? They sang songs, wrote memorial books. There was a general uproar of conceit. We saw dead eyes everywhere. In buses dignified women stood up for me. On every corner there was a dead man. I worked on a ship. To forget. Then I went back home. They forgot. They built new houses. There was talk of a miracle. Talk of the chosen people. The religious party joined the coalition. Buses stopped running on Saturdays. There was talk of pure blood. Of Thou has chosen us. Mira says nothing. I went to visit the mother of a friend who died beside me, his brains shredded over my face. He wasn't meant to die. I went to my friend's parents. And someone stood in the doorway and said, Who are you. I said, I'm Nahum's friend. He gave me hot tea. I wanted pity or hatred and I didn't get either. Mira looks at me. Then she started undressing. She started placing clothes on the edge of the gleaming white bathtub, meticulously folded. When she stood up naked I was scared. She had a marvelous body. How describe a marvelous body. Something amazing. I said, Maybe it's all a waste of time.

97

She doesn't answer. She waits. I didn't move. She said, You think I'll kiss you? There's no sudden closeness.

You think life's like in the movies.

God's caprice, I said. And she asked what that was. I told her it was the name of a French cheese. To fall in love, I said, is . . .

Don't speak about love, kiddo.

What if I won't be able to . . .

I stopped talking and she didn't answer.

The snow in the window keeps falling. I just couldn't imagine Aminadav getting on top of her. She and he. So I said, Maybe I can't, and I added, Mira. She flashed taloned eyes at me. How do you know my name. Who told you my name.

I didn't know.

She said, You're a liar, you know.

No, I don't know.

Who told you.

I don't know.

You said it.

She said, You sat there and told stories. A hundred men have already been inside me.

I started undressing. I didn't want her to see the quivering inside me. She came up to me, and licked the tears. I wanted to embrace her and she stopped me. The tears were salt. She said, Don't love, I'm protected, you have no idea how protected I am against seamen from Nicaragua. Whores in Naples are an old trick, don't press in . . . She stood there like that and stopped in midsentence. She said, Don't press in. She looked at me. The light was strong. You could hear whispers from the corridor. Someone was drumming now. And then she said, in a different, gentle voice, Pity me, Aminadav—

After that everything was violent and serene. Aminadav penetrated into a woman without being outside her, and remained inside himself. And she came to him. And then a third situation arose in which there was no Aminadav and no Mira. In Aminadav she awoke a sleeping king. She whispered to the murderer in him and to the comforter. He didn't think about the thing that penetrated into her arousing soft hillocks of feathers but became part of the motion, part of the penetration itself. Echoing the echo from the vase. Then she said, Don't look at me like that.

How.

Cheated. I didn't cheat you. Don't be disappointed.

I said, Mira.

She said, Don't say Mira.

She placed her hand on my mouth. She wouldn't let me say a word. She said, Love is a long, corrupted thing.

After we'd got dressed we sat down, she on the carpet and I on the toilet seat. We looked at the snow. She at the window and I at the mirror seeing the beautiful cabinet. I told her about my uncle the yarn-spinner from Tiberias. And how he went to hunt a lion he'd invented in the Dead Sea plain. So I told her in the calm that enveloped me. My face planted in the mirror. Seeing snow and storm in the window in the mirror. Her face seeing storm in the window. And then she said in a whisper: You wore khaki. Your face was kinda cute. You turned around, you sweetheart, you thought I could see the wall through you!

I loved you.

Mira laughed.

And then I said: But it isn't possible, you couldn't have been there.

She spoke to herself, perhaps to me: Every year he came, wearing a sombrero, he'd bought the sombrero in Guatemala, the show-off, your uncle was solid and muscular, a handsome man with a mustache, and he wore a dark coat. He was holding a rifle, and your knee was bandaged.

Right.

I remember.

Mira.

It was bandaged. Her expression was sharp and gave off a hidden dread.

Right.

Why was your knee bandaged?

I had sores.

I wanted to kiss her. She didn't let me. The tangle remained a mystery. How did she know. She didn't say. I decided not to ask her. Horoscope or no horoscope, strange and mysterious forces or strange and not mysterious forces. My eyes photograph the toilet seat in the mirror. I on it. She on the carpet.

回回

A large room. A wall all window. Beyond the window a snow-storm. On the floor is spread a canvas that takes up almost the entire area of the room. The canvas, twenty meters by sixteen meters. An ordinary painter could paint fifteen, twenty pictures out of this canvas. Not to speak of what a painter like Hieronymus Bosch might do. The party moved to this room. Frances kept her promise. The clown that I was waited for the command. Everyone walked on the canvas in a kind of bemused tension. Barefooted everyone, some even bare-bodied. At several points on the canvas stand buckets of paint, large paintbrushes, painters' brushes, sprays, rags and small cans of enamel.

Jerome, drunk, bleary-eyed, takes off his shoes and steps onto the canvas. Eight projectors light up the space. Frances Elliott, a concerto for divine body and red leg. Six foot three is her height. Amazing in her proportions. Who needs to be an artist with an ass like hers. An encyclopedia for child-making. Once there was a party. A man with one eye who used to write A Midsummer Night's Dream on an eggshell, and wandered around the Village with stamps on the other side of which he'd written the Declaration of Independence and the Bill of Rights, wrote the first three chapters of Dr. Spock on Frances's body, because she always aroused in everyone the desire to make children. She got bored at the end and then Kurt discovered her. And that was the overture to the marvelous relationship which had resulted, so far, in two private rooms for Kurt including a private bathroom in the establishment of Frances Elliott in the immortal kingdom. Waiters in bathing suits serving champagne. The corks being pulled out merrily. The woman with the mink crying and laughing in turns, chasing the tail she's decided she has. She suddenly became bare all over and she had some lovely things on her cold and petrified body. Kurt mumbles to himself and quotes things from his favorite articles by Kurt Singer. He proclaims his wares. Here

100

I am. Kurt awaits me on the canvas. He shouts: Domenikos Theotocopoulos of Jaffa oranges! Paint something! Kurt shouts: Aminadav Sussetz likes Nolde and Soutine and Schmidt-Rottluff. A painter of Prussian blue. Prussian and romantic! Like Hitler! Get up on the canvas and step into history, he said.

Mira appearing just as she'd disappeared earlier. She stood and looked at the clown trying to enter history through the back door. A girl dances without a bra. Kurt dances with her. I hear a whisper: *Don't be a fool.* I don't turn my face. Write something in Hebrew, says Kurt Singer. I write *qus imhem!,* your mother's cunt, an Arabic curse in Hebrew letters, with an exclamation mark.

He tries to read. He tries, *qu . . . ,* and gives up. I told him it was a poem. Kurt sinks his body in Prussian blue, on the huge canvas. Light glares from eight theater spotlights. He says, I knew the *breiha* by Bialik *lomadti* in Hebrew *shul.* I write in Hebrew: *Kurt Singer potz.* And then in the midst of the carnival I grasp what a genius Frances Elliott is. And not because of her big and beautiful ass.

Completely sober. Her cold eyes. At rest in the midst of the uproar. She's naked not because she's wild or liberated, but because by her nakedness she sends thrills through a large audience. Her body enforces pain upon everybody. Women and men caper around her. Because of her nakedness they too peel off. On her face is a dedicated freeze. Her painting is being painted by us. We are all her brushes. Without a word. She points with her hand and we paint to the beats of her heart. As if she's the brain and we the body's limbs. She pours paints tranquilly. Moves couples copulating for all to see, on the broad long surface of the canvas. The light is dazzling. The music bursts from the loudspeakers. Duke Ellington plays Take the A Train. Through us she coldly and serenely creates her chaos. She knows who we are. She invites people by their deeds. And now she rules from on high. She knows, she *knows exactly* what she wants. *In the lawless world which Kurt has created for her, she makes the laws.*

Serene. She puts white in a yellow place. Inspects it. Shows what. To do to people. Dolls in her hands. Kurt vomits on the canvas. He's sick. His body on the canvas. What a marvel. The clown weeps clown's tears. Frances lets him. Father was wrong. You don't paint only the concealed. There are also creators. Creations of abomination and exaltation. I want to leave the world. In which there are things. Like these. Waiters. Father administering Father. Father. Waiters without a trace of hair, Father. Champagne. Kurt on the canvas, Father. Tizzzzz, Father. Shame shame. Aminadav has entered history, Father. Frances came up to me, Father. She shouted into my ear, she was bare. Her breasts touching me. The divine nipples. She says to me, *I knew you'd write in Hebrew for me.* Hebrew, she said, Father. I remember the concentration on Bialik's face in the engraving by Hermann Schtrock. I'm lost, Father. I didn't go in and I didn't go out, Father. On the threshold. To die of shame. Frances. Engraving her eternity in me by me. Screw her.

8

The snow stopped for a while and it became very cold. The benighted city was white. I wanted Mira, to touch. I walked in a frozen city. The streets were empty to me. The cars in Madison Avenue were all stuck. On Fifth Avenue I was caught in a sharp gust. The thought of Mira, sitting on the toilet bowl, warmed. Next to the Plaza the carriage drivers were still sitting. Horses wept steam. The carriages were covered with snow. I didn't see where the hotel ended and the carriages began. The drivers in the rear entrance of the hotel were wrapped in a brown cloud that spewed outward and grew dense. They smoked and laughed. The reception clerk of the Plaza looked at me. I walked up to an armchair and sat down.

I dialed and Frances's voice on the phone was formal. She asked if I'd lost my way or maybe frozen. I said no. I could smell the party through the telephone receiver. The music came over at full blast. Tony Scott on clarinet. I asked her if she knew Mira's surname and telephone number. I said to her: The beautiful one that was at the party, with the most Jewish eyes Satan ever created, with the sick ascetic marvelous face, with the second-best body in the world, after Frances, with the marvelous nose, the black eyes and hair! She didn't know who I meant, and laughed at my description. I asked her, had there been more than one Mira there. She said, not even one Mira. I could hear the contempt in her voice. Maybe you masturbate, she said, even Kurt masturbates, I peep through the keyhole, what a sight, one hand holding the Art News, reading one of his own articles, and the other . . . No no, I said to her. Mira was there, what are you talking about? My voice sounded desperate to her. I knew by the silence with which she received it. Wait a minute, she said. I heard the receiver knocking against the side of the table, emitted a cold steam into the telephone, the receptionist who believes doctors and smokes Camels looking at me. After a few minutes she came back. Her voice was merrier than before: There's no Mira here and there was no Mira, no one knows her, Kurt laughed and said maybe you meant your mother. I checked the guest list. They were all invited by me and I was very careful, as you know, and there was no Mira and no one who brought a Mira, there was a Miranda but no Mira.

I went out into the street. The dawn was breaking pale, in masses of mists and snow. I went down into the subway at Lexington and put in a token. Wind blew through the tunnel. On the wall hung posters of Miami Beach. Someone had drawn a man and a woman copulating on the face of a beautiful girl in a swimsuit. Someone else had written: The blacks get screwed and the jews lie in the sun. Girls with hair flying free in swimsuits riding in motorboats. Water-skiing. I wanted to ride on a surfboard at Tel Aviv beach, to walk in the sun. To pick anemones. To smell the blossoming of citrus at Gedera, among the sabra clumps. To hear an orchard well in the distance *tik tik tik*. To hear the wail of drainpipes. To smell the sharp sweet aroma of coffee on a rainy night in Ben Yehuda Street. Someone at the end of the tunnel sang Stormy Weather. The train arrived. The car was empty. I fell asleep and dreamed I was walking through a field of anemones. I woke up and got off at the wrong station. I waded in snow, Division Street. Not far from the place where I lived when I worked at the Yiddish newspaper whose large sign could be seen even from here. The wall of the movie house was torn in the snow. The Hebrew bookstore was enveloped in darkness. An old woman selling bagels. I bought two. They were warm and crisp. An old Jew in a fur pressed me to go into a house where

someone had died. I was the tenth for the *minyan* and they gave
me a hot cup of tea. I felt a choking in my throat. I went to a
place where there was a Catholic hospital built of black bricks and
a tree with sick upthrusting branches like a hand with fingers. I
stood next to the hospital. The dawn broke. Nuns inside a large
and gloomy hall prayed their morning prayer and sang in pure
voices. I was afraid to go in. The doctor would tell me that death
is an objective thing. I stood next to the hospital and shivered
with cold. I thought: If I feel that death is trapping me and the
end is near maybe I'll be saved. The nuns sang to greet the
morning that was falling upon them. In black dresses and bonnets. The singing was pure and soft but a coldness blew to me
from it, and a closing of things, not understood. The morning
grew and I didn't die. I came to Division Street again. The
Hebrew bookseller called me. He said, I remember you. And
pointed to his bargain table in the snow. I asked him, Who'll buy
Hebrew books in the snow and he said no one buys them in the
sun either. He laughed and cried at the same time. I bought
Smolenskin's Burial of a Donkey in an old edition and Gnessin's
works at bargain price. I met people I didn't know but they
nodded their head in greeting and everyone thought they knew
each other on this face-contorting day. The wind blew fiercely,
pricking like spears. The whiteness slushed into gray and then into
black. The city was trapped. Old men with spades shoveled snow.
Even the policeman walking there blew steam like bagels out of
his slightly twisted mouth. On the night I met Mira, before I
went down the subway and rode to the Catholic hospital, the
famous painting Thumb Three was painted on the floor of
Frances Elliott's large room. To this day the residents of New
York live the dread of that moment. But they were not present
at the joy of creation. I was. And when I entered history on her
astonishing painting they were sitting at home, and between
electricity failure and sudden pain because of the heavy gusts of
snow, they were watching the little magic instrument. That night
thirteen stores were burgled. Five houses were burned. One hundred and two trees collapsed in the storm. Water burst into
forty-five offices. Five people committed suicide. The true life was

105

at Frances's. While in the fictional world, three million people saw Cleo Moore, famous winner of marathon kissing contests, trying to identify a face she seemed to remember from her distant past. At times she even succeeded, and the applause machine thundered with enthusiasm. The Oldsmobile company presented Lady in the Dark with Ann Sothern. They heard the young Polly Bergen sing Jericho. And the song: Five-year plan. They saw Hopalong Cassidy, and Charlie Chan burst into a mysterious den of burglars in Chinatown, with Sidney Toler. Art Baker introduced to his viewers a woman who'd met a man from outer space and had even talked with him. He was the captain of a spaceship that had arrived from Titaniac, which was one of the nine moons of Saturn, for purposes of reconnaissance and intelligence. Our friend Pop talked about creative cooking. And gave instructions on cooking Italian sausages, macaroni pasta and stuffed zucchini. Liberace sweetened the small hours of the night. In a pink suit, and a pink hat, with pink hands, playing a pink piano, with a pink picture of his pink mother, in a pink frame, on the pink piano, beside a gold swimming pool with pink water. He played There's a Girl in My Heart and smiled his charming spellbinding smile. Later the film There's a Girl in My Heart was even shown, with Lee Bowman, Elyse Knox, Peggy Ryan and Gloria Jean. But that was already just before morning.

Day chases day. Change of times, slow or fast. From their end you see a hasty thing. In the present things don't seem to move. Mira wasn't anywhere. All the telephone books were empty of her name. Mother writes about home, the smell of the sabra clumps, pine resin in winter, needles in a dress, the seamstress crying in the next room. The sea in the window. The Moslem cemetery gleaming on a moonlit night. You aren't there Aminadav. Once I looked for you and I found you with that girl. You were children and I pitied you. Later they told me that you smoked in the shelters. I painted a lot. I had an exhibition at Mr. Zwiegel's and I was written about, neither good nor bad. A painter of outdated things, I thought what was more beautiful than the pagoda of the Ise temple in Japan or the portrait of Philip the Good by Roger van der Weyden. I thought a lot about Paolo Uccello. Nights next to hospitals. I found places next to them. I have a map of New York. On the map are marked all the hospitals and clinics. I also found a book of the Doctors Association. With addresses. Walking from place to place with those lists, with the map. Always ready. And then I remembered Frances Elliott's party. I thought of Mira. Suddenly, not of Mira on a bed with a fleeing face, but Mira on the toilet bowl. There in Frances Elliott's magnificent bathroom. I bought twenty-one canvases. I primed them myself. I made a special ground. Who primes canvases today. You buy prepared canvases. Even mixing colors isn't in fashion today. I primed the canvases five times. The last three times very fine. And for many hours with a round and very soft stick I smoothed the ground until it was fine and nice and soft. And then I painted twenty Miras on the toilet bowl. Those were awful days. I didn't go out of the house, for two months, three months, four, I don't remember anymore. The kettle was boiling all the time. I painted her on a terra-cotta toilet bowl. Each Mira different from the others, different from herself. And above her the window. And in the window a storm. And in the storm snow. And pigeons on a roof. Fringed roofs. And a storm. And the room looked like a temple. On the toilet bowl. And Mira on it. And she, stripping in one painting and laughing in another. This Mira who was born twenty times one after the other, different and alike. Something beautiful had happened to me. The echo that had torn away from the vase and become something of form.

I brought Mr. Zwiegel to my room. He climbed the stairs and ran out of breath. This likable man. He had coffee with me. He didn't want to offend. But that isn't it, he said. So precise, outdated, it looks as if I've copied things from advertising paintings. Maybe you'll paint a bottle of Coca-Cola next, or a can of Campbell's soup. He laughed. Even I laughed. I thought of Jerome's Panamanian flags. Mr. Zwiegel clasped me around the shoulders and muttered something, maybe, maybe. I'd made twenty traps to bring Aminadav to perdition. And then I went to see Frances Elliott's Thumb Three. I'd read in Time that the painting had been sold for twenty thousand dollars and was hanging not far from Guernica. Soutine was farther away. Nolde isn't on this floor

107

at all. Guernica. White on white, Broadway boogie-woogie and Frances. And a crowd standing and looking at it in amazement. We're making ourselves a painting, I saw, and *qus imhem*, and *Kurt Singer potz*, Kurt's body in Prussian blue, the breasts of the telephone girl, the feet of Jerome, but the pleasure that hung there. The thing that gave everyone a spiritual thrill. A woman stood beside me and sobbed. She said, What a thing it is! What a thing it is! And people said, Yes, yes. And someone else said, The abysmal roundness! I read the articles, like arrows in my living flesh. Kurt wrote: In spite of this there is on this canvas a melancholy lacking in melancholicity, a serenity lacking in sereniticity, in other words, lacking the dimension of time. Rust is the effect of time on iron, and time is an a priori proof of the production of rust in iron. Frances Elliott's painting has its existence outside the sphere where rust and time exist as dependent or vitalizing factors . . . something liquid that continues to infinity . . . the effect is powerful because of the very liberation, because of the very spontaneity caught in its sources, a kind of meta-metaphysical meteoricity. . . . One could say of her [of Frances Elliott (A.S.)] that she paints with her feet, with her hands, with her heart, with her whole body, for she paints and doesn't paint at one and the same time, like sleeping and being awake at the same time. Frances Elliott does not describe the world as the journalists of art do; she *permits* her world to be itself.

Sitting in an Oriental restaurant, Mecca on Fifteenth Street. Pale light and neon competing with each other. Below, New York runs. I want to clear up some things for myself. The museum eludes me. I could have gone up on the balcony of the temple of sterility and had some coffee. With all the beautiful people of New York. The restaurant proprietor's an old friend. He asks me what happened. It shows on my face. I said that maybe not everything's destroyed . . . yet. He smiled. You and your Jewish envy. I asked him if he'd do me a great favor.

Depends what.

It always depends, I said.

He squashed two lemons into a bluish bowl and said, Not politics, I'm an anti-Zionist.

No, not today, I said.

What then.

Recite me a poem.

He recited me a poem. The words rang like music in his mouth. I like his gold tooth. We drank strong Turkish coffee with *hel*. I listened to the rhymes. So smooth. I don't speak Arabic well, but I knew the poem by the rhythm of the words, by the music of the rhymes, I knew.

It's a poem about a drop of dew in the Garden of Eden, I said.

He laughed with gold teeth.

Once I heard Charles Laughton reading the telephone book, I said to him, and the telephone book came to life for me. Every name with a special sound of its own. Great artists—and you're a great artist—don't sing *about* a wagtail or *about* a cow, they sing *the* wagtail and *the* cow. Until Frances Elliott came along . . .

9

I opened the door and the woman dressed in gray who had knocked on the door said her name was Donna O'Hagan. She came inside, into the pictures, but that was not where she'd come from. She found Mira on twenty toilet bowls of terra cotta and was shocked. Who's this whore, she said. I asked her if she'd have tea or coffee and she said whiskey. I poured her J&B. The face grew harder yet. Looking at Mira as if she'd found her enemy. She said, I heard that you have religious paintings. I said I haven't. She ferreted around and found some Ashtoreths and fifteen paintings of Sabbatai Zevi, the false messiah mounted on a horse, that I'd painted the year before. Donna, who was organizing an exhibition of religious paintings at the Theological Seminary, said that she wasn't looking for "religious" paintings, but (she added in a whisper with a deep and secret smile) paintings which had a religious significance. And she gave me a laugh, savage, she in knowledge of evil, a stylized savage. She told me that Frances Elliott had contributed a small painting but that mine was much more beautiful. She kissed me as if I were a sponge. My lips would bleed. I wanted to enter and she wouldn't let me. She'd catch the rising excitement and speak with it. She'd say to it, Sam—she called it Sam—the door's locked, only with a ring and a priest. I told her that whores kiss their lovers and screw with everybody. I yearned for the noble apathy that was Mira. But between Mira and Donna there were only Miras on a toilet bowl. The priest who was in charge of the religious exhibition wrote in the introduction to the catalog that David Dancing Before the Lord (my girl dancer) symbolizes a turning point in the consciousness of those who deny the truth. He saw a new wave rising. New-old, he wrote. A wave of dissatisfaction with the prevalent myths. Distress with the technology that has not fulfilled expectations. Despair of a civilization of disbelief which has only sharpened the dilemma of existence. A renaissance is approaching. The artists are always the first to bear the message. They themselves perhaps don't believe, but deep in their hearts they know.

Donna O'Hagan stopped cutting my lips, the exhibition closed and the painting was sold to some woman. I got drunk that night and Donna vanished out of my life. Afterward I used to wake up and think who'd cut my lips, and I didn't know. I tried to find out where she was and I didn't find her. She had told me about her parents and about her brother who'd got into trouble somehow, he'd killed a dog and tried to bury it, and an old man came along and wounded him, and after that he opened a store for sex accessories in Kansas City and they'd almost crucified him, she said, but he'd survived. And she vanished. There are women who aren't beautiful. Gray. They dress in black and gray. With white skin. You enter them as if this were a sweet sin. To enter her was mixed with a desire to kill myself. Maybe the choking, maybe it was that which wanted to be with the thing that was called Donna. Who vanished out of my life.

꧁꧂

Evening. The winter is mellowing and passing. Rain and sun alternate. I meet Dudu. There's an international house he discovers in Seventy-second Street, with women. A pretty Hawaiian receives me. She wants me to sing Hebrew songs, and to make coffee on a bonfire in a large room furnished New England style. In the morning we go down to the kitchen. A Korean girl and a Japanese girl, a German girl and a Danish girl, an American girl and an Israeli girl who was once a beauty queen, all eating an omelet. I teach them to make salad. They accept me. A house with a woman in every bed. At night I sleep upstairs, in a room with curved windows. I left a house with pictures of Mira on a toilet bowl. Looking for something to distract my mind. Dudu and I arrange a Middle Eastern evening. With felafel and a tambourine. They wanted me to put on a *kaffiyeh*. I refused. Fat people came, with cigars. The girls talk with the cigars. I sing *Ma yafim helaylet ekna'an,* How beautiful are the nights in Canaan, and Dudu makes coffee. At night they go up to the rooms and sleep with the fat men with the cigars. The Israeli beauty queen in the arms of a man who brought her a glittering diamond ring. She tells me, Come up to me later. Who made me a queen and took away my scepter? Her husband is studying to be a veterinary surgeon and has gone to Chicago. In the evening he comes. He plays for the fat man on a harmonica, songs of Russia. He's handsome, with a mustache. He believes in his wife. Who cries in the night in the arms of fat men so as to forget she was queen for a day and was then forgotten like the rest of us. A woman comes with a Yemenite dress and says her name's Dalia. She says she was once a singer at Li-la-lo. And no one remembers her anymore. She lives in a small hotel on Eighty-sixth Street. With a pension for life, from all her whorings. Once they acclaimed her and she keeps all the articles. With pictures that nobody can identify. She comes to the evening at the international house and hears me singing how beautiful are the nights in Canaan and says that Steve Allen is doing an Israeli night on television. Several days later, Dudu, I and Dalia are wearing the authentic garb of Israelis in a foreign land. On a huge stage facing eight television cameras. Steve Allen's wearing a big *abbayeh* and joking in Arabic which he thinks is Hebrew. I am to speak about Israeli art and painting, Dalia is to sing and Dudu will make coffee as in the jungles of Jerusalem and Tel Aviv; Steve Allen's hired a camel from the zoo. With a Turk who said he was an Arab. He's going to represent Israeli culture here. This is the public transport in the land of the Hebrews. Ah, camels and *ya hailili ya amali.* I stand with a picture of Sabbatai Zevi mounted on a horse. The camel's on the other side of the stage. Steve Allen plays an Israeli wearing an *abbayeh.* He speaks and makes the audience laugh. Four joke-writers run around behind the camera and write jokes on a large board and he improvises the jokes. About Israel. The camel grunts in the corner. Camera on camel grunting in the corner. I wait with the painting. Dalia sings an ancient Hebrew song. *Shalom Israel* after many years, *shalom Israel* after many years, to see the *yam lir'et ha'am, hashemesh* all day long . . . The camel discovers me, Steve Allen tells jokes to thirty million viewers. The camel goes *grrrr* and starts moving off. The Turk runs after the camel. The camera's on me. I with the painting, wearing an *abbayeh* or something, singing How beautiful are the nights in Canaan. Steve Allen asks me about art in Israel. I want to speak. I see a glimmer of light in the aperture of the camera. The cameraman makes signs to me. The machine in the studio claps hands. Dozens of people run about the huge stage. I'm speaking in front of thirty million viewers. I say that . . . Art is . . . And then the camel stamps its hoofs, it already dislikes me from a distance. It hates Sabbatai Zevi, the wonderful false messiah, and charges at him. I stand. The Israelis are all heroes, writes the joke-writer quickly. The camera stops for a moment on Steve Allen, who's saying, The Israelis are all heroes, they hit a hundred Arab states with seven Arabs, and the writer clasps his hands together, no, no, a hundred million Arabs and seven Arab states, and Aminadav beat them single-handed. And the camel stamps. It's already inside the picture. And I try. I say, Israeli art began with the exhibition of paintings at King David's Tower, which is a tower from the days of Herod in Jerusalem . . . Zaritsky displayed there, and Reuven, and . . . The camel's upon me. The camera catches Steve drinking Coke. He stops and says, Just a minute, maybe the camel doesn't like Israeli art. The Turk flees in panic. Thirty million viewers see Aminadav fleeing from the camel, who stamps on Sabbatai Zevi. The shame of it. The camera sticks to my behind. Dalia sings a song and tries to catch a camera's eye. Steve comes up to her and embraces her. Dudu makes coffee. Thirty million viewers. He tries to put out the fire in the studio. Firemen arrive and demand that the fire cease. Steve tells a joke. He seems drunk. Dressed in an *abbayeh*. I'm in the hall, running. The camel after me. Sabbatai Zevi in my arms. Israeli painting has been put to shame.

113

Steve switches the broadcast over to the commercial, they say it's really worthwhile to buy Mercury because it's better and more economical.

The spring waits between the suns. I went to the Theological Seminary and had a long talk with the old priest. He likes me. He doesn't know where Donna is. It was an enchanting day. I walked in the streets. Without knowing it I retraced the path I had walked on the day I arrived in New York. I went to Greenwich Village. From the same bus stop where I got off the bus that brought me from Hoboken New Jersey. From the shops there no longer blared Stormy Weather and Somewhere Over the Rainbow, but You Ain't Nuthin but a Hound Dog and How Much Is That Doggie in the Window. A world of dogs. A year is three hundred and sixty-five dogs. I reached Washington Square toward evening. The clock showed five. Listening to the ringing. Going on a heart of silk. An arch erected for a triumph that didn't occur here. The green is very green. Children in dark suits play hopscotch. A boy yells, Your mother. And the other one cries, cries. A girl giggles in a jerky voice. Very clear as only early spring can be in a city thawing out of a long hard winter. Mira Mira of the snow. The girl looks at me. Her hair frays out in the wind. She runs after a ball. Kicks. The ball lands on me. She laughs. This love. Her dress flies, she has little breasts, a thin face. Everything is crystalline and very clear.

By the side of the pool Aminadav. A young woman giggles to him. She isn't especially beautiful. But everyone's beautiful on this spring day. Legs aren't bad. Soon it'll be dark. The houses'll touch each other. The last transparent air of the day. A young man beside me, sitting with his feet in the water. Wearing short pants down to the knees, like the British policemen in Palestine (Eretz Israel), a tie around his neck, a Brooks Brothers jacket. A small Hermes on his knees. Writing a poem. Very concentrated. He doesn't see the woman, he doesn't see me. Our looks cross. I and the woman. Her legs say things to me. I thought of Mira. I turned my head to see if Mira disguised as the woman was seeing a wall behind me. I thought of a line from a play by Nelly Sachs:

"If I were your bridegroom I'd be jealous of the Angel of Death."
I thought Mira, Mira.

The woman came up to me and said, It's nice to meet you my name's Carolyn and you're Aminadav Sussetz.

I smiled at her. There also wasn't anything to lose.

I've been waiting for you for two hours, she said.

I didn't know I was supposed to be here.

But today's the first day of spring.

I didn't know.

You didn't feel it.

I did feel it.

Then why do you say you didn't know.

I didn't know it, I felt it.

All the painters have come here today. They painted in colored chalks around the pool.

I didn't know.

You weren't here. And I was sure you'd come to paint.

I didn't know they were coming.

They came and they've gone. And I waited.

Why.

I have a message for you.

From whom.

From Mira.

And where is she.

You're a nice guy, you have nice eyes.

But where is she.

If you go to your apartment you'll find a letter from her. She was born in Russia and she likes conspiracies!

And she went. I looked again for a wall behind me. There was no wall.

10

I'm writing to Aminadav—a funny name—Sussetz. Why am I writing to Aminadav. He has nice eyes, he has such a sad face and a forehead that's stretched tight like a drum, he has—you have? —a sweet body and a gentle voice. No, not because of these things. Maybe because love always lights up at the wrong moment in the impossible place. I saw a woman on a toilet bowl photographed in the Daily News, and it was me, Mira. Then I came here—you weren't here—and I saw twenty! I've been through terrible things. . . . Oh, there are different loves, people are born to love each other. But those who meet after all the collapses, after traveling all the paths leading to destruction, really come together. I'm sitting in a nice room. Too modern for my taste, but clean and sumptuous in a monastic way. Two big pictures by Gorky, whom I like, an African statue and a glass table. I'm writing my life to you. I won't make it long, I want you to know these things before we meet again. You entered me like one enters a ship or a wanton. But what was born was love in reverse, in contrast to the laws of matinee films; you entered first and only then asked me my name. Oh, I know that you knew. You knew because of things that stirred secretly inside you, but we became acquainted, the you and the I of today, only after you came out of me and I said to you, don't be cheated. I still can't tell you how I was there in your story about your uncle at the Dead Sea. After all, I know that you'd made that story up. You told me a made-up story and I was in it. One day, maybe, I'll be able to explain it to you. But then I'll also be able to die. I know that you're looking for me. They tell me that you call and ask for me. But I was afraid. Maybe I wanted to push aside the happiness because I thought I wasn't worthy of you. Today I'm writing to you. If you want to see me tomorrow, I won't hide myself anymore. I've broken down. The Mira who once was is no more and the new Mira needs a guiding hand, a friend. Let's start with the last thing. How I got to Frances Elliott's party. You asked and they told you I hadn't been there. I know Kurt Singer. I've known him for five years. Frances Elliott didn't know (and if I read her rightly, even if she had known she wouldn't have been too shocked) that after staying in her palace he used to ring me. I lived in Sullivan Street in a ground-floor apartment with a lovely little garden and weary aching soil that very little grows in. Kurt paid the rent.

He came to me so as to cheat himself, to let out his anger against himself, for I didn't belong to anybody, certainly not to him. Maybe he came to masturbate into me. Don't be shocked by my straight language, I'll tell everything candidly and you'll decide whatever you decide. I'm not as clean and innocent as I appeared. You know, I'll say even more, Kurt's love-making is really funny. He's excited like a child as long as he's penetrating inward, but when it comes to the screams he screams in Latin. We had a kind of game which seems ridiculous and awful to me today though once it seemed very natural. I would forget his name and he would remind me. Maybe that's what he came to me for. And paid the rent. Once he told me that he had a very wealthy friend, who kept a huge library of pornography in his house, perhaps the richest in the city. He took me to his friend's so I could read to him. I was then so debased in my own eyes that I found every additional debasement useful. Kurt used to wait in the corridor and I would sit beside the bed and read porno books to the old man. He paid me twenty dollars an hour. He didn't touch me. He didn't even look at me. The first time I came, he was lying in bed covered with a heavy blanket. He looked at me for a moment, then lowered his eyes and asked me to say something. I said it. He whispered, That's fine, and from then on I used to come—always with Kurt—twice a week. I'd go into the room—without Kurt—and read. Nauseating things. And he'd close his eyes, looking thin and ascetic like a saint, listening to the words as if they were prayer. I used to look at his face. It was an alarming sight. Such a beautiful face, old and full of sorrow and pity, listening to my voice, which Kurt claims is caressing, telling him unimaginably obscene and disgusting things. And Kurt, who brought me to this house, would make scenes of jealousy! Oh— did you know that he's jealous of you because of your memory?

He brought me to Frances Elliott's party for his own pleasure. He knew that no one knew who I was. He knew that Frances wouldn't know. He pretended that I wasn't there and in this way he was able to see me in Frances Elliott's rooms and think that only he knew who I was. In the morning he arrived at my apartment. He told me about how you'd phoned and asked about me. He wanted to know why you'd asked about me. I told him what had happened to us and he cried. I was drunk and not only on alcohol, and his crying amazed me. It hurt me that you'd phoned and they'd told you that someone had given you a made-up name. I ordered him to get undressed. I wrote your name on his chest in India ink he'd once given me so I could learn to draw. And I told him that he was you.

I met Kurt when I came back to America. Before that I was in Spain for a while. I have to tell you these things. I'm being long-winded but I can't tell it any other way. The Jewish girl that I was. I won't tell you about Father and Mother and my childhood. These are things one can tell later or not at all. But after I married I started finding a path or what the Chinese call Tao, which means way, in Catholicism. My husband was a nice boy from Boston. A good Jewish family and all the rest. His mother was warm-hearted and a little fat. He played the violin and studied physics. Quite good-looking, but without the sadness and the things that the years and troubles do to a man. He had a beauty that was smooth and white like a beautiful children's book. We got married and we lived in New York. I worked as a secretary and he studied at Columbia. And then I discovered Christianity.

118

I don't want to go into that whole thing now. It was nice to pray, to believe, to live inside such a solid and severe thing. I loved the dark churches, the ceremonies, the prayers, the candles and the smell of incense. I loved the New Testament and the Sermon on the Mount and I loved those smooth elusive priests. I met a priest who caressed me and said, What evil thoughts have you thought today. I knew the touch. I wasn't born yesterday. But his eyes were so gentle. I went deep into things. I even studied Aquinas. With the old teacher in the black robe I learned to love Saint Augustine and to suspect him at the same time. To believe and then to understand. To recognize the simplicity of things in such a strange and complex world. The Lord Jesus was for me more than salvation, or the Son of God who had descended to save man, he was the best friend I'd ever had. I too was from Bethlehem. I'd been born with every single beat of his divine heart. I went to Ohio to a convent. My father laughed. My mother mourned. I'll tell you about my parents sometime. My father's a Russian Jew. A refugee who came to America to participate in the creation of the atomic bomb, which he hoped would be dropped on Moscow. He was in despair when they dropped it on the Japanese, whom he idolized. My father loves me too much. That's another story. He thought: Ah, Christianity's good for Mira. It's better for her to sleep with God than with a strange man. My monastic life stimulates him. I think that only monasticism can arouse human instincts in him. But outwardly he pretended to grieve. I went to Ohio and studied. I was an outstanding student. More observant than the Pope. I believed in the sanctity of objects. If you'd brought me a nail from the cross I'd have kissed it. I returned to New York and found myself married to a Jew. I converted my husband. His name's Arthur. He followed me. His parents sat *shiveh*. And he played his violin and studied physics and at night he studied the principles of religion. Those were beautiful times. But I wanted to go all the way. I told him and he accepted the decision. I asked for an annulment of the marriage. Only the Pope can annul a marriage. I went to Rome. I won't weary you. These things are difficult and complicated. But I got the annulment. How happy I was. Arthur cried that night.

119

It's hard to believe, people had said, that the Pope himself will annul the marriage of two Jews who have only recently become Christians. But he did. The skill in speech and argument I inherited from my father. We returned to America strangers to each other. I in a black gown, dressed like a nun, and he numbed. We lived apart. We used to meet every day. He wanted to touch me and I wouldn't let him. He became even more withdrawn. Finally he went to a seminary in Rome and came back a monk. Then we were both dressed in robes. Whispering prayers and secrets. We tried to touch each other. I didn't love him but I pitied him. He used to look at me longingly. I'd say to him, I'm sure you're thinking of the Saviour, and he'd turn pale and hide his face behind his hands.

I went to Spain. I was in a convent there for three years. The mighty desolation of the Pyrenees. The convent was an ancient one and I found some Hebrew manuscripts from the tenth century there. I taught Russian to two old nuns. And English to some younger nuns. The convent raised grain. We had hard calloused workers who prayed whenever they weren't working their guts out. The convent was so cut off from anywhere that it was as if we were living in some other century, and the prayers were ancient and wonderful. Once an old man came with side curls on his cheeks and a suitcase and heard us chanting and he said that the melodies were very ancient. He said they'd been brought from the Temple in Jerusalem. The first nuns must certainly have been offspring of the forced converts, the Marranos, and these were the prayers that had been prayed in the Temple. On the eve of the Sabbath they'd light candles in the convent, and on Yom Kippur they fasted and no one knew why, a tradition of the order from its inception. I didn't say a thing. Arthur lived in Toledo and we wrote each other letters. Once he came to visit me. We prayed together. We walked through fields between the mountains. I was sorry for his pain. He loved me very much. He said, Look, we both belong to the same order. A monk and a nun. And how close we are. And I didn't rebuke him.

I organized the grain trade. I put order into the chaos that reigned there. Before I'd been there a year our convent had become the best organized and the wealthiest in the district. Bishops and heads of orders came, to examine and to marvel. Our contributions to Rome increased. In spite of the fact that we'd taken a vow of humility and modesty. We used to walk stooped. At nights the nuns used to groan and talk in their sleep and caress imaginary things with their hands and above the beds hung a cross and on it was Jesus and they gritted their teeth and moaned. I often traveled to Madrid. I arranged convenient selling procedures. I got credit from the church bank. The convent—forgive me, my good man—became a thriving enterprise. I didn't, though. The way always seems to me more beautiful than the goal. After three years I went to Madrid and I didn't go back. I wandered through the streets and I was suddenly like a stone that wants to be a bird. The other cheek wasn't offered. I humbled it. I wrote a letter to the mother superior. I told her I was leaving and I sent her the balance of the money I had been in charge of. I said that she could burn my few clothes and belongings. Who knows what they did with them. I took a boat to Morocco and I bought a large can of hashish. Then I boarded a ship and read all the movie magazines that could be bought in Casablanca. In New York harbor they didn't search the belongings of a pure pale nun dressed in black. I carried the can of hashish openly and no one noticed me. On the contrary, they did all they could to help me. A cop carried the can to the harbor gate and called a cab and crossed himself! I went into a bar and said I had a can of hashish. In a nun's habit. They laughed. I showed them. They stopped laughing. The price was twelve thousand dollars. I dissipated quickly. New York's a strange city. You can really fall here, and you can reach the heights. I've been every possible thing. Even drugs were already a joke for me, and reminded me of the incense of the priests. I've believed in Reichian therapy, in Trotskyism, in nonviolence and in violence. Arthur stayed a monk. To this day. He writes me a letter every two weeks. He claims that I'm a sinner and a criminal. Poor Arthur. Sometimes I cry about what I've done to him. But that isn't the end of the story. I came back from Spain with an empty womb and a big desire. I was insatiable. Whenever I laid with a man I'd have a mental picture of fifty-two worn-out nuns gritting their teeth in a huge arched room, with Jesus above every bed, embracing imaginary things in the air. And the man'd turn into a fly. They were afraid to come near me. But the very fact that I'd been what I'd been stimulated them. You know, men are so sweet, but they're such babies. I got sick of them. They used to come in and out with confessions and weeping and I'd remain cold. I wanted a full womb. I wanted a child inside me. I didn't want to attach my life to anyone else's. It was summer. New York was hot. I went to Jones Beach. I decided that my son's father would be a strong muscular man. I looked for a lifeguard. I thought with my mind and his body I'd have a marvelous son. Inside my womb I wanted something solid and spiritual at once, like that Jesus hanging on the crosses in the arched room with the moans. I went from lifeguard to lifeguard. I had a notebook. Don't despise me, Aminadav. I've never told this story to anyone. I sat hidden inside a beach chair. Covered with a thin blanket so as not to draw attention to my body which was—if I may say so—quite attractive in a bathing suit, and I made notes. I'd watch a lifeguard for a whole day. Noting down his body movements, his flexibility, the thickness of his muscles, his estimated intelligence. His estimated sexual potential. I had a number of candidates but the decision finally fell on Bob. Tall and blond. Eyes almost white, body tanned bronze. Muscles not too slippery, body not funny like a weightlifter's. Sexual potential seemed high. The things he said to the girls who admired him weren't very smart but not stupid. From a conversation he had one afternoon with a man wearing glasses who might have been his uncle, I understood that Bob had had two or three years of high school. I don't know if he graduated or not but at least he could read. The next day I let him discover me. He wanted me at once. I'm very talented at being liked. And if you want to fill your womb with a son you have to use what you've got. Forgive me, Aminadav, do you understand why I couldn't tell you these things face to face. I wasn't led astray, I led myself astray. And I loved every minute of it. The lifeguard, Bob. Yes. He ignited and within an hour we were talking. Within two hours he'd taught me the butterfly stroke, and within three hours we'd made

122

a date for the evening. There was a moon that night. And he was dressed so nicely, in a thin blue coat, and the bunch of flowers he brought me. He thought that maybe he'd get to kiss me. And that the next day he might be able to put his hand on my leg. And in a week he'd be able to squeeze me inside his big car and in two weeks he'd lay me. Hadn't I studied him a whole day and written down all his good points and virtues (and weaknesses) in my notebook? In Russian. So that none would discover me. But I surprised him. He laid a woman on the first date. That was something he wasn't prepared for at all. Poor Bob . . . He tried to be good to me. He was gentle and humble. For a man with such beautiful muscles. I told him my name was Lysanda and he whispered Lysanda, Lysanda. I slept with him three nights running in a small motel. Not far from the beach. The wind caressed the windows. He talked. I didn't. He said he loved me and wanted to marry me. He told me about his mother. He has an uncle, or something, in the neighborhood. Tomorrow evening we'd have dinner at his place. His uncle's an amateur astronomer. He's preparing his telescope for me, he said.

But the next day I vanished, with his seed inside me. How I loved the child that would be born to me from him. A blond and a brunette, muscles and sense, a gentle heart and my intelligence. But I vanished out of his life. I stayed at my parents' for nine months and I swelled up gloriously. I'd eat up entire refrigerators at night. My father wanted me to hand the child over for adoption. I refused. I was still his. The child was born dead. I went to bury the child. I bought him a tombstone. In a Christian cemetery—his father was Presbyterian—and I put up a lovely little tombstone and on it I wrote: Here lies the apple of my eye, who lived for one day, saw the world, and closed his eyes for another day. Life rolled on, Aminadav, between drugs and therapy, alcohol and Kurt. I went through several years of total fog. I read a lot. I tried to paint. I made ceramic pots. There were men but I've forgotten their names. Every month I go to my son's grave. I want a daughter, Aminadav. After I left you something happened to me. I saw myself for the first time for many years. Mira on the Toilet Bowl was a sign for me, a milestone. I'm no longer what I was. I waited long months to see if the change I'd longed for was really happening to me. I don't smoke anymore. I don't take pills. I'm clean and pure as I was when I was a virgin. But I'm sadder and wiser. I'm ready for a different life. With a man I really love. And apart from my father I never loved a man until I met you. I don't know why I love you so, but that doesn't matter.

I want you inside my womb. That's why I've waited so long. And now it's all in your hands. Tomorrow morning I'll wait for you in the park. At eleven. I won't be offended if you don't come. I'll be sad but I won't stop loving you. You loved me and I wasn't there, on the toilet bowl at Frances's. But from that moment you've been with me all the time.

Yours, Mira Brodie

11

To think she's waiting. To imagine the little park with the miniature arch of triumph with an avenue that comes out of it like an
outthrust knife, to imagine her body clinging to the paling around
the pool. Soon it'll be morning. A kind of spring without fragrance, without orange and jasmine blossoms. But spring that can
be interpreted through the coolness of the approaching morning.
You think that Mira, with whom you've spoken once, with whom
you've groaned on a rug which was wetter on the other side, will
be the mother of your children, the grandmother of your grandchildren, the great-grandmother of your great-grandchildren. Her
breasts pressing against you. Her elongated body, marvelous in its
proportions (how can you know what proportions are), next to
you, close, you touch it, you play on it. And this is the most
familiar thing. To tell her about Father. Shalom Aminadav, how
are you, I'm well, Love, Father. To describe Mother to her. And
Uncle Avner. Who hit David Vehetzi. So she'll know I'm incapable of stealing apples but I'm good at making up stories. To
introduce her into my fictional biographies. To find her a place
between Grandmother born in Tiberias of your imagination, and
uncles who never existed. To see how the wrinkles grow on her
forehead. To see the blue veins stiffening on her legs. To see a
flat belly become even flatter. To see flashing eyes and breasts
growing softer over the years. And nipples darkening and growing

125

with the children who will be born. To see a mirror and in it you and her. With breakfasts and sudden meals in the middle of the night. And to walk hand in hand. Like children. And to say again and again, I love you Mira. And to know that that's ridiculous at my age. And to think she's being unfaithful. And to think she's looking at a handsome young man. And to buy her presents on birthdays and wedding anniversaries and to kiss her on the birthdays of the children the grandchildren and the great-grandchildren, and on silver gold bronze and copper weddings. To see a divine spark in the twilight of life. And to embrace a back during a night of horrors. And not to be ashamed to be suddenly weak and full of dread and a choking throat and the terror of a night alone. And she's here. Beside you. Maybe in the children's room. Wiping away tears. Wiping feverish foreheads. And to see sickness come and go. To worry. Not to be alone anymore. All the Miras I'll have. Sitting in the garden. Waiting for me. Not now. Later. In the morning. Now it's only dawn. To write her love letters. To phone her in the middle of the night from a distant city and to wake her from the webs of sleep. To say, Here I am. And to know this togetherness. That forever. To know that she's anxious now. That maybe I won't come. That things are pressing. I drink coffee with a dry roll. Mira Brodie's Aminadav. Don't let her surrender. Let her stand up for her rights. And know them. And insist on being taken into consideration. She deserves it. She's beautiful. With her dark almond eyes and hair black as a raven. A white tormented face and a protruding nose, a suddenly long neck and broadening shoulders and thin thin legs and broad hips and soles of feet that I don't know. Who remembers the big toe of the left foot. Yet I'll get to know it.

And then to see her in the park. And the morning's still cool. And people walking, not hurrying. And children playing with mothers shouting no no no, and why why why. And dogs, primped and domesticated, and a man with a white mustache, white temples and a bow tie with a velvet voice asking me for a light and I give him a light and see Mira sitting downcast, yet with a majesty in her. She's never really downcast. She may seem to be crying or defeated, but there's a kind of mastery in her, a kind of strength that stems from some unknown abyss. And she smiles. Not in embarrassment. That I'm there. We make acquaintance again. Here's Aminadav my love, she said. We weren't cheated as each of us alone had always been. We spoke as if we really were Aminadav Sussetz and Mira Brodie. And then she changed her name at a municipal clerk's who asked me if I would honor and love her as long as I lived. And the ring I bought her for twenty-five cents at a five-and-ten-cent store. To exchange it for a real ring when the time came. With or without sanctification. And her father looking at me, pained. He does not mock in too loud a voice. And her mousy mother who tries to smile at me. And the apartment we lived in. And Naomi who was born.

回回

The director of the Tel Aviv Museum wrote me a letter. He'd heard about me from two collectors and had even seen a picture of Mira on the toilet bowl in Art News and why don't I do an exhibition at the museum. It'll be an honor for me. I wrote him. He asked for articles about me and a recommendation. The idea had to be passed by the committee, he said. He suggested I get recommendations from known critics, if possible, and to send them as soon as possible.

Kurt Singer received me in his new apartment. He now lived in an apartment that was splendid and attractive enough, with his new paintress Joan Faraday, who was known as the painter who had discovered, according to Kurt Singer himself, the visual correctitude of conducting liquidity. And that is how she paints. Recently Life devoted a large feature to her, with photographs of her dripping paint in a room like a church, in a bathing suit, with a real donkey in a corner of the studio.

Kurt didn't laugh on seeing Aminadav. His face was pale, and for a long time he looked at him and didn't say a word. I sat down and watched the donkey chewing a bucketful of hay. Above the donkey hung a small picture by de Kooning and beside it black with black dots by Reinhardt. The donkey chewed lazily and once looked at me as if it knew that I know about donkeys. I'd never seen Kurt without his armor. Even in his vomit he'd always managed to play Kurt Singer. Now it was as if he were naked. Joan Faraday came out of her workroom wearing a blue smock, filthied with paint, and said, Oh it's you. I said, Yes it's me.

Kurt played with a ballpoint pen he was holding and the donkey shat on the bordeaux-colored carpet. Joan said who'll take the shit down today. And Kurt said today it's your turn. She said she'd be back soon. On the way down she'd take down the shit. She was going to buy a battery for Kurt's vibrator. And she went. He remained opposite me fingering his ballpoint. He looked older than he'd been only a few years earlier. I sometimes forget that Mira and I have been married for several years now and that time is no granter of favors. I sense a kind of new sadness stamped in his face. Maybe things are slipping away from him and his control is collapsing. After all, Joan Faraday isn't Frances Elliott. And Kurt isn't what he used to be. His voice is still heard at the top, but other voices are heard too, underground, true, and the scene hasn't really changed at all, but there are painters who claim that the days of the exclusive dominion of abstract expressionism are numbered. That new days are coming. Only several months ago Mr. Janis said as if in passing that if Jerome's Panamanian flags are selling today at fifteen thousand dollars apiece, tomorrow or the next day people will want painted Coca-Cola bottles and perhaps they'll return to figures and feelings and who knew what might happen. But he didn't look worried. His connections with the museum directors are so firm that even if unimaginable new isms arrive, it will be Janis who will be standing at the cradle of the new scene that will be spread. It's a very small world, Jerome said to me, drunk and offended because of his success. Jerome's waiting for the day when he'll be able to take his pictures of Jesus, the ones with the stones, out of hiding, to show them in public and perhaps gain some grace after his long days of Panamanian flags which he paints full of self-hatred so as not to lose his place among what Kurt Singer calls the top contemporary painters.

But something's not quite right with Kurt today. The world continues on its way to nothing. The isms change. Is Kurt losing the compass. I pitied him. He spoke in a whisper. Joan wasn't there. No one brought coffee. I went to Canossa and the Pope was quietly venomous and refined. I wanted to be like Henry the Fourth. To stand shamefaced in the snow. Without shoes, without socks, without a shirt, without an undershirt, without armor, without a thing. And to wait for the Pope to do his worst to me. This memory would have about it a sudden joy, the joy that exists in very deep sorrow. Is Kurt dying. Why does he need an electric vibrator when he has a girl twenty-five years old as beautiful as Joan Faraday. I wanted Kurt to write me a letter of recommendation.

Picture:

My father sits on a chair reading Goethe. Light falls upon him. I arrive from school. And he asks something like: Who are you. The boy for whom he sought an epigram in the works of Heine, to bury him. Sitting opposite him and trying to arrive. His eyes rest on me. The painting you painted doesn't arouse wonder or admiration, Aminadav. There's arrogance in it, and self-satisfaction. And I expect more. In the Middle Ages, my father tells me, closing Goethe for a little while, they used to crown poets with laurel wreaths. The origin of this custom, Ami, is shrouded in mists. Dante Alighieri could have been crowned anywhere, but he longed to be crowned only in San Giovanni. The coronation was a ceremony of sanctification with religious undertones, very mysterious. . . . He wanted to crown himself with his own hands, while standing on his baptismal font! He didn't get to do it. Glory is a complicated thing, Ami.

I'm looking for forgiveness, not glory, I said to my father, I want you to forgive me the impudence, I said. And there was no mercy in him. Because of a love greater than I imagined, he wanted to save me the misery of standing before Kurt Singer, debased and contemptible in my own eyes, pleading for a good word. In Dante's Paradise, my father said then, the star circle is the place for the righteous who in their life on this earth aspired to glory and by so doing injured what Dante called "the rays of the right love." And these errant souls demand that the poet preserve their glory on earth and at the same time ask the souls that dwell in the golden sphere to pray for them, only that. . . . My father said just as a moving body aspires to be moving so a creator aspires for glory. And glory is his baptismal font. Whether he be Dante Alighieri or the least of men. Every man can choose between giving up or standing dejected facing fate, facing Kurt. In my mind's eye I see a small museum in Rothschild Boulevard in Tel Aviv. My father makes frames for Mr. Dizengoff, the mayor. On Saturday morning we go to the museum, Father and I. I see frames with pictures in them. The frames my father made. The pictures I would make. The boy I was. After ice cream in the Hermon Café with a glass of juice, for two mil. That Saturday. With people in suits from the synagogue. Father walking as if the world is really so pleasant. As if no one dies at night. And those groans. And Mother with her sad face. And we get to the museum. Five Ensors, one painting by Hobbema, not clear, a Rubens from when he was young, Gottlieb, and his large Yom Kippur, several Chagalls and Reuven. Yet all the museums in the world with all their treasures are nothing but delusion. A museum is a thing in the heart. Next to the water tower of the fire brigade. Next to the police station. Mr. Dizengoff's little house that grew and became a poor solitary museum. My father made the frames. With what love. A little city in the sands and it has a museum. A child I've nourished, Dizengoff called it. You walk on carpets. To hang here, on the baptismal font.

回回

Kurt looks at me. I paint demons inside bottles. And everything happens with diabolic speed at which you fly from black spaces to the pelvis of a mother with dark eyes and a Mongolian face. There was a pogrom which left not only afflicted but also beautiful cheekbones. Wherever there's smoke Jews burn, my grandfather said. Kurt smiles and writes.

He didn't lie. He wrote noncommittal things. Aminadav Sussetz is a painter with potential, meaning here not talent or knowledge but something different, something less important or perhaps more important, strange somehow, a something that can constitute a motivation for the creation of works of art, just as it can be a motivation for starting a car. . . . But he signed, the bastard. The signature with the golden rays. He asked if I was satisfied. We looked each other in the face. The sun in the window was setting. The gray house was suddenly illumined. The women's prison, opposite, switched on dim lights. Women walking on the barred roof, and screaming. You can't hear the screams. Below stand people sending kisses upward and making motions with their arms. Kurt approaches the window. Sees a woman on the roof. The woman raises a gray skirt. Kurt sees things under the skirt. He wants the vibrator. He withdraws from the window.

Kurt, I said, if there's anyone who deserves this letter, it's me. What I'm trying to say to you is that you and I deserve each other.

And then Kurt Singer burst out laughing.

Since Frances Elliott's party I hadn't heard the marvelous peals of his laughter.

回回

My paintings left for Israel some two months later and I was even invited to the opening. I sat in my room. My youth came and wondered. To celebrate the return of my dreams. I awoke at night from dreams. I emptied bottles of whiskey in a desperate attempt not to think. I saw black ants eating my eyes. A week before the date of the flight I was attacked by sharp pains. I thought: Again my imagination's playing tricks with me. I was too scared to go and be examined. Until I fainted. Mira ordered an ambulance. They carried me on a stretcher. Appendicitis, at an advanced stage. I was operated on at Mount Sinai Hospital. The nurse I'd had once was still there. Divorced twice, she said. She wanted to return to the days of our youth. I was brought clean and sterile food. Mira sat beside my bed and Naomi read to me from Dr. Seuss.

回回

The critics attacked. My father cataloged the reviews. Two of the reviews were not bad. But most of them were murderous. They attacked the directors of the museum and myself personally. They said what does he want to show us that we don't already know. What's the meaning of Miras on the toilet bowl and who

131

needs outdated paintings of Sabbatai Zevi. What boring and wearying painting this is. The reviews were quiet swords that cut me to pieces. On my baptismal font, there, at home. Next to the fire brigade, next to the Freund Hospital where I was born, next to the block of land my grandfather had bought for two bits and had sold for two bits. They sent me photographs of the opening. I came home from the hospital. Still in bed. Drinking juice and water. Portrait of the Artist as an Error of Birth. The essence of failure as a formalized joke. Father wanted me to give up. With nine words, perhaps he loved me more than any. He knew one should spare a bitter soul any bitterness that isn't necessary. In the pictures of the opening I saw Father and Mother. The mayor, a veteran actress and a number of painters. Jerome had recently set up a darkroom full of equipment. We went to Jerome's to get down to the backbone of things. We blew up the photographs as large as we could, my father's face was half a square yard. And so I could see my disgrace. What I saw in my father's eyes, blown up a hundredfold, was desire. I don't know how to explain, to someone, to myself, why on my father's face there was desire. Not desire for my destruction. His eyes were neither sad nor happy. There was neither disgust nor enthusiasm in them. It was the kind of desire you can sometimes see on the faces of old lechers when they're looking at books of pornography. Something that contains both apathy and longing at the same time. Apathy that's almost canned savageness. Like a professional executioner after his afternoon nap. Was his desire a restrained dread. The critical reviews clipped out and filed. On every review the date and the writer's name. Sometimes my father added some words of explanation. Like: This critic's very important, or this one's not so important. Someone tried to take pity on me and said I had talent.

Sitting in the room. Mira holding Naomi, aged five, on her knees, Naomi reading Dr. Seuss. My beautiful Mira. With the tormented face. With the pain and the love solid as granite. With the wisdom of simple things: to get up and cook during times of trouble, to answer the phone and tell Mr. Zwiegel that I've gone out and I'll be back late at night. With a bottle of J&B always ready. With ice. Hurting what suddenly doesn't hurt me anymore. Naomi cries. Mommy why is Daddy sad, why do you say bad things to Daddy. She doesn't say my child, she tries to leave things as they are. Leave the girl be, what does she understand. Failure is stamped in her toe. She too will fail when the time comes. You're funny Aminadav, when you feel bad you believe in fate. Like Stendhal, who was also incomprehensible, and claimed that every time his shoe hurt him he believed in God. You make use of God for your own convenience. Cut it out Mira, you're getting it all mixed up. Failure isn't a matter of smashed glory but of misplaced arrogance. A terrible thing. It's all a matter of proportions. Even hatred doesn't burn in me anymore. I twist my face in a smile, Naomi. Look, Daddy's laughing! Laughing. Why don't you laugh, Naomi. Once upon a time the elephant went to the river and the alligator bit its trunk and the elephant said with a closed trunk: vetty futty vetty futty. . . She doesn't laugh. My unlaughing girl. You have an uncrying father, my child. Reading the reviews to Mira. She doesn't move. She doesn't think these things matter so much. I remember twenty years ago. In the Jerusalem hills. I lay on the rocks. Ben-Gurion spoke on the radio, they said the state had been born. There were dead men. And crows waiting and vultures. And it was cold. The month of May, no more beautiful than all the Mays Mother Earth had ever given birth to. Armor-piercing bullets crisscrossed the darkness. An armored car climbed with its lights out. People cried. I was in the armored car. I left Nahum. Without his head. The blood that was on me. His brain pasted to my face. There was another dead man in the armored car. I drew the dead man's face on a pack of cigarettes. I thought: What am I doing. Myself in every joke. To see the end and to sing at one and the same time. To enter into that womb which one remembers with a kind of terrible sweetness. Why did I refuse to be born, I asked myself. Mira makes tea. With lemon. In a large glass with a copper holder. From Russia. A present from her mousy mother, as if again to ensnare my heart which will not be given to her. To her poor mother who cooks borscht for Mr. Brodie, my wife's father, and calls it cabbage soup, so that he'll eat it and not think that he's regressing to barbaric Russian customs. He wants to be American. Buffalo

Bill. Dreams in broken English. His daughter should marry a President and she married an Israeli. The things that happen to the wrong people. I'll go home. I'll ask them why we're born.

Frances Elliott. Motherwell. De Kooning. Reinhardt. Franz Kline who once threw me out of the club, asking who's this barbarian. Someone told him that's the guy about whom Hofmann said he's too much of a painter or not a painter at all. Glicky ficky fick fick. To spray paints. To feel the canvas. Feelings on the sleeve. Black lines. And monumental ugliness. The truth of cockroaches. Formica in the humming of veins. Batteries for their vibrators. To paint a horse. To paint a house. Not to paint what you don't see. To paint the things concealed in this little room. The tears and the laughter. They want concepts. Picasso is the Franco of painting.

My father is a lonely photograph, his eyes apathetic desire. There's no forgiveness, but there's dignified behavior. He was right, was Father, injustice is preferable to disorder. His Goethe by lamplight, on the porch, facing the Moslem cemetery. On a summer night with moths around the lamp dying to be burned. I thought to myself: The abortive exhibition at my baptismal font saved me. The very fact that my paintings are hanging there fulfilled the great desire. And there's no longer a need to prove anything. There are people who believe that syphilis saved Christianity. In the Middle Ages, fornication was rife among popes and priests, bishops and nuns, barons and kings, merchants and artists . . . millions were killed in mad orgies. Sex rites and mad revels reached their peak in the witch hunts that felled millions of victims. And then syphilis arrived in Europe. The disease was brought from Haiti to Portugal by Columbus's sailors, and spread at dizzying speed to Germany, France, England, Switzerland and Russia. In 1506, only twelve years after Columbus's sailors returned from America, the Archbishop of Crete died of the disease, and the terror of this illness that destroyed body and soul had its effects. Morality came later to justify the fear. What was not achieved by the exalted ideas of Holy Writ was achieved by the fear of organs falling off and damaged brains. To hang in the museum where my father framed pictures. The landscape of my childhood. A difficult disease cured me. The horoscope failed us, Mother. If I'd only known how to make use of the memory I'd been given. But I don't know how. I have no doubt at all that Mathias Grünewald remembered his days in the womb and the black spaces, and that Hieronymus Bosch certainly knew the memory of his coming to be. The canvases died before me. My hands were empty of painting. The mornings were awakenings into a long death. The nights were a longing for dreams. Art, the Chinese say, is the training of spontaneity. For art is nothing other than spontaneity in a cage of order.

I don't want anything anymore. I surrender. Become one with the tree and the sky, with the Milky Ways and the stars of Andromeda. And I depart at one and the same time, united and apart. I'm finished and therefore I've finished. I alone. I'm going to see where I came from. I'm coming home, Father.

12

To paint my last painting. Mira took Naomi. The house was empty and I found a cricket. The cricket chirruped. I don't know how the cricket got to the ninth floor. Maybe it had attached itself to us and we'd brought it from Fairfield Connecticut, when we were trapped in an old wooden house on a startling stormy summer night. When trees were felled by lightning and the rain fell in handfuls. I tried to catch the cricket but I couldn't. I drank red wine and tried to read Under the Volcano by Malcolm Lowry. I spoke to the cricket and told it that I was superfluous. That it was wasting its chirpings on the wrong man. I thought of my father's smashed violin. Why didn't I listen to him, why didn't I recognize his great love. I refused to accept with equilibrium the prospect for the days to come. Will I be able to get up early every morning to an office, to live a routine life. To keep books. To be insured. To take care of the future. The red wine Mira had brought from the liquor store. Something hovered at the edge of my mind. My head was heavy and light at one and the same time. But I was amazingly clear-headed. I was able to think about the cricket. And I caught the cricket. I placed it on the window sill. And slammed the window down. My hands wouldn't spill its blood. If it wanted to climb down from the ninth floor, let it climb. If it wanted to fall, let it fall. It looked at me for a long time until it vanished. The radiator hummed and stopped. I turned on the radio. A piano concerto by Schumann. It's nice to listen to music that my father doesn't believe exists. Schumann is so human.

One cannot imagine a gossip session between a chorale by Monteverdi and *Die Sieben Worte Jesu Christi* (The Seven Words of Jesus Christ) by Schütz, or between a mass by Palestrina and *Stabat Mater* by Pergolesi. On the other hand I find it easy to imagine how the melodies of Schumann and Brahms converse about the latest fashions in women's lingerie, or curtains from Damascus. There's something very human in the music that my father declared didn't exist. I listened to Schumann and had a kind of feeling of falling away from myself. Of pity for myself, for Mira, for Naomi. Through the windowpane where the cricket had been I saw a party in one of the apartments opposite. They were frolicking over there but I didn't hear. A woman stood, her face stuck to the window, and waved her hands in a kind of rhythm that was either pleading or joyful. A man approached her and stood behind her. I wanted to shout to her. The man kissed her earlobes as if he were gobbling sardines. She didn't laugh. She stuck her face to the windowpane even more than before. The squashed face of the woman in the window frightened me. I thought about death. I think about death whenever I meet a man in underpants or when someone beautiful and airy goes to the toilet.

That's the dread that's in the banal, Jerome once said to me. Here's the man in the window kissing earlobes. A woman with a squashed face in the window. Wearing earrings and trinkets. Her hair done. Her ears pierced as they should be. Invented by a ruler. Everything fitting: the right side resembles the left side. Outwardly, everything's so symmetrical. Two breasts. Two arms, legs, she stands. She moves, shifts, opens her mouth and closes it. A voice as gentle as velvet or as coarse as sackcloth. Lie with her legs raised. Two Aminadavs in her eyes. Schumann on the radio. Lovely *schmaltz*. My friend's brains smeared over my face. Life or death. A famous man in underpants. King or mosquito. For a second of eternity. Kindles and extinguishes. Everything. Once I had a girlfriend. We were children. We went to Shekh Munis, and we bought a white pigeon. I held the pigeon in my hand. In a field next to Shekh Munis. A boy was flying a kite. I remember a summer with stubble and sabras and oleander and bougainvillaea huge purple red like a drunken flame. The girl stood beside me. The Yarknon was there, not far, with a field of tall reeds. And I couldn't think about the girl who was my girlfriend and I wanted to touch her. I thought how beautiful the pigeon is. And then it shat on my hand, and its face didn't budge, a kind of quiet and divine expression. I wanted to be a porcelain man. Who doesn't die. Who doesn't have to undress. I didn't succeed. To be a glass soldier, on a shelf, dusty, living forever, not to feel. I didn't even succeed to not be born. Or to live in a different biography. I'm going back to my mother and father. How I wanted them to be different. With a single bedroom. And I didn't succeed. . . . The woman with the squashed face in the window. The fear. Maybe on Saturn or Uranus there are creatures without flesh and blood, without body. That is a great task for a god with a vision. Not to be needed and to be eternal. Of glass. The woman with the squashed face is the doomed finite. Is death the other side of life? Sitting in my room. Opposite the easel. Drums and trombones of Schumann. The woman in the window. I picked up some brushes and painted another Mira on a terra-cotta toilet bowl.

Alone all night. The radio didn't stop playing. I drank a little whiskey, my hand painted by itself. I thought about my life, about my father in his frame store, about my mother whom I hadn't seen these many years. About the wrinkles that must have deepened in her brow. About the boy I had been, whom it had suddenly become important to me to go back and find. The sea from the veranda. I didn't think about the painting, because it painted itself. From within me it came, I didn't even know I was painting. Tense and calm at one and the same time. I traveled to distant places and returned from them. I was at my parents' house and I drank steaming-hot coffee that my father prepared in a strange machine he'd brought back from Germany. I saw myself hanging on the walls of the museum with arrows sticking into me. So far I had painted twenty Miras on a toilet bowl. This was the twenty-first Mira and she already knew herself marvelously. No effort was needed. What colors. I didn't know I had those colors in me. Schumann, colors and whiskey. And Mira on the toilet bowl, with a window and a madonna hanging on the wall behind her and a storm raging outside the window.

And then morning fell on me. I saw it bursting in through the window. The woman did not appear in it. The cricket had vanished. Someone had closed the woman's shutters. I heard a plane. Everything panicked into stillness that became the sun shining into a weary man, whose life had crawled out of him, leaving him alone and clean.

I fell into the armchair and fell asleep. I slept about five hours. There was a strong light in the room. I didn't wake up. The smell of turpentine mixed with linseed oil and the sharp aroma of spray and enamel, guiding dreams deep into the brain. I dreamed of Giotto in an undershirt, he stood on a ladder and painted a fresco of Piero della Francesca. I woke up in a shirt. The undershirt remained in the dream. Mira stood behind me with Naomi beside her. Naomi said, Daddy get up.

With one blow the morning was on my face, aflood with light. Mira above me in tears. Naomi seeing her mother on a toilet bowl. I said in my sleep and with a smile that was still in me from the dream: That's how you were made, my child.

Mira kissed me and seemed a soft butterfly, her lips hovered above my face. She saw me in the painting and didn't see herself. That's how much she's inside my blood. Naomi saw her mother frightened and became alarmed. Mira's eyes were covered with remorse. Naomi went down to a neighbor who'd take her to school today with her son Freddy. Golden-haired and bleary-eyed. Mira led me to the bed. I wanted to take off my clothes and I couldn't. I felt heavy as stone and I said for the first time that I'm going away, I'm really leaving here. And Mira, you'll come over afterward. But not yet. She asked if I wanted to be separated from her. I told her that I'd never loved her more. But things are disintegrating inside me. The last painting. She said that it's especially beautiful. I told her, Like the peacock. The peacock is so beautiful. But the peahen is color-blind. That rare beauty that you see is not seen by anyone apart from you. And she said that

I'm a spoiled child who wants love and affection from everyone. I wanted to embrace that marvelous body. To know that she's mine. To say come, let's get married again. To say to her that I don't understand how I could have loved her when I didn't know her and really, only now I love her. She said thanks. I told her, don't thank me for that. She said, my Aminadav. I cried into her breasts. They're erect and the nipples want me. How I love to come into Mira. And to feel that thing that starts to quiver like a fish and I sail. And she laughs softly or cries. She always cries into my mouth and her tears with the hairs I swallow and try to get rid of when I have no hands because they so love this body which is a soul wrapped up in flesh and skin. Naomi will go to a matinee with the neighbor. A call from the store. They want to know if we need anything. I ordered beer, butter and rolls and went back to bed. And we gave ourselves to the terrible sweetness of bodies merging with each other. It was quiet and I heard cars charging along Riverside Drive. A pleasant breeze blew from the river, and we were together. There was silence. And then the phone rang and Mr. Zwiegel said that it's a nice day outside and why don't I come. I said to him, Clouds cover the face of the heart. Two days later I walked through the streets and I saw Aminadavs from all the lost years. Several days later I went and bought what I bought, parted from Mira and Naomi, and slept with my daughter's teacher.

13

In the morning I parted from Mira. She closed herself in the kitchen. I got into a cab and we drove through the thick mist of morning. Peggy, my daughter's teacher, with legs open, with Cutty Sark on the cabinet, with feet that sink into a sexy carpet. The thoughts that buzzed through me. Mira, the one woman I've loved. On the pier I stood bundled up in a blue sailor's coat, waiting to go aboard. Sunglasses on a misty winter's day. To camouflage fears. Foghorns blew on the river. A fishing boat's lethargy. This was how I arrived more than ten years ago in the city of men in the midst of mists. Try to know who you are and why. I give a steward my belongings and am led to a cabin. People waved goodbye and wept on the pier. Wet from the frozen rain. The windowpane of my cabin porthole is opaque in the rain. Opposite is the steel structure of the pier. Soon there'll be sea and space. I was saved and alone. I didn't know the exact time of departure, I knew that Mira wouldn't come to wave me goodbye. She thinks I'm leaving forever. That I don't love her anymore. Words, words. What do words say. I tell her and she knows how to laugh or to cry but what do words say. I thought that maybe Peggy from the Ziegfeld Follies might come and perform some marvelous feat with a tiny triangle between her legs and striptease on the gray background of the harbor in the rain. But today's an ordinary school day and my daughter's sitting facing her now and writing Honor thy father and thy mother. My country 'tis of thee. Mira'll come back from the school. She'll chain up her bitterness, sit in our room opposite the bookshelf that I built with my own hands out of planks and red bricks, radiating the light of a cheated martyr and silently slinging gentle words at me. The forgiveness that will be in her always. The fidelity to a moment that never returns. I cast a last glance at my city. A darkness was spread over her, like a blanket. Buildings were torn from each other in the black mists. All the edges merged and the sharp roofs protruded in vain, sudden towers from nowhere, goods yards, a store selling drinks, everything merged into a single dough. People came in and went out into low mists and tugboats tooted in the river. Smoke rose from the two funnels and a woman on the pier shouted. Look, she said, they're baking bread there.

I went down to the bar and waited. The barman's wiping glasses. With an owl's eyes. Wearing a dark suit, his eyes on the glasses. On his chest, a Palmach badge made of gold. And a big gold ring on his finger. Love at first sight. I read Palmach on the barman's chest. And he smiles at the drinker I'm going to be for him. An Israeli ship's a catastrophe for barmen. Two weeks of *mitz*, fruit juice, he said. I asked him what regiment he'd served in and he said the Fourth. I told him me too. He asked if I knew Bentz and Putzi. I said I hadn't seen them for years. Once I worked on a ship with Jan-Jan and Fat Menahem and Tarzan. He laughed. Hey, did you know Draw-Tooth? Yes, I said. He's got a daughter. Works in Haifa. He has a truck. Jan-Jan's vanished. To Brazil, they say. Chops down trees and plants coffee. Remember the Kastel, what a battle that was. What about today. We can't sell drinks until we're out of territorial waters, he said, I'm sure you know, but comrades or not comrades. He brought out a large teacup, and filled it from a bottle that was hidden in a secret place. Something for the meantime. I wanted to pay and he refused. Wait, you'll get your chance.

I started sinking. A sticky numbness of the senses. Something between, like despair. The ship penetrated into the ocean with great hostility. At night a storm began which tossed the ship about for seven days. The seamen stretched ropes along the companionways. The dining room was empty. The deck chairs were all wet. I sat on deck, wrapped up in blankets, I thought of my father and mother who were waiting for me, I sent them a cable. The sea was now above me now below me. I was almost alone on deck. Only some seamen were to be seen, walking around like drunks.

The sea was gray and white. Frothing wanton joy of water to fill the whole horizon. I tried to read, but the sea groaned in the billows. I closed my eyes and the time passed between certainty and uncertainty.

In the empty second-class dining room I sat next to a roundish golden-haired gray-eyed woman who turned out to be Dutch. Around her pupils were circles of red as if she'd been boiled in heavy tears and was now drying out on a line. Flushed cheeks, she was fresh and gay all the time. The storm didn't touch her at all. We drank a bottle of wine together and made each other's acquaintance. Her name was Beatrice. She thought I was funny with my yearnings for Mira on my face. I stood on all fours and showed her how Naomi played two dogs with me. Her laughter was wonderful. Two dimples sank into her cheeks and the voice that chirped out was like the crying of a goose. I told her that when I was a child I'd had frogs. That was when we lived in Qiryat Meir. The frogs had multiplied in an alarming way and it had been necessary to destroy them. They'd destroyed the tadpoles with sprays, but they hadn't known how to get rid of the frogs. Frogs, I told the Dutchwoman, have an angle of vision of one hundred and eighty degrees and they always discover their killers. We talked about tadpoles, how they become frogs, swallow crickets and regulate nature. The Dutchwoman called nature this cruel thing, and I tried to explain to her that her pink cheeks and the patch of water in the lake reflecting the sun are also nature. To her, nature was a terrible and threatening thing. But she smiled when she spoke of the cruelty of nature. We spoke of big fish eating little fish. I told her that in Africa there are insects whose mothers produce them as eggs and they emerge in different colors. Reds, greens, yellows, and more. They live for all the world like ordinary insects, but when a certain bird approaches they fly

143

to a tree trunk nearby, glue themselves to it and within a second turn into a flower. The green insects become a stem and the others arrange themselves upon it as petals. They make a flower that even emits a special odor repellent to birds, and what's interesting is that in nature there is no flower anything like the one they pretend to be. Do they create rather than imitate? The Dutchwoman didn't know.

And then I was drawn into the unforgettable argument about orange yolks. And to tell you, Beatrice, to meet a woman like you during a storm when everyone's hiding in their cabins and vomiting out their guts. After all I was a seaman once and you could have looked for salt on my body. The moss that my body grows, and this early middle age. She said that orange yolks are also called Dutch yolks and therefore she knows more about them than I do. I tried to reach her. I said that for the yolks to be orange the hens had to be fed a mash of Peruvian anchovy mixed with ordinary feed. We played a game, what is Peru, why and when. I claimed that the Peruvian anchovies are caught out in the open sea, and her version was that they're caught in little streams that are full of coral. I said, how strange and perhaps more cruel than nature that in Peru people die of protein deficiency while in Holland hens gobble up Peruvian anchovy rich in proteins. She said I was smug. Her eyes darkened. They became suddenly transparent. After all, she said, in Calcutta people die like flies. They lie down on the banks of the holy Ganges in disgusting postures of death and destruction, and this doesn't disturb your traveling second-class, drinking excellent French wine and talking with a strange and sexy (so she said) woman about injustice. As if you're really clean yourself, with a kind of dryness that came over her with the same suddenness with which her eyes had become transparent before. Injustice depends on location, she said, it depends where you stand, when and why. It's very easy for you to be moral. But to be immoral and right is a lot harder.

From the argument about what's immoral and right, with the Dutchwoman, to the Israeli-Arab conflict. In the suddenness of a ship on a raging ocean. Beatrice is going to Israel on this stormy sea because her fortuneteller from Houston Texas has prophesied that this year, nineteen sixty-seven, there'll be a war between Israel and the Arabs. And she has to be there, to see the miracles that will happen. I argued that this was a ridiculous prophecy. I read the papers, American and English and Israeli, and I know something. What do you know, she said. You know what you read. I know things that are more secret. She told me how once she'd gone to Europe, and she'd been ill, and her fortuneteller had told her not to travel and the train had turned over. Once she went to the Valley of Arcadia in the Peloponnesus, looking for a Greek shepherd playing a flute, as beautiful as Apollo, and she hadn't found him. But her life, she said, fulfills a supreme command, and she has hardly ever been disappointed. My life, she said, is arranged in advance, though open to change, requiring choice from time to time according to the meaning of things and the choice of the right way within the computed and ever-branching field. . . . Her fate, which is known in advance, does not explicitly define every single step, and she has to be attentive to the correct interpretation, which is also the only interpretation. To lay her life on a line, to walk like a tightrope walker, like all of us, but to know the possibilities precisely. A fascinating tension, she said.

Huge waves tossed the ship about. Devout Jews fill the synagogues and sing to God. They don't want me to drink milk after beef Bourguignon. The barman's my closest friend. We count the Dutchwoman's virtues; he takes an interest in her lower parts and I in her upper parts. I spoke of her spiritual virtues and he said he suspects me and we drank gin and tonic. He tells me that people who take an interest in the exalted spirits of big women with magnificent asses are suspect in his eyes. I told him that this was like the gallery owners I knew who often spoke about art. Painters who talk about money make more sense to me. The officers joined us and we discussed the storm and the barometric reports. When we crossed the Gulf Stream the ocean sent up vapor and the sky was caught into the sea and created a rainbow of foliage and the water trembled. The sea was slaughtered in sudden heat. Then the Dutchwoman cried. She said that loneliness is a physical thing. At night we got together under a thin blanket. The heating in her cabin worked perfectly. Outside the porthole the sea seethed with a cold storm lashing against its face. Toward morning a girl ran in the corridor. A huge wave tossed the boat suddenly and a terrible creaking sound was heard. Then the bow slapped into the sea and a thick door which for some reason had been left open closed on the right big toe of the little girl, who screamed in pain. The noise of the storm didn't drown out the scream. I took her in my arms and asked her who she was. She cried and couldn't answer. The toe was completely squashed. At the information counter I was told that her father isn't on board and her mother is seasick and in a very bad way. I took the girl to the ship's doctor, who sat in his cabin manicuring his delicate fingers. At breakfast he'd told me that he was a navy doctor. His wife had been dead for several months now. He'd gone to sea looking for adventures. He liked the sea and the women in the ports. He sat there doing the manicure, looking like a scarecrow with silver hair and a delicate face. I wouldn't trust him. On the wall a picture of Marilyn Monroe in the nude. The man's fifty. I sat the girl down on my lap and the doctor treated her. I thought of Naomi my daughter. How three days ago we'd gone to Riverside Drive to buy The New York Times in the snow and a strange dog had wanted to be ours. The girl cried. Her tears seemed to be mine.

The doctor finished treating her and I took her to Shoshana's kindergarten where they were singing *Tze'na tze'na tze'na habanot ure'ena hayalim bamoshava,* Come out come out girls and see there're soldiers in the village. Shoshana was smiling through her seasickness and taking care of two little tots who were vomiting in the room. My little girl in a bandage with dry tears. Naomi at school learning striptease. Diamonds are a girl's best friend. I'll buy her beads of dew and she'll scoff at her father. I couldn't go back to the Dutchwoman, who was waiting for me under the blanket with physical loneliness. I went out on deck. The sea roared and waves launched themselves as if for battle. Everything was one single vortex. I found a rare beauty in this picture of eruption. I heard the ship's engines humming and a smell of food cooking came from somewhere. The deck was washed with waves.

In the stern stood a woman wearing a plastic hat that came down to her neck. Her face was wet from the spray of the salt water. Agitated, she said we have to do something, we have to all band together, she said, and take the helm into our own hands. The captain's going the wrong way, she said, he doesn't know. She pointed at the curling wake and said that she'd done this trip six times and she knew the way well. The captain's mad, she said. I saw his eyes. Reads the Bible all day long. I don't trust him. Then a huge tremor ran through the ship and the propeller emerged as if it was being separated from the ship and the woman fled inside with a thin birdlike scream. A Chinese proverb says: Three things one mustn't rely on: king, sea and time. The mast sways. Am I enjoying the destruction of the world. That may occur. Maybe not. Like the cars that grind to a stop at the traffic lights near my home and give me a demonstration of my death. The woman's right or not right. The captain's a king, time is waves. Go and be Giotto in these conditions. I laughed to myself. Thus die people who have never been born. To tell the truth I laughed at myself with typical pity. It was cold and a fierce wind whistled. Waves up to the funnel. In one of the lifeboats sat a man and a woman. I stood with my back to them. They looked out to sea. The din separated us. They didn't see me. The woman may have been older than the man. Her voice rang melodiously as if time wasn't a problem anymore. Perhaps she was his wife, or his mother. I had made grave errors during my life about who is whose mother or wife. The woman said she was afraid. The man, her son or her husband, said that fear is a specific psychological condition which can be trained. He spoke about liberation of the self. About alert posture. Unification with the all. Since he had learned the hidden secret of things, said the man, the separation from the ego and the delight in being part of everything and separate at one and the same time, he's hardly afraid anymore. There's a black space, he said, and everything is swallowed up in it. Stars, entire galaxies, vanish into antimatter which is black spaces in the immeasurable universe. Nonlife is life in its more perfected edition. He feels things at his fingertips. This storm is perfect. He's willing to sing hymns to it. How beautiful and pure it is. Silence that has donned a mask. The woman trembles, her voice expresses lack of confidence, she has sought the all and found lies and vanities, she asks him in this storm which is all around me, has an answer been found to the fateful question, *is is?* And the man answered without a pause, *is is because isn't isn't.*

I sang: Ocean, how hidden is thy night, encasing thee in a cast envelope, engulfed in spaces, stars spreading and vanishing, signs, into antistars. I come from spaces and return unto them. From woman to woman. From pain to pain. If I sleep all my life I will dream only about things I've dreamed about before because there will be no life apart from sleep. There will be no separation between the real world and life. And when I die I won't know I've died. And I won't be so sorry about dying. Or so alarmed. The sea has no borders. Movement is slow. The noise of the engines is dull. Is that a secret message or conclusive proof that we really are going somewhere. Perhaps the woman was right and the captain doesn't know. I was encompassed with new fears. As if those I'd had before weren't enough. Mira Naomi. The paintings I smashed. The fear of the Aminadavs waiting for me in the homeland.

I went back to kiss the Dutchwoman as proof that is is. I wanted to return to my cabin. To dream alone. With Mira, not with the Dutchwoman. Her body is beautiful but this fierce yearning. I drank cognac. A little numbness. The ship sways like God praying. His face offered to Mecca. Darkness descends. Enwraps the ocean. The ship drives into the night. Bells ring the change of watch. Seamen pass along the companionway and tighten ropes. A man cries in the synagogue. Stars glittered into the storm. At first there were chariots and magnificent horses. King Henry II crowned at Notre Dame. The huge canopy. Swiss soldiers dressed in red and white holding swords. The Bishop of Paris reading the holy certificate. Then Marie Antoinette ate cakes with blood. Because there wasn't any bread. And the chariot of the Empress Theresa stopped beside a beautiful house, perhaps a palace with innumerable windows. Then a long row of palm trees on the road from Atlit to the seashore. Slim-figured Washington palms. Wind moving the fronds. A grenade exploded. The brains of the world splattered over my face. So I said to myself in my dream. A man whose head was sewed filled empty heads with brains that he pulled with tongs out of preserves cans. On each can was written: Danger Poison! Then they sewed all the heads with thread, put the people into drawers and filed them. Each of them had a file. A name and Roman number. And then there was sea. A different sea. Quite like a tear blown up a millionfold. I was sailing in a ship. On the empty sea. There was no wind, and no sound could be heard. Only quiet ringings inside a glass bell. We stood on deck, the Dutchwoman, who in my dream was taller than usual and had orange eyes, the captain and two faceless people from the lifeboat, who muttered, is is because isn't isn't, is is because isn't isn't. And I. With Jews with bundles and sticks migrating to Eretz Israel. On its blue deck, silent and unmoving, stood the girl whose big toe had been squashed, wearing a red bandage, my cat Kadarlaomer, the woman I'd seen in the stern wearing a plastic hat, and the barman. The barman wore large sunglasses. His heart was exposed through the torn glass window on his bare chest. I saw cogwheels and an enema shaped like the enema in the poster opposite my house in Division Street opposite the ruined moviehouse. The cogwheels drained the blood and filled the enema with fresh blood. Our ship was returning from the Western world, which had been destroyed. The ship sailing toward us was returning from the Eastern world, which had also been destroyed. The sea was flat. As if it were covered with an invisible roof. We sailed on a flat sea in a world that had been destroyed. Nothing remained save two ships.

And there was a moment when we sailed ship beside ship, touching and not touching. And each of the ships continued in the opposite direction. And when we were close we sang a song together.

> The west is destroyed
> The east is destroyed

What'll happen when the fuel runs out
What'll happen when the fuel runs out.

I awoke drenched in cold sweat. The doors groaned in the storm. Everything seemed to be begging to be torn apart. It was dark and tiny lamps lit up the companionway. I fled to the Dutchwoman's cabin. She received me nicely even though she was sleeping. She poured me sweet Drambuie. I had to tell her about the dream. She wasn't alarmed at all; she told me that her fortuneteller had told her that there's a language in which the words for dream and window are similar. I told her in Hebrew dream is *halom* and window is *halon,* and in Hebrew the final *n* is often transformed into a final *m.* She wanted to know how she'd sung in my dream, soprano or alto. I told her she'd sung beautifully. And she let me get into bed.

You're sweet and tell me again how I sang.

You had a fine thick voice. You sang as if you were concentrating on the singing. And on nothing else. There was something stirring about it.

You're sweet.

I'm going home, what awaits me, Beatrice.

Who knows. Why don't you press harder, sweet violence isn't illegal.

I'm in her and she talks about her trip to Greece. A Greek flute-player in the Peloponnesus. A disappointing trip, she says. I suck her breasts like one deceived. She spoke in a dry voice of night. After waking up from sleep and finding Aminadav in bed with dreams and dread. And the sea outside beats against the ship's walls. On the Peloponnesus she lived in an ancient fortress that had been turned into a hotel on a little island near Nauplion. She saw ancient monasteries climbing up the mountain. Don't turn me over, Ami, I like it under you. She went to the valley of Arcadia, and didn't find the love of her heart. Who does. She climbed to a frightful monastery on the cleft of a canyon, she'd drunk a special wine that tasted like raisins soaked in water.
. . . You frighten me, now it's time for gentleness, Ami. In the toilet of the convent. You laugh? She got undressed and stood

naked in front of the window. Looking down at that divine valley. The trees there grow downward. The sky's inside the canyon. She thought she was a goddess and she loved her own beauty in the window, which is also a dream in Hebrew, yes yes Ami, kiss me and I'll be quiet. Yes yes. Two Greeks told her afterward that she ought to be in the movies but it was terrible. Dry rice and fat mutton. The mountains are all alike. She flew to London, Olympic. Ships spoil you. You meet Aminadavs. There's time. You dance in a different dress every night. A world divorced from the world. With no newspapers. You see old movies. You laugh at nothing. Oh, do you like being inside me. Ships are lovely. You meet people. Without obligations. She calls it the Friends of the Month Club. You're beautiful, you! You!

Afterward she ordered coffee. A steward staggered in. She received him in a floral robe. He smiled. His lips twisted, as in pain. We drank coffee together. The grounds remained. She turned my cup over and read my fortune. You don't need to worry about the dream, she said. You'll live many years, you have to beware of quicksand and of people with harelips. The cruelty will vanish. Children will be born to you. She refused to withdraw the prophecy of her patroness about the chances of war in the Middle East. There'll be one. And it's connected with water. The Jews will win. I said, Whom will they beat, where. She said that in certain places new blood always has to flow according to a predetermined pattern. I told her that the Moslems believe that a war breaks out whenever one of the walls of the Garden of Eden cracks and is about to collapse. It has to be repaired, and the good Allah needs good Moslems to repair the wall. They die and go to the Garden of Eden direct from a holy war and repair the Garden of Eden where I was twenty-five minutes ago exactly. She kisses me for the compliment. I wanted to ask her if I was better than a vibrator. Beatrice says that this year perhaps two walls in the Garden of Eden have broken.

The storm didn't stop until Madeira. In Madeira we disembarked in a large boat which came to take us and we saw an island which was a mountain. Everything was calm suddenly, and gentle. The mountain was a carpet of flowers. At night, before we weighed anchor, the captain had read some chapters from Psalms. He said that not far from here was a sunken continent.

After Madeira we sailed to Gibraltar. The sea as smooth as silk. The synagogue emptied. And at night they danced dances that were quite daring for a middle-aged ship. An Israeli singer called Shashet Sasso suddenly broke out of hiding and organized a whirl of social activities. He's a hit parade star, said the seamen, and asked for autographs. To fill what we'd lost the last seven days. We'd paid and we'd eat our fill. Stomachs swelled. Steward bring me two steak tartares and some potatoes, lots of them. Aminadav sits on deck wrapped in a thick blanket, and the sea over his head is coated with lacquer. Releasing me into a pleasant languor. There's a lot going on on deck. A plump woman who bought twenty black Banlon shirts in New York is exchanging with a woman who bought twenty yellow Banlon shirts. Then each of them changes her shirt, one with a woman who bought twenty orange Banlon shirts and the other with a woman who bought twenty white Banlon shirts. Later still the black shirts return to the first woman and the yellow ones to the second. There's an atmosphere of good business in the air. Someone who'd brought a double toaster exchanged it with someone who'd brought an electric mixer and an electric blanket, General Electric. A rumor spread that I hadn't filled in all the items in the returning residents' questionnaire. I became the apple of the passengers' eyes. I was flooded with invitations to coffee and smiles. I, who walked about on deck with a *goya*, with a bare back and blue eyes like a whore. The mother of the girl whose toe had been squashed, cured of her seasickness, claimed that after all there was a special relationship between us and why wasn't I willing to sell her my right to a television set and a refrigerator. She could buy them on board. Only the customs clearance would save her. She lived in a small apartment, she said, and she didn't have a thing. She sends me her daughter with a bunch of plastic flowers she bought in the ship's store, with a letter attached to the bunch of flowers: "Mr. Sussetz, do me a favor. Everyone has a Philco except me. And I can buy such a nice television. I'll pay you a hundred dollars for the right. Thanks. Yours, Mrs. Avinoam." The girl came and said,

Uncle Aminadav, my mother loves you so much. She talks about you all the time. She says what a good man you are.

I took some toilet paper and wrote: "My dear Mrs. Avinoam. You have a magnificent ass. I'm dying to part it. For one fuck you get a Japanese toaster with an alarm clock that kisses you in the morning and makes coffee too. Two fucks (not in succession) will get you a Philco refrigerator—two-door, fifteen cubic feet, with automatic ice-cube maker. Three fucks—a television."

The girl brought a letter. "Mr. Sussetz. It isn't nice to speak like that. I'm quite amazed. Is it nice to say such things in the presence of children. I don't want to understand what you wrote. If you wish to discuss conditions, I'm willing to pay, we can speak in the bar this evening. I ask you not to be funny."

I wrote a letter and the girl took it, the sweet postman she was with her squashed toe. "Dear madam. I'm sex-mad. Erect all the time. Dying to get into you. How many refrigerators do you need?"

This time there was no answer. In the dining room she held her face in her hands. Dressed in glittering elegance, with false eyelashes. Her eyes gleamed. I saw her peep at me.

I sat in the dining room. Approaching Haifa. One more day. A festive meal. Candles on the tables. They're already serving *humus* as hors d'oeuvres. Everyone's waiting for me to give in. To sell rights. I'm not willing. Don't I want to love these people, my people. I thought, here's my daughter Naomi in a white dress, coated with lacquer, her hair in curls, coming up to a man with silver sideburns with a Mona Lisa smile and saying to him, I'm an orphan. My father ran away with a Dutch whore. I have a pair of pajamas with elephants on them. I'm asking you for your right to a General Electric washing machine with an electronic dryer. Oh, my father's a horrible man. He left me starving. My mother's crying. I'm an orphan. My schoolteacher makes pornographic films at the Ziegfeld Follies. I want a Philco refrigerator, two-door, thirteen cubic feet, with a small freezer. At night they danced *Am Israel Hai.* The band played *Hora Hedera.* Old men in Banlon shirts, wearing ties with the Empire State Building and Marilyn Monroe painted on them, with handkerchiefs in their jacket pockets, danced with old women on high heels wearing funny silk dresses, their faces smeared with youth-searching creams, fifty years our settlement stands, sing the praises of the founders of Hedera.

My father and mother are waiting for me in the port. The returning son. The years that have passed. Perhaps my father's waiting for someone else. I recited to myself a Latin poem Kurt had once quoted in my honor: "I don't love you Lyssini, but I cannot explain to you why." The years that have passed. The letters of their letters dancing inside my eyes. Mother's letters full of scolding, stories, silent weeping, yearning, and the nine words on the cross of Naftali Sussetz. Will he forgive me. I'm no longer the boy who left home. I lay back in a deck chair. Night, quiet, on the sea. I thought: Here's the boy I was when I was ten. Coming back from planting trees. The teacher Mr. Erlich asking us to write a composition. The topic: I planted a tree in Eretz Israel. I chew the pencil. The eraser at the end of the second pencil already digested in my stomach. Scratched into the table: AMINADAV LOVES SARARINA. I must have loved them both. The place where we hid tea and sugar in case the Germans broke through the line at El Alamein and invaded Eretz Israel. The oaths we swore. Sitting and thinking what I'll write. I wrote: "Today we were asked to plant trees in the yard. The teacher said that to plant trees in Eretz Israel was a *mitzva*. I planted a tree in the yard. The yard was sandy. The children sang *Be-tu tu tutu be-tu be-Shvat*. I didn't sing because I was hoarse. The children laughed and the teacher sweated. He had a handkerchief and he tied it around his neck. The headmaster came and said, how beautiful it is that we're planting trees in Eretz Israel. This is how we build and are rebuilt in the homeland. I dug a hole, planted the tree, sang, and filled it with earth. Then I took a watering can, stood in line, and together with everyone else watered a tree in Eretz Israel. The water entered the earth of Eretz Israel and fertilized the tree. One day the tree will grow and flower and will make shade over all of Eretz Israel."

The teacher gave me barely Fair. My mother said, actually it's a nice composition but teachers like prettiness. I didn't know then it wasn't only teachers. Half a year later I wrote another composition. I wrote how the lights dimmed from among the clouds and the earth became covered with soft dewdrops and a tree lowered its head and my heart stopped beating and the silent ship of Israel crashed against stormy waves and the sun vanished from the treetops. I got Very Good, plus getting to read my composition to the whole class. Thinking of Jerome. The same story. He painted Jesus with stones. They said it wasn't a painting. He painted Panamanian flags and became the greatest painter of the moment. I look at the sky. Night, and the ship whispers toward Haifa. The wake behind the propeller is beautiful and straight. Restless people sing to themselves, hum old melodies. Stars spread out in grandeur. Empty sea. Sitting inside a huge universe with tiny lamps of stars glowing, lighting up my way. From the stars above, my life looks like the single glow of a flashlight. Born, lives, dies. Once I read in a book a sentence which really frightened me and remained engraved in my memory. "From the end of the eighth century B.C.E. until the sixth century C.E., more than one thousand years, the inhabitants of Jericho did not know the craft of pottery, but they sculpted and painted on skulls." Hundreds of thousands of people. Inventing carts and wheels. Dying and living. Giving birth and loving. A thousand years, and all the information is a few words.

I think about the bridge through my window in Division Street. Only one side of the bridge can be seen through the window. Cars would burst out of an invisible point and appear on the bridge with fascinating suddenness. And then drive on toward the Pepsi sign. What'll be the other side.

The woman of is is because isn't isn't passes me. She walks slowly. Arms folded behind her back. She points to a vacant chair beside me and asks if it's vacant.

In her voice I hear, is is. I say to her, vacant because vacant. She looked at me for a moment and laughed weakly. It sounded as if she were passing her laughter through a sieve. She said, What do you mean, sir.

I said to her: Madam, if one discovers a deck chair on an enchanting night like this, then apparently it's vacant or not. But

155

if you ask, madam, surely that means you want to know if the *vacancy* of the chair is illusion or reality. As to that, I will answer frankly that I cannot know for certain. Perhaps the vacancy is an illusion, and in the apparently vacant chair there now sits an antiman whose source is antimatter and whose essence is antinumerical.

She takes out a pack of cigarettes, offers me one, I point to my pipe, she lights a cigarette, sits down in the deck chair and doesn't speak. After a while she bursts out laughing and immediately subsides into silence. Her face is like ancient parchment, pleasant in the sharp sea wind.

I've seen you before, sir, in the dining room. . . . And on deck. You're very funny. . . . Are you especially sad?

I didn't know what to answer her. To calm myself until we entered Haifa port. Father Mother. There's something cruel and pure about returning home. There's no return except to a different place. Where am I returning to. The place I came from no longer is. I too am not the same man. Thus Aminadav, attempting to fish up some last minutes before the point of no return. She wants to know why I speak so funny. Where I'm going. What my life has been. I tried to explain. Try and explain. Nothing makes sense. About herself she's resolutely silent and I don't ask her embarrassing questions. I said to her, My fair lady, let's leave ourselves some mysteries, so that we can have some material left for sweet dreams.

I got up. I straightened my clothes, which had got crumpled because of the moisture and my prolonged sitting in the deck chair. I took her hand which was not young, not old, kissed it courteously and said, To a proof that everything still exists. I walked away from her and thought she said something. Maybe not. It didn't seem to matter, during such gentle days, such clear nights of sea.

Morning on deck. A ship in the distance emitting smoke. Beautiful on a sea as soft as butter. Savor the last moments of serenity. Here, I'm emerging from the womb. Any moment now. The memory of the black spaces. How nice it was in the bosom of nothingness. Not to be is better than to be. There is no end to not-being. There is an end to being. I want not to be. A tear on the cheek of a dead God. The woman appears far off, wearing the mystery of the is is. I'm nicely dressed for Father and Mother. Far away, the land draws near. Not the same land I left. Mira and Naomi. Eating toast. Now they'll eat as much as they like. The great toast-hater has sailed off far away. The heart the heart. The captain shoots orders into a tube, and the machine room hums. The smell of cooking. The last meal before returning to Mother. Now the Carmel slowly comes into sight. As if it's swimming toward you in a dream. The Dutchwoman stands on the deck. My Beatrice. Draped in a long white dress down to her feet. Waving a blue-and-white flag. Casting sidelong glances at me. I wanted to say, You, with your Friends of the Month Club! What has been no longer is. A ship and friends for a moment. Playing the famous game, who when and why. Expert on orange yolks. But I understand, she's a girl. Playing the game of possibilities. Inquisitively checking if the expected things come true. My daughter Naomi did the same sort of thing with the sunrises and the sunsets. The Dutchwoman translates cosmic reality into psychic mazes. I'm afraid for her. Offer a hand. Refuse politely. Refused and refusing. A blue-and-white flag. Where'd she get it. The chutzpah of it. In the ship's store. The navigator guides the ship confidently. I suddenly feel national pride. Hell with it. We've learned something. The dome of the Baá'í temple gleams in the distance. The sun touches it. Gold on every side. A wound. Beside the pier we become dwarfed. Large ships pressing around us. Tying up to the pier. The sailors sweat. Soon it'll be women and wine. And I—Father and Mother.

The machines slowly stop. People on the pier. I see Mother. Father's probably looking for a cab or something, frightened of the actual meeting, trying to arrive later. A stubborn effort not to be hurt. He cried because of me and didn't forgive. The epigram I prevented him from putting on my grave, by Heine. A meeting is demands. Difficult questions. The steward came into my cabin and asked me to hurry. Mother through the round porthole. She doesn't see me and I see her. I go through the inspections with an air of indifference. The customs men are relaxed, eating apples and smoking Pall Mall without a customs tab. Here is their kingdom and they celebrate it. A single system, controlled and filed. Madame Is Is passed by me and said Mr. Funny Man, shalom. Beside her walked the man in glasses, small, with a bag on his back, like a Jew migrating to Eretz Israel during other days. He smiles and wipes his glasses. She says something to him. He waves to me. See you in the Himalayas, sir. My tears will be crystal crystals. To place on the cabinet of my dead grandmother. Must conserve energy. The things that await me. How will I explain. And why. Suddenly my heart starts beating at dizzying speed. I feel a choking. Familiar symptoms. I'm dying. The porters terrify me. The plank is high. The yells, the growing heat of a winter's heat wave. If I get a stroke now I'll be ridiculous, where will I fall. Into the narrow plot of water between the ship and the pier. This filthy water. And my mother, what'll she say, he arrived and died, just like that. To kill me dead. And Father . . . where the hell is he. The eternal surrenderer. Here I am, your son. After the failure. Broken, ready to be put together again. Be my glue. Like the grace of God. I'm an expert on diseases. I diagnose my disease. Dread. Choking. A flawed heart. My father who isn't standing there below used to tell about a man in Berlin who was always feeling sick or thinking of sicknesses and had many books on medicine which he read night and day. He could file any pain in its place. They said later that he got a stroke from a misprint.

Mother's waiting alone. On the pier. The horoscope inside her, surely. She knows I won't die here now. I'll come down to her. I went down.

14

The strip of always turbid water was lit up by a beam of light. And where did it come from. A window slammed, the gleam glittered, a startling prism, sharply contrasting with the side of the ship. My mother discovered me and there was no way of retreat. She ran toward me but met me with shyness, calmer than I'd expected, she kissed me and cried. She turned off the tears and a customs official threw down a butt of Pall Mall exempt from customs which landed next to my feet. The water whispered against the pier. Porters yelled *yalla yalla!* and rushed past us with carts. She asked how are you. How could I be. I said it was a good trip. A heavy storm that stopped near Gibraltar. At Gibraltar there were monkeys. All the shops belonged to Jews. I bought her silk from Hong Kong and a little gold watch with a lovely chain, and for Father some nice shirts. She received this as if I was trying to hurt her. Measuring her son, this blood-enveloped thing that had come out of her, and there's silver in his hair. Wearing a blue sailor's coat and Polaroid sunglasses. She drew back for a moment and fingered the cloth of my coat and only then said, I promised you Father'd live. And he's alive!

To fish for the malice that wasn't there. Something bewildering and demanding, gnawing and accusing. Heavy suspicions, what does she mean alive, had he been dead? I spoke around the point.

159

Trying to grasp her. I have to know something that I don't know. She didn't understand my hidden intentions and without further thought told me that Father's fatally ill, that she'd written me three letters and I hadn't answered. And then she got the cable that I was coming and understood how worried I'd been about Father and I hadn't been able to write, with no words to express my pain, and she knows, she knows how much I love Father, I came, and soon Mira and Naomi will come and we'll all be together and maybe Father will come through. We'll do everything, she said. Hadn't she promised me in her letter to keep him alive for me? And he's alive! I remember dimly, three letters lying on the telephone table. Last days. Painting a last painting, meeting a cricket, going to buy a car, laying a dancing girl from the Ziegfeld Follies, my daughter's teacher, riding in a cab Yo ho ho. Why hadn't I opened them. How will I explain to her. In my pain I say nothing and she misinterprets my silence.

Gray warehouses and officials smoking Pall Mall. With rolled-up sleeves, drinking tea between nine-thirty and ten. Suddenly it was all so familiar. People sweating, with *Davar* in their hands, with glasses of tea, smiles and anger alternating. I could know what I hadn't known for ten years, what they'd given birth to in the night, what they'd dreamed at night. What they'd do on Saturday morning. Their windows open onto the street. The radio at noon before the news, with a hallah on the table and the Friday evening paper rolling around the armchair or the carpet. Children smoking in the toilet. The wife warming up chicken soup with cold noodles. Pot roast and potatoes and carrots. Vegetable salad and stewed fruit.

Mother sweats. The world that is against her with characteristic hostility. People who were with me on the ship walk behind her as if they believe in her power. From warehouse to warehouse. A permit in Warehouse Five. A permit for a permit in Warehouse Ten. Back to Number Five to get a permit for a permit for a permit and then to Number One to get a signature. It's hot. Haifa has grown, it melts in the stifling winter heat wave. The Carmel becomes pink and distant. Houses float above its head. Stella Maris and navy antennas on the convent. The sky is full of dark clouds full of haze. A mountain hanging over me. Cars climbing it. The red roofs of the German colony are soothing. Hills of oranges on trucks. Mustached drivers yelling at each other. A clerk makes tea and says what's the time, time for action, and laughs. Outside are taxis, Be'er Sheva, Ashkelon, Tel Aviv, Nahariya, Qiryat Shemona, Dimona, Qiryat Gath. Something pessimistic draws a smile. Everything hums love. Home, home. The clocks show different times. A customs official in a suit says, Mr. Abarbanel, here are your papers. And smiles. He stretches out such a delicate, cultivated hand. A man pays to bribe. People shove in the queues they've discovered. My mother gets angry. She's built this country and nobody knows. Everyone shoves. Smell. Felafel in a corner. A Yemenite chants. Eating a pita with olives. Sitting in a corner under a wagon and eating. My mother recounts her pedigree. She shouts, wages wars. We'll take out our things even if the world turns over. I'm home. Officials nip off my head. My son shed his blood for the homeland, and here officials do me a favor, my mother says.

We were saved by a porter who arrived at the end of the travails. He carted our things to a taxi. The ship's captain, in civilian clothes, walks beside a tall woman who's painted herself up for him. She embraces him, he looks like he's strangling. Pale, dwarfed in civilian clothes. I didn't want to see him disgraced like that. He tried to escape toward a small car that was waiting for him on the pier. His wife drove the car toward the gate. I hid my face.

In the taxi my mother got caught up in her thoughts and said something about life. She spoke of the path of sorrows. I asked her if there really is a path of sorrows. Mother said, Of course there is. I spoke of the inadequacy of words and of my destruction of things. What's the meaning of career, or a ladder of ranks. Is there a ladder like that, which one ascends and descends like Jacob's ladder. My mother changed the subject (you've always got something different to say) and spoke about the State: You haven't been here for such a long time, the State's been through some severe crises. It's impossible to stand up to our enemies and be perfect. She told me she'd bought me a house. Surprised, I said nothing. Then I mumbled thanks. She said, A few months ago

I suddenly thought what'll happen if one day you come back, and now there's a recession and it's possible to buy a house. Opportunities don't last forever. And our apartment, your father's and mine, is so big. . . . No children in the house, and who comes to visit already. I found a small house, a bargain. With trees and bougainvillaea that you like. Lovely flowers and three rooms, a marvelous kitchen and a new toilet, a fine bath and food cupboards and wall cupboards and everything. . . . I sold our apartment, bought a smaller one, and with the difference I bought you a house.

She said, If I don't look after things, who will. You don't know your right hand from your left hand. And then you cabled that you were coming. After Father got sick. You see, I know everything in advance. I feel things in my bones. You think I didn't know you'd come.

I didn't know how to thank her. She said I'd be able to paint in a little room which could make a fine workroom. I said I don't paint anymore. She looked at me in amazement and the radio played a song about Simona from Dimona. And then we saw Ze'ev Rotman. He was standing at the end of Kings' Street. Writing something in a little notebook. In a suit, with a pleasant smile and white hair fluttering in the wind, without a tie, like the workers of bygone days. The driver laughed: Bet he's a spy. Standing opposite the ships and making notes. We stopped. My mother laid her head on his shoulder and cried. Her burden of sorrows. Who'd understand. He put his notebook in his pocket and smiled at me. The driver fixed something in the carburetor and knocked on the hood. Ze'ev said that he writes down the number of ships coming in and going out because since he retired he has nothing else to do. But only until noon, he said. In the afternoon, he went on, I listen to the tape recorder. My daughter brought me one. I record myself and listen. It's really amazing how my real voice is nothing like my voice on the tape recorder. How are you Aminadav. How many years haven't we seen each other. Ten, twelve . . . I speak into the tape recorder, says Ze'ev, and tell about all sorts of things that have been. You know, about those days when your mother and I were, how do they say it today, friends,

162

you know, when we were you know what . . . and he laughed. My mother cried more and more and he embraced her and stroked her hair.

We escaped from Haifa. My mother transmitting, Give, give. I have nothing to give. They drive like madmen, maybe because of the gravity of the defense situation. My mother sings the praises of the new road.

What've you got against the road. It took them so long to build it!

I have nothing against it, Mother.

But you have nothing in favor of it!

Not especially, Mother. It's a road.

But it's a wonderful, wide road, you must admit. At least give credit where it's due!

But it's only a road, Mother.

A new road. In the sands. You know what the road was like before.

I know. I traveled on it for many years. So what?

You're against it again.

I'm not against it.

And not in favor of it.

No.

Electricity poles. The sea vanishes from my sight among trees. My mother speaks, with her own hands she built the roads of our land. I tried to imagine myself years ago. Traveling along the old road. To Haifa to get on a ship to Paris, and from there to New York. I remember the suit we bought at O.B.G. The sight of my face. With the hair that was black. The things evade the words. Sometimes you say house house house and the house disappears. I try to hold on to something. House. Blow and caress. Was my return not written of in an obituary by Mr. Herzberg. At the Kfar Syrkin intersection I'm filled with a great self-pity. I think of Naomi. Has her tooth come out. I choked again. My mother looked at me and asked what happened. I told her my throat hurts. You're always imagining sicknesses, she said. It was terrible to hear. Suddenly I couldn't take it anymore. I said, I had someone to inherit that from.

Her eyes a film of tears. A hostile silence ensued. I understand
"I promised you Father'd live" is an accusation. All the sons of
my mother's friends are properly established and love their mothers. They work in good places with great chances of advancement.
They have bank accounts. They come every Sabbath eve and eat
dinner at their mothers'. They love their wives. They bring grandchildren to mother. They let them say to them, Don't do that,
and don't put your finger in your nose, and they bring flowers.
They have black James Bond attaché cases and new cars. And an
expense account and tax deductions. And they don't want to
paint crazy things. They don't remember the womb. They don't
hate, and they don't love too much. And there are time payments.
You're the only one who's different. You come to me with nothing. Where's my granddaughter. Where's my daughter-in-law.
Where are the important things. Why not a washing machine
and a vacuum cleaner. Shadows from the trees. Sun of winter. In
New York it snowed. You have a nice house. Look after it. It's
yours. From me to you. Who'll look after things if I don't. I know
how deep her grief is. Despite her great bitterness. Smoke rises
from a blue house with a veranda shaped like a tear. The driver
apologizes and explains to my mother why he's driving with this
wildness she detests. How much can one keep driving back and
forth: Haifa–Tel Aviv, Tel Aviv–Haifa. Is that a life. Sometimes,
he said, there's the smell of my wife in the air.

She suddenly embraces me. Cars fly along the opposite lane.
The driver apologizes and explains that his wife died not long
ago. Every Wednesday they used to go to Dizengoff Street.
How he loved the doll she was. With a face of glass. And suddenly she died. The radio says that on the coastal plain it would
be hotter than usual for this season. The cars look as if they've
been painted with dust. The winter heat wave strikes mercilessly. The driver speaks about his wife. My mother listens. His
troubles soften bitter things inside her. The doll used to dust
the apartment with peacock feathers. The driver said, we had
armchairs with plastic covers! Children he'd kept for others. So
as not to crease her lovely body. He drives as if he's rowing a

boat. My mother's angry. But softening. Bitterness on her face. But gentleness, gentleness . . .

The driver says, Every time I turn on the gas or open the refrigerator the house fills with her. My mother understands. She speaks about how life is sad. And young people don't understand its sadness. And she steals a look at me. On the verge of middle age. I'm alone, lady, he said. I know what it means to be sad. Her smell everywhere, the refrigerator, the gas. The armchairs with their plastic covers. My mother smiles with a kind of melancholy mixed with a dash of scorn. What does he understand. And thus without my noticing when or how, the two of them started discussing who suffers more, she with her sick husband or he with his dead wife. What do you mean, I'm alone without my wife. No children. She went to Beilinson Hospital and died of an early pregnancy. And you, you've lived and you have a son and a granddaughter, what have I got.

You have life, you're young.

But she's gone.

I understand. It's sad. But I and he, my husband, the two of us alone. He's sick. I have to look after him. No one comes anymore. The hospital. I'm keeping him alive. I alone. The doctors kiss my hand. They know. If it weren't for me he'd be dead already. To see the life seeping out of him month after month, the beautiful person that he was.

The argument flares. I smoke my pipe. The landscape flashes past me rapidly. The driver increases his speed. He's angry. My mother's alert to everything. She tells him when to turn and when to stop. He says, When can I even go to the movies, driving Haifa–Tel Aviv, Tel Aviv–Haifa every day. The house is full: refrigerator, a new cabinet with shellacked pigeons, covered armchairs, a solar heater. Who needs it. Once a week the laundry. And the debts . . . And she isn't there. The gas and the refrigerator . . . The washing machine. She wanted a Westinghouse, I bought her a Westinghouse. They come every month to collect. Vouchers I have, but no money. Eshkol and the recession . . . A taxi license isn't what it used to be.

I understand.

He isn't sure that she understands.

The journey drags on. The driver blows his horn frequently and harshly. He complains, alone all day long without the wife!

And I without a husband! she said. She wasn't making fun of him. She was absorbed, deep in the relish of her pain. I thought: Where did I inherit the relish of defeat. I sat with Mira and stuck needles into myself. The driver glows with a sense of sharing. Only real enemies are capable of love. There is satisfaction on both their faces, in the form of gnawing despair. The funerals to which I used to go with my mother when I was a boy. The aching faces and the delight of participation. My mother's friends competing with each other to be the first to arrive. And the flowers on the grave. With faces of dry wax. With hearts open wide. I wanted to say to her, Mother, I'm back. Look, I'm here. The cemetery of my childhood. Of sins that I wanted to sin more than I sinned. You're all right, Mother, you're strong as iron. Pretending to be a broken thing. If only we all could. You've lived for my sake. And the rewards, hell, why aren't they more beautiful. She's bought me a house. Fluttering in the net. As if I have an alternative. You come to ask forgiveness of the womb and it buys you a house with bougainvillaea. The stars of Andromeda are far away, what I have here is you. Keeping my father alive for my sake. The sacrifice. The driver understands my mother better than I do and that's unfair. The heated argument about who suffers more. They count their pains. Mother says, When you see Father, kiss him! I wanted to kiss her but her face wasn't offered up in that melancholy posture of a neck offered for slaughter. That day I lost you, Mother, remember? And an Arab boy with blue or clear eyes slung a burning cigarette butt at a wailing cat. You remember. That's you, you whom I lost. Of all the people in the world it had to be you! She can't remember. Here's the marvelous sea again. They're building a chimneystack at Reading. Tel Aviv from the distance is like a sweet cloud. I was a beautiful baby, they say. I lay on my back beside the gramophone. I heard Mozart. I knew Schubert by heart. At the age of three I read and wrote. I knew arithmetic. At the age of five I drew. Mother with a smile and love. Father with a kind of upside-down anticipation, not to try and not to be. To live. Only to live. To live with loves on the side and not in belonging, not to suicide. Not to search for a kingdom and find asses. It was then we moved from Balfour Street to Mendele Street. There was a big flood and I rode in a boat down Ben Yehuda Street which was in the sands. With my little love. There were things. The two years that are a mystery and only Mother remembers.

One can cut one's life, I said to Mother, and give it a meaning. She didn't reply, and then said, We'll buy you new sheets. I have enough blankets. Your house is really nice, Ami. What'll happen with Mira and Naomi. I've never met them. Don't you think that's cruel? I'll die and I won't know my grandchildren.

You will, Mother.

Maybe you think that Mira and Naomi won't want to see your old mother.

You aren't old and you look wonderful.

I went to have a medical examination. Tomorrow or the next day I'll get the results. If I die before Father you'll have to look after him.

You'll live many years more yet.

She smiles a sad smile. The driver mutters something to himself.

No no, my mother says with repressed pain, I'm sick. But I'll try, for his sake, to live a little longer. I want to see my granddaughter before I die, Ami.

Why talk about dying, Mother, you're very alive.

You think they hate me?

They don't know you.

You haven't told them about me?

I have.

Only bad things.

No, actually only nice things.

What do you mean actually. Did you lie? Did you want to tell the truth and you told lies.

No, I told them everything, Mother.

You told them how I tormented you. What a terrible woman I am. That's what you told them.

And she cries.

I kiss her. She dissolves into me. The scorn that was in me dissolves. Mother. I want to be something for you. Maybe not a son. It's too late. Maybe a comforter. Maybe Father's sickness has happened so as to heal the wounds, maybe now what has never stuck together will unite. But she's afraid for her life, tells me about her weak heart, about cardiograms. About high blood pressure. Sleeping pills. Aldomin.

I've thought a lot about my actual birth, Mother. Was it really so terrible.

Thirty-eight hours the child fluttered, my mother directed her words at the driver. Thirty-eight hours I struggled to bring him into the world.

He refused to be born?My mother is grave. One doesn't refuse her love. The driver understands that he's made a mistake, and it's easy to see this by the way he turns the dial on the radio and looks for different music. What do you mean he didn't want to be born, of course he wanted to. I smiled to myself and we entered the outskirts of Tel Aviv. And there, entering the city, I felt a kind of serenity that I hadn't felt for many years. Maybe it was like the moment when you wake up from a nightmare. The momentary relaxation. And then the accounting and you see, well, you've been saved from something awful in order to return to something awful, only a little less awful. But that one moment was so pleasant. They're destroying a wonderful wilderness, I said to my mother about the outskirts of Tel Aviv. She didn't like to hear it. A bridge is not a poem. Naomi and Mira are sleeping now. An upside-down world.

15

By the door to Father's room Mother said, Go in by yourself, he's waiting for you, he'll be so happy.

The doctor in a green gown, so young. He said I should prepare myself emotionally for the fact that my father will not know me.

His room is pale green like the doctor's gown. Beside him lies a young man who weeps in his sleep and is connected to an artificial kidney. Rubber pipes, blood dripping into a plastic tank, a bag of urine filling slowly. My father's bare as a babe, very soft, inside a sheet, his face looking at the window. His hair has thinned, his face is plowed with creases. Only his eyes, the same sweet burning. When he turned his face to me it wore the amazement of an abysmal apathy. His face was beautiful even now. He waved a hand as if wanting to say something but then turned his face back to the window. Through the window one could see a tractor slowly plowing, a plane landing at Lydda airport and two dusty cypresses. Don't you know me? Shalom Father. How are you. I'm well. Love, perhaps, Aminadav. You are daring in your retreat. A tractor in a window that is a frame, and window is also a dream in Dutch, or Hebrew, I no longer remember which, a plane landing and two cypresses. Shadows on your forehead, Father. You've become like the earth and the earth doesn't need you. What injustice. Does the body become like the earth, plowed with creases, so as to copulate with the earth. Your face is happy to copulate with the earth. Hallelujah. A smooth and cunning coupling. To see that on your oh so noble face. Is all this nobility nothing but a pretense of dark instincts beyond measure. My mother says you'll be so happy to see me. Your face looking at the window. This nurse emptying urine for four hundred pounds a month, after taxes. What do I know about you. Aminadav sits at the head of the bed. The room whispers death. The plane has landed, the tractor's still plowing. The cypresses are dusty. A hot wind blows. I know so very little about you, Father. Nine words of love. You were born in Galicia. During the First World War, what happened exactly you never told me. You were an officer, or something. You fought against your father's army. Son against father. And you didn't shoot at him. Then Berlin and Heidelberg. Philosophy and violin. The teacher you had. With his young wife. In a boat. I saw a picture. With a woman in white, her face pale, her eyes marvelous like a whisper. The teacher wore a white suit with a bow tie, a drunken hat and a gray cloak like Sherlock Holmes. The threesome you always were. Mother hinted once. You loved the wife. And he, her husband, loved you. Living as three. And Dr. Neidler bringing love letters from her to you and from you to her. And the glances. Maybe you accidentally touched. Father don't turn your face, I'm here, Aminadav. Mira's husband. You don't know me, Father. To know that you get to the same tree. For the apple, you know, doesn't . . . How you adopted Germany. The language. How does one adopt a country. I don't understand. Eleven years in America. Haven't I remained the same little Tel Avivian. You dreamed in German, Father. Thank you, madam. The nurse brings me coffee. One spoon of sugar and a little milk. Yes, in a small cup, I can't stand coffee in large mugs. There's something monstrous about them. I like my coffee pure. Without distraction or decoration. You taught Hebrew. Your brother who disappeared in Siberia. He wanted to migrate to Eretz Israel. Was it because of him that you left everything and came to Palestine. After all, you knew the Meistersinger by heart. The blood of Henry the Fourth flowed through your veins. The division of the duchies in the sixteenth century made bone of your bones. I try to reach you, Father.

There are things in the blood. Don't mock. Say that blood is a hackneyed thing. But who better than you should know that it isn't true. Your fathers were secret Sabbatarians. They believed in the messiah even after he'd changed his religion. You inherited from them and passed on to me. Zealots of a God who betrayed. You studied violin and people prophesied a great future for you. A prodigy, they said. Why did you come to Eretz Israel to make frames.

I remember, Father, years ago. I went to Dr. Neidler in Gedera. There were sabra hedges and almond trees. It was hot and a wind blew from the sea. They said the air was good for asthmatics. Patients with rheumatism sat in the shade of the trees and read German newspapers. He told me how you smashed the violin I'd never seen. For fifteen years you played, and dreamed. He told me about coffeehouses in Berlin where they used to put on women's clothes and paint themselves up and sing lewd songs. Carrying candles, and the city laughing in white. About the forest in Heidelberg. You went walking in the forest, Father. In the black forest without wolves. To see trees destroyed by storm. Stricken by wind, to stand and dream. Goethe as a violinist. And to return to the attic. To dream about your beloved in the arms of your teacher. In a boat on the Rhine. The love the three of you had. And polite coffee in the morning. To tremble in a vague fear. To dream in German. To give birth to a Fatherland full of history. To enter history as I entered eternity in Frances Elliott's painting, when I wrote *Kurt Singer potz.* How you went to hear Huberman. On a winter's night. You in a black coat and Dr. Neidler in a hat. And Huberman played the Concerto in A Minor by Johann Sebastian Bach. The glaze of your face slightly disconcerted Neidler. Who thought, here is a divinity revealing itself in all its beauty. Like the sun in the morning. Here, said Neidler, Huberman is showing us what we always knew without noticing, just as the law of gravity was always here until Newton came along and pointed it out, so too Bach revealed what has always been. And Huberman revealed what Bach revealed. Then the two of you went and you were silent. What does this Galician think, why isn't he stirred. Afterward you went to your room and you picked up the violin. And very slowly, you smashed it into small pieces. To give up, to give up. Thanks, nurse, I don't smoke cigarettes. No, really. I'm thinking about my father. He's a handsome man? I know. He's a good patient? You all love him?

Dr. Neidler, did Father cry?

He didn't know what to answer me, Father. Perhaps, he said. And I tried to imagine you crying. I'd never seen you miserable or wretched. Everything was always closed and sealed. You evaded me and remained a flutter. You read me Schopenhauer and Kant. You spoke to me about humanism and the categorical imperative. From that day when you smashed the violin you didn't read a book which had not been written before then, you didn't listen to music that had not been composed before that. Thinking Goethe Schiller and Jean Paul. Listening to Bach Scarlatti Monteverdi. On Dr. Neidler's table there was a Japanese picture. A painter sitting next to a table opposite a window. I went up to the picture, Father, and looked at it for a long time. I said to Dr. Neidler, Now I understand the painting. Here the painter sits opposite a window bathed in sun, wrapped in a magnificent silk robe. In his hand he holds a fine brush, and on the table is a piece of very thin parchment, and he waits for the desired moment, to go into battle. Dr. Neidler told me then, Father, of Erno Daniel the troubadour, who said, I gather wind and hunt a hare with a bull and swim against the current. The window the window. You can allow yourself to be tempted by it, Father. In your eyes I see a plane landing, a tractor plowing and two dusty cypresses. If it weren't for the window you wouldn't know about the existence of the dusty cypresses, the landing plane and the plowing tractor. Everything has to be framed. That's why I didn't understand your sorrows, Father. For you allowed the frames to guide you. To pour gold on the wood. To listen to the humming of the wax and the glue. You would fix the message of the rivers and the lakes in the making of frames. Father, perhaps you saw forgiveness for the arrogance that had pulsed in you when you were daring, young and passionate.

I went to him, to my good Dr. Neidler. Who saved me from a certain death at the cool and elegant hands of Dr. Fabrikant.

We walked along shadowy paths. An orchard well wept in the distance, *tik tik tik.* The smell of citrus blossoms. He made bold, that gentle man, to say you had something in common with the professor in The Blue Angel. Service to immortal creators, politeness and a face of excessive humility. Hating the chaos. Detesting things that aren't enclosed in stocks. How you restrained yourself in Palestine (Eretz Israel). My first paintings looked savage to you. There was no forgiveness in you. Perhaps that was true love. Not to lead astray. And here you are. Erased. Not alive and not dead, the orphanhood on your face. Mother's in the corridor. What's she hoping for. If all great works of art are produced by obedience to severe laws why does your sadness lack form. The proud man that you were. The man who gives up. A frame of a man. I understand my lady of the black notices. I never told you about her. Beautiful, as your face is now. Dressed in black. Erasing the dead from a book, in purple. She refused to acknowledge my existence, Father. Existence is a name. Isn't that what you proclaimed too. I'm looking at you, Father. You don't know who I am. Know me. Recognize me. I've come because I'd reached the end of the road, the very end that you kept for yourself. See a broken man. A wife and a daughter. A car in customs. Mother's bought me a house. Bougainvillaea. How will I know the riddle of my failure when I don't understand my life. Who are you. What were you for me. Everything's in you and I don't understand. Window to window. I see a tombstone in your eyes. Proud doormat, not trampled down, for the daring of others. They live. Too innocent to know how great their shame is. And you know and keep silent. With a smile, and jokes in Old German. To kill demons. To strangle them while they're still in the bottle.

How vapid to engrave a tombstone in your eyes. The courage of it. To erect it before my eyes. Who have returned to you for forgiveness and mercy. To pass on yourself a sentence which is also my sentence.

Father, this is me, Aminadav, your son!

To know that the voice betrays, damn it. The tombstone in his eyes looks at me. Suddenly there's a movement. My father's trying, what, perhaps, to say to me. His face is turned to me. My

173

father said, *Ein unnütz Leben ist ein früher Tod!* which means A useless life is an early death. I knew that this was a passage from Goethe's Iphigenia. He spoke and the words came out stuttering and very slow and there was a dread to them. My mother attentive in the corridor. Measuring the tiles. Blue on a greenish background. Asking the head nurse embarrassing questions in a voice washed with gentleness. She bursts into the room. She whispers to me, Did you understand?

He said that—

No, you didn't understand. He can't get the words out. He wanted to say one thing and it came out different. For one who doesn't understand . . . I know him. I've been caring for him for two months now. . . . He meant to say that he's been missing you and how happy he is that you've come. That's what he said, isn't it, Naftali, my sweet.

Yesssss . . . whispered the man who was my father. My Naftali. Suck your thumb. Forty years of marriage. He never even condescended to sleep in the one bed with her. His independence. Now he responds to her. His face is open to her. As if at long last . . . But all those years measured. And one mustn't kiss in public. Who knows what goes on behind closed doors. I was born. Fact. In the dark. What a wonder. He detests affectionate nicknames. And now, my Naftali. And his pale smile. A child with a tombstone in his eyes. My mother mumbles to him, words of pity, of joy diluted with a kind of sorrow, and he draws near to her. He knows her. But he doesn't know me. And I suddenly understand the meaning of A useless life is an early death. His brain is damaged. What remains is not his personal memories. . . .

Father, I said, I understand. And had I only known German well perhaps I could have conversed with him. My father remains with a landscape that is barren to me. What remains for him is passages from books. Quotations from poems. Maybe he wanted to say, I'm glad you've come, Aminadav, but you're a man I don't know, and instead he said, A useless life is an early death. My return is therefore nothing but a momentary incandescence of Goethean consciousness, creation is epigrams. I do not exist except as a mysterious acrostic of passages. Perhaps all of us are

nothing but a profuse and astonishing lexicon of German poetry.
Goethe spoke about Aminadav. Tomorrow I'll ring Mira and I'll
say to her, O my dear one of the modest smiles. How to pity you,
Father. Standing beside him. Looking at the broken thing that
was my father. I want to kiss and to kill. But I came to ask
forgiveness. Why didn't you wait for me. I yelled, FATHER
THIS IS ME AMINADAV YOUR SON.

This time he repeated my words. Perhaps because I yelled.
THIS IS ME—
THIS IS ME.
Aminadav!
AMINADAV.
I screamed at my mother. What do you mean he loves me.
What do you mean he's happy. He's dead.

She shuddered. She slapped my face. Trembling all over. She
went out of the room.

I went out after her. To gnash my teeth. To say bitter things.
She calls him my sweet. My Naftali. By what right. A dead man.
Büchner doesn't exist. *She doesn't recognize the existence of
Büchner.* Büchner says, Rivka Sussetz, fair thou art and beautiful.
How we walked together forty years in the wilderness. You and
I. Arm in arm. Giving birth to Aminadavs. Waiting for things.
Speaking to the dew early in the morning. Swimming in a sea of
affection. I come out to her. My father turns his face to the
window. To see a plane landing, a tractor plowing and two dusty
cypresses. She stood pale under a landscape by Holzmann. An
aquarelle on good terms with the walls. She whispered, How can
you speak like that, you're cruel, just like him! You always were.
Heartless. I work hard. You think it's easy for me. So I call him
my Naftali. Why not. Why mock me. And if I don't understand
what he says, why shouldn't I want to understand. . . . You're hard
and bitter. Your bitterness, you inherited it from me, I know, but
you also inherited good things. Why not pity, Ami . . . To pity,
to sense things, to know what pain it is to see the lover of your
youth dying before your eyes. All your life all you do is complain!
It's all my fault. My fault, my fault. You accuse and insult me.
After the war, it was my fault that friend of yours died, that

Nahum. . . . It's good that you're alive, and it's a pity that he's dead. And that's the whole truth. So you went to his parents. And what did they say? Where's my granddaughter. This man whom I love is going to die, Ami, and I don't want him to die. What's wrong with that? I've lived a bitter life, I waited for you and you didn't come. This man was hard and strange. He never embraced me. Once he said to me, I love you, and he thought that was enough for a lifetime. And I waited for him to say it again and he never said it. Maybe he thought it. In German epigrams. I speak Hebrew, not German. My father was a Hebrew teacher, not a German intellectual. What a descent for him. To marry the wild and beautiful Rivka. In the wilderness that is called Palestine. I waited for tenderness and it didn't come. I wanted to say my sweet and he wouldn't let me. You think it's because of *me* that we didn't sleep in the same bed? All these years you teased me about it. Do you think I don't know about your private biographies. Ami, I had yearnings too. I lived in a false biography too. I thought I was married! He was a block of ice. But after forty years this is what remains and this is what there is. And I love him. And he's become a child. Maybe he'll recover. I'm doing all I can so he should recover and you know that when it comes to will power I have plenty of that. And he lets me, now he lets me call him my sweet, and he lets me misunderstand his German proverbs. Why does this matter to you so much. Have pity, Ami. . . .

The next day I went to Haifa. It was a hot day. I went to the port to get the car out. A man there said come back later. I went to Bat Galim. I had a girlfriend there. Twenty years ago. With a sweet face. She didn't live there anymore. The sea the sea. I saw women in bathing suits reading telephone bills. To kiss their eyelids. Sitting on beach chairs facing the sea and reading telephone bills. One woman said, The house cost us thirty-five thousand. We made a kitchen for ten thousand. The car cost twenty thousand. The washing machine and all the rest another ten thousand. Now all we have is debts. Children build castles out of wet sand. Castles for women who read telephone bills by the shore. Smoke rises from a chimney. Here they don't roast Jews. My grandfather said that wherever there's a smell of smoke there's fire, and Jews are being burned. Here Jews aren't being burned. An old woman with a very beautiful face, dressed in blue, pushes a handcart with bagels on it and calls her wares. A man with a horse sells hot sweet corn. In the bus a young girl in torn jeans with blond hair in a tangle sat reading Allen Ginsberg. Up on the Carmel, with trees and the scent of pine resin. The air is clear. A sudden breeze. The radio says that the heat wave's breaking. Women emerged from the sea with telephone bills.

I took the old road back to Tel Aviv. Next to Bet-Lid there was an overturned car, lying on its roof with its lights on. There was no one in it. Later there was a dead cat on the road. During the night my mother woke me. She was wearing a white nightgown. She came to sit on my bed. Her son had returned. And I wanted to embrace her. To tell her don't worry. That life isn't so bitter. What do we have. Only ourselves. My father is a map of all my failures. Why hadn't I learned them years ago. In the creases of his handsome brow. His high and so intelligent forehead. My mother laid her head on my shoulder and cried. She whispered and said that life is impossible. That there's no escape. That everything's ruined. That she tries to take hold and she can't. I wanted to kiss her long eyebrows. I took her head in my hands and held it. Her nightgown was made of white silk. Around her neck she wore a purple cord. Her tears were salty like all tears. I asked her why an overturned car lay next to Bet-Lid with its lights on, glowing into nothingness. And where had the wounded vanished to. I asked her if she'd ever wondered about the great question whether is is. She replied twice no.

She said she doesn't understand what I'm talking about, she never understands.

She got up and looked at me. Then she walked to the wall. Hanging there was a picture of Naomi when she was one year old. I'd sent it to her from America. Naomi standing barefooted. On a carpet. In our home. Holding a plastic ship. That Jerome had brought her from Japan after exhibiting his Panamanian flags there. In a white dress with burning eyes and golden hair. The tears now were for the things she could have had. And then I asked her in what language Father speaks to her.

She whispered as if she didn't want me to hear. German, she said.

But you always spoke Hebrew.

Yes. Always.

And German he only read.

He always read German. But he spoke Hebrew. What questions you ask. As if you didn't know. The years in Heidelberg and Berlin were good years for him. He played violin then. But you know that.

Yes.

And when you made me in Heidelberg, Mother, thirty-eight years ago, what language did you make me in.

She turns to me. Anger and surrender both. She wants to smile or to go on crying. I said to her, Mother, I'm a big boy. I've made children in lots of women. One of them came out not bad. Here's her picture on the wall. I *know* how one does these things. . . .

Then he spoke German, she said. And blushed. My mother. And then she laughed. My father would have been horrified to hear her wild laughter. His wild Rivka from the Middle East. Whom he'd brought to Germany in '29, to show his friends. And he'd gone into a *pension* in Heidelberg. There was thunder and lightning and she'd been frightened. And she broke a vase. Then he got into her bed and I was made. Her wild open laughter. How beautiful to see her laughing. A man dying and a woman laughing. What could be more marvelous, more right.

Then we sat and talked. She told me about my childhood, about the years before I found myself in Jaffa near the clock when I was two years old. She told me about Father. How she met him. His polite courting. Later we opened a window. A cool breeze blew from the sea. Her nightgown frayed out in the breeze. Her hair was suddenly disheveled and wild. A young woman, standing by the window. A troubadour will sing her songs of love. But there was no troubadour, only a son returned. I asked about Father. And she sat on the bed and shaded her face with her hands. And she said, Don't speak about him today. I said, Today I've come back and everything's strange to me, Mother. I have to confess. I didn't read your letters. I didn't know that Father was sick. I came back because I'm finished. Everything's finished. Mira and Naomi don't know if I'll come back to them or not. I don't know myself. I'm not a painter anymore and nothing else either. Suddenly I see a dying man speaking about a useless life being an early death. Was his life a life without hope. And you and I . . . I want to understand myself. Maybe I'll search for who I was, for who I was meant to be. Did Father ever ask, *Mehr Licht?*

She hadn't expected this question. Without hesitation she answered, yes. And then she was alarmed. She said, Yes, yesterday before I went to Haifa to meet you. And she stared at me with alarm in her gaze, as if seeing something she didn't want to see, got up, went to the kitchen, put on a kettle and came back. Her eyes had become cold. The kettle hummed and then whistled and whistled. She said, Why did you ask.

Nothing. I'm tired, Mother. I don't know why. And really it isn't important.

Let me be the judge.

No, no.

Tell me, Ami.

There's no point.

I fear there is.

Those were Goethe's last words, I said. *Mehr Licht*—more light.

I thought I took a wrong turn on my way to my new house. The winter suddenly so pleasant. Something fresh in the air. Before morning rain fell. Children walked to school and shouted. A milkman with a donkey and cart. Ringing the doorbell. On the porch of the house opposite a woman shakes out a huge carpet. My house. Bougainvillaea blossoming fire. A palm tree in the yard. A well-kept lawn. The kitchen spacious, with Formica. My mother wants me to cry with neon in every room. She's even prepared a child's bed. The phone rang. I hurried to reply to my mother. A man's voice. I thought: The doctor, bad news. I lit my pipe. The voice said, are you 779808? Just a minute, let me see, I said. I read the number on the dial. Yes, that's me.

And your name's Aminadav Sussetz.

Right.

And you're a new client.

Whose client. Is there a house of that sort here?

He was silent. I heard a panting, a heavy breathing at the other end of the line. Then he took courage and said, Are you a relative of Mr. Naftali Sussetz.

He's my father.

Very good, he said.

He's fatally ill.

Sorry to hear it. Heart?

Stroke.

Very bad. Give him regards.

From whom.

The post office director. We used to go for walks together. He was an excellent man, your father.

He's still alive.

I'm sorry.

What for.

You speak somewhat strangely, said the post office director.

Maybe. I've just come into my new house.

Mr. Sussetz. I'm speaking to you as a new client. I wanted to wish you much joy with your new telephone. You have joined the list of proud telephone subscribers of the State of Israel. And we are happy to inform you that— He was very excited.

I didn't ask for a phone, sir, and so I didn't wait for it. So I have a telephone. So what.

But we're speaking to each other, aren't we? Do you know, sir, that a hundred years ago the wise men of the time not only claimed that it was impossible for sound to travel over wires, but also objected to the idea because no one would prefer to speak with someone else over an instrument rather than face to face. Wasn't that absurd? Sudden glee. I told him that I was of that opinion even today. It's true that there were times in America when the telephone was my only friend. But then Mira came.

Who.

My wife, Mira.

Give her my best wishes.

And I'm grateful, I said, for having been annexed to the list of telephone subscribers of the State of Israel, and with God's help we shall be consoled and redeemed and there will be an end to our suffering and the arising of Israel will come to pass.

He considered for a moment. He mulled it over. I could hear the screws in his brain unscrewing. Then he said, Amen, Amen, and slammed the phone down.

I dialed a number at random and heard a curt woman's voice. She said, Hello! I said to her, Dear madam, this is a new subscriber, who has just this day been annexed to the list of proud telephone subscribers of the State of Israel. And I wish to take satisfaction in the fact that at long last I can also speak with you, madam, and by so doing create an unbreakable bond between one Jew and another, between one human being and another, and let us say amen.

She said, I'm not a madam, I'm the maid, I don't understand what you say. The madam will be home in an hour. Her husband's in bed. You want him?

How is he in bed.

Who.

The husband.

What you talking about.

What're you doing at eight o'clock.

I'll call the police, she said angrily.

I wanted to say hello, baby, and you get angry.

She slammed the phone down.

My next-door neighbor, wearing a suit and tie, knocked on my door. He'd brought bread and salt. He blessed and welcomed me and immediately sat down and started condemning his brother-in-law, who'd lived here before me and from whom my mother had bought the house. His brother-in-law thinks that a car is more important than life and that's why he built a magnificent garage and chopped down all the pine trees so his yard wouldn't fill up with needles. And now he's gone to live in Ramat Gan. It's good that you're living here. You're an artist and that's nice. I too sin sometimes, at writing, in Yiddish. I wrote some things and they're all at Yad Va-Shem. If you're free sometime I'll read something to you. . . . He said he'd had three children. Two daughters and a son. The daughters would have been about your age, he said, but they remained "there." He took me to his house and showed me wood carvings that he does with a knife and chisel. He'd taken part in a hobby competition. How does one send a carved table to our esteemed president as a gift, he asked. I didn't know, but I promised to try and find out. He gave me yellow roses from his garden. I went back to the house and put them in a vase full of water. I went out for a walk in my new neighborhood. Children stood behind a fruit booth and smoked cigarettes. A jet plane flashed past suddenly and set windowpanes trembling. I bought an ivory back scratcher. One thing that my mother hadn't bought. My home was full of all good things. I rang to thank her, and arranged that later on I'd come to the hospital. To visit my father who was waiting for me, according to her, impatiently. To drive to the city of sands called Holon. To arrange a car license and a driver's license. The white houses of my childhood have become covered with grayness, they look like rubble. Signs in diverse languages. Warsaw Sewing Salon. About to collapse. I walked like someone walking along the paths of his own blood. Only the smells were still what they had been. A strong aroma from the cafés. Flower shops with their fresh smell, bookstores and the smell of old paper. Peanuts and almonds. The smell of felafel and peeled oranges. I went down to the beach. Old houses hiding in the shade of ruins. Rust on the houses. A closed sea. I sat in an empty café. Once this was Nussbaum's. After Naples we used to come here to hear Beethoven's Fifth on the gramophone and drink cold beer. Dolls used to smile at us. There was something astonishing and young in a city on the sea. Ships on their way to Tel Aviv harbor, new immigrants with hundreds of watches on their arms. They sold watches and bought cameras. We thought of sailing off to dry the Amazon in Brazil. To seek a future. To plant coffee. To return with panache. The fierce waves beat on the concrete wall of the esplanade. Two tourists in the wind, photographing the ugliness Tel Aviv had become. A man on a bicycle beside the paling of the esplanade. His back to me. The coffee au lait isn't au lait and isn't coffee. The man takes a notebook out of his pocket and writes something. The back isn't familiar. If so then why are my eyes drawn to a strange back. A girl shouts in the wind. And the man's ragged and unkempt. Wearing old gabardine trousers and patched worn-out shoes. Instead of laces he uses string. The bicycle is old, faded. Instead of a bicycle seat he's fixed himself a car seat. He finished writing, put the notebook in his pocket and turned to me. His hair is thin, most of his forehead is exposed. His nose is fleshy and he has a harelip. His mouth looks as if a scream had frozen on it. He came and stood facing me. A ship sailed among waves. The sea froths.

183

The man looks at me. More sugar in the coffee. On the bag it said: Look after your city! The man with the notebook in his pocket waited for me. He came a little closer and said, Shalom.

Shalom, I answered.

What a place, he said. What a dead city.

I said, It's a pity. Will you have a seat?

He didn't answer and stared at the sea. The waves lashed and beat against the concrete. A boy climbed onto the paling and walked along it, juggling a schoolbag on his head, like Arab women carrying pitchers of water.

The two tourists slapped hands. The boy came up to them and they gave him coins. The man leaned on his bicycle and said, You can call me Ansberg even though I've got different names and even this one isn't precise.

Aminadav, I said.

He paused for a moment, I thought he tried to smile, and his cloven mouth seemed to deepen, and he said, Yes, I know.

Know what.

Sussetz.

I said, Shalom, friend. He said, No, no. Not a friend. We were never friends, you're exaggerating, and there's no need to make an effort to be too nice.

I waited.

He asked, Have you any idea what I was doing next to the iron bars of the esplanade.

You wrote something in a notebook.

His eyes lit up. Yes, yes. Licentiousness I despise. I smiled. Then he said, I'm doing research on sexual behavior at the beach. We weren't friends. Remember Monsieur Ketzele.

Badim badim, I said.

Monsieur Ketzele was a person I loved. He was perhaps the last person who ever loved me.

I said, There's something wrong with that sentence. If he was the last, then how come you say ever?

That's O.K. People with a lecherous face and a talent like yours will never be able to understand.

I said there was no reason to use such strong language already and perhaps no point in touching on intimate and painful things. . . .

Only those, he said. And his voice hinted at some hidden warning.

You're a bit like him, I said.

May I join you.

Of course, sit down.

Listen, he said to me. I'm a poor man and I don't have the money for the luxury of elegant cafés.

He leaned his bicycle on a tree, came in and sat down. He spoke with nervous fervor: You went to North School. Your teacher was Nehama. Then Hedva. Then Dvora. Then Erlich. You went to high school, your father makes frames. Your uncle's branch manager of Barclays Bank in Haifa. You're a painter. We expected more from you.

Who?

We. Those who remember Monsieur Ketzele. You were supposed to be a consciencist. What do you mean, you became a painter. Do you really think there's room for painters in this crumbling world. Listen, maybe you don't understand, but everything's going to ruin. You know the purpose of man. No. How would you know. Who knows. Who thinks, Here goes a dream down the drain. Something people dreamed evaporates. Who cares. They fuck on the beach. So what. A painter. Who needs any more soap bubbles. You decorate walls for people. Who needs them. Can I also drink something on this occasion?

I said, Your lack be upon me.

I don't lack much.

The little you do lack, Ansberg.

That isn't my name, either.

What should I call you?

Ansberg.

So be it. What will you drink?

You must remember, Aminadav Sussetz, that I lack means.

I called the waiter. A face like a tubercular bulldog's. Eyes for seeing prostitutes in the street. Ansberg studied the menu meticulously. The waiter shifts his weight from foot to foot. Two women smile at the waiter and raise their skirts. A clear sign of hard times.

185

Ansberg says, Cheesecake. Iced coffee with whipped cream, and a glass of soda. The waiter shrugs his shoulders and vanishes. Ansberg asks if he isn't exaggerating. I tell him that his order is quite reasonable. The two women burst out laughing. I look at them. Ansberg gazes at me. One of them, ash-blond with a lot of stuff on a squashed face that looks as if trains have run over it, says, Nahum blows my mind. What does he want. Really shits me. What, didn't I see him in a taxi with that fat piece with bandy legs from the bar and she made eyes at me and took his hand and put it on her flat chest as if I'm r.i.p. here and can't see what I see with my own eyes?

A name's a personal thing, said Ansberg. It depends on what and on whom. Depends on all sorts of things. Mood for example. I was a year ahead of you at school. And you don't remember. You don't remember the mathematical genius that I was.

I said that the moment I saw him I'd thought I knew him. But I have a poor memory. Why had he expected me to be a consciencist and what did consciencist mean. Why we and not I.

We simply thought you'd be more than you turned out to be. Who's we.

I!

He's offended. Shows me a pained face. We simply thought you'd be something special, an example, and we'd all follow in your footsteps.

I said, I didn't even save myself.

I'm the man who disappointed this wild and likable sex researcher. Beware of harelips, Beatrice had said when she read my fortune in a coffee cup on the ship. He sucked his spittle inward and said, What do you think of all this sexual licentiousness in our days. Life's landscape has been debased. I liked his expression life's landscape, as if this stinking life has a landscape at all. And Ansberg spoke. His speech flowed feverishly, constantly on the brink of boiling. Like someone walking to an abyss and not taking that extra step. The sea stormed. The wind covered the esplanade with dust. Two girls with thick thighs in trousers and boots invited passers-by to come into the Athens Cellar. Only its doorway could be seen from here. Like a black jaw. The girls laughed.

186

They glittered. And their hair gleamed. There was a place there called Acropolis with pinball machines. Boys came in and went out. The women from the café went into backyards and came out again. Men went in with them and came out alone. At the end of the backyard I saw a woman kneeling on the sand. In the yard. Among broken stones. A man crouched over her. She raises a hand and looks at her watch. He dances on her. Ansberg speaks. The waves beat against the concrete wall. The woman lowers her hand. The man shudders. She gets up. He tries to get up and stumbles. She giggles. Two young men wearing tight trousers stand at the corner and look. She waves to them and laughs soundlessly. The man pulls up the trousers that were let down before. The woman tinkles over toward the two men. One of them pokes his hand into her skirt and her face contorts with pleasure. A smile and then a scream. The man who was with her comes out shamefaced. He gets into a car parked outside Acropolis. A woman calls him to come into the pinball machines. He leans on the steering wheel. He starts the car and drives off. I look at Ansberg, who's writing something in his notebook. And in my mind's eye I saw my father's eyes. Something sounded in me: *The tombstone in my father's eyes is the most living thing in his face.* Ansberg speaks about licentiousness in beds, on the beach, in literature and in the theater. Sex sex sex. My research . . . will prove that . . . The waiter brings iced coffee with whipped cream, cheesecake and soda. Ansberg swallowed the cake with one gulp. Then he sucked up the iced coffee through two plastic straws. His wheezing was alarming. When he'd finished sucking the iced coffee and swallowed all the cake crumbs he gathered up in his hand, he drank the glass of soda. I asked him if he'd like something else, to drink, to eat. He said that I was forgetting who he was.

I'm not forgetting.

I'm a poor man.

I know. What would you like.

Visionaries die of hunger in the land of Israel, he said.

You're my guest, order whatever you want.

He raised his hand with majestic grace and the waiter hurried over. Chewing a piece of bread and cheese. Ansberg said, Please bring me soda, iced coffee with whipped cream and cheesecake. Then he turned to me. Monsieur Ketzele was my friend and none of you knew!

I admitted that I hadn't known. But, I said, at least I owe nothing in the case of Monsieur Ketzele. I'm sure you remember that he even refused to shake my hand. After it was discovered that I returned apples and that it was other children who stole.

Of course, said Ansberg, that's why we called you consciencist. Hell . . . again. Who's we!

I.

So, I.

I'm not even sure my name's Ansberg, Mr. Sussetz. You know, he said after a brief pause, during the month of December, here on the beach, between Gordon and Allenby, I counted four hundred and fifty-four acts of fornication. I can prove to you by statistics that this number is only a small part of what really goes on. First of all I count only twice a day, two hours in the morning and two hours in the evening. Secondly this is only one section of a long seafront that is rich in places for concealment and whoring. If fifty people were to count acts of fornication during the course of twenty-four hours, along the whole beach from Reading to Jaffa, the number would be astounding. I'm afraid to even utter it. Frightful dimensions of fornication, and there's no one to say how far it really goes!

I asked him what was so terrible about it and why he used the word fornication.

Again he sucked the iced coffee that had been brought to the table in the meantime and said, Because love is dead. That's why. We're waiting for someone, for someone to come and exalt it again, to raise it up out of the dung, Mr. Sussetz. I can't grant these animals—and the word animals is too good for them: lots of animals know what love is—I can't grant them a better word than fornication. If only Monsieur Ketzele were alive today.

What could he have done, he was such a poor old guy and all he said was *badim badim*.

He'd have written letters. Brought the police. Just like he did when they caught you.

And you knew?

Only at the end. I didn't know that you. Were a consciencist and all that. I thought you were like everybody else. And then it hit me. At nights I dreamed about you, Sussetz. And they said you'd gone away, Aminadav. You disappeared, and I wanted to find you. I did some gematria on the numerical values of the letters of your name. Some terrifying results I got. I said to myself, He mustn't be allowed to be an artist. Art is a luxury and we can't afford that luxury. But you'd vanished. Then there was the war. And they said you'd been wounded. And then you became a seaman. I followed your career. I read about you in the newspapers. Painting. America. Paris. Tel Aviv, at the museum. I went to see the exhibition. I thought: The consciencist has arrived. I saw paintings. What do you paint. Will you move one heart with those paintings. Will you be able to change something. To raise the level of morality. To bring people back to belief in themselves. No, no. Sabbatai Zevi was a false messiah. And your paintings were false. They lied. They said nothing to me. Even in the place where I live I have a souvenir of you. What do you think—you think I didn't wait for you, Mr. Sussetz. For you to understand you'd made a mistake, and to lend a hand. I knew you'd be here. But I would have found you. Every now and then I talk with your mother. I tell her that I'm Yehoash Gover. The one with one arm missing. Who was a friend of yours, and now lives in Eilat. She doesn't recognize my voice and she tells me things. I knew you were arriving. By the way, you remember Mad Max.

Of course. We used to go looking for sea anemones together. He had a weather vane on the roof. Ansberg, do you live in Max's house?

In his cabin.

On the beach.

North Tel Aviv.

He had a great beard and gaping shoes and ragged clothes. He was a kind of prophet, wasn't he?

189

A great prophet and he died and no one knew that he'd died. They killed him. The bastards. I went to the funeral. There was only me and an old woman who said she was his aunt. And Aminadav thinks of him, how he was thrown out of class. To go to the hills. To the cave. To the place where we hid tea and sugar against the Germans who were at El Alamein. And Max always there. Waiting. And going to the sea to look for sea anemones. Eating seaweed. Measuring the force of the wind with his weather vane. He had a sandglass. Cloth shoes because he didn't want a cow or a deer to be slaughtered because of him. And there was a girl there. She lived next to the cabin. Rina Faktorovitz. On the hills. With her one could learn anatomy on the sands. With her legs raised. In the Turkish ruin, not far from the Moslem cemetery, I'm sure you remember. . . . Ansberg says that once he found a letter of mine. I'd written to Max in English class and a boy named Yohanan K. who'd gone to Rina Faktorovitz to learn anatomy had brought him the letter. "Dear Max, you are a saint in a world of locusts. Steal everything from them. When you steal from them you bring them grace." Ansberg had wondered a lot, how come a consciencist like me had written such a strange letter. Until he began to understand things and now he sells postcards to whoresons and sons of whoresons to finance his research which will save the city from this terrible licentiousness.

I smiled to the sea which was beating me with its waves. The sea frothed. It put on marvelous hues of purple green white and black. And Ansberg handed me a parcel of postcards. I ordered beer. A faded poster on the wall, Give your man Goldstar, the man's beer. And a woman with a ring on her navel and a fabulous bikini giving me a glass of beer. I drank her health, To you, baby doll! The froth tasted good. On this stormy shore. On the first postcard was a photograph of a frightful fuck. A man with a huge thing. And a woman.

From Turkey, said Ansberg

His face was sad as he spoke.

Beneath the Turkish gall was Ansberg's answer to consciencism. From all the garbage cans of all the institutions he gathers postcards. His chief supplier is the Jewish National Fund office

190

in Tel Aviv. Postcards of the settlement of Hanita. Nineteen thirty-eight. The planting of a forest in the Jerusalem hills. Navy women in white uniforms. An Israeli armored column in action. The President of the State shaking hands with the ambassador of Upper Volta. The centenary of the settlement of Mikveh Israel. At night it's sad, he said. All this shining paper. To finance research. To save a nation from perdition. To place the piece of gall from Turkey with the naked things on top and to walk through the streets of whoredom. To employ the methods of the enemy. He yells and I'm forced to ask him to lower his voice. The waiters point at him and mutter. The venom in their eyes. The gold teeth of pimps.

Sometimes they beat me up, he said. They look at the first postcard. They buy. They walk into a doorway and put a hand in a pocket. They look at the postcards. They find navy women in white uniforms and chase after me. And they beat me. How they beat me. But mostly they buy and go away. They wait until they're alone. And then it's too late. I defeat them with their own weapons. And I learned that from the letter that you wrote. My consciencist. To Max the Saint who was killed by those bastards . . . I'm financing a research project to wipe them out at the root. And I sell them purity and beauty. I am tied to Nahalal and Hanita with holy strands. I love the mythos of Eretz Israel: onward we drive, the valley is a dream, we have come to inherit, to build and be built. Jews with a bundle and a stick, to conquer a place in the desert, to drain the swamps, and this becomes a world of sex maniacs with sixteen-year-old whores with painted faces and rouged cheeks. With pictures of Hanita in my pocket, as if they were pictures of Egyptian fucks. Once they caught me. And beat me. I said to them, You're not the only ones who have a right to cheat. I have too. I told them that not every Faust achieves Hell. And that's a sad thing, Aminadav. . . . Do you know that Aminadav was a king of Ammon.

I didn't know, that is, I didn't remember.

A king, said Ansberg, and laughed. For Ansberg can't smile or be sad. He can cry or laugh. With his cloven face. He lives between terrible extremes.

191

I'm no king, I said.

You're a consciencist, he said. Very soon now I'll publish my report about the savage sex life on the beach between nine and one in the morning and between six and nine in the evening between Gordon Street and Herbert Samuel Square, in nineteen sixty-six and -seven. If the messiah doesn't come by dint of prayers he'll come with the aid of statistics. Someone will have to see. He'll call the pamphlet Where Has Love Gone.

Perhaps you'll write the introduction for me.

Perhaps, I said.

One must cry out. You know, like a prophet in the wilderness, a seer. Those who see the fornication rising must cry out. . . .

I buy postcards of fornication from seamen. There's no local production yet. But there will be, don't worry.

I'm not worried.

In your place I'd be worried!

I say nothing and look at the sea. You know, says Ansberg, there's been a rise of nine percent per year, here on the beach, of fornication, and that's more than the rate of increase of the gross national product.

I told him that the word fornication annoyed me.

I don't have any other word. Love is something . . . like consciencist. Once they used to hide, he said. Whispering love. Remember? How beautiful it was. A bench among the trees. The air around love, the enchanted atmosphere, the glances.

I said, I'm getting nostalgic.

I'm nostalgic for something I never knew, Mr. Sussetz, he shouted now in a trembling voice, and you I'm sure are nostalgic for something real. You've known it, I haven't.

I'm sorry, I said.

He gazed at me for some time and then two tears dripped from his eyes and stopped on his cheeks. It's all athletics, he said. There's no tenderness, no gentleness, no shame. . . . They go to the beach. She raises her skirt, he pulls down his trousers, they finish and smoke a cigarette. Is that love? That's filthy fornication, Aminadav King of Ammon.

King of himself in vain.

192

That's because you didn't become a consciencist as we expected. And this time his yelling was so loud that even the waiters
shuddered. They didn't laugh.

You could have been, he said. We expected it of you.

Who?

I!

Say I.

He said it. And laughed. There's no affection, he said. Girls and
women. Something cries in me. You hear? All of them, mothers,
girls, soldier girls, all of them, on the sand, on the beach, or in
a car by the sea, waiting. There's no silent anticipation, no refined
play of instincts, no glances, no restraint. You're a painter, aren't
you? Can there be a painting without a frame, a sight without
bounds, a dream without borders. No. Everything has to be
bounded.

I said, That's my own problem.

I know your father. I went to see him, you weren't in the
country at the time. He used to speak about you with a lot of pity.
Maybe you thought it was love, maybe it was. The way he pitied
you. He didn't know who I was. I said my name was Nahum. He
didn't know that Nahum died in the war. Your father was smearing hessian and breaking wood and smearing carpenter's glue.
That wonderful smell there. And thick volumes of Schiller and
Jean Paul. And records in the shop, Vivaldi and Bach. A man who
knew what frames are and loves only in a stylized manner. And
you. You don't? What do you . . . I waited for you, Aminadav.
Girls do that, Aminadav. On the beach, as if it were eating ice
cream.

You remember, he said, when they found out you hadn't stolen
those apples. And *badim badim* refused to offer you his hand.
They had a parade at school.

I remember, I said.

You remember what the headmaster said. Ansberg laughed. I
sipped the beer which was no longer frothy or cold and Ansberg
quoted from memory: "In these anguished days, when the people
of our nation are bound to stand shoulder to shoulder, prepared
for any objective, when it is our destiny to gaze with alarmed eyes

193

at the ship of Israel crashing against the rocks, when stormy waves rock it from side to side without cease, when we are stormed and savaged from within and from without, and the enlightened world stands watching while the boats founder in the darkness and speculators drive up the prices of land and the long-suffering and meek teachers of Israel give their souls for the sake of Israel's children, when we endeavor to elevate the spirits of our youth and to imbue them with the awareness of Jewish brotherhood, in these anguished days . . ."

At the end of it he stepped toward you a little, said Ansberg.

I said that I remember how the children stood there with their heads down, shamefaced.

Your mother was proud, said Ansberg.

And you, he added, you didn't even look at her!

Because they believed I'd stolen. And I hadn't. Even she, maybe.

Monsieur Ketzele was my only friend, he said. Everyone laughed at me. Because of my mouth. He didn't. You and he. Who else. Who else did I have or will I have. . . . You're a consciencist. And he was such a wonderful person.

What was so wonderful about him?

He was. You wouldn't understand.

I might, I said.

Afterward I sneaked into the lavatory. To hear what the lady teachers were saying, said Ansberg. I had a secret hiding place there. I waited. The headmaster stopped speaking and the lady teachers went to the lavatory to talk. As usual. I stood and listened to them. They said that you know, you, Aminadav, that pinching things is just as bad as stealing. And that it isn't just cute and sabraish to be a *shvitzer,* a show-off. To sneak in . . . That everyone pinches from the British as if that's O.K. and afterward they'll steal from each other. And then the teacher Nehama said you'd be a consciencist. She must have made up the word. I remember how it thrilled me to hear it. Consciencist. I was exalted, I felt as if I'd grown wings.

I said to Ansberg that he'd be recompensed somehow. He chews a straw methodically. He says, I'm already recompensed,

194

and he bursts out laughing and stops at once. From the American embassy a black car emerges. To take the ambassador to a fateful meeting. Girls peek at the gleaming car, and open their legs behind shattered buildings.

And that isn't everything, says Ansberg. And that's why I didn't become a mathematician. Who needs mathematics in this degenerate world. I'll let you into a deep secret. Actually I'm ready now to reveal to you my main occupation. And you yourself will be the judge whether I'm worthy to be the friend of a consciencist.

I proposed that he order something more.

He drinks iced coffee and tells me how he discovered that the light in the homes of the wives of Tel Aviv workers doesn't go on when the average worker (so he said) goes out to work.

One can prove, on the basis of this, he said . . .

On the basis of what.

You'll understand in a minute, Sussetz.

He drinks the coffee and follows it up with some soda from his glass.

I can prove, he said, two theses with one stone, which is to say . . .

Which is to say what, Ansberg.

My name could be different.

I know. You spoke of theses and one blow.

Stone.

Yes, stone.

Two theses and one stone. That the wives of Tel Aviv, Mr. Sussetz, including members of the Histadrut and Working Mothers, noble and base, don't receive true love.

And the second thesis?

Aha, he chortled, but his cloven mouth writhed. That the rate of fornication at Tel Aviv beach stems from Fact A, which is that the wives of Tel Aviv workers do not get the love that is their due.

I waited. I sipped cold coffee which was supposed to be hot. On the esplanade facing the sea. Once I stood here and thought: Ah, always be yourself. I remembered the Socrates I was then, with a wounded leg at night, with clouds over the stormy sea and my leg in plaster. Behind me the noise of the hotels. At Café Piltz,

Menashke Baharav played *Be-arvot Ha-Negev,* and Klatzkin, with a smile, sang with him, and embraced him, and afterward they sang *Arye Arye,* off you go and volunteer and join the Hebrew Brigade—and a woman who took me in her hands and said she was from "over there" and embraced me and we walked arm in arm and she took my wallet from me in a little room while I waited to be a virgin no more, and she didn't come. And the rain, how it rained then. The waiter came up, brought Ansberg what he'd asked for, and wiped the table. Taking his time. He too wanted to hear. The wind whistled fiercely. Ansberg drinks and talks. There's no love anymore, what are the husbands looking for. Fast fornication. Physical pleasure. Athletics. And then . . .

Oh, then I go out. Every morning. While it's still dark. I spy out the average worker's apartment, Aminadav. I see him leave home at five-thirty. And I see that there's someone reliable here. The light in the bedroom doesn't go on. That means the wife's sleeping. No?

No what.

No matter.

It matters, go on.

The light doesn't go on. That matters, Ami.

And then the long-awaited day arrives. And at three minutes past five-thirty, after the average worker has already reached his bus stop, Ansberg leaves his bicycle against a tree, takes the tin can from the bicycle and goes up to the apartment of the average worker, opens the door with a skeleton key, places the can with its wire handle on the floor, takes out of it a pair of old slippers made of elephant skin, and walks toward the dark bedroom.

What are you doing, Ansberg?

I'm walking to the bedroom, says my brother, staring wide-eyed at me. Ansberg doesn't walk into that bedroom willingly. And then, he says, I get into the warm bed, to my beloved, I get into the warm bed that the husband has left five or ten minutes earlier. The heavy smell warms me, he says. The mustiness of night . . . the man's absence. And I fill his place. I put on his image. And then he raises the nightgown of the wife of the average worker and enters her with great tenderness. I slide into her, he

196

says. And I can count on Ansberg on this. Mostly I do it from behind, he says, but I'm sure that they don't open their eyes. And if they open them they don't see, and if they see what do they understand, and if they understand they don't say a thing and that's discouraging, Ami.

Yes.

They don't say a thing. How concealed are those depths. Do you think they're dreaming.

I told him I don't know.

It's complicated, he said. And I wasn't surprised by the sadness in his voice.

You must understand, Mr. Consciencist, that the husbands of the average wife don't know how to love. For true love is only in the morning. And his face glows now. I see a laugh that wants to be a smile. The mysterious face of Rudolph Valentino. His eyes mist over. After all, he's speaking about love now. You understand, love in the morning. Not at night when the instincts burn and there's a numbness and you do the animal rites by rote. In the morning . . . At dawn. After the dreams and the long sleep, maybe still in dreams, in a kind of tranquility, a kind of silent slow lambency, which comes out of you, and your beloved is in your arms, and you become one in truth, you truly touch, in a kind of sleepy wakefulness, and the tenderness . . . Nocturnal sex life is vulgar and simple, like cats. They sneak out of their wives' beds. Love in the mornings finishes after the honeymoon. If at all. And then the statistics start rising on the beach. One depends on the other. Even the Swedish and Danish women who've started arriving recently with their long blond hair and their exciting swimsuits don't help. Listen, I'm not a fool. I know that this is love and at the same time it isn't love. They don't see my face. If they were to see it they'd faint. And Ansberg's face is sad sad. But, he says in pain and a sense of great responsibility that finds a response in my heart, *through me* they love their husbands and that's something. Their stupid husbands, he added as a second thought. I embrace them, he said, I'm gentle with them. I kiss the napes of their necks. I play with the roots of their hair. I stroke their earlobes. I enter them with a kind of dread. Not as a conqueror but as one conquered. I ignore the staleness that comes from the mouths of night with uncleaned teeth. What do you know, Mr. Sussetz, you who love women who clean their teeth for you! Did you know that no woman ever polished her teeth for me? And to live with that. All your life. And to know that I love them and they don't know. And I tickle, I play. I caress. And they smile. Not to me! To their distant husbands. And you ought to see the husbands. I see them for three mornings in succession before I get into their wives' beds. Their morning faces. Unshaven. Yawning. Waiting in line for a bus with a lunch bag in one hand. Mr. Sussetz, the general atmosphere of licentiousness, I want you to know, pleads for some new beginning, for a change, for a true consciencist who'll take things in hand. . . .

You understand, they smile at me. And actually they're smiling at their own husbands. Who are at the bus stops. And I'm inside. Who's inside. They're inside, I'm always outside. Even when I'm inside I'm outside, with a mouth like this. And the husbands go to work. And then, in the evening, they come home. They take off a shirt. Put on an undershirt. In the summer. In the winter, a sweater. They sit, eat an omelet and salad and read the evening paper. Who killed, who fucked, who raped whom. And politics. That we're still the best in the world. And then they hear some pacifying stuff on the radio. They play cards. They sit on the balcony, and look at how the neighbors are playing cards and looking at them. They scream at the children everything that's piled up during the day. They drink coffee, beer or fruit juice. And they go to bed to sleep. Three times a month, with eyes closed, with sleep at their fingertips, they turn to their marvelous women, who long for love, and enter them like a donation to the Jewish National Fund. And come out quickly. They wipe their things on the blanket. They put their pajamas on again, and snore. In the morning the wife dreams. And the man goes out to his bus stop. And I stand opposite her house and wait. When I enter her like a true lover whom does she dream about? About him. And do you know who brings up my statistics? Those husbands! There's a point of no return. Ansberg swallows cake crumbs. The wind blows fiercely. Women women in boots to lead tourists into dim caves. So far, he said, I've had thirty-two women. He spoke this last sentence dryly.

Thirty-two?

Thirty-three.

Thirty-three.

Thirty-three. The thirty-third doesn't count. By mistake I entered the bed of my landlady's daughter. And she screamed. I was caught. There was a trial. The trial was publicized in all the newspapers. Now he spoke in an awful sadness. *Not one prosecution witness turned up at my trial,* he said, *apart from the mother of the girl with whom I hadn't been.*

Thirty-two women, not one of them turned up. Can't they read. Of course they can. I have evidence. I saw newspapers and books beside their beds. On the woman's side. Better evidence than that isn't needed. They could have testified in camera. They could have received court protection so that their names wouldn't come out. They didn't testify. They didn't come. They didn't write letters. They maintained absolute silence. How do you explain that.

I think about Mira. The esplanade is flooded with light and clouds play with the sun. Are you lying in our bed now. Turning off the television. And some lipless Ansberg enters you pretending to be me. That's why I said, I understand.

I don't, Ami, said Ansberg. I don't understand!

You know, he added, in court . . . they were merciful. I'm sad to say. They even had some kind of admiration for me. I got nine months. I think the nine was a result of the judge's sense of humor. Maybe because he was incapable of imagining that I entered his bed too. After all, he gets up at seven-thirty in the morning. And leaves home at eight-twenty and by that time even tired women are up. And thus he is saved from the crimes of people like me. Did he know? Before you asked about prison. Now it's coming. Only for you, Sussetz. In memory of Monsieur Ketzele. Do you think Monsieur Ketzele ever knew a woman? I don't rape women, I don't go to them because I'm a sex maniac, I hate sex, Aminadav, I hate sex that's separated from love, I'm a love maniac, Aminadav, I don't deny it. And the bourgeois don't understand. The prisoners understood. I taught mathematics. I had a study circle of wonderful rogues. One had killed his wife because she had looked, for one moment only, at another man. Could the judge have understood a love like that. Would members of the Histadrut and those who aren't members of the Histadrut be capable of killing a woman because of one look. Love . . . that's love . . . that man who killed because he was proud. We lived in the same wing. I taught him geometry.

Ansberg got into bed in slippers made of elephant hide that he'd bought from a Swedish seaman in Haifa near the port. The reason that he got into his beloveds' beds in slippers made of elephant hide is that his father used to make all the little Ansbergs in slippers made of elephant hide, he told me with characteristic fervor. Ansberg's father too used to sleep in a separate bed. But toward morning he used to wake up with a great love. And it was cold. He'd put on his slippers and get into his wife's bed and make little Ansbergs and laugh. Ansberg used to lie in his room and listen to the laughter.

And Ansberg's afraid of arousing too much attention. If he were to laugh they'd really wake up. To be inside them was a sweet dream. Laughter was too dangerous. High above their understanding. To laugh and to love. And maybe even with the light on.

17

On the esplanade, close by us, two girls walk. One swings her ass in a pale green raincoat and has bluish hair and the other wears a short skirt and white boots. She says, let him go, I've had enough! I said to him, what's he say? A fist in the face. Shit, I said, with his fist in my face. I said, sweetie, I'm crazy 'bout ya. Put it in again. At the beach he got on me. It was wet. He pulled my hair. I said, I've had my hair straightened and tomorrow's Shabbat. He said, shit on your hair. I'm like your father, he said. And ran off. What shit. I said to him, take your money. He took it. What d'ya make of that?

He writes word for word. Avid for words. I call the waiter. Up on the second floor there was once a gramophone, they played Beethoven. During the days of the drying of the Amazon and the coffee planting and the Greek ships winking at us from among the waves. Now they were counting last night's takings up there. I could hear the ring of coins. Ansberg turns his face and says, Sex sex sex. In the theater, in the movies, in literature. In the distance a ship sinks in the water. Vanishes. Toward Ashdod. I remember Zarathustra saying that chaos must rage in you if you aspire to give birth to a dancing star. I'm a returning son, Ansberg, will you be my childhood friend.

I paid and we left. Ansberg isn't willing to forget the look on my face when the headmaster made his speech. You didn't look proud at all, he said. Maybe you're modest!

Not modest, Ansberg. Maybe shy. I wouldn't be able to get into a strange bed. You're a brave man.

With a face like mine it's easy to be brave, he said, and shuddered. Suddenly he started shuddering. I asked him why he was shuddering. He asked if I'd understood what he'd said just now. I said, Yes, but you can say what you want, I believe in you.

You really believe in me.

Yes, Ansberg.

That was only partly true. I don't even know what I look like. When did I last see myself in a mirror.

I said nothing. And he said, Thanks three times, for the cake and the coffee and the soda.

At Vitman's we ate ice cream. His bicycle rattles. The tin can tied with wire stays. The streets bustle. Angry. What hurts me. A woman runs, with a little boy on her heels. With a basket. To market. In a shop they sell tobacco. And a butcher slaughters chickens, sidelong, from the market. And hawkers wail. Ansberg complains, The beach used to swarm with love, remember. . . . Under and on the esplanade. At nights. An autumn breeze blew. Let's sit down quietly and count the stars, little girl. . . . And sand sticking to the body. And beauty queens were chosen in the Casino. Women are a mysterious thing. An old man cries, My wife wore a crinoline. I didn't know she had bandy legs. But the marvelous mystery. My mother used to tell about the Casino. Dr. Bugrashov, now a street, was the teacher. They used to walk in rows, singing How beautiful are the nights in Canaan. Mother used to tell and Father didn't listen. Now he weeps in Hölderlin's German. Wants what. Love or a sword. Maybe he smashed himself instead of the violin. The violin that my father was, to smash his son, his only son, whom he loved, Aminadav. Here on the esplanade. Where I was. Allenby Street. With the knight of fornication. Seeking love in vain.

After Kapulsky Cakes, Bialik Street. Named after my dear godfather. Who wrote me in rhymes. From there to go to wherever my feet take me. To seek out the city that was, opposite here

202

was a shop called Hefzibah. There were rulers and erasers and pencils. Made in Czechoslovakia. Always stolen by studious boys. There was stealing. And going to the Allenby Cinema. After that to go up Shenkin, a renowned Zionist leader. Past all the little shops. Making a detour around my father's frame shop. Who's sitting in there now. I'm not willing to look and see. Mother's waiting with Father. He's expecting you. His face looking out the window. Seeing the tractor plowing, two dusty trees and a plane landing or taking off. To walk in this street is to melt the boundaries between things. Like the enemy that I am to myself. In this street Father walked. How many times did he walk up Shenkin Street in the direction of Balfour to our house where I was born thirty-seven years ago. Did he see what I'm seeing. To repeat this injustice. Ansberg doesn't sense these things precisely. You boomerang back like a fired shell shot that fires back at the one who fired it. Once we fired a Davidka on Shekh Jarrah. It exploded. The men shooting were killed. I lay in a trench. With a rope tied to the Davidka. The fragments were huge. Father used to walk here. Dressed like a poet of the twenties. With his handsome hat and purple shirt, bow tie and carved walking stick and white hands. He'd have his shoes shined at the corner of Ahad Ha'am. And from there two minutes' walk past the blossoming branches and beautiful treetops of Rothschild Boulevard to the house with beautiful verandas on the corner of Balfour Street. And from there Mother. With me, inside her, to the Freund Hospital, to bring a gift to her wound. To bring salvation to the things already extinguished in her. And I didn't light up. Ansberg stumbles along beside me. He measures the houses. I measure the city's weariness and mine. And my heart goes out to it. Cloven people like us, Ansberg. Hell, if you only had a simple name. Like Patrick or Henryk or Thornton Alfredos. Later on I'll go to Father. He'll abuse me in Goethean. Is it my fault that Rivka Sussetz isn't Charlotte von Stein. Or that I'm not Wilhelm Meister, the eternal yielder. Like him. Like my dear father. The violin-smasher. I remember things. Ansberg hears me talking. He thinks that a man whose memories are so literary hasn't really lived. Maybe I haven't lived. Father didn't believe in the existence of Beethoven's symphonies. Did the symphonies exist despite his disbelief. I tell Ansberg about Thomas Mann. Mr. Naftali Sussetz took care of my weary education. And he read me Mann's essay on Goethe.

Mann wrote about the Goethean synthesis between the monstrous and the divine. The son of God and the monster are both beyond man's power of conception, Ansberg. Mann struggled, my father told me, the problem troubled him, but the contempt for man is a profound inheritance! Ansberg walks beside me. My father studied in Berlin or Heidelberg and for his living played at the Kinematograf. Behind wild clowns. He stood there on summer nights and played Brahms even though he didn't believe Brahms had written symphonies. Am I capable of understanding my father. Mann claimed that people aren't capable of conceiving the monstrous without coupling it with divinity and thereby worshiping it. The exalted, he said, is charged with dread. Instead of saying to me, Aminadav, let's play Bring Some Bricks on the record player, and let's take a boat ride on the Yarkon, he told me Schopenhauer's hatred of women and read me Goethe. And he sat me on his knees. With the terrible restrained love of a man who has erased himself so as not to take someone else's place. The apology for existing. Mother was always pleading for love. Now she calls him Naftali. Mann says that the exalted, and I hear my father's voice speaking to me in Shenkin Street next to Ahad Ha'am Street, near children with side curls who go to the yeshiva and yell, Whore! Whore! at a woman in a mini with a little girl in a mini and a minicar parked nearby holding a bunch of red and white flowers. Mann says that the exalted is suffused with dread. A great loneliness full of grace . . . My father's voice. The quiet, solid voice. My father's Goethe conquered demoniac impulses, distilled them, polished them, purified them, and thus the polite and the demoniac were wedded. And that suits my father better.

To walk along the boulevard. People in the shade of trees and sky. Sun between clouds. David Bustanai's house. With a bright garden, among large buildings. To cross Allenby Street at the corner of the boulevard. To drink *gazoz* at Rovanenko's. To see the Tel Aviv Museum with Father's frames. The lovely building with the iron gate. To note with amazement that there's no more

fire brigade tower on the corner and no police station. And to walk
in Herzl Street. What for. And Ansberg leans his bicycle against
a post and says, Upstairs here there lives a woman with squashed
breasts who screamed *thief! ganev!* and wept bitterly. And I was
inside her. And she screamed *ganev! ganev!* as if in delight. And
I wasn't at all. To see the window with a flowerpot and gray
curtains. And beside it a sign saying Diplomad Pedicurist. And
a dental practitioner in a house about to collapse with a woman
in front of it, daringly dressed, offering things with a smile, to
come with her behind the house into the yard where not long ago
a huge and dusty berry tree died. And to arrive. At the Freund
Hospital. To retrace a lost journey of thirty-seven years ago. The
end of Yehuda Halevy Street and suddenly a respite. Behind the
yard there is still the Eden Cinema. Then they'd shown The Jazz
Singer, with Al Jolson. Paper fragments of him were opposite my
house in the street of the professional mourners. Man, says Hermann Hesse, is a momentary intersection of nature. And for a
moment I was united with the heretofore. At the Freund Hospital. And the façade of the Freund Hospital still looked like a
Greek temple. Filth on the marble steps. Faded during the years.
A godforsaken street. The hospital, a part of it is a storehouse of
the National Bank and a part of it a storehouse of nothing. The
houses are bare. Opposite the Lands Registry office a gray-faced
man sits at a little table, with a sign behind him: LETTER WRITER.
FIVE LIRA PER LETTER! Two lira it had read before, now that was
crossed out. And on the crossing-out there was a three, and on top
of the three, a five. Even at five there aren't many buyers. The
request writer smoked a thin squashed cigarette. He introduced
himself by standing up and bowing. He wore a suit and tie. With
the smell of sweat and eau de Cologne. He clicked his heels and
said, Hefetz-Haim Abutbul! Very ceremoniously. He asks if we'll
have coffee with him. I refuse politely. He was born, he says,
during the Hebraization of Rishon-le-Zion. They brought a
Sephardic midwife especially from Jaffa, sir, in a carriage drawn
by four strong stallions. And what one comes to! But in the
upbuilding of the land is our consolation. He complains that
everyone's fled from here. Once there was a courthouse here,

205

people used to congregate, a nice crowd it was. What happens today: some young guy met an Australian girl at the beach and another guy met a French girl at the movies and they write her letters. And I lie for them in flowery phrases. I don't have the heart to throw their letters right back in their faces. With the brilliantine. Once all the aristocracy lived here! And now, he said, troubled times are here. If the sword were in my hand I'd hew it all asunder! And he drinks his coffee, with loud measured sips. And smiles at us. Lone cars straying along their ways. Not far from here are the lanes of Neveh Tzedek. Women in aprons covered with shawls steal into dark houses. Locked houses wearing a shattered nobility. Here was the shout of joy of the first ones. Here my mother danced on the hot summer nights.

A house with its shutters closed by boards. A red curtain lights up a street. A hexagonal kiosk, the only one of its kind still in the city. A Lucas lamp that no longer shines. The man pours red *gazoz* into a large glass. Father's waiting for me. Will Mira be able to understand. Now, opposite the house, I thought, I who I was and who set out on all those ways, I've come back with me! I want to know exactly what was here. Suddenly I must know. Aminadav sits. In the yard of the Freund Hospital. Time dies. Father waits for me at the Eden Cinema. Al Jolson sings Sonny Boy. Bialik walks out of the hospital and says, Naftali, the moment Aminadav's born let me know. And then one gets born. And they cut the cord. And there's *badim badim.* An Arab boy slings a burning cigarette butt at a cat. The cat howls. He has pale blue eyes. The kindergarten teacher says that all Arab children have black eyes. Father leads me to the museum to see a painting by Chagall. Frames with the smell of glue. And the molten gold. And Goethe. And then people and New York and Aminadav painting superfluous things. And Mira and Naomi. And coming home Father sick. Dying. Don't let him die. She wants to raise her a new son. Ansberg jumps from bed to bed to bring salvation to the female species. They love their husbands through the man with the cloven mouth. The Dutchwoman told me to beware of quicksand and of people with harelips. I sit and wonder what happened to the man of conscience that I was supposed to be. Trying to fish

206

up something. The moment of birth in advance. To paint houses; browns, whites, oranges. A red window, a hexagonal kiosk, a Lucas lamp, a woman in a shawl. A whore in Pines Street. Neveh Tzedek. Here my grandfather Nehemiah taught. A childhood friend of Bialik's. Through him the poet became my godfather. And named me Aminadav. The letter writer writes a letter to Kurt Singer. Maybe to God. Like me in Fifth Avenue. On an Irish cop's ticket. A bridge isn't a poem. I'm a painter. It doesn't matter, same shit. The Greek for journey is the Hebrew for book. There was a moment, the waters broke, a great bubbling, and here I am, the potential that became actuality. One o'clock in the morning, the second of May, nineteen thirty, here in this place. I became, for them. For Father, for Mother, for Bialik, for Mira, for Naomi, for the Dutchwoman. And for me?

Father skips from the entrance hall to see the King of Ammon enter the world. Air-conditioned weather in a city of forty-two thousand inhabitants. A wind blows from the sea. And the memory ends. The womb is gone. Black spaces swallowed. Memory returns two years later, in Jaffa, what happened in between. Does it matter. Why am I so eager to know. The death of memory and the emergence into the world at one and the same time. One moment in which I know all the women I've ever known. I evade them, slip out of them, knowing there's only one Mira whom I've really loved. Whom I knew how to love. Did I really know? The paintings I will paint are already painted inside me. On the walls of my consciousness. The choking was always a momentary reminder that it was also death that I knew when I was still a baby. How does one return to this forbidden region. Will words be able to create for me this sweet and bitter moment. The words will pass beside it. They won't touch. Paintings have died for me. What's left. Ansberg chews a straw. A man yells, *Veissen kesslach! Veissen kesslach!* On a cart, with a face of distant days. Fragments of sky between houses as in a jigsaw puzzle. And Washingtons spreading disciplined fingers to the sky. Women on balconies knitting jackets for death. Philip the Second, King of Spain, sits in a house filled with funeral accessories. His rooms are sarcophagi. On the way to the prayer house lies his coffin. Always ready. Dressed in black walking to mass. Equipped with all the necessary apparatus. The monks at Latrun don't speak. They only whisper to each other all the time: Remember death! Remember death! Aminadav in the coffin. He is not mourned! Born, born to his death. Mother smiles. Here is my child. May he fulfill my desires. He'll do everything I didn't do. And my father smashes his violin for me and expects me to be Wilhelm Meister. Not to challenge fate. What will I do, what will Aminadav do on the day he is born. Like all real strangers, I seek connections. Here Father stood. Here Father still stands. I was born and here I go on being born. I died and I continue dying. We found a girl's exercise book. On the ground. In the yard of the Freund Hospital. Worms had gnawed the exercise book. It was old and yellow. Hidden pimples of puberty between the words. We leaf through it. Ansberg's ascetic face. A true monk. What dedication. We sit on two limestone slabs. Soon the quick hasty twilight of Eretz Israel will descend on us. I said to Ansberg that I feel like Fang.

He doesn't know who Fang is. He wants to leaf through the exercise book. I tell him about Fang.

Fang was a Chinese policeman. He brought a prisoner from a village to Shanghai. They walked all day and evening came. They sat down to rest at the outskirts of a forest. Near the mountains. The prisoner was tall and bald. Like all the prisoners in China. Tied with ropes. Fang, who liked a drink, wanted a drink. But he's a policeman. The prisoner's eyes are closed. Fang thinks: Why not. The prisoner will fall asleep. I'll drink a little wine and I'll feel good. He waited until the prisoner closed his eyes, took out the bottle he kept in his bag and drank it all down in one gulp. He got drunk and fell asleep. The prisoner got up. He undid the ropes. He shaved Fang's head. He tied him with the ropes and fled. In the morning Fang awoke. He saw that he was alone. He rubbed his head because a cold wind blew against his bald head, and discovered that he was bald. He rubbed his neck because he felt something strange hanging around it, and felt the ropes. He smiled and said, What luck that the prisoner hasn't escaped, but where am I. Ansberg laughs. The Complete Works of Charlie Chan, Volume Five. Ansberg wants to know why the prisoner didn't kill Fang. I have no answer that might be satisfactory. During the war I was at the head of a large convoy. Behind me drove armored cars with blackened lights. Before me was a mystery. To lead a nation to the besieged Jerusalem. Fear, a marvelous curiosity and a very dark night. Full of mines. And now in reverse, the same road but backward, from the mines on the way to the pure and the clean. I came, I said to Ansberg, to try in some way to paint this place.

Not to paint, something like painting, not painting, to understand.

To write.

No. Why does a consciencist leave a wife and daughter and come to the cradle of his childhood. Why did he break his paintings.

You broke your paintings.

Into little pieces.

Madman.

Yes. To make a movie. Maybe. A movie about the day of my birth.

How does one photograph in advance.

I don't know.

And you know how to make movies.

No.

And you have money.

No.

And you want to.

Very much.

I'll help you.

We left the hospital. If one may dare to say so, different from what we'd been. In the girl's exercise book we read the names of the boys she had loved. She loved Amnon. The next was Amihud. And if not Amihud, then Ehud might do. But not Nahum, she hates Nahum. Ansberg of course decides that she had married Nahum. He, who knows women from behind in the early morning. With his face to the window. In a dark stale-smelling room. With a crumpled nightgown. To wake up to Ansberg's tongs. He accompanied me as far as the El Al Building. We parted deciding to meet again tomorrow. I went to see my father. Who was expecting me. Mother was outside. Next to the pink bushes. She says she worried about me. I said I lost my way. Try and tell her about Ansberg and the Freund Hospital. A doctor sweats with a severe expression on his face. A nurse runs through a corridor with a catheter. My mother speaks about shooting at the northern border. There had been casualties. Our forces had returned fire. The Arabs will divert the sources of the Jordan and we'll be short of water. Beatrice on the border. Waiting for a miracle. She knows there'll be a war. "Our forces returned fire" isn't a war. The Garden of Eden is cracked. Two walls have broken. There's no need for cheap labor. The excavations are in a terrible state. It's sad and cold in the north. They shoot at innocent farmers. They're building the land at the feet of the Hermon. An ancient mountain is Mount Hermon. Beatrice waving the flag of the Lord, thirsting for salvation, and soldiers mount her in turn. With her white breasts, her dimples, the hair in the enchanting place, blond. I want to weave dark intrigues with her, together among the folds of a blanket. Old people bent over sticks. In wheelchairs waiting for their offspring. With a smile ready for the meeting. People shrinking so they can take up less space in the earth. Young nurses passing by in line. A doctor in green, young, with a beard, measuring them through the wheelchairs with catheters hanging and urine dripping. I go into Father's room. His face is to the window. A nurse changes a bag of blood hanging above the bed.

Blood drips into his veins. My mother said, When you go in, kiss him! For my sake, she said, after my face had expressed some amazement. She didn't understand how much I wanted to kiss her and him! The young man beside my father mumbles through his faint. Everything here is slow and quiet. In the window are two tractors, a plane landing and two trees which are no longer dusty. I want to reach my father, to actually touch him. To know what quotation marks I have been to his life. I see the tombstone in his eyes that look at the window and the window is a mirror, and in it I see Aminadav looking at his father, seeing a tombstone

210

in his eyes in the window. I try to imagine a different life. Not for me. For him. Married to a different wife. And she to another man. I would have been born half of me to him and half of me to her. But the smile the two of them could have had. I think of my little dog in Naples. Maybe he could have married her. What a life they might have lived together. She liked artificial flowers, those an Englishwoman had given her in Pompeii after feeding her sardines and kissing her on the mouth. Kisses and artificial flowers. Father's Goethe did not marry Charlotte von Stein the fool's wife but Christina Wulfius, who worked in a factory that made artificial flowers. Father, who often told me about Christina Wulfius, wanted me to be a restorer of paintings if I so much wanted to do something connected with art. Why not repair and restore old paintings. Why not clean off the mold of years. A fine and respected profession, what could be better? For by becoming a restorer I would give, as Goethe had done, legitimization to given conditions! He refused to see me as an artist. He thought I wouldn't have the courage to smash a violin. Why didn't you believe, Father, that I'd have the strength to play a violin? One could say about you, Naftali, that if Goethe were alive today he would have written you. Because, Father, it was Goethe who said that only the law, in distinction from emotion, makes us free men, and therefore *injustice is preferable to disorder.* The subtitle to Goethe's The Sorrows of Young Werther is The Resigners. Oh, resignation, resignation. Resignation that comes not from despair or incapability, degrading defeat or surrender, but a noble inner triumph that comes from the recognition that "it is in contraction that maturity is seen." In the Prologue to Faust Goethe says: "Man errs so long as he aspires." You aspired to harmony! To resignation, Father. You resigned everything. We were all erased. What did you hate most? You aspired to the highest and you knew it was unattainable. What does Faust say about my father: "The blood of human sacrifices has flowed, a night of lamentations and wailing." Goethe sought a total harmony. "Nature, like art, creates forms," he said, and the form is what matters. My father, who framed the demons of others, pushed himself aside, contracted himself, created humble forms, so as to stifle the aspiration inside him. And he found a marvelous and cruel restraint. But the tombstone in his eyes isn't restrained.

For it is nothing but my reflection. Everything that grows organically, says Goethe, is also legitimate because, he said, *frames are produced.* And frames are necessary for the proper development of society, art and life. In that order. The destruction of existing frames is an inestimable disaster. A catastrophe in the process of the universe. An explosion beyond repair. And that's why Schiller said this of him: "Quiet waters but deep."

18

When my mother telephoned her voice was gay. Within ten minutes she'd told me what had happened. Dr. Kovalski is really nice just like I thought and see how Father's condition has improved and there's no point in leaving him in Tel Hashomer Hospital. So we have to take him to a convalescent home and we can actually move him to Gedera. I've pulled all the strings and really, just imagine, they'll accept him into that palace, you have no idea what a wonderful place it is. . . . Sick people get healed just by seeing the building. Everything's so clean and beautiful. And in Gedera too . . . the town where he spent such beautiful years, which he loved so. And my mother ties everything together on one thread. Dr. Neidler his boyhood friend who rescued me from the hands of Dr. Fabrikant has been living in Gedera for many years. The marvelous clinic he opened there. The trees in the yard. The conversations on the way to Meshek Peter. A well in the orchards. And Lili is still there even though the good friend is dead and Mother will be able to sleep at her place two or three nights a week and together they'll go to see Father. The joy in her voice. I felt relieved.

Mother sat beside him in the ambulance. I drove behind them. Is he thinking now. Thoughts more profound than we can imagine?

Gedera and sabra hedges. Orchards with orange oranges. Down a side road, to take father to the palace. Old houses surrounded by thick trees. Acacias and bougainvillaeas, cypresses and margosas. In the distance naked almond tress, black, *badim badim*. Don't pick up hitchhikers. I think of his eyes in the window of the ambulance. Mother drips honey into his veins. Is he nourished. We arrive and here's Aminadav looking at the castle that was built on a lovely hill surrounded by pine trees. Beyond the hospital are fields and beyond them hills and mountains and sky. From within the mountains. Spread out. The building commands a landscape but is not a part of it. Nurses in short skirts wash old people. With fallen faces, like mummies. A man prays, the skin stuck to his bones. Yellow faces and white pajamas. White walls and wheelchairs. Mother speaks with the head doctor. I kissed Father, who wept or laughed. They sat him up in a bed. They tied a catheter to him. A man with brain paralysis moved his head from side to side like a mechanical doll. A woman sat on a chair and smiled. Who are you, she asked.

I said, Sussetz.

She said, you have the bed of the man who died during the night.

I said, I don't know.

She had a clear bright voice, something with alternating sharp and soft syllables, and polished gutturals.

I asked her if she's from Rosh Pina.

She said, Very close, from Metullah, and how did I know.

I said, It's a secret.

She laughed, exposing false teeth.

A corridor and nurses pouring medicines into tiny saucers. A male nurse leads an old man, his head lolling. He mumbles. And the woman says in a different tone, her face a mask of sudden opacity, Every night they die here. Don't bring a healthy person here!

I left my mother at the hospital entrance. She'd sit in the corridor. She'd wait. She doesn't trust anyone. She'll watch in awe for millimetric improvements. She'll count the snores. She'll wait like a serpent, for awakening. She'll be merciful and she'll sacrifice her life. She loves him. Maybe because he lets her call him My Naftali. A little tenderness, nu. I drove to Tel Aviv. The girl I picked up asked if I didn't mind if she slept. I said no. She slept with her mouth open and the sound of her slight snoring blended with the Light Program which sold me washing machines and fruit juice. On the news they said that there was again tension at the northern border. In Belgium a baby had been born with its twin's head stuck to its chest. The operation had been successful. And then, in the space of five minutes, they told the people of Israel the life story of Voltaire. Of the five minutes two and a half were devoted to the subject of Voltaire and the Jews. It started raining.

The rain was heavy. The wind blew mountains of water. Cars slithered. My hitchhiker slept. The breaths were rapid. Vapor rose from her mouth. The windows were closed. The car filled with vapor. Aminadav could have resigned, could have given up about proving something that is nothing, but I didn't. The gutters howled. A washed city, a girl hitchhiker from the air force, snoring slightly. Clouds flying quickly. Trees praying in the wind. I went into my house and my neighbor brought chocolate and tea in a Thermos. He looked at his watch when I left the house. Measuring my hours.

Scene:

Aminadav, come to Father . . . here, sit here. I brought you a globe for your birthday. It's not my birthday today, Father.

But you've just finished the fifth grade.

The seventh!

A nice globe, isn't it?

In what language is it?

Greek.

What will I do with Greek?

Don't you learn Greek?

No, nor Latin, Father.

I didn't know.

Only Hebrew and English, Father.

Good, well then, in any case, here you are.

Thanks, Father.

215

I drank tea from the thermos. My neighbor observes my lips drinking. I phoned Gedera. To hear from Mother that Father's getting acclimatized. When he dies you'll get messages from the next world: He's on his way, he's passed the gate, the Angel Gabriel is registering him, he's gone inside, he's beside the footstool of the Throne, hop, he's gone past it, he's walking among people, more beautiful than all of them, intelligent, they know, they bow to him, he's sitting down, he's *acclimatized,* Ami. I slammed down the phone. And said to my neighbor, The troubles of raising parents! The man with the gold teeth who had left his "there" laughed.

Somebody rang and asked if Father had been transferred to Gedera. I said that the place is marvelous, the landscape fascinating, the treatment excellent, his bed is beside a window, and he's getting acclimatized. Ah, what a man he was, said the other end of the telephone.

I said that he still is.

The Ford started up at once, despite the wetness. I waited awhile for it to warm up.

Children walking, schoolbags on their heads. Aminadav always used to get to school first, with his schoolbag on his head. In races by the beach. I drove to town. I parked the Ford in Ranak Street. My father was born in the city of the Ranak, Rabbi Nachman Krochmal. My grandfather discovered his long-neglected grave. In Tarnopol. Once we planted trees in this street. I walked up to one of the trees and measured myself. My mother had planted trees in Keren Kayemeth Boulevard. Everyone here enters eternity with a tree in his hand. I go into the Café Vered and Nadiv Israeli who's waiting for me is quite a funny man. He's shaking his head all the time as if in disbelief. As if to say, you came back and I didn't know. Really, how can that be . . . maybe you haven't come back. After all, is there something that Nadiv doesn't know. No, no, there'll be no war this year and not next year either. Look, he says, it's true that things aren't so quiet up north, but the Egyptians are quiet and we have no interest in a war with Syria alone. . . . The Jordanians aren't moving because they're afraid to make a move. . . . Don't worry. The Russians don't want a war and they're putting pressure on the Egyptians. The Americans don't want a second front on top of Vietnam and they're putting pressure on us. The forces on both sides are too strong for just a war. That's why there'll be no war. At least not in the next few years . . .

As against his confidence and assurances I had only the word of the Dutchwoman of the orange yolks. Try to put up facts against the prophecy of a madwoman from Houston Texas. The Dutchwoman's more naïve than Nadiv Israeli, but something about her makes me put my trust in her more than in him. As if wars are determined by rational causes. Last night I'd rung Nadiv. Since then he's been laughing.

This is Aminadav.

No.

Aminadav Sussetz.

You're kidding.

How are you, Nadiv.

You make me laugh. When did you arrive?

A week ago.

Now you tell me. It can't be. I didn't know. Rina, Rina, Amina-dav's here (I hear him say to his wife). The bastard didn't tell me. . . .

I heard her laughing. As if he'd told her once more about Cohen the spy. Rina who was my girlfriend in the eighth grade. We slept next to each other in the youth movement hut. And it was cold. And I played with her. And she with me. And it was dark. Her face in the window and my face on her. She was afraid to look. The pretty fresh nipples she had.

And then Nadiv came, in the second year of high school, and he told her that she was unique and beautiful. She waited for me to say something real. What could the son of Naftali say? Already in seventh grade she knew that she'd get married the moment she could. She wanted a home and walls. Her youth she wasted on dreams of being grown up. Always living in the future. Why didn't our sages say that he who doesn't live on the Sabbath doesn't live on the Sabbath. We were children and she wanted explicit things. I quoted one of Rachel's poems to her. We were on a trip to the Gilboa. The mountains of Gilboa with dew and rain. It was hot. We sat on a rock. The sun blazed down. And she said, Ami, what'll be. I quoted: "Atop the mountains I'll yell out loud, hooray for youth, and an echo replies!" As a parting gift she gave me a picture, and on the back of it she wrote For Labor and Self-Realization, For Kibbutz and Hachshara.

And Nadiv married her. He wrote me a letter to Paris. Then to America. Then the two of them wrote that they'd called their firstborn after me. But we call him Ami, they wrote apologetically. Afterward Nadiv left the kibbutz and came to town. They bought a broom and a small one-room apartment. Later they increased it to two rooms. And then they lived in a hut and Nadiv built a house. And sold it. And then they bought that villa. And after a deal with the government there came the first car and then the second one. Then the journeys overseas. When Nadiv came to America with Rina dressed like Mira's mother. She went shopping at Macy's and I introduced him to a chick in the Cider Bar. He took the chick out and told her that his name was Yaacov Perah-harim, Mountain-flower. She laughed, because I'd told her that his name was Nadiv. He went up to her room and she stood by the fireplace, she told me later, weaving a wreath of flowers. He stood in the doorway and yelled, I'm going to screw you tonight! He gazed into her eyes with a Gary Cooper look and she burst out laughing. Afterward he went to a striptease show on Fifty-second Street and told me that Rina's sexier.

Nadiv becomes serious when you talk about money. He claims that the recession will heal the economy. And I understand from what he says that his situation is good. When he speaks you hear a man talking about his home. These roots. With a floral American shirt and cultivated sideburns and the smile of a man who was born mature.

He heard me out and said, To make a movie of twenty to thirty minutes in color, thirty-five millimeter—actually I don't know why not sixteen millimeter and not in color but you were always a bit crazy—you need to invest at least thirty thousand lira. And that's a modest estimate. What do you want to make a movie for.

Just like that.

Just like that isn't an answer.

I think about Nadiv who was my friend, his cold face, his clothes that look bought even after he's worn them. The smile that looks like it'll turn into a drawn sword. His obedience to some distant pulse, to a basic disinterestedness. I said to him, I want to make a movie. I had a terrible year in New York. Can Nadiv know what those bitter days were when I wanted to be a painter, he knows that Aminadav sits in New York and paints naked chicks. He fucks bodies from Birmingham Alabama. During the year in which you diverted sources and built an empire of air, Nadiv, I walked hungry in the great city called New York and did a painting of Charlie Parker. His face was tormented in the painting.

Nadiv finishes his coffee. He wipes his lips. The practical face from my childhood now extended, he gives me wise and practical advice. My whole life is wonder about Aminadavs who want so much, wonder about Aminadavs who died at night and woke up in the morning new.

I did a pretty ugly thing (Nadiv made the suggestion and I accepted it gladly). I mortgaged my house. After I'd done it I told Mother. In Gedera. In the yard. Next to Father in his wheelchair. Her ascetic face smiled a bitter smile and she said, Speak with Father. We bought your house together.

But how did you talk about it, he was already sick.

In his name. I spoke with him and he agreed.

But he doesn't understand and doesn't . . .

Aminadav!

I look at the landscape and say nothing. Then I told him that I need money urgently. Something important. To save my soul. A bitter smile on Mother's lips. I said that the tombstone in his eyes is my birth. That's how I feel. I don't understand why. It was from there that the plea reached me. It stemmed from there. His eyes gleam. Do they withhold tears. Outside there was a rainbow. And the world was bright. The green very green, and the red on the bougainvillaeas so very red.

Later we brought Father back to his bed and the woman from

219

the next room said in a Galilean accent, Ah, you're the son of the man in the bed of the dead!

What can one expect from you, Aminadav, said Mother, just don't sell yourself cheap. I calmed her. If someone were to offer me a hundred lira for myself she'd know someone who'd buy for a hundred and ten. Two days ago I bought another heater. First of all she scolded. I said, Mother, I'm a grown man, and I can heat the corridor too if I want to. She explained that at her place she had just one heater going and that's more than enough. And she's older than me. When Father was healthy, she said, we hardly ever used even the one heater. I said that I was born old and she answered that I was born beautiful and strong, I weighed three and a half kilos and there was hair on my head and everyone was amazed. Then she asked me how much the heater cost.

Later on she phoned and said, I just happened to go into a shop, and I asked, just like that, and you know how much a heater like that costs? And she quoted a figure. Twelve lira less! She can get shoes for the price of a matchbox. When I was little I bought a bargain. A Mickey Mouse watch for two shillings. She was shocked. The next day she showed me a Mickey Mouse watch and said half a shilling! But the salesman said two and a half. She had ways of her own. Why do I do things like that to her. Buying expensive heaters, wasting money, when *Father's so sick and there's no knowing what might happen.* And I wanted her to say to me to forget about the movie. She didn't. That too is revenge. Who'll say it to me. Mira and Naomi are so far away. I sense them through the distances, I touch them. To take revenge on myself. And there are so many people wanting to help you. Whom will I tell. My neighbor . . . My neighbor writes poems in Yiddish about Buchenwald. Before they went to Buchenwald, they were taken to a high school. To the gymnasium. And there they were beaten with sticks. They broke his ribs. And then they took his daughters. Since then he hasn't seen them. But he doesn't reproach me. He won't be the one to brand me with enlightened guilt. Which is why Mother was able to say several days later, I bought him a house. I kept his father alive for his sake! . . . I'm also financing the movie he's making. The movie about me! And

220

so you think, Lifshe (my aunt), that he'll invite me to see the movie when he finishes it? Wait and see!

The movie too she financed for me.

The studio manager had heard about me. The studio will be glad to enter into a partnership, after the initial investment. Editing, machine plus editor, sync, developing! For fifty percent of the take. He picked his teeth with a broken match and looked at me. Thick-fleshed and smiling, with a thin mustache and side-burns and receding hair. He doesn't know that I remember how he ran in the Jerusalem hills, after the Kastel, in a state of shock. He screamed, They're screwing us! And he wept into the mountain rocks gleaming in the remorseless sun. He refused to move. They had to drag him off by force. He cried and beat his head against a soldier who was dragging him. Once we sat on a mountain. There was a dead man there. In his coat there were cigarettes. I took out the pack and found two cigarettes. I lit one for myself and one for him and he refused. I smoked. After the war he published memorial books on Amos and Nahum and sold them with a big publicity campaign. I was in Paris. I sent him a letter and on it I drew a burning cigarette and a vulture. He didn't answer.

I told him that I wanted to make a movie for myself only.

What do you mean, for yourself only. He took the match out from between his teeth. To ferret among the heaps of paper. On the table. To discover any secrets. Just like I say, for myself! I'll show it to four people. To myself, my father, Mr. Ansberg from the Government Bureau of Statistics and whoever edits the movie.

A fat man, yes, to say it simply, fat! In the mountains he was a thin melancholy boy. He had grown in width and gone to fat. The fat man extinguished his eyes. Wasting his time with Amina-dav. He grumbled under his breath: A man's wishes are his own. *Want want*, Father. If you bring money we'll make a movie, if you don't we won't. No partnership under such conditions. I'm sure you understand. And he meant, Why don't you go. Can't you see I'm busy. Phone calls to two secretaries. To bring fruit juice and coffee. How many? One coffee and one fruit juice. For me!

The hell with it, not for Aminadav. Sussetz . . . I don't want to know. Then he got up, and sat down again. What will you do with the movie, he asked, his eyes piercing me out of the mountains of fat, after you've shown it to your father and Mr.—

Ansberg.

And Mr. Ansberg, and yourself and the editor. What the hell will you do with the movie.

I'll burn it.

You say I'll burn it as if one burns films today. They're not celluloid and they don't burn.

So I'll bury it.

Why.

Because that's how I want it.

It'll cost you a fortune.

The vanity of mammon.

That's nice. I'm dying for a laugh. Bring me medicine. Listen, I know you from someplace.

Yes.

Where.

In the war.

You were in the Fourth.

Yes.

And we saw each other.

Yes.

When. I don't remember. Only the name. I read about you in the papers. I don't remember what.

On the Kastel.

Ah.

And afterward in the mountains. There was a dead man with a cigarette. You didn't want to smoke.

I don't remember. Who was the dead man.

I don't remember.

From the regiment.

I suppose so.

And you'll burn the movie.

You said it won't burn.

You'll bury it.

222

Yes.

You're funny. Even if we were in the same regiment. Despite the fact. You understand, I have sentiments too. If you want help, look . . . you think I'm a bad man. There's a recession on. I have a studio. I pay wages whether we make movies or not. I have to pay them. So it's hard. . . . If the situation were different I'd make allowances. . . . It isn't every day . . . you understand. The regiment . . . that was something. That war . . . See, we've built a state. But what . . . Shit! Everything's got messed up. Why. How can one know. Maybe sixty years isn't enough. Now there's jokes about who's going to be the last to put out the light at Lydda. Eshkol says we have to build the country quickly and get the hell out of here. . . . So what went wrong. The wind has gone out of the sails. Everybody's become shit. Nobody gives a damn. You know, they want washing machines and cars. And the Arabs . . . they'll come. What we need now is just one war. See how everything's starting to move. We'll win as usual. And then they'll start making war movies. Then there'll be something to do. People will get up for us in the buses. Things will happen, this farshtunkene state needs a war every few years and then they'll make movies here and I'll have what to pay with and to help a man who wants to make a movie to bury.

There'll be one!

When.

In another few months.

What're you talking about. Who said so—Nadiv?

No. Nadiv thinks there won't be a war.

If Nadiv thinks there won't be one, there won't be one.

But I know.

How.

I have my sources.

Who.

A Dutchwoman.

What is she.

I don't know. Believes in horoscopes. Travels around the world. She has money. She knows about orange yolks. She has a magnificent ass.

That's something else. But Nadiv knows. What's this Dutch-woman stuff. Listen, maybe she's a spy.

I go outside. If I only knew how to steal. *Badim badim.* How.

My city. Drainpipes wailing. City sealed to me. Her stepson who has returned. Father, a great darkness. A tombstone glowing from his eyes. Sufferings of gods in frames. Who hears.

The rain hadn't stopped. Ansberg stood pressed against the paling of the esplanade which was washed with water. He got into the car and dirtied it with muddy water. His movements were clumsy, like those of one who occupies himself with deep thoughts. Last night I was at a baroness's, he says.

Did the baron go out to work at five in the morning?

He works at Tnuva. A porter, I think.

I wiped the windshield, to clean off the vapor sticking to it.

Five mornings I watched him. He has a sensitive face, Ami. The baroness is something rare. . . . It was monotonous and pleasant. From behind her, I slid into her and she started trem-bling. Do you think that all baronesses cry when . . .

I don't know any baronesses!

Oh, men of conscience sleep with baronesses, that's a known fact, he said. And quiet women prefer love with a little touch of violence. They love to surrender. They want to surrender. The struggle they put up . . . There was a window there. In the window it was raining. I thought of you, Aminadav.

It rained for four days. Then it cleared up. Ansberg sells post-cards. Thinks of me in baronesses' houses. Mother waits with a face of pain. Father peers through a window and stammers. *Danke schön,* he said yesterday. The studio manager waits for me. With his editing girl and editing machine. What I lack is money and a point of departure. I sat in libraries and read about the day on which I was born. Ansberg helps me. But the money from the mortgage sale isn't enough. Anyone with a life like this one doesn't need dreams. Ansberg tells me about windows and gentle women and in the window lies Aminadav, the man of conscience he could have been. On the roof of a house stood a boy flying a big balloon. Ansberg examines the windows so as to familiarize himself with a new area of yearning women. I went up to the roof because the boy was standing there. In the house where lived the girl with plaits who played the piano and her father caressed her hair. And wrote books that nobody read. The trees had grown too. One of the trees had been planted by Hadassah Klemenovitz on the day she heard that her brother had been killed in the riots of '37. And the tree was called Amihai. My people lives. The balloon was as large as a cow. The boy told me he'd bought it in a shop that imports goods from Japan. I have a weakness for Japanese things. I like Japanese lampshades. Zen. Samurai and Japanese movies. The boy said there are three balloons as big as this one. And they're filled with hydrogen. I wanted to fly a balloon. A balloon as large as a cow. I bought a balloon and went up to the roof with Ansberg and flew the balloon. We were gay. I let go of the string and it meandered soft and slow out of sight.

I'd mortgaged my house. I mortgaged my mother's house too. Her terrible smile of Ah, who doesn't know you, Aminadav my son. And the money isn't enough. The Moloch who gnaws inside you mercilessly, incessantly. And now to Café Vered. Nadiv Israeli. Expert at all things. An emporium of things with the face of a fighter. Ansberg with his tired cock inside his pants measures the woman at the espresso machine. You're used to seeing tents rising at the sight of alluring things, not at old women in blue pouring espresso. Nadiv talks with three men. And eats cheesecake. He claims that there aren't better cheesecakes in Israel than the ones at Café Vered. He winked at me. And then he saw Ansberg measuring with the tent between his legs. An expression of disbelief spread across his face.

He furrowed his brow at my friend and brother. I twined my arm around Ansberg. Aminadav, says Ansberg, I have to warn you again, I'm a poor man, without resources. . . . And again I said to him, Your lack be upon me, man.

We sat and ate cheesecake and drank coffee. Ansberg suddenly said that we had incredible merchandise of our own.

Nadiv's willing only to give me names of people. So Ansberg and I cooked up something. I took him to my house. My neighbor saw the car approaching and stood there with a watch in his hand. He saw Ansberg and closed a shutter. Ansberg was carrying a typewriter which we'd hired at Koenigstein's in Allenby. Thirty lira a month. We'd bought a ream of white paper. We would write a movie script based on Ansberg's life: "When they bury you, every minute is terrible." This title was from a conversation in Ansberg's notebooks.

First old man: How come we haven't been seeing you lately?
Second old man: I was in the hospital.
—Sick?
—For the insane.
—Did you go mad?
—Yes.
—And were you saved?
—No.
—What happened?
—I died.
—What's it like to die?
—Cold.
—Why? Isn't it easier?
—When they bury you, every minute is terrible.

And we wrote the story of Ansberg's life. We improved on the story a little, adding some beauty spots here and there. One has to give an Israeli story a little phony splendor, for the truth frightens. The story of Ansberg has to be sleek. We need money. *I* need money. In the story there was Ansberg. With his harelip. But polished. In the form of an allegory, so that the things would be understood by the policemen of Israeli culture. I diverted the story about *badim badim* to Ansberg. He returned the apples. To tell the truth, he deserved that. It is in him that the vision of morality burns, not in me. He became the consciencist I was supposed to be. This meager gift filled me with affection for myself, and forgiveness. And then the obscene postcards in Ha-Yarkon Street. The beatings. Ansberg beaten, taken to the hospital. A beautiful nurse. She likes him. He doesn't know. Whores in yards. He standing on the esplanade and noting down fornications in natural colors on our seafront. Weeping over the loss of the beautiful days. The Casino that was. Ginati-Yam. People in

227

suits who loved songs. Daring loves in the mornings. Early in the morning, creeping into warm beds. Opening doors with a skeleton key. Wearing slippers made of elephant hide. Pouring love upon wretched women, who love their husbands who stand in line waiting for their bus. The error. The girl who screamed. The prison. Teaching mathematics to hard embittered men. How they love him, suddenly, and, for the ending, a nice winter's day. Ansberg walking in the street. A woman meets him. He doesn't know her because he never sees their faces. She's been looking for him. She *knew*. It wasn't her husband that she loved. Ansberg objects. He says that I'm falsifying, but I am adamant. The woman, facing Ansberg with his monk's face. She says she has looked for him. She loves only him. All his life he has wanted to love with laughter and the light on. Early in the morning. In the light and with laughter. And now she wants too. She loves. The dawn breaks. A new day. She smiles. In bed. Or on the grass. Or on the beach. In summer. Early morning. Chilly. Fresh. And on the smile THE END.

He thinks they'll smell the phoniness from miles away.

He's wrong.

And then he asked, If so, then why the name. What's the name got to do with the story. I said to him, Ansberg, with all due respect to you and your great experience in love, which of us has been married, you or I? And I told him what a nightmare marriage could be. Sigrid, Queen of ancient Norway, I told him, invited all her vassal kings to a feast in her palace, and when they had eaten and drunk she set the building on fire. She said, That'll teach my petty kings what it means to court Sigrid Queen of Norway. Ansberg, who loves women from behind, in the dark, and doesn't know their faces, bows his head to my experience. I move with my mind's eye toward Mira. It was beautiful being married to you. But everything gets so confused, Mira. Ansberg says, I see you really know the Sigrids in and out. And that was some compliment from the great lover of the century.

Nadiv gave me a list of film producers. He phoned them and sang our praises. As if we were merchandise. When we saw Producer A we were a trifle embarrassed. We hinted at a scandal that

228

would arise and gather steam. And he immediately saw the potential. That must be said to his credit. He bent over and stroked a row of colored felt pens. There was talk of interviewing some of the women . . . and a thorough treatment of gossip column writers. We signed a contract for a film script we would write and we received money for the rights on the story. Not bad.

Before we went to Producer B, we drove to the Acropolis Bar. HaYarkon Street. A man comes outside in driving rain. What do you want here. Ansberg whispers something in his ear. After five minutes a silver-haired man comes out of the bar and embraces Ansberg. A pale thin face like those you find in libraries, wearing spirituality and a gray suit. The burglar, who was Mr. Adler, likes Ansberg with an almost physical affection. He calls him Teacher. He said, So listen, Teacher, I don't mind. . . . It sounds funny. . . . I don't want no money. . . . No favors . . . I owe the Teacher a lot. . . . Those were fucking awful days in jail and he taught me. . . . I didn't know a thing about mathematics and things. . . . You think I don't know now?

And then a beautiful local girl came out with a floral skirt and a short fur coat and he kissed her on the face. And thus Mr. Adler became an Israeli writer from the United States who had just come back. He had written two scripts for MGM. I taught him to drop names with expertise. Ansberg says that Adler can learn with devilish speed. Producer B was no less excited than Producer A. Now there was talk of an international market. Tax rebates, a budget of five hundred thousand lira. Sync. An editor. Two cameramen: Greenberg or Goldberg. Impressive prospects. In addition to a high advance payment we were hired as experts. I as art expert, Ansberg as authenticity expert. I didn't go. So as to maintain an alibi. Consciencist. Adler spoke in my name.

Adler said, What a pity that there won't be a war, because if there'll be a war, he said, and we win the war and we get caught, there'll be an amnesty.

I thought of Beatrice. Bring me a little war. Break a wall in the Garden of Eden. So we can get an amnesty.

The money was in my hands. Father's in Gedera. Mother's crying Give Give. I'm with my nakedness. Late at night. No pictures to smash anymore. The movie hasn't been made yet. Nothing to burn. And there was the smell of smoke. From the Ta'as factory, not far from my house, a heavy gray cloud hanging on the night. Two heaters burned in my house. I almost burst from self-hatred and self-pity. I drank cocoa. Then cognac. Which entered the throat like a polished sword. Then I mixed a little olive oil and lemon into a container of sour milk, and ate it while nibbling at a clove of garlic. I dialed the overseas operator with the taste of garlic in my mouth. My sweet little girl in the pajamas with elephants on them answered. Who's there?

She sounded alarmed. I said, It's me, Daddy, sweetie . . . how are you?

She said, Daddy . . . Daddy!

I said to her, Let me talk to Mommy. Afterward I'll talk with you, my love. She was silent for a moment and then said again, Daddy . . . it's Daddy!

Hurry Naomi.

Where are you? Come home. I'm sculpting, with Plasticine. You want me to read you a poem? Granny brought me a paper house. And I'm doing puzzles. I know how to write Aminadav.

Give me Mommy, sweetie. It's nice, what you're saying. . . .

She started crying and Mira took the receiver from her. Her voice, I know the tones of her voice. She wanted to know what's with me . . . what am I doing . . . how . . . I'm speaking from our house. Near Tel Aviv. It's a nice house, I said, with a bed for Naomi and a lovely room for us. Windows facing a palm tree and lawns and the sharp smell of pines. I . . . Mira . . . I'm making . . . a movie . . . about myself!

A silence. I heard her breathing, thousands of miles away breathing in and out into a strange and distant city. I wanted to ask, What's new in Central Park. Is it snowing. Is steam rising from the carriages at the entrance to the park. Have they arrested all the robbers. Is Fifty-seventh Street celebrating noble winter days beside the Russian Tea Room. Does the line outside Carnegie Hall extend forever. Have they caught hares and jaguars in the Black Mountains. And Mira said, Very interesting. . . . Naomi doesn't stop asking about you. What's going to happen, Ami. The last words she said hurriedly, as if she hadn't wanted to say them.

Mira, a terrible thing happened to me. I felt that I was finished, that the failure was grave, and I came home. I had to come alone. To fill a vacuum and to wait for you two. I'm searching for who I was. I'm searching to know Aminadav. When I find I'll know or I won't know. What? What will I know? Are you still so beautiful, Mira? . . . I want to touch you, to embrace you.

I cry a lot, Aminadav. Everyone calls, they ask where you are; Mr. Zwiegel calls every day. At ten-thirty . . . What should I tell them?

What are you really asking, Mira?

We have no money, Ami. Your flight, I thought it was from me. I knew it wasn't . . . but somehow you lose your self-confidence. What should I tell Naomi?

Mira.

And to listen to my father tell me that he always knew you were like that and here's the proof. . . . It's hard. And he wants Naomi to hear. And I'm terribly afraid. That she'll listen and think that . . .

I just had to go.

Don't worry, Ami, she said after a short pause. And her voice changed suddenly. I've got a chance for a job . . . that is, there's a job . . . but it's strange and new to me. And I—miss you.

Me too, I said. But I have to be alone—for a while. You understand?

Yes, Ami.

There are things, I can't explain them in a Transatlantic call. . . . My father's very sick, Mira. I didn't know because I didn't open my mother's letters. They're probably still on the telephone table in the corridor, Mira. He doesn't know me.

There was another silence and I heard Naomi yearning to speak.

I'm sorry, Ami.

Mira, everything was a lie . . . an invented biography. Tiberias and all the rest . . . You understand. You always knew. *I wanted to have been born different.* Now I'm examining my real birth. . . . I'm looking for Aminadav in the place where it hurts to be Aminadav. When I was a boy they thought I'd be a consciencist.

231

A what?

A consciencist. From the word conscience.

I heard Transatlantic chirrupings. Waves, maybe ocean waves. I heard the voice of my daughter in the pajamas with the elephants on them, oh so sweet, and her voice demanding, Mommy, give me, give me. . . .

She took the receiver and said, Daddy Daddy Daddy. And then she cried. Come to us. . . . Mommy hung up a poster of the Beatles. . . .

Mira whispered something and Naomi said, See you later! I'm sending you a kiss. And Mira took the phone from her and said, We're waiting, Ami. If you want us we're always here, waiting.

Thanks, Mira.

I'm sorry about your father.

Thanks, Mira.

Write to me.

I'll write, Mira.

Say something else, will you.

How's the weather there?

Cold. It's snowing today. And there?

Warm. Sometimes it rains. Shooting at the northern border. Do you know what the date is today?

I didn't know.

The eighth of January. Nine years ago today we met for the first time. At Frances Elliott's.

Bye. Give yourself a kiss, and Naomi too.

回回

I sat in the room. Debased and privileged in my own eyes. Thinking of Naomi in the pajamas with the elephants on them. Clean after a bath. My arms embraced air. It hurt in the embraced air. I said to myself MiraNaomiMiraNaomiMiraNaomi in what became an incessant chant. With my right hand I beat the rhythm of MiraNaomiMiraNaomiMiraNaomi, a small fugue MiraNaomiMiraNaomiMiraNaomi.

20

After I'd chosen Bustanai as cameraman for the movie, there remained the problem of the editor. The studio manager said that there was no doubt: Nelly Braun is a bit crazy, but she's the best. For a movie intended for destruction, he said, excellent editing is necessary, and the fat man laughed. But, he added, she's very busy, she's editing Gav Rapp's movie for me, a monumental Israeli movie. The studio manager is expecting an Oscar. And he told me the story of the movie in a few words, noting that a good movie is one that can be told in one sentence: A typical Israeli soldier goes home from the border after receiving divorce leave. On his way to his wife and to the divorce he screws a girl soldier in an army shower room, a woman doctor in her home, a woman sergeant in a helicopter, and then he gets divorced. It's quite a sad and meaningful ending, he said. They showed me some selected rushes and I was one of the select few who saw Gav Rapp naked in a helicopter. The studio manager was very proud. He sweated like all very proud people. To the premiere, he said, they'd invite the chief of staff, the generals, ministers and presidents. I said to him, A premiere of nobs and snobs. He smiled and asked, Are you sure we met over a dead man's cigarette?

Sure, I said.

I don't remember, he said, and smiled again. A world premiere. If it weren't for the army and its generous assistance we wouldn't

233

have been able to make the movie, he said. And all I could think was: Beatrice, my queen of orange yolks, please write to your knowing woman, lest she start a war on the day of the premiere when our chief of staff and all these nobs and snobs will be sitting in the one cinema, will be extending their auspices to their dear Gav Rapp naked in a helicopter.

Meanwhile, said the studio manager, I'll give you Ivria. Deputy editor, and Nelly will be free in about a month.

To meet with Bustanai. To go to Café Vered. And to meet Ivria. Who came wearing a red dress and you immediately liked her. Because her face was round and granted unlimited trust.

Everything came wrapped in invulnerability. Her dress looked as if it hung on a hanger. Her femininity was hidden under the folds. She had no wink or mischief. Everything faded as if on purpose. You don't find her pretty. Her body's too round. She has a virginity lacking in radiance, like a puppy or a singing doll.

To ask her when it'll be possible to rent her. To hear her say, without batting an eyelid, Right away! And then she took a sip of her coffee au lait and asked, As merchandise, may I ask when right away is?

She doesn't hide that she isn't like all the others. And I was glad of that, Mira, even though I said that I don't know all the others. She smiled as if in disbelief. Something nestled inside her and said, Every man knows the others. But she held back from saying it and I respected her for it. Not every nice round woman needs to fall into the trap of bitterness. And so I knew that Ivria came from a good home and, she said, Actually from a religious home, but a poor one. With us, she said again as if warning, it's very important to preserve things.

What things, Ivria.

She didn't say. And I enjoyed the hidden accusation. With a candor that was not lacking in grace she said that she has a revulsion to what she calls the world of the movies, a concept which sounded vague and satanic. Everyone kisses everyone, she said. She spoke with a shyness that didn't lack firmness. Warning me. I don't like flirting, she said, and she has no boyfriend or fiancé. The word fiancé sounded fearful. She doesn't like cheap pleasures. She doesn't go out often. She likes to work hard, for a director who knows what he wants. And again I heard a hidden warning. This severe recession doesn't frighten her. She never goes, she says, to what she calls night dens. She can't stand mutzi-putzi in the editing room. Kisses aren't coffee au lait, she said, and she'll get married only with her husband.

A sweet smile, as defense not only against the world but most of all against herself. She laughs like a bell whose clappers are drunk, my friend Ansberg will say one day. I wanted to kiss her sweet mouth but I never kissed Ivria even once. I thought maybe women from religious homes become pregnant from a kiss. She told me with a smile, but with sad eyes, how she would get married only with her husband. For she knew, with some affable cunning, that it's quite alarming to hear things like that. With a round body like hers, ready for children, ready for all the possible pleasures, beautiful or not beautiful, there is something soft and feminine about her. And it's absurd and perhaps admirable that she's keeping it all for one man. She said to me that it's frightening to marry a strange man.

Ah, the terrible things they do to love . . .

In the night dens?

Everywhere.

I said, Have you any idea what goes on at the beach?

Her sad eyes responded for her.

I try to reach, Mira. At a certain moment. What can be more noble. I calculate my sorrows with the same caution that Father measured the sorrows of others. Most of the time I sit facing the Steenbeck machine. On it I see fragments of the day of my birth. I spoke with Mother. With Aunt Lifshe. With the librarian of Bialik House. With the shopkeeper from whom Father bought bagels. With the landlord in Balfour Street. With the nurse who brought me into the world. I read all the newspapers that came out in Tel Aviv during the week I was born. I went over all the stories and all the items it was possible to glean. I was spread out before my eyes. I made of myself a movie.

235

It was one morning. There or here, I don't know, one way or another, I was with Father. I clove to the Goethean formulation of his being. A nurse gave me a cup of cocoa. Participating in my grief which wasn't as deep as it should have been. In the evening I drank whiskey in a little bar in HaYarkon Street near the old port. A woman sat beside me and drew Mickey Mouses with her lipstick on a small round mirror.

She said, you look like a Taurus, one can see straight away. . . . You're right, I said. What'll we do about it. This whiskey. And she looks at me with a meaningful look and a voice like Tallulah Bankhead's and says, I'm an Aquarius. You know what happens to a Taurus and an Aquarius when they meet?

The Aquarius eats the Taurus or vice versa?

She said that I must be a comedian. Am I professional? Before I answered, into the bar came Amiram Sheloni, the singer of the new hit Stars on a Dark Night, with sideburns and a muscular body. The Aquariuses I lose on these weak nights.

I finished the bottle by myself. Clouds in my head. A thing inflated to infinity. Where am I in all this released tension. It was a powerful and very fine night, like nights of drinking can be. The white Ford floated through the empty city. I thought: Tomorrow I'll see my reflection in the mirror. On the screen. It was nice. I returned home. It was late. I rang my mother, and woke her. I asked her if I can come and see her now. She paused for a while, perhaps she looked at a watch, and said, Aminadav, have you the slightest idea what the time is now?

I said, Four.

She said, Four in the morning, Aminadav!

I said, What's so bad about four in the morning? The cocks are crowing. Milkmen are driving carts pulled by donkeys. There're trucks on the Geha Road. Soldiers are cocking rifles at the northern border and waiting for a command. . . . An enchanted hour, Mother, it's as if the world has been created at this very moment. A kind of light, you know, like the crown of God.

I don't understand you . . . and I'll never understand.

Should I come?

But you don't need to come today, Ami, you came yesterday, and Father was very glad . . . and you took me home and we had some tea. You don't have to come today. The day after tomorrow is your day!

I banged down the phone with something like sudden joy. I have no reason to be sad, I said to myself. I lay down to sleep with my clothes on. It was nice in bed with clothes on. I smiled into the dream that started painting itself in circles. That whiskey. A kind of mental clarity, polite at first and later demanding, impudent even, penetrating inward, into the secret system of internal communications media and in complete darkness. And then I heard the clock. I suddenly didn't know where I was. I thought: Maybe I'm dead. Maybe I'm dreaming I'm alive. Maybe I'm an old man in a prison. Maybe I'm my father on his deathbed. Waiting for that angel. To take me. I peeped at my hands. It was six o'clock. Someone inside me knew I had to get up. My head felt dizzy and a sharp pain pierced my temples. Like Mira, I saw fire inside my closed eyes. I groped my way to the kitchen and put on a kettle. I drank black coffee. I sat in the dark kitchen. The coffee in my hand. It was five minutes after six. It was dark and the milkman was putting milk bottles on my neighbor's doorstep. Soon he'd get to me too. A dog barked from a nearby house and another dog answered him. Children shouted that they were late for school. I stood next to a public park. I saw children playing and I said, Now I'm playing. As if years hadn't passed. The memory was clear and pure. It somewhat soothed the headache which was bothering someone, I didn't know exactly who. My head rang. Sometimes after drinking a bell rings inside your head. This dark kitchen. I must open a window. And cut a tomato. And drink orange juice. Wash my mouth out. There's no need to dress. I'm dressed. I didn't take my clothes off last night. Who was here last night. Who was I. I know people who emit colored smells. A poem of my godfather's came to my mind. The child playing in the public park recited in the monotone of kindergarten teachers:

237

A flower grew in a flowerpot
And he peeps all day at the garden plot
All his friends are merry there
And he alone is standing here

I tried to think of other things. I thought of my neighbor's
daughters. The way they'd become smoke. I thought of the S.S.
men eating omelets and looking at the smoke. I thought of the
beating he got in the gymnasium in the high school building. I
thought of Nahum's brains plastered over me. And myself sitting
with the studio manager somewhere, smoking a dead man's cigarette. I thought of the vultures. None of these thoughts softened
my sadness for the flowerpot. Its loneliness was dreadful. And
then I heard the alarm clock. I got up and looked at the wall. I
wanted to open the window. To feel myself like Fang and make
sure that I was here. That I was me. I was afraid. Maybe an old
man in prison. Tomorrow they'd put me on the pyre. Or tomorrow the judge would pronounce: You will hang by the neck until
your soul leaves your body and may God have mercy on your soul.
My soul, may God have mercy on it, was a pretty wretched thing
in the presence of that lonely flowerpot looking at its friends
growing outside. Will butterflies find their way to it. Bialik was
my godfather. That I remembered. But who was I. Slowly memory returned. Like out of amnesia. That whiskey had penetrated
dark chambers in my brain. And instead of opening them up and
bringing me a wonderful lucidity, it had brought me complete
oblivion. My head buzzed with dull ringings. To take a pill. To
drink tomato juice. To kill the hangover. But I didn't move. I was
a boy and then I knew who the boy was. But I couldn't connect
the boy with the I standing here in the kitchen. Maybe I'm really
an old man awaiting his sentence. But the boy that I was was
bright and clear like a thing engraved on soft skin.

I was a boy, I traveled to visit Uncle Avner in Haifa. In the
afternoon to go up to the Carmel. On the steps of Balfour Street
to sit on a stone. To go farther up. Next to the British army camp.
To see Australian soldiers in broad slouch hats, drunk, next to the

fence. The city spread out before my eyes. The sea below quiet and smooth. Two ships sailed toward the harbor. Looking at flowers around me and seeing how they grow. Rain fell in bursts all that day. Clouds flew about a boy's sky. On the mountain the rain suddenly stopped. The towers of smoke all around the bay started smoking all at once. Defense against Messerschmitts. Smoke from two hundred small gray towers. From the ground now rose with exaggerated slowness some hundreds of huge silver balloons. I knew that the defenders of the city were setting out war, quietly and with restraint. The smoke along the bay. The balloons. They gleamed in the light of the setting sun, looking like enchanted mirrors. A rainbow suddenly stretched across the bay. The two ships sailed slowly on a sea as smooth as oil. The driving rain stopped and started. The sun sank slowly. The smell of flowers washed by sun and rain rose from the fragrant earth. The pine leaves emitted a perfume all their own. Next to Stella Maris walked a long line of nuns dressed in black, draped in cloaks, with white bonnets, walking slowly in the driving rain. They whisper prayers in a monotone and hold palm branches in their hands. The sun in the water. Half of it out. Red like blood. The nuns turn gray. Their song recedes. The balloons glisten in the last of the sun. Behind the clouds a blazing red world burns. Again rain falls. Every drop suddenly larger as through a magnifying glass. The rainbow grew smaller and vanished. The line of nuns passed beyond the arch of the mountain. The flowers started drooping their heads. The smell of rain and moss. The washed leaves. The pine leaves and the sharp resin. The roofs of the city below me. White, red, gleaming in the last of the sunlight. Poured into the bay that smokes with its hundreds of towers. Wearing silvery balloons. This sight is preserved in the mind of the person who stood in the kitchen that morning as the sight of the world *as it should be.* I have always seen this specific sight with all its details as a potentiality that became actual only once in my life, when I was ten, in the year one thousand nine hundred and forty, in Haifa. A line of women appeared in the darkness. Each woman held a candle in her hand. They walked with great weeping

239

toward the grave of the prophet Elijah. And then the memory ends with the darkness lit by the candles in the women's hands. I remember the sight.

My neighbor knocking on the door. That's all I need this morning. Dressed in his usual elegance. To pretend I'm not at home? I owe something to his daughters who remained "there." I got up with a cup of coffee in my hand and opened the door to the sun that burst savagely into the house. He was fresh, one with the blue sky of winter. In his hand was a block of chocolate, as usual, and on his face a dog's plea. I tried to smile. I thought: Here's a man whose life isn't imaginary. A man from the fire. Beside him I'm a boy who returns apples, making a career as a consciencist. The teacher Nehama reads a poem about the heroes hanged by the British. About Hannah and her seven sons. How they stood up to the cruelty of the Greeks. And the children were burned on the pyre. One after the other, and the Chemelnicki pogroms. And Kishinev. And the Slaughter. And Jews on gallows in Mayence. And I in the corridor. By the sea. Yohanan learning anatomy from Rina Faktorovitz on the hills. I standing in the corridor, breaking a coat hanger. And through the door I hear "Heavens if there be a God in you." My neighbor is very grave. This morning he read an article he wrote once for Yad Va-Shem about his daughters. B. B. Bella and Bluma. My head's bursting. We went to sleep very late, he complains, and you weren't home.

Always we. When his wife goes shopping and he meets me by the fence between our two yards he says, We're going shopping. We write for Yad Va-Shem, we're planting a walnut tree. We've become farmers in Eretz Israel, see, we've planted a nice garden. He says, The house is empty and they're not here; or, If you have time come and see us, we're making wooden plaques. How he saw his daughters the last time. His wife buttoned up their coats. It was very cold. She said, Bella and Bluma, tomorrow I'll sew on new buttons. That's what we said to them. There had also been a son. We hid in a bunker. That was after they'd escaped from the camp. And hid. There were ten Jews there. And a rabbi who cried. They whittled something out of wood because there was nothing to do. The girls had been taken away already. The baby was a year old. He cried in the bunker. German soldiers passed through the forest. They marched over the bunker and sat down to rest. They took out food and ate. One of them played a harmonica. Maybe he'd stolen it from a Russian prisoner. My neighbor looks at the closed window. I open it for him and the blue sky bursts in. My baby, not B. B., who went up in smoke, burst out crying. Will you have time to read what I wrote about this for Yad Va-Shem? Ah, the Germans on top of the bunker ate and sang. And the baby cried. They would have discovered us. And then I strangled him.

How does one strangle Naomi, Mira. What would have happened had Naomi been in the bunker with me in her pajamas with elephants on them, with her sweet smile and her white teeth and her wonderful eyes. How does one strangle Naomi pressed to me in her pajamas with elephants. Embracing her father. Crying, not crying. Could I have done it. Ah, since he's been in Israel he lectures on wooden synagogues in Poland. He has a rare collection of photographs of beautiful synagogues built in the sixteenth and seventeenth centuries which were destroyed by the Nazis. Wooden synagogues, with slanting roofs. Lectures organized by the Histadrut, for weary branches, speaking a Yiddish that fears for itself to an audience of aged pensioners. Sometimes ten come, sometimes twenty, the women knit and tears drip from their eyes though their hands don't stop knitting jackets for grandchildren who won't wear such old-fashioned jackets. People nodding their heads all the time in a kind of sadness and a distant light of noble memories lights up in them. We are witness, he said. To those synagogues. They strangled a baby in a bunker. Their wife goes shopping. He brings me chocolate and sweets as if I were a baby. Shows me wooden plaques on which are engraved synagogues from Tarnopol, where my father was born. The two daughters who became smoke. How much suffering can be indifferent in one man. He looks like a cucumber, so fresh, as if nothing has stuck to him, the numbers on his arm, blue, peeking at me, who gave me the right, the numbers ask, like the refined voice of my father.

I finished my coffee and my neighbor went. Measuring on his

watch when you'll go out to work. It's funny that they call what I do work. And could I explain to him. He advises me to give my laundry to Aharan Shemesh and not to Nahum Betzer as I'd done until now. And tomatoes in summer he buys only at Reuven's. And in summer they sell watermelons here as if by eating watermelons the world will be saved. And if I ever want to go with them to Yad Va-Shem they have a good friend there in the library who'll show me and he . . .

I read the morning newspaper that had been left on my doorstep. A tractorist plowing near the northern border had been shot at. Kurazim and Ha-on had been fired on. The prime minister had said on the radio that the book is open and the hand is writing. I saw my neighbor's hand folding with his eyes on the distant, invisible border. His fist clenched. I thought: Unjust . . . My kindergarten teacher Mrs. Kotzelman who said that all Arab children have black eyes, the cigarette slung at the cat, a baby in a bunker, against the threats of Damascus. From the north the evil shall break forth, said my teacher Mr. Erlich. I sat and laughed in the classroom, Grade 6B, and he said *hosheym robeyv ol ov kal*, der Lort ridez upon a svift cloud, and from the north come the wheels of evil. And they pour over upon the Jews. And we have a prayer in the heart. With the *Shulhan Aruk* we offer a neck to the slaughter and sing: Heavens ask mercy for me, or scream: The mountain will evade the judgment. Has the teacher Erlich seen Mount Hermon beside which evil is being designed against innocent plowmen. And what does innocent mean. Is a Hebrew plowman, plowing beside designers of iniquity, evil, is he not a designer of evil, has he not come to inherit. To inherit the land we have come, said the teacher Erlich and then added as if on second thought, to build it and be built by it. From whom at whose expense. And they're threatening in the north. I have no other place. My neighbor's bunker was burned. The Germans peeping through every hole. And there's nowhere else save this rotten border to flee to. To the fragments of Little Tel Aviv. Narghiles and gramophones in the Casino where Mother was elected beauty queen of Judah. And they went to the Workers Club and then there was Cassit and Cancan and the Theater of the Singing Kettle. Streets of sand and sun. Sabra hedges. Father smoking a narghile in an *abbayeh*. He's funny, this *yekke*, they say. A land of *khamsin* and *shus*. Which means a land of heat waves and donkeys. In Ginati-Yam they hear the satirical songs of Avigdor Hameiri. And Alexander Penn is a *halutz* in Mishmar Haemeq. And they create a land in the wilderness. Bedouins on camels. Tel Aviv of the old water tower. Where am I in it. The river is never the same river. I wanted to say to Mira, if she were only beside me, life was not meant for revenge, and certainly not for victory. Where is the life that was not meant for a kind of victory and where is the place where death is not defeat. I rang the studio.

I was told by a sleepy secretary that the editing rooms were all occupied this morning. Because of Gav Rapp's film, you know, the one that's going for an Oscar! I was angry. I started a noisy argument. The secretary switched me to another man, who didn't hear what I said. He just repeated my words like a parrot. I said give me the manager. The manager sounded exultant. He'd received assurances, he told me, he has a friend, the head of something in the army, and this guy had seen rushes of the movie last night, and he said it's a wow, man, it's a bombshell! The best movie ever made in the country! What's an Oscar? The Nobel Prize! And the manager's exultant. So wait another day . . . what difference does it make . . . you understand, Sussetz . . . we're friends and all that. The Fourth Regiment, you're sure we met? A dead man's cigarette and I don't remember.

I'm sure I'm sure.

So tomorrow then.

But I want to work today.

Listen, I've got nothing, so fix something else, Aminadav, a Nobel Prize doesn't come just like that, you know! An Oscar!

And Cannes and Berlin and San Francisco. What do you know. This will make Israel big, it'll give us . . .

I slammed the phone down and marveled at myself. With this awful hangover. This maddening headache. Children strangled in bunkers. Girls becoming smoke, for you count your life as testimony, and you get angry about one day lost in the studio, ah

243

boychik. . . . I phoned Mira. Her voice was old, like my mother she asked, What's the time?

I told her.

Now it's the middle of the night, Ami. . . .

By you. By me it isn't. And afterward you'll be able to sleep, Mira.

Thanks . . .

Don't mention it.

Let me wake up, man. . . . Listen, I'm a working woman, and soon now Naomi will wake up. It's hard enough to sleep in any case, and for her . . .

Mira, you know Naomi's pajamas, the ones with the elephants?

Ami, I have to wake up. You sound drunk. In the morning? That's something new. . . . Let me have a drink of water. And I heard water being sipped thousands of miles away. I know Mira's glass of water, with the sleeping pills, next to the bed, in a direct line with her breasts, she puts out her hand with eyes closed. What's happened, Ami, what exactly has happened, what pajamas?

The ones with the elephants.

What are you on about?

What?

What about the pajamas? They're torn.

When?

Tonight. Naomi tore them. How did you know? Wait, now I'm really waking up. Listen, you know what she did tonight? She took a pair of scissors and cut up the pajamas. From the pieces she made little flags and hung them on her bed. . . . Wait a minute, Ami, how did you know?

I didn't know, Mira. All I wanted to ask you to do was to take a pair of scissors and cut up the pajamas. I wanted the pajamas with the elephants cut up, that's why I phoned. I'm not drunk. But now I'm no longer sure that I'm not drunk. . . .

The tears flowed out of my eyes and softened the headache. Suddenly my head was light and the dizziness passed and there were no bells ringing in my brain. I said to her, I'm crying because I can only hurt those I love. And that's sad, Mira. . . .

244

And then I told Mira that there'd been shooting at the northern border. That the prime minister had said that the book is open and the hand is writing. In Texas they think that there'll be a war in the Middle East. What do you think?

After we'd put down the phone I went outside. My head was clear. I vomited in the yard and watered the garden even though it had rained yesterday.

I drove through the streets. Ivria waited for me at her home. Her mother gave me a cup of tea. We went to a Hungarian restaurant for lunch. I wanted to see Ansberg but perhaps he hadn't received the message I'd left for him at the studio. The restaurant proprietor suggested a Czech cake for dessert. He tried to explain its quality to me and then he said: It's easier to eat the cake than to explain it. We went to a matinee. In the evening to count anguishes at Mother's. To ask about Father's health. To know that he's expecting me. To drive to the hospital in Gedera, to sit beside his bed and say Father Father Father Father. And then to sleep like a stone, legs folded, like a baby.

I went to the studio, Ivria was already at the Steenbeck. She switched off the work light, turned on the lights in the darkroom, in which a strip of light danced in the frames of the blacked-out windows, and said, I didn't sleep all night, Aminadav.

Why, kid.

I'm not a kid.

Baby.

Don't call me baby.

Ivria.

That's better.

Why didn't you sleep.

I thought about you.

That's bad.

Not the way you think.

That's even worse.

I thought why do you need me.

Because I'm a lost child and I need a woman's pity.

No ooey gooey. You have a wife in America and you love her. So don't be smart.

245

She was agitated and paced back and forth in the little room.

I saw things were buzzing inside her. I kept silent and let her speak.

You want to make an experiment, she said. I'm afraid it's going to be too cruel for my liking . . . at least the part where you want to photograph your father and see . . . forgive me the frankness, Aminadav.

It's all right, Ivria.

It's your business. I mean you've got money and you can do what you like, as they say. . . . What I don't understand is the frame. . . .

I smiled.

She looked at me and wondered for a while. She'd lost the thread of her thoughts. Then she remembered: frames! No, that wasn't what she meant. The general framework, Aminadav, look, you could have photographed with an eight-millimeter camera, black-and-white, whatever you wanted. To edit the pieces on a small editing machine, to cut—anyone can do that, there's a splicer and I could have shown you in five minutes how to cut a film and how to stick it together with Scotch tape. The whole thing in five minutes! The movie would have cost you two thousand lira! You'd have put together the fragments, spoken, sung, danced, I don't know what else, you'd have shown the movie to your Mr. Ansberg, your father, and even to the studio manager. Then you'd have cut the movie to pieces and gone to have some iced coffee. What's wrong with that? It's your money. It takes my father three months hard work to earn two thousand lira, but if you want to, O.K. . . . But thirty thousand lira . . . to take a cameraman like Bustanai, the most sensitive cameraman in the country, and an assistant cameraman, to hire zooms, to take a quality sound recorder that costs a fortune, to make a movie in color, with a professional editor and assistant, an editing room with a Steenbeck, in thirty-five millimeter, all for one single screening—hell!

She chain-smokes Broadway cigarettes. She's sweet, dressed in white. White boots. White dress white sweater. Large white glasses on her face as a mask. And her eyes gleam through the glasses.

Look, Aminadav . . .

You can call me Ami.

Look, Ami. One makes a movie in color, in thirty-five millimeter, because one wants to make a movie. So people can see it. It's art, a movie is art, like painting. Not less. And one doesn't make a movie for one day for a sick father and a Mr. Ansberg whoever this Mr. Ansberg may be.

Art!

Yes, art!

Like Gav Rapp fucking girls in a shower in a helicopter and in green fields only because the chief of staff gives his auspices to all that rubbish that makes it art?

Look, I know. But Gav Rapp wanted people to see the movie. He wanted lots of people to see it. . . . So it isn't exactly art. But there has to be good and professional cutting and acting. And good recording. And sync. For art movies and for movies that aren't art. But not for a movie like yours! Look, Kafka didn't write his books so as to burn them.

He wrote because he wanted to burn them, I told her.

Maybe, but that makes no difference. Why won't you understand what I'm trying to say.

I understand very well, Ivria.

Maybe you understand and you seal your ears? Maybe you're not telling me the whole truth? Do you forgive me?

It's all right, Ivria.

Maybe you do want to create?

Now she'd reached some climax, all night she'd been conceiving something, and I saw her eyes, through her glasses, gleaming more than usual, to kiss her eyes and sink myself in her hackneyed charm . . .

Maybe, maybe yes, to create, you . . .

What's happened, Ivria?

I don't know. The words slipped out. Look, maybe you want to take your own private life, which seems to have been a failure,

247

or even really has been, and to try to succeed in the story of your failure?

I went out into the corridor. I drank a glass of cold water. To cover my confusion. To crumble into words. I went back to Ivria. Suddenly I was filled with a frightful savage fury, as if all the polite clothing had been forgotten. My hand rose to slap her but it didn't land. Later Ivria told me that at that moment my eyes had been dark like those of a man exploding. Terrifying, she said. The blow that had almost landed on her was so obvious that at the moment I raised my hand I was conscious of the blow, of the potentiality, as if it had been something physical. Ivria smiled, crumpled a cigarette into an ashtray, and suddenly I was enveloped with a great calm. The change of energy was a cold shower. I beamed at her. My face expanded, I felt. I said to her, Ivria Ivria . . . You see I'm asking for help!

And then I tried evasion. We were in a closed room. Like in the elevator. The choking in the throat. Mr. Herzberg's obituary for me in my veins. I ran through the convoluted streets of my existence, looking for a typewriter, to write a poem to God. Oh, how I wanted to wallow. To be unworthy to live. To be a mirror for what I had never become.

I said to her, Ivria, you mentioned my wife before. . . . I love her very much. More than anyone in the world. But who left her? And why? So as to find Aminadav? And who did I sleep with on the last night before I left her? With my daughter's teacher, Peggy, a very sexy thing, with a body like Brigitte Bardot's, and breasts like Jane Russell's, you know Jane Russell's breasts? And with this magnificent female I ate dinner and went to her home, and under a Buddha, a Shield of David and a crucifix, we made, as they say, love. And Mira, my beloved wife, sat at home and waited for me, for the knight of her life, the joy of her eyes, for the man who had saved her from a life of deception and lies. The man who had given her a gift, a beloved little daughter. Why isn't she here? My beautiful daughter. Damn it . . . I'll die from some stupid shame. Aesthetics! What's more detestable than aesthetics. What's uglier than a beautiful thing. A beautiful thing is true. A true thing is beautiful. That's why destruction is beautiful.

Because it's true. Like a tank. Or a Boeing. Or a screw in a state of exaltation . . . Yes, forgive me, my sweet. I tend to forget, after all, night dens and all that. . . . . I'm seeking Aminadav in the destroyed world. Is Aminadav destroyed? The search is meant to give cover to the loss. But there's no cover and who knows better than I. I have a neighbor who strangled a baby, Ivria, with his own hands he strangled his own son. Who strangled the baby? Goethe? Himmler? What is my father? My sentence, what is my sentence? Failure? A false birth? When is birth false? There's a firm promise by an astrologer, Mrs. Kantorovitz. Can I lodge complaints against her? Or against Mother, or Father? Against whom? I'm asking for help. . . . I had a friend, we called him *badim badim,* I was his closest friend and he didn't know. Is it possible to return apples, Ivria, apples that have been eaten? It's impossible, of course, but I tried.

I pace the floor. Waving my hands. I don't answer her. Her question needles inside me in a kind of sweetness, a kind of passion. I said, Is there a value in suffering? My mother's always suffering, my birth's an infinite suffering that goes on to this very day. . . . And the hopes that they pinned on suffering . . . Twelve churches, Ivria, keep the foreskin of Jesus, among them important churches like the church of Hildesheim and Cologne, to every suffering there must be some value. No? There must be. But there isn't. Is is because isn't isn't. Failure is a value thing. And this valueness is measured by form, by its form a thing works, or exists. . . . Injustice, said my father's Goethe, is preferable to disorder, which is formlessness. Did you know that the hydrogen bomb is a beautiful thing. I try to imagine the man who sat in the plane that dropped the atomic bomb on Hiroshima. He photographed the huge cloud, the dreadful mushroom, landed at his base and went into a darkroom and developed a beautiful picture, he cut, he edited, just like you, Ivria, he contracted and darkened, intensified and made it thrilling, didn't he? The mushroom that killed seventy thousand human beings. And this movie too will be beautiful. That's all. Beautiful for me, not for others. For if for others, then I've surrendered. For then I've continued to rebel against my father, Ivria, and I want to smash my violin quietly

. . . with the lucidity of a man who's weary and wise, a little wisdom won't do any harm. I'm adding up for myself what my life has been, why, how and when. And that will be beautiful, for without the editing, without the beautiful photography, without thirty-five millimeter and color, this miserable movie about Aminadav Sussetz won't be beautiful, and if it won't be beautiful it won't be true and if it won't be true I won't know a thing. I won't understand. Is it possible to learn something from chaos. Only when you put chaos in fetters. And this was beautifully understood by Naftali Sussetz, my dear father. . . . Beautiful is that which cannot be otherwise. And what I'm trying to know is this: Could my first days have been different? Could I have not been born? Socrates studied playing a musical instrument during his last hours. Why? Couldn't he have played badly if he wanted to? But he studied. No, he wanted to attain to a perfection several hours before his death. And can I do this forced and tasteless deed, to photograph my birth thirty-seven years after the event without it being beautiful, unbeautiful, as much as possible? When Horace said, If you want me to cry for you you have to be sad first, he was talking about aesthetics. And that's what we're left with. Bombs, paintings, movies, stories, strangled babies, tears, fire, smoke, God, Satan. All of these are, after all, aesthetics. For they do not exist as such in a reality whatsoever. They were created for the purpose of clarifying things. And that's why, my dear Ivria, I need a good editor and Nelly Braun can stay on Gav Rapp's movie as long as she likes, because my movie's going to be edited only by you.

21

Mrs. Kantorovitz lived in Bilu Street, in an old, even stately house. She wore a blue dress, she'd heard that on television one looks more beautiful in blue. We told her that for a color movie there's no reason to . . . and she smiled cunningly as if she knew. She made up her face, her eyelashes grew longer, her eyes took on a bluish tint, and she refused to be photographed with glasses on. As we photographed we realized that she didn't need them at all. She was looking at me and talking. She read off my face the horoscope she had given my mother one week after I was born. She spoke and we photographed. Bustanai photographs her with love, I can see it on his face. She has a kind of gentleness, innocence, as she leers at Bustanai, who could be her great-grandson, or at least her grandson. She wobbles her hips when she walks to the bathroom. She drinks tea like Madame Pompadour. Crosses her legs and draws up the hem of her dress as if she were a girl of seventeen. And the delighted smile doesn't leave her lips. As if to say, I'm playing something but I'm also living it. I know I'm making a fool of myself but what else have I left.

And thus spake Mrs. Kantorovitz when she read the things off my face: Tel Aviv. May second, nineteen thirty, the fourth of Iyar 5690. One A.M. The gong in the damaged clock in Allenby Street will strike once. In five minutes it will be one o'clock. People will grumble, why isn't the clock mended! Some people have clocks of their own. Look and behold, a child is born. A nervous type. Tense, the influence of Mars and Uranus which means a tendency to high blood pressure and more or less good, though not ideal, health. The dominant planets in Taurus are Venus and Jupiter. Venus is close to Mercury, at the beginning of the House of Gemini. Although the birth is in the sign of Taurus, the Gemini element is very strong (the twenty-sixth degree of Taurus!) and the planet of Gemini is Mercury. Taurus points to a solid temperament, close to reality, but the proximity to Gemini under the influence of Mercury will give the personality an intellectuality which may well be called unique. Venus is in a good (?!) aspect with Mars (sixty degrees) and points to great spiritual energy and alertness. Venus plus Mercury means versatility, interest in various spheres, mainly artistic I would say. A good but disputative character, hyperintellectuality, a capacity for sharp thinking and as a result deep sorrow.

Mercury and Venus are in a negative position with respect to Neptune and that complicates matters. Many artists find themselves in such complications. The complication does not affect the talent but makes the artist's life very chaotic. Sometimes it causes a lack of clarity, in intentions, directions and aspirations, outwardly and inwardly. A situation of insincerity to the surroundings, to others, may arise. A kind of lie, I would say, maybe intensive pretending, very interesting, rich, sometimes bewildering, mostly painful.

For a certain type of artist this kind of condition is thought to be useful. The condition is called "divine discontent." It is a condition that provokes search, quests for new and varied goals. In a practical sense this is not very pleasant. Insincerity and chaos disturb the proper course of life with others.

Between the moon and Uranus, sixty degrees. At the moment of Aminadav's birth the sign of Aquarius was on the horizon and the dominant planet of Aquarius is Uranus. But you know that, no? (She smiled a childish smile, twisting her face like a young girl on the beach toward an approaching Apollo.) What I said points to a good aspect, when the moon and Uranus kiss! That's

252

a situation which helps creative thought, uniqueness, originality, a life full of surprises that's very varied, but it gives little hope of peace of mind and spiritual or personal stability. For Uranus occurs in the sign of Aries together with Mars, which means great impulsiveness, firm power of decision, sometimes too hasty, you need to beware of deviations, of hasty steps. Complicated and unnatural relations with others, inability to make natural ties, long-range friendships doubtful. Respect for others on the one hand, and withdrawal, reservations and extreme inconsideration on the other hand. Yes . . .

Spiritual life aspiring inward. The framework doesn't always matter. Many moments of financial lack and misunderstandings, ups and downs, terrible disorder in life but improvisations which will save every situation at the very last moment.

Despite the versatility, there is a lot of solidity. Seriousness, sometimes as an expression of protest. The sun in a triangle with Saturn produces a similar situation for everybody, because the sun is the center. The sun in the third house points to deep spiritual activity, so does Saturn. Taurus in the third house is in a good aspect with Saturn and endows life with much meaning. Aminadav's sun is in a good aspect with Neptune, which hints at mystical, even religious tendencies. . . .

Venus plus Mercury equivalent, art. Sun plus Pluto are energy. After each failure will come consolidation. Like a doll with a lead bottom. Personal charm mixed with impatience. Inventiveness anchored in much melancholy. Incessant new ideas and an unbearable ferment, a sharp critical sense and a tendency to new techniques and risks, and at the same time a perpetual dread. But Mars in a negative aspect with Saturn means disturbances in the operations of the energy. Sometimes he will be too exhausted. Sometimes he'll be full of energy. Mars is energy; Saturn, caution. These two produce conflicts. There'll be problems with Father! The factor of cruelty toward others and toward himself will be decisive. He'll suffer from a wild imagination. Knowledge of limitations will be a blessing and will bring harmony at a later age. The surrender to the limitations and to the suffering involved in this knowledge will bring a late rebellion which will give a monstrous, even horrifying dimension to the talent which will turn from a way of obstacles to self-realization.

Mrs. Kantorovitz on the screen. She gives a precise description of all the things that have happened in my life. She speaks of a meeting in Naples without mentioning the name of the city. She mentions the apples and *badim badim* without excessive detail, tells about the war and New York, Mira, Naomi, there's nothing she doesn't know. She tells about a man. She doesn't know details. The stars sing her my life. Everything's true and yet isn't true. She smiles. She asks if she was right. I'm not willing to answer her. Everything's true and not true. The details are true, the trees are in their places, but the forest isn't the same forest. She's grasped everything except the failure. Building hills on hills on a flawed foundation and I don't know where exactly this foundation is. She's gaudily painted like a Berlin whore in a painting by George Grosz. Her face is like a clown's. Beads of rouge on her cheeks. She speaks about my life as a program that must come about.

From here, Ivria, I want to cut to Nahlat Binyamin and Yehuda Halevy Streets, the Freund Hospital. I want a bird's-eye view of the city.

Little Tel Aviv from a helicopter looked like a dream that was dreaming me. Shenkin Street crawled, then Balfour, Mazeh, Montefiore, and we got to Yehuda Halevy and Ahuzat Bayit. And thus from the gaudy face of Mrs. Kantorovitz I see on the screen straight into crawling streets from above. Aminadav comes out (quick cut) from the smile of Mrs. Kantorovitz asking What, did it all come about? Am I right? And from the make-up of a beauty queen of Tel Aviv in the year 1929 to Tel Aviv, May second, nineteen thirty. Collage of fragments. Forty-two thousand residents in Tel Aviv. A warm day. A seashore like lacquer. Sand golden and pure. Casino with two weather vanes on its head. Funny, beautiful arches. And balconies like a toy castle. Strong colors. A beauty queen. Vintage nineteen thirty, smiles with a mouthful of snow-white teeth. Shemen toothpaste, destroys microbes! A drum beats, sand sand. Forty-two thousand inhabitants. Jews disembarking from a ship in Jaffa port. An English official in a white pith helmet with a khaki band around its hump gets into a boat. He smiles between the ends of his thin curling mustache. An Arab shines his shoes. The holy land is kissed by an old man dressed in stripes. Close-up: a red sweating face. The burning earth. Barefoot vendors sell *burrechas*. Potatoes. Peppers. Lettuce. Someone strikes some little cups and sells tamarinds. The best there is, *the best there is.*

22,978 rooms in the first Hebrew city. 2,693 trees. Hermann Schapira on a postcard. *The Golden Book of Trees.* Apart from me, in the year 1930, 2,100 babies were born, 510 Jews and one non-Jew died. Where did they bury him. 695 were married, 129 divorced. Not one violin was smashed. An average family's needs for subsistence came to four lira and three hundred mils per month. Sixteen automobile accidents as against 122 bicycle accidents. Twelve abortions.

Cut to a woman screaming. Her face is contorted. A doctor sits beside my mother's bed and reads *Doar Ha-Yom,* the revisionist newspaper. LET US NOT AID THE TROUBLES OF ISRAEL, LET US NOT PUT OUR SPIRITS IN THE HANDS OF THE BOLSHEVIST SATAN. WE SHALL NOT STRIKE ON MAY THE FIRST. The doctor wipes beads of sweat from his revisionist forehead. His eyes burn in anguish for his Jews who are making a fraud of the aspirations of two millennia. Someone yells: *Hebrew immigration!* In the Bata shoe store they laugh in Czechoslovakian. Marvelous Czech shoes pass from hand to hand. Outside people are demonstrating against Bata in blue shirts. *Buy local products!* A woman cries, They tore my shoes, I paid twenty-five piasters, what are they doing to me. A pogrom in Eretz Israel? I want Bata shoes, the best what there is, why they burn my shoes? And people shout at her: *Shame! You should be ashamed!* One hundred and thirty-seven faintings this year, mutters the head doctor of Hadassah hospital with an indifference worthy of note. The head nurse has been in love with him since Odessa. She wrote her mother a letter: "Dear Mother, he's here and I'm here too, but the parallel lines *nekagda* will meet." Only sixteen cases of hysteria in the pioneering city of Mr. Dizengoff, who rides a white stallion, with a good broad face. Out of 11,059 animals slaughtered in Tel Aviv in the year one thousand nine hundred and thirty, there were *only* four buffalo. Every hour zero point eight children are born. My cousin Ahuva and I are one point six humanity. Early draft. I. Publish a notice on the tablet of the heart, seeking connections. Mira cries. Why why. Naomi my daughter dressed in tatters of blue pajamas. No elephants. In the Yom Kippur prayer, I want to read into the film, is written: "Until I was created I was not worthy and now that I have been created it is as if I had not been created. Dust am I in my life, how much more so in my death." Sweet roofs of toy houses. Jews came from Russia and built houses. One of them saw the palace of Graf von something and built himself a miniature palace in Bialik Street. Another saw a castle of noblemen in Germany and built himself a castle in Florentin Street. All the old houses are but castles that have turned into marzipan houses. And how beautiful and sweet they are in their childish innocence. Verandas like tears hanging out to dry on chocolate box houses. Cut to an Arab newspaper, *Al Sarat al Moussoutakim,* the face of an Arab astrologer, a dervish, a big smile shining on his face. Black teeth, turban, dipping a peacock feather into red ink and writing, May the second one thousand nine hundred and thirty according to the count of the infidels! At one o'clock in the morning in Tel Aviv, a Jewish suburb of glorious Jaffa, will be born a king of Israel. His mother will mix water with her milk and he will die of intestinal typhus. . . .

A quiet street. Young trees in Rothschild Boulevard. Slim-figured palms sway in the wind. The sixty-five dentists, eleven dental technicians, fifty-one lawyers and two masseurs of Tel Aviv walk, just like that, spring and all that. Mourning notices on the untimely death of the wife of the father of our city, the exalted lady Zina Dizengoff. A mourning notice flutters in the spring breeze. It tore off the wall of Mr. Donkblum's house, opposite the new municipality building, and flew off. A gray notice. Rain and water will dissolve it, what do they mean by untimely. Aminadav will die of typhus at the age of three. Says the Arab astrologer. And his eyes are black, damn it! Notice, when will they fix the clock in Allenby Street! Will it not come, the mending of the clock? Vote for a workers' municipality! Long live international working-class brotherhood! Long live the revolution! Long live Socialist Zionism! Down with the imperialist exploiters! Mr. Dizengoff our mayor, mourning the untimely death of his wife and giving out candy to children and taking me for a ride on his white horse. The founder of the city. The dreamer of the city. Where to cry this evening?

At the Eden Cinema: The Mad Singer with Al Jolson.

At Gan-Rina: The Burning Volga.

At the Mograhi Opera: The Mysterious Tear.

A procession of shoemakers, demonstrating against imported products. Jewish policemen out of a Buster Keaton movie disperse the demonstrators. The demonstrators yell: Hebrew labor! Hebrew shoes! Down with Bata! Down with Eckstein! And a Hebrew policeman shouts, Chomsky, what's got into you demonstrating here giving me trouble. . . . Go home, Chomsky. We'll talk in the evening. . . . Yesterday when you were sick you weren't ashamed to ask me for an enema and today you're doing this to me! What'll Mashka say. . . . You have children, Buchsbaum, aren't you ashamed of yourself? You're carrying on like a *goy*, Pachovsky. . . .

The soloist Giulini will sing this evening the melody by the late Dr. Mazi for shofar, the famous song by our national poet Imber. To delve into the tissues.

Kisses in Rothschild Boulevard. Scattered weeping, quiet, and cut to . . .

A man hanging in a leather shop.

"Yesterday Mr. Baron, proprietor of a leather shop, hanged himself. It is thought that the suicide is connected with the suicide two weeks ago of one of the owners of the Keter tanning factory.

"The owner of the Keter tannery owed Mr. Baron a considerable sum of money. Feeling deep contrition at his inability to pay his debt, he put an end to his life. When Mr. Baron learned of his debtor's fate and of the reason for his suicide he too felt deep contrition, sank into black despair and put an end to his own life. . . ."

Fragments: The society for climatology and balloonology announces a lecture by Dr. Binyamini on the climatological characteristics of Tel Aviv. On the screen: my father's face. Naftali Sussetz. Still. Thirty-seven years younger. Tomorrow I will be for him. His son, whom he neither expected nor wished for. Why complicate life, it's complicated enough as it is. An enlarged eye pupil, enlarged even more. Birthmarks, gleams, maybe ants are devouring his eyes? Old photography by Susskin. In his eyes there is no tombstone. That appeared one day much later. To make comparisons. Speaking Goethean. The fabulous landscape of the smasher of violins. I see my father's eyes superimposed. A warm spring day. The third of Iyar, May the first, May Day, Arise ye workers from your slumbers, sing Hava Halprin and Leah Ficki, and are fined the sum of seven lira.

A sad young communist girl, golden-haired, blue-eyed, with a neck like a swan's, swims out into the sea. Black flag: swimming forbidden. She asks the sea to take her soul but it can't because her swimming is better than her desire to return to the infinite. And a dark sadness pulses in her. In a playing sea. She sings a delicate Russian song on the sand, in a bathing suit of the thirties.

To kick my mother's belly. From inside. To try to see the world from inside. The world, for me, is sounds. Is food in a tube. Is the inside of my mother's body. The maze of kidneys and liver. The intersections of the veins. I kicked her and my mother said, Listen, he's cute, this stubborn kicker! She thought I wanted to come out from inside her. She didn't know what a blow was awaiting her. Sitting on a tear-shaped balcony in our house in Balfour Street and sending waves of pleading. My father is in the frame shop and C. N. Bialik is beside his worktable. Bialik is elegantly dressed, as usual, an expensive tie, brown suit, checkered, combed, after eating salt fish and drinking lemon tea. A wise face, a carved walking stick in his hand. And he goes out toward my mother's pleading. He walks in the boulevard toward Aminadav who will come into the world shouting. Father pours a fluid resembling gold on a frame for a painting by Hobbema. Suddenly he put on his green corduroy jacket, closed the shop and hurried up Shenkin Street toward Balfour. He stopped at the Tradesmens Center and drank soda water. Saw a flock of birds flying north.

Had his shoes shined at the corner of Ahad Ha'am. Even to Mother's sufferings Father wants to come with his shoes shined. The early spring caresses my father's cheeks and he doesn't know it. Bialik's face glows in the intoxicating spring breeze. A sharp smell of life, of tree resin and foliage. Of a city being built. Houses in frames. Bricks being cut in oblongs. Workers on scaffolds building a homeland. An Arab on a donkey carting vegetables. A blue veil wraps the city for them. And I stopped fluttering. In the midst of Mother's agony. She sits on the balcony, awaiting her loved ones, I scoff at her from inside her. I'm in you and you aren't in me. And very soon now, cut; Father and C. N. Bialik will meet in the boulevard on the corner of Shenkin and the trees drunken with spring. They'll turn right toward the house of S. Ben-Zion and from there to our house.

To photograph things that were a long time ago. A bird laughs inside me. Time is not as real as all that. My father's path from the shop we photographed with the assistance of Ansberg.

At first he said, How can I be your father, with a harelip and a criminal past? But afterward he liked being my father. Bustanai doesn't hide his contempt. I know the mockery of those who see only the end of their nose. Early in the morning the streets are empty. Little Tel Aviv, where we did the photographing, is not very different in the early morning from the Tel Aviv of my childhood.

Only the cars! Karl Netter Street without the stream of cars is still Karl Netter Street. Only the trees are higher, and antennas on the roofs. With Bustanai's help we manage to disguise these defects. To speak about April twenty-ninth, the first of Iyar 5690, thirty-eight hours before I was to be born. Ansberg dressed in my father's clothes walking toward my mother, whose pains have suddenly stopped. I found him a bow tie and he looked so sweet. He shows me his back. And Bustanai photographs from ahead. He reaches the boulevard and meets Bialik with his carved stick. The poet walks with delight toward my mother. Ivria splices fragments to place on the screen: Bialik. Streets of Tel Aviv. Zina Dizengoff who died untimely. A torn poster. A coach and pair make a marvelous pounding of hoofs on asphalt. A model-T car, black, belonging to my uncle Avner, manager of a Barclays Bank branch in Haifa, the city of the world as it could have been. Workers yelling, Hey ho labor, from every care it'll save us, and turning into a doctor, reading *Doar Ha-Yom* Mother waits on the balcony, ashamed that her pains have suddenly stopped. What will she say to her saviors. She feels pity for Bialik and Father. She knows they'll come. She has counted day for day, nine whole months. She counted the hours, 6480 hours, waiting for Aminadav. Learned in sorrows is my mother. Once she was younger. She rode horses in the Jezreel Valley. She sang God will build the Galilee with Young Guards who yelled In blood and fire did Judea fall/In blood and fire will Judea rise by Yaacov Cohen. Fun at nights in the barns. They made coffee and sang How beautiful are the nights in Canaan and said Love there is in the world/Where is my love. Later she returned to Tel Aviv and found a pale man wearing a corduroy jacket smoking a pipe, who read Jean Paul, listened to Haydn, played the mandolin, smashed violins, always wore shined shoes, sought epigrams in the works of Heine, spoke of Cimabue and Cimarosa. At night he sat in an attic room listening to the seven words of Schütz, *Die Sieben Worte Jesu Christi* or *Pouray-je avoir Votre Merci* by Guillaume Dufay and the *Iste Confessor* by Palestrina. The horses roared and she was trapped. The bird my mother was. She waited for him to say to her I'm a man and you're a woman. He looked at her as if she were a wonderful crystal and told her about the tempestuous life of Goethe and said we'll get married on September first. They went and got married, he to a fluttering woman and she to a frozen fire. Fire and water. The man chilled everything. And there was a framework. A shot was fired inside her and became still. Since then she waits for me. For me to be for her what he wasn't, emotion, joy, something with exalted and destroying words. He loved her as one loves an efficient nuisance. What he loved was the idea that in the house where he lives there is a beautiful woman who looks human in the morning. And she wanted a different man, one who destroys and broadens horizons, different from her horse-riding friends in the fields of the Jezreel

Valley, in the Galilee hills, all mad for the earth. And he scoffed. What earth? What nation? He wanted to listen to the mad stillness of dead music, he wanted to wrap old pictures. To live until death, in a whisper, was what he wanted. Not to disturb the forms of politeness. The house was always in order, for him. Crumbs and scattered papers are a sign of a stormy life, of an apocalyptic vision. Clean utensils were rinsed a second time. Showers twice a day. No dust and no upsetting things. Like spider webs and everything flowing like a stream in a book by Jean Paul. She extinguished herself inward and waited for me. In quiet fury he stood guard on her life. Not to allow abandonment. Not to say things. To be silent. Not to try to spoil the artificial cleanliness. My mother wants to be embraced. All these days counting my becoming in her while he listens to Pergolesi. All those hours. 6480 hours she waited for me. My mother knows that Bialik and Father will come soon.

She called them in the night.

They heard.

Bialik and Father meet. Together they walk in the boulevard. Here Ansberg left the picture. Ivria puts in fragments I gave her. Arm in arm they walk toward me.

The parliament of idlers on the bench now debates the significance of the visit of Sir Simpson, from the Indian service, in Eretz Israel. They debate the White Paper. The new decrees. They greet Bialik and my father. What's new?

What will be?

Have you heard anything?

Who's this Simpson?

Good for the Jews, bad for the Jews.

A new Jewish boy will be born, says Bialik; more important than a hundred Simpsons.

The old men smile. What does he know, the *poète!* He sees clouds. Muses. Here in Eretz Israel the pogroms continue. Jews are killed in the Chosen Land. What will we do?

After passing them Bialik looks at the maddening spring that envelops everything. At the birds. At the leaves, with their mad fragrance, and says, Once the Jews of Eretz Israel asked Pascanius

261

Niger, the competitor of Severus, to lighten the burden of taxes upon them, and he answered them that if it were up to him he would impose taxes on the air they breathe as well. This fragrance that awaited me in Rothschild Boulevard, to be born in spring.

22

Bialik embraces my father and says:

What do you want, Naftali, a son or a daughter?

It makes no difference to me.

Nevertheless . . . ? (And he has no children!)

Not a rogue.

Call him Aminadav, says Bialik, and Ami for short. My people.
My Ami . . . A woman, in a moment of desire, will call him Ami.
And she won't know it's his people she's calling.

For all festive occasions my mother wears white. The white also
suits her tan coloring, the pale tan of Rivka, says Bialik. On the
balcony she sits, in the yard is a many-branched casuarina, climbing vines, bougainvillaea, and the fragrance of the spring is wine.
The scent of jasmine mixed with the fragrance of citrus blossom.
Mother is white. Father in a green corduroy jacket, Bialik looks
like a diamond merchant. Bialik is festive like a Sabbath reception
at Ohel-Shem Theater. In Naples I will see pigeons shitting on
the statue of the national poet while children wait for dung. Bialik
is a fantasia of himself in gray, mastering dark instincts inside
him, like Goethe linking civility and the demoniac. For this
reason my father links arms with the poet, he knows what folly
the poet would like to express.

An argument arose, I heard it from inside her. Should Rivka
be taken to the hospital even though her pains have stopped. My

263

father, of course, preferred to wait. Bialik, the childless, demanded that they go at once. He related to me, before I was born, as to a poem. And a poem must be preserved, placed in unguents, one must fear its death from the slightest error. Apart from which I am to be the grandson of Nehemiah Feldman, of blessed memory, C.N.'s friend. Beloved friend. A man wears a body of words. I was the words that Nehemiah and Bialik wanted to exchange between themselves. Ah, C.N. used to say, Rivka will grow up, she'll marry some *chalutz*, a new Trumpeldor, and then . . . the hills of Galilee will see a new generation growing from the ruins that we are, Nehemiah my friend. And Nehemiah plows the furrows of the Bible, seeking hints of my coming in Second Isaiah. He died untimely, like everyone. And we, what are we, chaff blown in the wind. . . . In what language does the greatest knower of Hebrew of our times speak? Yiddish. And Father answers him in German. Bialik says, and quotes Dr. Fabrikant, it's better to take Rivka to the hospital, for if it doesn't help it won't hurt. They take the suitcase that has been packed this last month and go down into the boulevard. Mother in white, I in her. Pulsing. Going to my doom. And I am not quiet. The time is five in the afternoon. The first of Iyar, April twenty-ninth, one thousand nine hundred and thirty. Evening embraces treetops with a cheer. Bialik thinks to himself: Aminadav ought to be sung in anapestic pentameter that relates the whole poem (me!). But, says Bialik to himself, I've never written a poem that is anapestic pentameter from beginning to end! Where I do use the meter I generally follow a pentameter line with a bimeter, or perhaps a trimeter, and, he muses, leading me to the sacrifice, I tend to slow down the speed of this metric pattern by adding an extra syllable in the middle of the line, after the second anapest, thus diversifying the rhythmic complex. The unloading of a spiritual burden is achieved, always (at least with me), by a repetition of a complete syntactic form, and of course I can't forget the structural overlapping, and so, here's Aminadav: *Yelad katı/Aminaı/dav* (Little boyı/Aminaı/dav). And C.N. smiles to himself. Now the poem can be written. With a bimeter line. So fine. A tremor in the shackles. A substitute for Goethe's iambs. What am I, who am about to be born, like billions of others on this planet, but a fairly weak line of tension between Bialik's anapestic pattern and Goethe's iambic structure. And I smile from inside my mother who is about to rob me of myself very soon now, yes very soon now and I'm a poem, the title: "If Is Is, Isn't Isn't." Which is: "If is is′/isn't is′/n't. . . ." They've choked me, shouts the poem. But like many anapestic lines, no one hears.

At the entrance to the hospital C.N. leaves us. He demands forcefully that he be informed *the moment* I'm born. We'll come at once, Manya and I!

Here Tel Aviv ended for me in the place where it began. From here on Neveh Tzedek, Pines Street, Third Street, the girls' school where my grandfather Nehemiah taught poems by Bialik, with what love. Withered trees. A vacant lot surrounded by sabra hedges. A hexagonal kiosk. A man pouring red *gazoz*. Torn notices about events long long ago. A man laughing. A cart harnessed to a horse. A man writing requests. Shin Shalom wrote during the week when I was born: "We are building Jerusalem like men ascending to the gallows." Tel Aviv is a city. And there are many cities, says Ivria. And I say: There's only one, my grandfather Nehemiah was among its founders. On the sands he built a city.

As the measure of humanity her measure is. Not exalted, not an error like Jerusalem.

In her are no diadems, squares, towers, history or distress.

Flat, broad, spreading, fleeing from the sea that lusts for her.

Cleaving to the sands to tell them a huge story she has forgotten.

Bursting forward and leaving herself behind.

Rust is her forgotten splendor.

Consumed with decay and coquettish.

Pampering and prettiness, without brilliance or madness. Vaguely deceiving under her modish dress, merchandising herself for appetite, imprisoning every groan with appeasement.

Ivria splices with Scotch tape the front of the hospital, my face, superimpositions of a fragrant spring day reaching its dusk. Bialik returns to his national house. Dressed like a merchant. With a cunning smile. He sits beside a large table covered with a white tablecloth and lethargically eats soup with knaidlach. There is a knocking on the door. Who knocks in the still of the night? The poet Fichman knocks in the still of the night. An intoxicating night, it sends people out of their minds. Ah, Ansberg, during those times the spring nights raised romantic statistics! On the sand, among the houses being built. On the scaffolds. Bring us bricks, they sing, while their hands secretly seek a white breast. In dread of remorse no deed will yet be done, no act of love for man as man. Fichman is no longer young. A kind of wakefulness traps him in the incisors, something pure is being distilled inside him. They say there's love in the world, where is my love. Fichman walks through the streets and thinks, Ah, C.N.'s eating soup with knaidlach! We'll talk about spring in the Hebrew poetry of Spain. We'll talk about spring in the poems of J. L. Gordon, we'll dig into the spring and discover our wasted bones. And he knocks on the door. Manya opens and asks, How are you Fichman, Ravnitzky was here before, there's a new article by Lachover and C.N.'s eating soup with knaidlach. He says, That's nice, that's nice, but you ask how I am—well, I have pains, if you particularly want to know, particularly on the right side. And she says, Pains shmains, it's old age Fichman. . . . And they sit on the porch and ask sweet questions of the sun setting into a spring night of scaffoldings, with Hebrew workers who have stopped inverting pyramids and are asking where is their love in a world in which they say there is love. The happy sing songs, Fichman, the miserable write them. And the difference is smaller than it appears. What is misery if not happiness gathered inward into pain, into madness. . . . *Chalutzim* in Ben Yehuda Street are building the land. C.N., will we go there? Bialik's tired. He's waiting for Aminadav. He walked a long way in Rothschild Boulevard with Naftali Sussetz and a woman who is very pregnant. C.N. is bewildered by the spring. Fichman says decisively, No, I'm not hungry, Manya. . . . But he swallows down two plates of soup. Manya's knaidlach, they're irresistible. The lady Manya knows the souls of her poets. They sit on the porch and sigh over the world's sorrow in the poetry of Ibn Gavirol or Hasdai ibn Shafrut. Spring! A bird

266

brings the message and suddenly it pulsates! Ahhhhhh. Bialik lets out, Nehemiah's daughter is about to give birth.

That's nice, says Fichman, on a spring night like this to give birth to a sabra in Eretz Israel. . . . He'll chatter in Hebrew, swear in Hebrew, make mischief in Hebrew, fight in Hebrew, ah, who needs poems when there's a night like this, why, you can explicitly smell each separate smell, while together they're a kind of concoction that is unparalleled by anything. And you really think it'll be a boy?

That's what they say.

Tell Rivka, says Fichman (he too is expecting me), that Fichman suggests a name. If she wants she can take it, if not, not. I suggest Aminadav!

A nice name, mutters Bialik after a short pause. Which arouses heavy suspicions in me that they never understood the man they interpret, those fashionable barbers of poetry. A nice name, Fichman . . . Ami and Nadav. "My people" and "gave (generously)." Nadav Ami. He gave Ami. What did He give? My people. And what is my people? With his body he will give, generously volunteer, his life. Love is a giving, though giving is not love, right, Fichman?

Manya washes dishes in the kitchen. I kick inside my mother. Father in the yard walks up and down up and down. Manya looks in the window. On the window sill stands a flowerpot, it peeps all day at the garden plot. She sees a flowerpot weeping out of a poem by the man she loves, with a clay city at his feet, as if it has been burned from the inside. And my father walks up and down the yard and mumbles, What will be, why do they take so long here . . . spring spring. . . .

Waiting for me: Bialik, Fichman, Father, Mother, Dr. Freund, Mira, Naomi and Kurt Singer. We're drowsing, Mother and I, I rustle and hide in her, charge about inside her, bring her the message of the quiet streams, the message of the black spaces. Eyes, hair, body, sex organs, stomach, fed from inside her. Breathing from her. Fichman left Bialik's house to walk to his own home. Red and purple flowers in Rothschild Boulevard. Secret kisses on benches. A cart with Arabs in it passes along the sands of what will later be Dizengoff Street, close by the silicate house, large swamps and the croaking of frogs. A quiet night closes its fragrance for the years to come. A gentle breeze blows. Jasmine and citrus. From the stars drops a cosmic dust. The number you have dialed is not connected please consult the new directory. Aminadav weeps into veins and a man's voice says, Error! Error! Wrong number. A mélange of voices like a sea. Bialik tries to sleep. Who can sleep on a night like this. He writes on a clean white sheet: Nadav, *rav, gav, av, sav, kav* (gave, rabbi, back, father, grandfather, line), *Nadvivahu ki ye-nadev* (God-given that he may give), *Ami mi mi* (my people, who who). Calls Aminadav by another name. What is the name?

The city tosses restlessly. As if she has fallen in love with herself and knows how useless that is, because she hasn't a mirror. The sea is closed. Lovers don't have precise mirrors.

23

Mother's teaching Bible to Dr. Freund, who's bent over her much-kicked belly. She's teaching Bible in suffering. As a woman-who-sacrifices-herself-all-her-life should do. Dr. Freund complains. What a language . . . gravel! Born on stones, harder than hell. My mother calms him. Dr. Freund stammers Hebrew in a hospital resembling a Greek temple in Yehuda Halevy Street. At the Eden Cinema the technicians are preparing The Jazz Singer for the early evening screening. This evening is the gala opening. The aristocrats of the people will come to see the voices and Al Jolson will sing them Sonny Boy. Sonny will be born and his name in Israel will be called: Ami-nadav. Ami-boy. Father returns to the shop. Aminadav isn't ready to be born yet. Before leaving Father kissed Mother's hand. In the streets carts traveled. Someone yelled: *Alte sachen, alte shiyech . . .*

A comb-hawker sang

> Combs combs for hair and baldies,
> Combs combs for men and ladies!

A Hebrew policeman, wearing short pants and socks up to his knees, wipes sweat from his brow. The sea hums from far off. Dizengoff rides his horse and stops next to my father's shop. His face is still sad over the untimely death of his wife. And Father

frames pictures for the museum. Child of my nurturing, he'll call
it. In a city with no towers, a museum will be built on the sands.
Forty-two thousand inhabitants in a nice suburb beside Jaffa.
Father frames him a painting of Marie Laurencin. And then the
mayor asks him if I've been born already.

He's late in coming, says Father.

The late in coming live long!

May it be so.

How are you?

Will be fine.

Boy or girl?

Boy, they say.

What name will you give him?

Well, you know . . .

Listen, Naftali, I woke up at night. It was spring, what a spring.
. . . In the bones it was. I sat up in bed, drank tea with sugar and
thought: Naftali is to be a father of a son. What will be his name
in Israel, and I thought . . .

What, asks Father.

I thought Asael, or Amiel, and then I said, Why not Aminadav? A name full of grandeur. That is, grace . . . No?

A nice name, I'll tell Rivka.

Father parts from Mr. Dizengoff and runs again to the hospital.
Al Jolson proclaims my arrival in the world: *You ain't heard
nothin' yet!* The only sentence that's spoken in the miraculous
movie. Ad-el-Arsalen, the head of the Arab delegation in America, has declared that there is no room for a Jewish-Arab agreement in Palestine on the basis of the Balfour Declaration. There
will never be peace between the two peoples, he said, as long as
their aims are diametrically opposed. . . . Thus they prepared my
entry into the world. My life. My fate, if I may be allowed a more
elevated language, Ivria. They spread out a carpet for me, Ivria,
and said, Go kill Arsalen because he's killing you. I don't know
who Arsalen is, I said. But on the other hand, they said, he doesn't
know who you are either. And he said, Aminadav? King of Israel,
the one who'll die of typhus . . . The forecasts of the honorable
dervish proved false, so we shot at each other. He at me and I at

him. We saw sights of rifles and through the apertures of the sights we fired. Then we said, with one voice which was quite bewildering, He started! I didn't. . . . Arsalen is old today. Maybe he's already dead, Ivria. He said, You came to inherit, and I said, No, no. I came to bring you culture and technology. I came to sit beside you. And he said, I'm quite happy in my own shadow, I don't want any partners. I said to him, I have no other place. He said to me, That isn't my problem. I said to him, Look, the whole world expels me. He said, That's the world's problem. I said to him, What about God's promise, and he said, Where was your God these two thousand years. For one thousand three hundred years I've been sitting here and I haven't seen him around. I said to him, As a guest. He said to me, How long did you sit here before that. I said to him, But this is my land. He said to me, No, this is my land. I said to him, Come on, let's divide it up. He said, Why. It's mine. If you're willing to divide it that means you don't really feel that it's your land. I said to him, I'm a man of conscience. He said, If so what are you doing with a rifle in your hand. I said, But at first I had a hoe, and you fired so I fired too. And so fifty years passed. Who'd want to be born into such a noisy marketplace. And he said, Look, I'm speaking to you now as an individual, really who? But we fired and each of us thought his cause was just. And you know what Goethe said about disorder being worse than injustice. That's why we'll live like this. With rifles in our hands. And flowers will grow on the graves. And Mother said, A Hebrew hero will be born to me. He will build the land and be built in it. In blood and fire did Judea fall, in blood and fire will Judea rise. As long as within a Jewish heart does beat a Jewish heart. Strengthen the hands of our brothers redeeming the earth of our land. And Arsalen sings, Falastin oh Falastin. . . . In an ancient Indian poem called Sho-do-ko, Yoko Daishi says: "Now I know my true being has nothing to do with birth and death." And the koan, the mysterious Zen riddle on this subject, goes:

"How will one liberate oneself from birth and death? What is your real being? No no no! Don't think. Examine it from close up." A Sanskrit proverb says: "Shadows of bamboo sweep the steps, but the dust doesn't move." Who am I in all these, Ivria, help me. . . .

Gathered up into myself. The sanctity of the blood. Who loves holy blood. There's only holy hatred. There's not even any holy love. Phony phony. Dust gathered on my way from myself to myself. And I didn't arrive. Why. The climate, the gleeful corruption of the Turkish bureaucracy, pogroms expected and unexpected, Mongolian cheekbones. Serfs working the lands of effendis in Beirut. Capitulations. Sales of rights to foreign consulates. Austrian post in the Turkish empire. And so settlements were established. And there was Jewish capital. And pioneers came and inverted pyramids and built a city and I was born in it. A piece of land. Mine and Arsalen's. Is Heidelberg an ironic station in my life? In the light of all we know today. Jews on roads, in forests, in camps. My neighbor with his two daughters who became smoke. What's Arsalen's argument. That he's not to blame. Am I to blame? And thus the two most blameless of all remain with rifles in our hands. And all that world laughs and sends us both arms to kill each other with.

Bialik sleeps. To regain what was not caught the night before. In the spring night full of splendor. Quiet street of night. To bring aristocrats to the gala premiere tomorrow. A mottled cat skips over garbage cans. Naomi my daughter is enveloped in me. I in my mother. My mother in her mother. All the generations in one seed. An old carter sits on a cart and drinks tea from an aluminum cup. A woman whispers a fine-venomed Russian toward a woman in a window opposite me. Sabra bushes block a vacant lot.

Empty balconies from a hospital resembling a Greek temple. The Northamptonshire team, the best in the British Army in the Middle East, has been defeated by Maccabi Tel Aviv, champions of Eretz Israel, with the surprising score of two-one. The Maccabi team yell with joy. And the crowd roars: *Long live Maccabi Tel Aviv!* Consolidated, united, as one man they strike at the British, on the football field, beside the Yarkon. Thus does a nation become consolidated. Once I went to an Italian circus. With Mira and Naomi. We sat and they did amazing things. People walked on tightropes. And jumped. I felt pity for the trained

272

animals who were given sugar and secret doses of drugs but the trapeze was a fascinating thing. And then a clown came and told jokes. The Italians in the audience laughed. Mira didn't. I did laugh. Mira asked, Why are you laughing, do you understand Italian. I said, No, but I trust these people. Ivria, are you aware of the fact that flowers have a pulse?

No. Ivria doesn't know.

She gets up. The room is dark. She walks to and fro. She's had it, she says. What do we have here, Latif cigarettes, Bialik and Manya, Fichman and a comb-hawker who's a poet, football and an old carter, why the carter?

There used to be lots of carters.

The Kita-Dan Hotel. Where's that?

Buried in HaYarkon Street.

Does it really matter, Aminadav?

It really matters, Ivria.

But where are you in all these. Three years now I've been editing films and I've never edited anything as crazy as this. You know, Ami, I don't understand a thing. So there!

A religious home and the eyes of a rabbi. Cute body and sweet soul. Hates night dens, and marriage is to your husband only. All these beautiful things. And suddenly bitter words. Give, Ivria, give me your hand. Wait, patience, everything will become clear to you. Maybe to me too. In the books of your religion it is written: "We shall do and we shall hear."

My religion?

Yes.

And yours?

I have no religion. Maybe I'm a Buddhist. But to tell the truth I don't know what Buddhism is.

You're crazy, Ami.

I'm crazy, Ivria.

All crazy people have some religion, don't they?

But I don't believe in dogmas. I mourn them. They've withered inside me. Have you any idea, sweetie, how many Jews turned Christian during the nineteenth century?

What does that matter.

That matters damn it, I suddenly raised my voice, and she yielded.

How many?

204,504. And all those, Ivria, escaped Auschwitz.

You're heartless.

Maybe.

That's a terrible thing you said.

She spread her hands as if in pleading. A woman is a complete and absolute thing. A woman is the most unaccidental thing, so experienced, strong, knowing, touching with ingenuous intuition on the right points, deprecating her own value so that the world may not be empty of children. She waited. A dazzling light in the window. Clamor outside. People traveling to all places. We're closed in the room. Bustanai has gone to Gedera to look for good locations. And I'm playing with my inner fire. On the second of May we splice again—the Indian scientist Sri Bossy announces that plants have a blood circulation and arrives at the conclusion that for this reason they have a pulse. (Flowers with broken hearts, Ivria, taking ECG tests, committing suicide because of contrition.) But Dr. Pearson, renowned American researcher, claims that although he has managed to listen to the pulse of cotton dipped in cabbage water, the theory of Sri Bossy has not yet been conclusively proved. Sri Bossy, asserts Pearson, found blood circulation in plants because he *wanted* to find blood circulation in plants. Ivria wants to understand why the famous movie (at the Gan Rina Cinema) of the divine Sovkino, The Burning Volga, belongs to The Failure of My Life as an Error of Birth. (Temporary title). I told her, Wait.

Who's this Sovkino anyway.

She doesn't know. Hitchcock yes, Sovkino no. Look, Ivria, by a special agreement signed today, the second of May nineteen thirty, Austria (in whose army my father fought against my grandfather's army) promises to buy from Poland a specified number of pigs in exchange for a hundred Polish tourists who will visit Austria. Invisible links, Ivria.

Father's outside. In the hospital yard. To bring salvation to his Aminadav. Hearing Sonny Boy. The aristocrats of the people come to see Sonny Boy and Father in the yard behind the cinema listens to the song. Twenty times Father heard *You ain't heard nothin' yet!*

In the evening to go and see Father. To see nurses emptying urine. To see the holes in Father's veins. The place is frightening. A woman weeps in green. To die with a young and heartless world. Father loved Gedera. He said the air there smelled of wine. And Dr. Neidler fell in love with the place and opened a clinic and then another clinic. He cured Bedouin children with swollen bellies and protrusions. A transparent branch of melancholy spreading across his wise and beautiful face. There was a lovely hill in Gedera, not far from Meshek Peter, among anemones and narcissi, citrus orchards and almond groves. We walked there, three of us, Dr. Neidler, Father and I. I was a boy. After *badim badim.* Donkeys carried milk to the dairies. It was after the rain, the earth was washed and an orchard pump went *tik tik tik* in the distance. And the hills united into a sky like a disaster averted. We picked oranges, we swallowed them like wine. Father and Neidler spoke about Büchner and Heine. Cows lowed farther away. A donkey bellowed with a savageness that was frightening. Young Arsalen rode a horse and cracked his whip near us beside the sabra hedge. The sabra was green and on top of it a hoopoe cleaned its feathers with characteristic arrogance. Everything was fresh and washed clean. Yellow mimosa trees led into a grove. From the grove the orchards appeared indistinctly, green foliage and golden patches. The red clay soil stuck to our shoes. Büchner emerged triumphant from the jest. And then we arrived at this hill. From it we could see the sea in the distance. And the sun shimmering into it. To the east the mountains, and closer, green fields. Pines and wattles. Father always used to say, Ah, to build a café here . . . You remember, Hermann, in Berlin, the café of Hammelfugen? A big white veranda, wooden tables covered with white tablecloths. Cheesecakes and chocolate. Cream. Coffee with *schlagsahne.* Good wine. Here I'd build a café. Aminadav will be the waiter, and you and I will wear white aprons and receive the guests. People will come from all over the country. Here no one will speak loudly, it will be forbidden to raise one's voice. To call the waiters there will be little bells made of delicate glass on every table. At five in the afternoon there'll be Schubert's Trout, people will drink coffee, eat *kuchen* and then listen to Mozart's Quintet for Oboe. Every afternoon at five. Until sunset. That's what my father used to say. I don't know why. He never had any known aspirations, at least not since the day he smashed his violin. Everything was according to measure. I was according to measure. Once he looked at me for a long while to remember my name. He respected my mother. He related to the world at an astonishing distance. But on this hill at Gedera he dreamed such a wild dream.

Now Father lies in bed and looks. Through windows which are frames he sees the Judean hills, Meshek Peter, the pines, the gold of the setting sun. The temple that they have erected on this hill for Father is not as quiet as the café he wanted to build. Patients in white. Nurses with bright faces. People constantly at their dying. At night they vacate the beds of the dead in whispers. I look at him. The tombstone in his eyes. Suddenly Father says—I'm leading him in his wheelchair, we turn into a gravel path, to go to an enchanted place, to see the Eretz Israel that doesn't exist except from this hill, and the sun is about to set, that terrible and marvelous gold— and he says suddenly, *Ami . . . I'm cut off from my life.* And falls silent. I try to stimulate him to more, but he says nothing. On his face is the coy smile of one who has been done a grave wrong. If I could only cry my father's tears I'd cry my father's tears. But I don't have my father's tears in me. For so many years you've forgotten, I said to him, am I to blame? He didn't leave me his tears. He sits. Caged in the frame of himself. Suddenly I remembered two lines by Wilhelm Bösch that he used to recite:

> A father to become
> is not hard
> A father to be
> is harder.

Wilhelm Bösch, Aminadav returns to the beginning. Nine months before Aminadav. Was it as an ironic jest that Mr. Naftali Sussetz took Rivka Sussetz to Germany to meet his friends? Nineteen twenty-nine, by ship to Trieste and from there by train to Germany. It was a year of crisis. People ate soup and paid nine billion marks. Lotte Lenya sang in a dark bar. In a nightclub where men, pale and made up with lipstick, wore dresses to dance the Charleston, and the awful streets with fear in children's eyes. A streetcar named obscenity. Father smiles. Outside a house he stops to tell his young bride, Here I played in the Kinematograf. Here Frau Schpatz lived. Beside the river somewhere they drove in a black car, he thought of his love, of the teacher who used to row and look with yearning eyes at his beloved. And Father's friend, Dr. Hermann Neidler, invited them to stay at his house. They ate lobsters and Mother screwed up her face. She didn't know how to eat foul things. They said, Ah, the beautiful Rivka from the Orient, black she is and beautiful. And they quoted the Bible that Father had taught them in their youthful days in Heidelberg. They listened to Mother's stories. Father smoked a pipe and didn't speak. A stranger on the background of Liebermann and Franz Hals, Kirchner and Schmidt-Rottluff. They sat in an elegant salon, a fire in the fireplace, on the wall a picture by Oppenheimer which Mother thought especially beautiful. On the gramophone they played Brahms, ate roast potatoes with butter and parsley. Porcelain plates with illustrations by Dürer. Father was silent. What could he tell them? The frames that he makes for Mr. Dizengoff. An Oriental country, *khamsin*, no manners, open-necked shirts, in the evenings they sit on the balcony in pajamas eating watermelon, what's a watermelon? Their eyes light up. Jews on horses, conquerors of the soil, plowers, free love in the barns. Father smiles through smoke rings and they say, Yes, yes, Palestina. Very important. But we are here. Jews in key positions, the elite. People say that if it weren't for the Jews there'd be no theater, literature, cinema, education. We might not be great creators, says Hermann, but we're the best audience. We, he adds, are the central pillar of culture, the stratum of

277

criticism, for example. . . . Mother scoffs. Clubs where men get painted up like women, screeching with candles in their hands. What happens is that at night Mother smells fire.

Naftali there's a fire here.

There's no fire Rivka, sleep.

It was a nice evening Naftali, your friends are so nice. . . . But I don't believe them. . . . You think they're happy here?

Very Rivka. And I have to sleep.

I can't sleep. Naftali, I want to talk!

But I want to sleep.

I smell fire.

There's no fire.

That was in Heidelberg. Before that they went to the forest. Animals roared in the distance. And all the time she smelled fire. Something dark and vague suddenly in her nostrils. She didn't know what. She was scared. She clung to my father who doesn't like being touched. Who likes the fine space between people. People slept in marvelous houses with sloping roofs of red shingles and smoke curling up. They went to a beer tavern by the river. They ate sausages which they dipped in the most excellent mustard she had ever tasted. And the fire in her hostrils. In the tavern she sat on a bench on which was inscribed in Gothic letters: GOETHE SAT HERE. And she pretended, for his sake, that she found this exciting. Father pretended it was a joke. But in his eyes, deep inside them, were tears of real emotion. In the forest, later, he asked to be excused. He must go off among the trees for a moment. She thought: Ah, he has to piss. What's happening to Naftali, is he becoming *human?* And she was so happy. But only a few minutes later (and the smoke, the fire, in her nostrils all the while) she heard her husband yelling a savage roar into the forest. She was horrified. She wanted to run to him, but remained rooted to the spot. The trees stood dense. She didn't know where he was. Farther off there was a fortress. She thought he'd been bewitched. What would happen if the devouring hounds of the tyrant fell upon her? She stood and heard my father scream the only scream he ever screamed in his life. And he returned to her, pale.

Why did you scream.

I didn't scream, he said.
But I heard.
You didn't hear.
I did hear.
You also smell fire.
I really do smell fire.
So you also heard a scream. I didn't scream.

Why did my father scream into the forest of his youth? Mother didn't know. At night they lay down to sleep in the *pension*. And the beds were separate. Between the beds stood a small cupboard, and on it was a lovely vase of gladioli. And Mother smelled fire. She started trembling. Then she remembered that once her father had told her, Wherever you go open your nostrils. If you smell smoke you'll know that there's fire. And if there's fire it's a sign that they're burning Jews. And my father's friends were so friendly. They went to the Schocken Department Store to buy shoes for Mother, they took her to a concert, and all the violinists were Jews. Everything was open. No one shouted or insulted her, and she wasn't in Palestina. There Jews who rode horses were returning to a lost homeland, among swamps and eucalyptus.

Naftali, I can't sleep, this smoke . . .

There's no smoke, he answered sleepily. There's no fire. Everything's quiet. Listen to the quiet.

And there really was a wondrous quiet. Everything was breathing in a marvelous opacity.

And she cried. My mother cried. My father felt pity for her. In a strange city. The place where Goethe sat and ate sausages, near a petrified black forest. And there were sudden lightning bolts and rain poured down on the trees. My father stepped toward my mother's bed and the cupboard fell and the vase broke and Father got into his beloved's bed and tried to soothe her: There's no smoke, no fire. Look at Dr. Neidler, he's the most famous children's doctor in Berlin. Look how people cluster around his door. It's true that a plate of soup costs a billion marks, but they aren't blaming the Jews! They have a Jewish minister, and Einstein. And Mother said, I'm scared, Naftali, hold me tight, I've been longing for you. And Naftali said, Ach, your

279

father's stories! It's they that have ruined you, puffed up your head with nonsense, every bit of moss looks like a cedar of Lebanon, and she laughed at the biblical simile of Naftali Sussetz who hadn't used a simile out of Goethe or Hölderlin. Dogs barked in the street. And she embraced a pale and sleepy man. The wooden floor was smooth. Father stumbled as he went to get a handkerchief and fell into her arms like a baby. It was cold, the rain beat down outside, and then he entered her and she thought he'd say to her I love you Rivka and he didn't say it. He swallowed something and said, You're smooth as a fish, the floor's smooth and so are you, and he said something astounding: You're mine, mine, all mine! As if he'd formulated a mathematical equation. And then I suddenly came from the black spaces, from the antistars and through his ejaculation I penetrated into her. Afterward my father fell asleep and she drank from the water that remained in the vase and the water tasted of gladioli.

From there they went to Switzerland and there were lakes with skies inside them and they didn't know which were the lakes and which the skies. And the white mountains. And Mother longing for the *khamsin* in the street about to fall next to Jaffa. Father takes off his shoes and wades in the water. Everything longs for exalted words. Summits of culture. What am I doing in the Middle East. Why am I framing pictures for men on horses. But Father's riddle is not open to interpretations. He was a frame to some dream that had no interpretation. Show her Piero della Francesca, and Paolo Uccello in Florence. They ate Tuscan *lasagna* which resembled *strudel*. And then you vomited, Mother. You were pale and he didn't understand. He thought, My caprices. And then you felt a kind of choking because I came into being in you. And he didn't know.

You returned. You in a white glow: the boy will be born, he'll pay the tickets for all the trains I've missed. And Father didn't know. Had he known, he would have laid a broken violin on her belly and said (to me): Look, don't raise your sights, don't aim for the skies, don't be too daring, be polite, humble and yielding, and your life will be a perpetual triumph. Whoever aspires lands in the pit. God isn't forgiving, art isn't democracy, whoever can stops,

whoever can't gets burned or turns into a son of God, like Giotto.
Who are you that you should be a Giotto. And so one tries to die
at the moment of birth. Mother with a wondrous glow, and I
inside her, be a man for me, she said in her heart, build the land
for me, bring me grandsons in my old age, smile to me in a sad
cold house.

24

In the morning Mother rings. Why don't you come to Gedera, Father misses you, it was such a clear day. . . . He sits in his wheelchair and reads *Der Spiegel.*

Tomorrow after shooting I'll come, I said, and I'll be able to bring you back to Tel Aviv. There was a silence, I peeled an orange. She said, Tomorrow's the anniversary of my mother's death and I want you to come with me to the cemetery, it's many years since you visited her. . . . Apart from that, there's something important, I have to talk to you, come to me, take me to the cemetery, and we'll talk. Again there was a silence and then she added quickly, And dress warmly, and hung up.

My neighbor brought chocolate and grapefruits fresh from the tree. We squeezed them and I poured the juice. He'd found me a photograph of an old synagogue from the town of Tarnopol. This was the synagogue of Rabbi Nachman Krochmal which was burned by the Nazis, he said. He and his friends always say Nazis, not Germans. Once I dared to say that the Lincoln Continental and the Rolls-Royce were better than the Mercedes, and he didn't believe me. I ate *halva* and he drank juice. He said, Look what a wonderful synagogue. The wooden boards aren't joined by nails but are interwoven. Inside it's hot. The ceiling's low. All Israel are friends. No heights like with the Christians, everything's woven to the sides, there's room for everyone. God is here between man and man, while with the Christians the contact between man and man is by way of God. Hence Gothic towers and exalted art. For to be good means to behave correctly toward God while with us to be good to God means to be good to others. I said to him, There's no more Judaism like that. And he answered, Maybe there's no Christianity either, Judaism and Christianity both died in Auschwitz. I said to him, If anyone died it wasn't Judaism or Christianity that died, it was you and I. And that's much worse. But he doesn't appear to accept my view. He scrutinized the kitchen, and said he'd make new shelves for me. One day my wife and daughter will come and there won't be room to put all the things. I didn't know what things he meant.

Before my neighbor left he said, Wear warm clothes today even though the sun's shining outside! Wear a hat, and warm socks, and most important of all, put on warm underpants! People make a grave error, they dress warmly on the outside but next to the body they wear thin light underclothes. That's one of the gravest errors there are. . . . Look at the increase in cases of influenza! (He too with statistics!) And I thought of the Dutchwoman. There was a woman you could talk to about subjects like these. My neighbor looks very concerned as he talks about warm underclothes. I asked him what was worrying him. And he was pleased that I'd noticed his sorrow. He looks at his watch to check my departure. He refused to answer. I said, Let it be so. I put on a coat and a hat and was about to go when he said what had been worrying him all this time, Hershel went to Haifa and they haven't come back.

Who?

Hershel, my friend. Who comes and plays cards with me. You've seen them. They said Shalom to you one time. And they have a big wife what shakes the hand all the time.

Yes, I remember, but why are you frightened about his going.

Not because they went. Because they haven't come back.

I told him that most people who go to Haifa come back. There's statistics on it, the Egged bus cooperative and the Israel Railways have them, and he smiled wryly. My neighbor changes the direction of his concerns: the roof has to be cleared of pine needles, they block the drainpipes, the wall will fill with mold and there'll be leaks.

And then, as in an unavoidable love for this little man with the torn sweater, I went into the bedroom and put on warm underpants that Mother had given me from Father's collection (for the scene where we'd photographed Ansberg as my father walking in Shenkin Street), I put on warm socks and drove to the studio.

Outside the sun shone and a fierce wind blew. It didn't rain. I had coffee with Ansberg who during the night had visited a woman in Bograshov Street. He hums something to himself. Iced coffee in winter? The waiter puts ice in the coffee and adds whipped cream. There's no ice cream. Anti-Semites, says Ansberg and sucks through his straw, as usual, with a noise that sounds as if he's sucking outward and not inward. Ansberg tells me that Ivria phoned the studio, before that she tried my house but the line was busy, she isn't coming today.

That's impossible, I said.

She tried and the line was busy and then she rang me at the studio.

And you were there so early.

Yes.

And how did she know you'd be there.

She knew.

My line wasn't busy, Ansberg. He twisted up his face and sucked some more iced coffee on this cold winter's day.

What did Ivria want.

Sickness, no, not she, Nahama.

Who?

Her mother, he said in alarm as if trying to conceal something.

I don't want to go to the cemetery with my mother. A man's dead or alive. I hate cemeteries full of grief cultivated with flowers and death like cans of preserves.

Ansberg says that there's no point in going to the studio. Bustanai's photographing newspaper clippings.

And at night, he said, it rained torrents.

Torrents, I repeated, drank coffee au lait and ate a croissant.

I stood at the corner of Bograshov and Ben Yehuda, and the

husband was late coming out. Finally he came out and I went in. The corridor was warm. . . . Before that I'd sat opposite, in a kind of garden, maybe a kindergarten, I don't know, Bograshov, next to Ben Yehuda, with seesaws and trees and lovely plots with scarecrows in them. I sat there and watched the entrance of the building. I wanted him to come out. . . . I thought about you.

About me, Ansberg, that's nice of you.

Yes, about you. I thought what a pity that you aren't with me, among the trees, and when I thought of you, Ami, I stopped thinking about the rain. When I went upstairs you vanished. The key creaked, I was afraid I might wake everyone, but no one woke up. I heard the snores of a child with a cold. I know children's diseases by their breathing before morning. If I ever find love, Ami, and know happiness, I'll have children who'll be conceived with laughter by lamplight, and they'll breathe like all children, and by their breathing I'll know what diseases they have.

One should wear warm underclothes, I said.

Who told you?

I know.

Know know. Suddenly everybody knows, says Ansberg sorrowfully and liquidates the iced coffee. So get this straight, they don't know. They think they know everything and they don't know a damn thing. I know, I know because of the woman, she slept in warm socks and underpants. Her husband's. With the slit behind. Get it? The fly groin . . . What could be more exciting? Nothing. A deceiving game. A woman in a man's underpants, with the fly in the back and her husband running to the bus stop, the things you find in the beds hidden in Bograshov and Pinsker Streets! Who was Bograshov?

A teacher at the first Hebrew high school. He taught my mother.

Ah . . . Everyone says State Circle, where the top people live, or Smuts Boulevard or 29th of November Street. . . . It's rubbish. Pinsker and Bograshov. The window was open and she mumbled: Nahum my dear.

And drops of rain sprayed into the room. There was a transistor there, next to the bed, and suddenly I wanted something ceremonial, this magnificent woman. . . . I turned on the transistor—there was a smile on her face—and quiet music came, maybe a mazurka by Chopin, I looked at her again and her eyes were open and on the transistor! That was exciting, she too was happy, I was afraid to laugh, I tried to smile and I made a sound like a broken faucet and then she whispered to me, when I was already inside her, through the slit in the warm underpants, *Don't be crazy, Nahum. . . . You'll be late for work and Kupfermann has already warned you.* But you know, Ami, her voice wasn't very convincing. She didn't want me to go to work! And then she whispered something in Rumanian or maybe in Hungarian, she whispered to the transistor! And that was a compliment, she enjoyed it. She breathed deep and short, she was happy with the air filled with raindrops that caressed her sweating face, suddenly she raised the upper half of her body, as if she's woken up, and let the wind with the raindrops embrace her! And the music changed into a waltz and suddenly I thought: Ansberg, you're raising statistics with Swedish girls on the beach because of a transistor named Nahum. I thought about myself in the third person while I was still inside her. She raises her body and I'm inside her, from below. And then she turned her face to me and her eyes were closed and her face was that of the Queen of Holland with her husband's warm underpants and the sad smell of morning in her mouth and I loved her from in front, I on top of her, like some Aminadav or studio manager. And then she turned her face and body to the window and fell asleep. And her breathing was the purest and the quietest thing I've ever heard in my life.

I thought about Mira, I thought about Naomi becoming inside a body behind which a man with a harelip rocks inside it to the rhythm of a mazurka. What woman could resist such a marvelous rhythm.

I said to Ansberg, I know that yard.

What yard.

The yard. The kindergarten with benches and plots of flowers. I know it.

Next to Bograshov?

Next to Bograshov.

What did you do there? Peek at the woman?

I went to kindergarten there, Ansberg. The place where you waited in the rain and saw Nahum leave for work and then you went up to her. Don't fool me, Ansberg, you know I have a wife and daughter. Sometimes you remind me of Jerome, who said that Stephanie fucks like a motorbike. I never understood what it could mean to fuck like a motorbike and I thought, what, who, and now, the happy end, she was fucked like a motorbike, this queen of yours, and how? With a transistor. A transistor fucking a motorbike. What a world! And now, I didn't give him time to say the words that were on the tip of his tongue, let's talk about the yard. . . . You remember the nursery school run by Mrs. Cukierman whom we called Mrs. Kotzelman who said that all Arab children have black eyes?

Yes.

Afterward, I said, I went to a real kindergarten. The teacher's name was Hava, and that was the yard where you sat in the rain. . . . In Bograshov Street. She was the wife of a Hebrew author, did she know that Bialik was my godfather? And that author was killed by Arsalen! Who slung a cigarette at a cat, burning. And said, You've come to inherit the land. But Arsalen didn't have black eyes.

How do you know?

He was the official representative of Arab nationalism, and he surely had display eyes of green or maybe almond color. And the kindergarten, where you stood last night in the rain, one side of it bordered on the Beit Ha-am Theater on the ruins of which they built the El Al Building. We used to peep into the Beit Ha-am, and watch the rehearsals of the Kumkum company, and after that the Matate. They sang songs against the British and there was a song about a shoeshine man.

◫◫

In the kindergarten entrance Ansberg looks upward. There was a balcony and on it a plump woman hanging laundry out to dry.

And he blushes. I can swear that I saw a smile creep over her face and he made gestures with his hands. Afterward he took out the notebook in which he kept the beach statistics, and wrote:

12 March, 1967. Love in Bograshov Street.
A queen and a harelip (the undersigned). Full of remorse and
   exaltation. From behind. Through the slit of a man's warm
   underpants. Rain outside.
—Thirty-two minutes.
—Index, 43.900%.
—Ashkenazi, thirty-nine and a half (age). Clothes: Grade C.
He took off his shoes, put on slippers of elephant hide. Took off
   his clothes. *She didn't.* From behind.
And for a moment even from in front, for thirty-two seconds.
Not one word of love.
—Without laughter. Without a lamp. A transistor!

He put the notebook back in his pocket. The woman went inside and closed the shutters.

You see, he said, that's what they're like. Who cares who I am and why?

I do, I said.

Hava the kindergarten teacher laughs. Short brown hair, before total destruction, the Golden Age still on her face, for some time. Within two minutes the obstacles were removed, she understood that this silver-haired man named Aminadav had gone to kindergarten here and that his teacher's name had been Hava. And so we smiled at each other. It was hard for her to grasp that the little kids running about behind her leave this place, stretch their muscles, grow paunches and become thieves or prime ministers, high officers or teachers, professional rapists or merchants. They're so little, she thought, with their short pants and their "Hava I want peepee" and "Chaim did peepee on me" and "My peepee's bigger'n yours." In my mind's eye I saw myself alone and weary. About fifty-five, life finished long ago, waiting for the redemption of silence, for death, when you can see it coming. With black bags under my eyes, like those people who are finished. And Naomi would walk past me and I wouldn't know her. She's grown, no longer the girl who ran about the yard, but a woman. Wearing make-up, a short dress, and I say to her, Hey baby, you remind me of someone. And she'll say, Yes, your Naomi, Father, and she'll slap me in the face. Or she'll say, Father Father, and embrace me and put an end to my aloneness. Or maybe she won't recognize me and she'll give me alms: her body, or money from a gilt purse. Or I'll be immensely wealthy. I'll live in a building with fifty stories all of them mine and there'll be fifty private elevators and fifty exclusive limousines waiting for me in the underground car park. A hundred secretaries sitting on efficiency chairs and typing my name on their typewriters. AMINADAV AMINADAV AMINADAV AMINADAV. For I won't have anything for all those beautiful secretaries to do. Money will flow from taps in the wall, people will sit and count the money, Brink's armored cars will bring the money to the banks and fill the vaults, I'll be an old man and smoke a cigar.

A new cleaning woman will come from the cleaning women's bureau to clean away the two grains of dust that have accumulated in my hermetically sealed room after two weeks of money-counting. The cleaning woman will be Naomi and I'll make her into a queen, I'll buy her a kingdom for her birthday. There will be no bounds to my generosity. And she'll be Queen of Holland and she'll get screwed from behind, like a motorcycle. No, I'll be dead and she'll stand over my grave and cry. Or laugh.

回回

So what exactly do you want here, asked Hava the kindergarten teacher.

I said to her, When I went to kindergarten here, the place was quite some way from the city.

A wilderness, she said, this was a wilderness. Buffalo charged about, Bedouins drew knives, Turks took baksheesh. She spoke mockingly.

I liked her. Ansberg sensed it. His horns, or tendrils, are like antennae. Her face is mischievous though with some sadness in it, and you can't tell exactly where the sadness lies. Between the eyes, or at the corners of the mouth. Afterward the fornicator said

289

to me that were the kindergarten teacher married, and to a husband who got up early in the mornings, he'd pretend he was me and go into her.

She's willing to let us in. I, for example, despite the wilderness and all that, impress her as an honest person. She'll let me sit with what she calls quite seriously "her cute ducklings." A little boy asks, Who are these uncles?

I said Aminadav, and introduced Ansberg. A little freckled boy jumped off his chair and started screaming more than singing. Huge laughter in the room. And before the poor beauty could hush them another boy yelled out a funnier version of the same song. There was an uproar which subsided only after several scoldings.

Hava the kindergarten teacher is speaking. She says that today there'll be an unusual talk in our honor. For unusual she uses the common Hebrew term *yotze-dofen,* a compound whose separate words mean coming out of and wall.

What does *yotze-dofen* mean?

Coming out of something, says a cute duckling.

Something to do with food.

It's clothes.

Hava explains. The children get excited. A very pale girl says in a dry quiet voice, That's wrong! *Yotze-dofen* is the offspring of an animal born an unnatural birth, and taken out by an operation from the wall of its mother's stomach!

A silence ensues. Ansberg writes something down in his notebook. A little boy bursts out laughing. The pale girl emits a single tear. Hava asks if there are any questions. And so it began.

What are you doing here? This is a kindergarten for little kids.

My name's Nehama and I live at my house.

I had never spoken with forty children at one and the same time. Naomi burst out of all the faces.

Children, I said, many years ago I went to this kindergarten. I lived in Mendele Street, not far from here. My teacher's name was Hava too. She too was a good teacher. I played with my friends in this yard . . . your yard. I swung on your swings. . . .

That was a long time ago.

290

When I was big I never went to no kindergarten. I was a footballer. My name was Spiegler, said one, sticking his thumb in his nose. With fuzzy hair.

My father was in overseas. Auschwitz. He never went to kindergarten.

And I added, You'll all be big one day too! Uproar and again my Hava, hushing her ducklings.

What I really wanted to say was: Naomi my love, my sweet, my pajama cutter, my deserted daughter, don't ever grow up. Stay a child. Everything's surer. Don't be big and sad, don't come to know death. I stumbled. Again there was uproar. Ansberg drowsed. Hava very awake. A girl got up and said bitterly, Not me. I don't want to be big. I don't want to grow up. I'll never grow up. My mother promised me I wouldn't! It's better to light a light than to complain about the darkness, says a Chinese proverb. I quickly told them about Peter Pan. To save something. And I added, But there are children who want to grow up. They'll grow up.

The girl cried. A boy says, She sucks from her mother. Ansberg wakes up and looks at the window. The shutters are closed.

After a new uproar, a new silence. And I say, And I played football. I climbed fences, I sang Passover songs and Purim songs. After that I grew up. I traveled abroad on a ship and I came back. Now, please, listen to me, what I'm asking is important to me. Do you think that even though I left here many years ago, I can still be here?

But you are here!

The pale girl cut through the chatter and the noise with her monotone voice. Her eyelids closed and opened, like a magic box. She says, You kids don't understand. He asked if the kid that he was can be here when he's big.

She doesn't look at me. She doesn't ask if that was what I meant. She knows.

The children become alert.

You got a car?

Yes.

Then sure.

I bet you're in hiding.

Hiding shit! yells a boy with green eyes and his mouth twists into a smile.

No it isn't.

Yes it is.

Hava's agitated, restless. I soothe her. Ansberg photographs the closed veranda through the network of his eyes. Hava likes Coca-Cola. She says, In America they drink a lot of Coca-Cola. And then:

You married?

No.

Why?

Didn't happen.

Why?

There was no one to marry, and no time.

It's worth trying.

Who hasn't?

Tonight at the California, a movie or something. Will you come?

Why not?

Nine?

Nine.

God is the king of all the places, says a boy with reddish hair. He lives in a huge hideout and has lots of servants.

No He doesn't, He lives in the sky and comes down with the rain.

A girl: My daddy says there's no God. My brother Noam doesn't know.

God has arms and legs, He walks . . .

He's got wings. He walks on the clouds. He cooks for Himself. What He likes best is ice cream. He's got no wife.

A boy: He's got no wife, He's got no prick, He doesn't fuck! Great uproar.

Hava tries to hush the ducklings. I wait.

He's got no shirt, He's got no pants.

He's rich.

He doesn't eat. When the rain comes down He drinks it.

He farts!

Who said that?

It was Itamar, say the kids.

And Itamar says, It was me. What about the lightning and the thunder?

The pale girl: Lightning is an electric line of light that flashes across the sky because of the collision of two clouds charged with electricity. Thunder . . . And then she concludes: He can't fart 'cause He hasn't got an ass.

Itamar: What's your name.

Aminadav.

Ahalibama . . .

Who?

Ahalibama, who knows everything, she said He hasn't got an ass. . . . I said that He hasn't got a prick and that He farts. If He hasn't got an ass He hasn't got a prick. I like words like these. I'm the biggest in the kindergarten. You know, I've got a secret hiding place, and you can stay there if you like. That's about what you asked about before. And then he thought for a moment and said, What I wanted to tell you was that afterward I was born.

After what?

After the farts. Not because God wanted. Because my uncle came home and told my sister I'd been born, and she cried.

I was born from my mother's stomach.

From her cunt.

Mothers don't have cunts.

From her cunt.

Hava was very quiet. Ansberg drowsing. Here was what Mira calls the revenge of the grownups. They still haven't been avenged.

And then Ahalibama got up and said:

I remember. It was sweet and frightening, yes. There were machines . . . like things that make things. Transmissions? Maybe knitting needles and a loom? And suddenly it was dark and light at the same time. And then hands, I think, white hands, maybe knitting needles and not hands. And the machine had an antenna like in a car, of wire, like they stole an antenna and put in some wire, and then we crashed. They sprayed water, I don't know, and some huge thing screamed at me, and I said Why, and I was awfully scared, and I cried. After that there was this kind of gentleness, like my hands after a bath, Daddy calls them duck's hands, and he was there, yes. With his face. Without all the other things. Days poured over me and again I was very scared and I screamed, but no one heard because they were all dead, maybe not dead, but they didn't want to hear, they didn't want to, and I wasn't anywhere either, maybe I was, maybe it was some place, but I don't know what place. And then there was a voice which caressed me hard but also gave me a slap on the face, and I came out of a tunnel and was pulled along. I was pulled and pulled. I remember, it was like I was swimming. Like I was drowning. Maybe not, like in a whirlpool. I saw light, there was a crack, and then all the waters fell on me and the knitting needles stabbed me and closed something. I had a voice and suddenly it stopped. I had a mouth and it didn't open. I had a body that had been torn. And I cried and cried and cried.

And she cried and cried and cried. They tried to soothe her. I knew that she had spoken from within me. A marvelous thing had happened. I, she, Ami and Ahalibama. I smiled. I knew her. She ran outside and I went out after her. I stroked her. She sat under Ansberg's tree and cried. I stroked her and kissed Naomi's forehead. I told her how wise and special she was. I said to her, Look at the hats flying off people's heads in the wind. She smiled through her tears and there was a rainbow in her eyes. Beside us a procession of ants marched in exemplary order. I spoke with her, I told her about myself, about Naomi, about the hats blown by the wind. Very slowly she calmed down and then she even laughed because I told her that once the lion went from animal to animal and asked, Who's the king of the jungle, and all of them said, You are, Sir Lion. And the lion went to the elephant and asked him and the elephant, who'd been drowsing, said, Why don't you leave me alone, can't you see I'm tired and sleepy, but the lion stretched his muscles and said, Tell me.

He didn't want to tell him, I said to her.

And the lion tried again and again. Until finally the elephant slowly got up, approached the lion, raised his trunk, picked the lion up in his trunk and threw the king of the jungle into a very distant tree. All the lion's bones were broken. He crawled down from the tree, returned to the elephant and said, Tell me, Mr. Elephant, if you don't know why didn't you say so. And she laughed and laughed.

回回

I'm like the Japanese whose wife ran away from him and went to the beach and raked the sand and people asked him, What are you doing, and he said, I'm looking for my wife, and they said, But she surely isn't here, and he said, She has to be some place, why not here.

25

Hava was there before me, smiling at me from the cola. I approached the table, struggling with sweating backs, and ordered a double whiskey and a glass of soda. Outside it was raining. People spread evening newspapers over their heads and ran. Beams of light from display windows refracted golden in the screen of raindrops. A policewoman in a yellow hat and slicker directed traffic, shaking her head as the rain fell on her nose. The window steamed. Electric heaters burned over our heads. In the California, the usual tumult. Voices swallowing each other like after a fast. Nine-fifteen, between the first show and the second show at the movies. American students and a young Indian laughing around a glass of beer. We sat and talked about marriage. She said, I had a boyfriend, he had a fishpond that he loved, every morning he'd feed the fishes. He had a rifle and a pistol, he liked security matters. He was nice, a good dancer, with a lovely home and a ten-thousand-dollar stereo. And two dogs. But most of all he loved the fishes. I lived with him, I cooked for him, at night we'd go dancing, him and me. My mother made me a lace wedding dress. One morning I fed the fishes, I had a fishing net, I tried to fish out a fish my love especially loved, so he could caress it, because I used to do that every morning and afterward I'd put it back in the water. I injured the fish. My love came out in his pajamas and shouted at me, and after that he beat me. I cried.

I said to him, I didn't mean to hurt the fish, but he swore at me. He ran into the house and phoned his veterinarian in Jerusalem. I said to him, Call a veterinarian in Tel Aviv, it's closer. But he said that the veterinarian from Jerusalem was better. Before the veterinarian came the fish stopped breathing. I tried artificial respiration on it and my love screamed. Then the veterinarian came and said that nothing'd help, the fish was dead. After the veterinarian had gone my love said to me, Take the fish and cook it. I took the fish and cooked it in a piquant sauce. He came to the table and ate the fish. Then I took my clothes and left his house. Since then I'm not getting married.

We skipped over puddles to see a movie. I looked at her back in the dark theater, a small back, very brave, maybe defeated. I was tired but I caressed her back. She told me afterward that after I'd gone her little ducklings had looked for me everywhere. They said, The uncle's here, he's hiding, here he is! He's a little boy hiding under a tree. They said that you're little and big and that you're in kindergarten and not in kindergarten. How did you make a thing like that tangible to them? I myself don't understand how you can be an adult and a child at one and the same time.

We sat in her rooftop room. She took off her shoes. She was wearing black trousers and a green sacklike shirt. Her breasts were firm inside a thin black brassiere, more outside than inside, and the nipples didn't show. Two wondrous curves. Her face was like that of an intelligent boy who had not become wise. She folded her legs and wanted to know how. Instead of a bed she had a mattress covered with an Indian carpet with a goddess with many breasts and many arms. Beside the mattress were stools and beside them a small table and on it a vase with daisies and on the walls reproductions of Juan Gris, Abel Pann, Paul Klee and an enlarged photograph of Cassius Clay. I found no common denominator among the pictures and tried the bookshelf. There were the writings of Berl Katznelson, two Perry Masons, The Crusaders in the Land of Israel, the abridged *Shulhan Aruk,* a Spanish-German dictionary, Vilnai's Tours of Israel, a novel by John Updike, The Journeys of Benjamin the Third and a Hebrew grammar. And then to drink cognac and to say, Perhaps there are many times, not just one time.

The children, I said, intuit. Later on will come what Mira calls the revenge of the adults, I said Mira, I didn't say my wife. I told her about the Japanese who raked sand and said, My wife could be here just as she could be anywhere else. And she smiled the same smile: the smile that Ansberg was incapable of smiling. Suddenly I saw the absence of Ansberg's smile appearing on her lovely lips. And I thought how there's no justice in the world, something that only a child can say to himself, or an old man weary of life. I made her laugh as I probed toward her, into her via her arched breasts. She accepted my kisses for what they were, something better to do than the nothing else to do on a rainy night. She was no less bored, but no more, than the other women. There was nothing exciting about her apart from her breasts, but she wasn't unexciting either. The sorrow on Ansberg's face when he claims that women do it like they eat ice cream. He wants there to be a radiance. Faces aglow. An inner silence. Shoes dropping off by themselves, clothes burning on the hot body, breasts speaking, stomach singing, he'd like every love to be a miracle, because it really is a miracle, but go and explain that to a kindergarten teacher whose boyfriend loved a fish and he called a veterinarian from Jerusalem and the fish died and he ate his beloved while the stereo played the Swingle Singers.

Rain outside. Aminadav's drainpipes wailing. She wants to understand how I made the children grasp that there are two different levels of time, but she'd probably be just as interested to know the difference between the ways the Irish and the Scots distill alcohol if I were a liquor merchant. There is love in my heart, Mira Mira. How many people can truly give themselves? Only monogamists like me can truly be unfaithful, the others do things to each other like toothpaste. Monogamists feel remorse, pain, guilt. Ah, Mother, the guilt you filled me with, sometimes I love you only for that. Sometimes I die, really die. Do you know what it means to die because I'm guilty guilty guilty and I'm incapable of living with that. Guilty of being born, guilty of you bringing me up, guilty of you sending me to school, guilty of not loving and not giving, guilty of your not having a better life, of Father's, Mira's, Naomi's, of this pitiful Hava's who lets me suck her breasts and thinks of a hundred distant things that aren't even a dead fish. Into the pupils of strange women's eyes I look to see and know that I exist. In Mira's eyes I don't see my existence. There I give myself. There I love. There I don't exist because someone dear to me is sharing life with me. Real monogamists fall in love with women whom they betray.

I lie on a mattress on a roof in Dubnow Street. Wind blows on the roof. The drainpipes. The arched breasts. Frances Elliott's painting. Steps on a floor paved with broken hearts. Kurt Singer writes: Aminadav Sussetz has found his way. He paints with his miserable prick cut the Jewish way, in the boat of a bored teacher, and later a poor kindergarten teacher, in order to know that he exists. I beside her. She beside me. Night. We've finished the physiotherapy. We've breathed deep. Now we rest. We drank coffee. We ate grandmother's biscuits. We lie next to each other. She moves. Strange women move too much. The strange man doesn't become a friend after the physiotherapy is over. Thinking: Who was here before me. Not jealously. More like looking for friends. Liking them. After all, men have been in her before me and will be after me, and we're all brothers. We've penetrated into the same place and we've come out of it wrung and mangled the same way. Her sweat that dripped onto me is surely known in its sweet aroma, mixed with Chanel No. 5, to liquor merchants, doctors, soldiers and the geography teacher who gave her Vilnai's book. I thought: Maybe here were fathered the children I saw today in the kindergarten. A diabolic idea. I recalled Chaplin walking in the street and calling out Glazier with the kid who a little earlier had broken the panes.

And so I penetrated into her again. With a certain tenderness that was answered with a sigh of contentment. Maybe I wanted to father a new Naomi. To be liberated from Mira and Naomi, from New York, from the guilt always inside me. But Naomi cannot be born of a technological exercise, but only from absolute love, which begins on a toilet bowl in a magnificent bathroom and ends in an endless wedding of myself and Mira, every morning when I sanctify and wed her and she me. And that miracle of the two of us together, in bed, unmoving, loving, together, with the something that isn't me and isn't Mira but the two of us together. And a Naomi is born with flashing eyes and pajamas with elephants. Where is love, Ansberg. Once I walked in HaYarkon Street to look for Ansberg at the beach. A woman in a short skirt, with a purse, asked me, You want? I said, Yes, but only in love. She laughed. The awful laugh that came out of her. Something scorched. And the young man standing on the corner with long curly hair, tight trousers and delicate manicured hands also laughed. I thought: The list of my predecessors' names, all those men who fathered the kindergarten children here, might be inscribed under the mattress. We drank tea. It was morning. She said, Go before my mother comes. Every Wednesday she comes to check who's been here. I asked her who had been here before me. I was stirred. I laid her in the morning the way Ansberg dreams about love. She was cold and detached. And she told me names. She didn't need to inscribe them under the mattress. She told me and I was jealous and that was a blessing because this thing in the morning, with bodies burning in the characteristic chill of Tel Aviv, was something special. I and all my friends. Whose names I've already forgotten.

My mother waited for me outside her house. I was forty-three seconds late, there'd been a traffic jam in Reiness Street. From some distance I saw my mother peeking at her watch, her face pale as if all the injuries in the world had already been piled upon her today, as usual. Dressed in white, hugging a bunch of flowers.

We drive to the old cemetery. I called you yesterday, you weren't home! All day I'm alone. I come back from the hospital and sit home alone. No one comes. You don't come. I called you and you weren't home.

I'm sorry, I said. The traffic light turned red. I gave her a light. She blew out the cigarette smoke and the window clouded.

And then she said, I bought you a house! You can sleep in it occasionally!

I didn't answer.

You can answer me, she said. You think it was easy for me?

300

Mother, every night I sleep at home.

Last night you didn't!

Last night was the first time.

That's because last night I called you! Aminadav, you're a
grown man and I don't want to interfere. I sold the apartment
in which I saw joy with Father, because I thought, Aminadav
needs a house, he'll come, he's coming home, where will he live.
. . . It wasn't easy! And now you have a house of your own so you
can sleep in a different house every night, and wander around in
cafés.

I don't wander around in cafés.

You were seen at the California.

By whom? Aunt Lifshe?

As it happens, yes, but it could have been by others too.

When?

What does it matter?

Because yesterday I went to the California. And after that to
a house where I slept. It all happened yesterday. And yesterday
was one day, no more.

Coincidence, eh?

Coincidence, Mother.

Drive carefully.

I'm driving carefully.

Coincidence, I call him and he isn't home. Eight times I called.
At one o'clock in the morning I call and he isn't there. What's
that? Coincidence? And then along comes Aunt Lifshe and says
to me, Where do you think Aminadav sits whole nights? At the
California with all the entertainers. . . . A chain of coincidences.
She smoked nervously. I drove among cars, careful in guilt. Don't
kill me, she said. And we were driving to the cemetery. Look, she
said, as far as I'm concerned you can do whatever comes into your
mind, you're a grown man and you know what's good and what's
bad. But in your place, if I may say this, I'd sleep in my own house
at least once a week. Just so as not to forget it.

I switched on the radio and heard the weather forecast. The
sun shone on the wet road. The lovely thing my mother is in her
white dress. All the trains she's missed. With the red flowers in

her hands. We're interwoven, it's not a strange womb I remember, a world full of beautiful women, every morning a beautiful woman is born, every evening a new one comes out onto the street. To be woman-blind. Mother tears me apart with her silence. When she talks she kills, when she's silent she strangles. The hostility on her face. Forty-three seconds late! Last night he didn't sleep at home! He never sleeps in his own nest. We reached Trumpeldor Street and I parked the car by a parking meter. They should put up parking meters beside the graves until the resurrection, I said, but it didn't make her laugh. I took out some coins for the meter but she beat me to it. She refused to let me put coins in the meter. She'd pay! She asked me to come. We're going to her mother's grave.

But she's my grandmother.

So what? You feel anything for anyone? Family's a dirty word to you. You say grandmother as if you really cared. I'm paying, Aminadav. And apart from that you're short of money, you're under pressure, and I, you know, calculate my life properly in moderation and don't carouse in cafés when I don't have money and so I always have enough and have no need to ask favors, it's a pity that you don't know how to live in moderation and then you wouldn't always be in trouble.

What trouble?

Trouble, she said. And stuffed the coins into the meter. We heard a click and the dial showed one hour. We walked to the cemetery.

On the right an old wall of limestone blocks, on the left houses pressed against each other. On the other side my kindergarten and next to it the El Al Building rising above us. Sheltering the old cemetery of Tel Aviv. In the kindergarten they're singing a Passover song now and someone, maybe, is looking for Aminadav hiding. My beloved kindergarten teacher says, What are you looking for, he isn't anywhere. Even in me he was and isn't. Like a mast of sugar. Melted. And the dears shout, He hasn't got a mast, he's got a prick, and she says, Maybe, but he snores and shoves all night. Talks about love in the wrong places. Stock '84 doesn't suit his breathing. Talking about her all the time (I didn't), making a movie about himself, seeking links with the womb. He has a car, a little house near Tel Aviv, divorced in usable condition, not brilliant.

And they look for me in different time levels. My mother looks for her mother and does not hear my musings of remorse. I think of Mira. Of Naomi. What I did last night. Why did I say love. Is it impossible without a phony glance of pain. But there was pain. And in the morning, that smile on her lips. And Mother walks and penetrates into the cemetery, and I walk after her. Her flock. To pass from outside in. To the hard earth with the graves, and under them the dear ones of Tel Aviv. The now legendary figures. Uncles and aunts, Levontin and Izmozik, Natanel and Hoffein, Luria and Matmon Cohen, Grandfather and Grandmother. Here's fat Meirowitz who used to spray water on us and here's his wife who used to hide the wig. They don't bury here anymore, for many years now. Graves exposed without shade, houses with plastic shutters all around with music for housewives. With women in hairnets hanging laundry, with television antennas to receive—why—Jordan and Cyprus. A woman in a long dress and shawl wants to rent me a skullcap. I said that I'll stand with my hand over my head and she gets angry.

I walked with my hand on my head until my mother said, Take your hand down already. The dead don't see anyway. I saw that she too had given in to a kind of mischievousness, which was unusual for her, here among the old people and the adults who had filled her youth in Little Tel Aviv. I thought: Here we go again. We'll hold hands and dance. "I'm standing in the circle and looking round about me,/I'm reaching out my hands,/Who'll come and dance with me." But we didn't hold hands. Mother walked on in her white dress, like a bride. Holding flowers. Here are buried Bialik and Ahad Ha'am and . . . they were all friends of your grandfather, she said. We stood beside Bialik's grave. She was tired, maybe she wanted to wait a little before appearing before her mother. They hadn't seen each other for quite some time. My mother's mother was a distinguished woman with deep wrinkles and the face of an ascetic angel. At sixty-four. It's hard to be an orphan, my mother said gently, and I hugged her back.

She trembled. We were standing beside C.N., the man who whispered to me A flower grew in a flowerpot/And he peeps all day at the garden plot. The man who saw a bird from the warm-lands come to his window. Under the stone lies a man hungry for sons, who received me from Mother's womb. I felt I belonged to the earth under the stone. I saw birds. I felt I could fly with them. I didn't want to. Or maybe it was the other way around. Mother said, He was such a generous man. . . . People said he was mean, it was they who were mean. . . . He was a great poet, and a human being. How he loved your grandfather. How he loved this people. Does this people deserve such a love. And I knew she'd spoken about me and her. And I wanted to say to her, Let me love you, don't ask, don't command, I'm only a human being, and a failure. I'm looking for some connection. And you're in it. Like Mira and Naomi. We're a single seed that has put on many faces. He too. C.N., and your mother, and your father, that prince of the de-tached. She said, C.N. smiled at you, you were a sweet baby, you had hair, you had a perfect nose when you were born, you even had eyebrows, he held you at the circumcision until the *mohel* came. And then he turned his face.

When we left the grave (Mother laid two flowers on C.N.'s grave) I asked her to go on alone. I'll come in a minute, I said. She smiled bitterly but with an unexpected tenderness. Not here, you shouldn't, Ami. . . .

Just for a minute, Mother.

What's happened?

An infection or something. Just a minute.

She looked around her and saw dead men, all her friends that she used to visit on festive occasions. All her teachers from high school, all Grandfather's friends. All this uniform, monolithic landscape in which she had fluttered, beautiful and special and distinguished, acting with the Lovers of the Hebrew Stage, and not one of them was still alive. We heard buses stopping with a grinding of brakes at the bus stop in Trumpeldor Street. The woman with the shawl was far away, behind a kind of thin mist. A boy ran with a hoop, far away, among graves, at the other end of the cemetery. She said, But be quick, Ami, and went.

I saw her seeking the grave of the woman she loved. I stood
behind my godfather's grave. No children waited for manure, no
pigeons had left their droppings in his tomb. I closed my eyes and
waited. I heard the music for housewives from a nearby house and
thought: The Japanese don't say I have a headache but There's
a headache. Just as we don't say I have a bus at the bus stop but
There's a bus at the bus stop. I concentrated, and then a terrible
pain flashed through me. Everything misted over. I wanted Bustanai to photograph me with this sudden pain. But there was no
Bustanai. Everything misted over, I sailed off inside Aminadav.
Arsalen put on flesh and blood. He said, Shoot at me, shoot at
me. Like a man called Himmo whom I knew in a monastery in
Jerusalem, without eyes, and without legs and hands, and he had
a lovely mouth and a nurse fell in love with him and lay beside
him so as to ward off death, because she loved the divine mouth
and death crawled out of her hands and she gave him an injection
of love and he died beside her and she rang the monastery bell
which once used to be rung to call sinners to repentance and later
on not. All the time he said Shoot at me shoot at me and the
wounded beside him, I with a split leg, hating him and loving the
king that he was. We called him Himmo King of Jerusalem. I
knew I was returning to the same pain that wedded me with the
fate of incinerators and sad eyes and exhilarating victories in chess
or theoretical physics. My godfather beside me, only bones. They
say there's love in the world, my godfather sang in an Ashkenazi
accent. And then, without my knowing why, a sentence penetrated into me from the outside: *I have a naked address.* And it
repeated itself over and over: I have a naked address, I have a
naked address. I don't know why it kept returning to my consciousness. It was like an old friend who had found a home, or a
whispered prayer. The pain cut me like a sharp Samurai sword.
It cut into my back, along my spine, shook my being and shrunk
me into the grain I had been once. And again, like then, when
I was eight days old, I didn't know that the pain was so fierce. The
blade joyfully piercing me was a meeting with something. Maybe
with that naked address. The pain became a kind of joy. The joy
of defeat. I celebrated it with my legs asplay. Stubbornly sidelong

beside an elegant tombstone. I thought: Here's all the innocence that C.N. wasn't, here are all the Aminadavs, together for a moment. It was amazing. Out of the silence and the pain I returned to a forbidden region of cruel innocence.

Not far from here children are telling their kindergarten teacher what fancy-dress costumes they'd worn last Purim. Each of them was someone else. All of them disguised to themselves. Or to someone else. Birds fly in all directions, theaters are pulled down for high-rise buildings, plastic shutters are the national façade of the city, laundry on lines, MiraNaomi far away, a bus stops at Trumpeldor, who fought Arsalen, just like me.

Soon the coins in the meter will be used up. A Jewish policeman will come and write a ticket. The pain passed. Death against the pain. The policeman against the kindergarten teacher. Coca-Cola against Pepsi-Cola. What will you do, enter the womb with a pocket flashlight? What are you seeking, son, tubes in a thinned-out condition, a liver saturated with sorrows, you know, son, we decay . . . false teeth. Withering toward cemeteries, the earth waits. I shouted: I have a naked address, and I didn't even have a naked address.

Walking to her I thought: Here's Bialik, a man who wasn't forced to smash his violin. She stood beside her mother's pinkish tombstone. I said what I always said, How nice the tombstone is. And she replied with her sad and bitter smile.

On the pink marble it said in almost invisible letters, Shoshana Feldman. With no date of birth or death. That was my father's idea. My aunt Lifshe put up a desperate fight. But my father won. He said to her: Passers-by won't see it, and doubters will be able to call her name. Why should anyone want to know from when and until when. In another hundred million years the world will be destroyed, the sun will explode, our planet will become a naked mass and the sun will destroy all life, and then the moon will break and everything will vanish. I remember the words, because they filled me with a dread that has not passed since. Even though a hundred million years is a considerable length of time. My mother bent over the tombstone. Mother wears a bridal dress, her voice catches, it all looks to me like stage décor for a play, the dead don't keep here, among strange tombstones, among houses buttoned with plastic shutters, phosphorus in the earth. I think of my grandmother. Maybe with regret, regret not that she's dead, even though it's a pity to remain in the world without witnesses, but because in all my biographies her place is missing. For thirty years I didn't see her even in my imaginings. Now her wrinkles are engraved in my imagination. Her white hair, as if she'd been born with all the sorrows to come. My mother's sad smile came from her, and from my mother to me, and from me to Naomi. We ate Shabbat dinner, she was grave and wore a long dress. Father said, White hair is lovely but not in soup. And she didn't laugh, a dark anger fumed inside her against my father, and his Goethe and his Schiller, the darkness of heavy ignominy. There was a film of disgrace on her face, as if everything was in vain. She taught me to eat soup without making a noise. She believed that the love between her and her husband had deepened since his death, on both sides. In Father's Goethe she saw a bandit who had come to rob us all. Father sat in the shop and read Fichte or Hegel and she didn't understand. She tried to explain things to me and I didn't understand, she told me that my grandfather had arrived in Eretz Israel in a coffin because of the decrees. She sat opposite his picture and refused to let my father frame it. Her image suddenly finished, I heard my mother muttering to her.

To see yearning on my mother's face. Yearning to be her mother's daughter. To be embraced, little, lifted in her arms. And her arms, without her knowing it, embraced the cemetery air. She stood embraced in imaginary arms and wanted Mama and Papa, like everyone, to be lifted up suddenly, to be mounted on shoulders, days that don't return. To enter that sweetness, to be sick with the grippe. To lie in bed with Mother feeding you honey and sugar in a spoon with warm milk and butter melting in milk. To hear old women saying, Garlic is good for all diseases, to medicate tea! To breathe in sweet steam. On a roaring stormy night. My mother is embraced by a mother whose memory is white and wrinkled, in a melancholy before the end. In her bridal dress she looked like an actress in a Yiddish tragicomedy on Second Avenue in New York. Here, in the place that Jews call the House of Life, she had come not to apologize, but to return to a wonderful moment that had been, perhaps to return into herself. I seek a way to my mother, she to her mother, my daughter to me, and my mother's mother to her mother, and so on to the first seed that is in us all and that we are in.

And then we walked down the cemetery path and my mother complained about the neglect: neglected and broken graves. I said to her, Actually, who cares? The third generation can't remember. She said, What a pity, what a pity. We stopped beside my grandfather's tombstone. On it was written: Here lies a scholar of wisdom, beautiful of spirit, the humblest of men, who passed away while still in his prime. . . . In pictures he looked like a prince. Maybe the same prince I was meant to become. A glow on his dead face. I told my daughter Naomi that my grandmother lives in Tiberias and rides camels and that my grandfather's a Jewish Robin Hood from the Golan Heights. Mira was born from out this false biography, and now, facing them, I felt the same remorse that I feel toward God. Perhaps if I could believe in Him He might be able to exist, or at least be less cruel. And we left the cemetery.

A Hungarian café. No vapor on the windows. The smell of coffee and cakes. Big thick-bodied women sitting and reading German magazines in cardboard bindings with advertisements on them from twenty years ago: Sail Shoham! Strand Special Cigarettes! Fly El Al Super Constellation! Quiet hubbub. Waiters in white jackets with gleaming mustaches and hair wipe tables, emitting the scent of eau de Cologne. Moist hands wiping tables with towels that aren't clean. A waiter produces a menu. His stance is at once wonderment and a challenge, the mustache stuck to his face with glue. I asked for a clean towel. My mother suddenly smiled. The waiter grew angry: What do you want? I said, First of all a clean towel! He said, Very smart, you'll probably order coffee and sit for two hours. I said, We'll sit three hours, we'll drink soda if we like, this place doesn't belong to your father. The cemetery does things to me. My mother says nothing and inspects the walls with renewed interest. Outside the window walk people dried out in the heat wave. Another waiter came and asked,

What's the problem. I said, No problem, I just asked to have the table cleaned with a rag that isn't less clean than the table. He smiled, brought out a clean rag, wiped the table and returned with a waiter's face. I said to him, One espresso and soda and one iced coffee and cake. Mother drank the soda thirstily and I mixed the iced coffee and the whipped cream. Outside stood a woman selling flowers. She had gray hair and was holding heavy baskets and a man tried in vain to make a call from a public phone. Suddenly I saw Mother's lips move, she spoke (so I guess from the fragments of words that I heard) about her mother's grave and who'd look after it after she too was gone and sundry other things about graves. But I don't hear the words, I hear what her heart is saying without words:

My marriage was a great sadness, Ami, for your father I was an ornament, for convenience, something else, to be together, I was unique in some way, maybe in my inner cunning, in my unlimited energy. . . . And he sat with all that was dead and I was a miracle of life on his arid desert. He's sick, will he recover? I believe. I know you don't believe, recover to what, everyone asks. Recover to what. To be a stone. But with a stone one can speak, the sadness of old age. Do you understand it at all. Someone who doesn't come on Shabbat eve because one should come with the granddaughter I don't have. Someone who sits at home and one can speak to him. The bitter ornament that I was, Ami. The life that spilled between the fingers. He loved with no tenderness, no pacification . . . no pathos. With no declarations or madnesses. And I yearned. All my life . . . And you came, the most apathetic of sons. I was a lamp in the house, I llumined for you a life in which there was no room for me.

Where were you. Habitualized estrangement. You weren't there. Tombstones. I and he. Everything died in him. Music died, things died. Delight in life in an immense shadow. Why. Coffee in the morning. Every morning the same coffee at the same time. Glasses arranged in straight lines in the kitchen. Slippers under the bed. Forty years. The same form. Pillows, this one on that one in the same order. Fresh-brewed tea in the evening.

To see a man get up in another room every morning at the same time. Reading Goethe, at five in the morning. I in my bed in the next room. Winter, cold. And you aren't there. Who is. He says good morning as if he's saying cheese. The dead books stand beside each other. With ornate bindings. With deerskin book marks. A kind of glass man. Go live. You're getting old and becoming dependent. What'll happen if he's late getting up. Instead of at five, at two minutes after five. No. But you hope. But no. And Aminadav isn't there. Gone to America. The shame. And I'm alone. There's no one. Who'll answer. Is there no love, no forgiveness, no understanding. . . . Lights switched off in anger. Don't waste electricity. Every night to part like two enemies. And in my dream he isn't there. I grope to seek him in my dream and he isn't there. And his snores beyond the dream somebody else is dreaming. Not I . . . You were late coming to me. And, after coming late, you refused to be and then you vanished again. . . . You're grown up. You have a daughter. He is never hungry. Never thirsty. He doesn't sweat. Doesn't complain. Smashes a flowerpot in anger and returns to Schiller. A legend about gilded frames. Why. Emptiness in separate beds, to wear out life, it's good against bacteria and snoring, good for the mattresses, they last longer, bad for the human being . . . that I was and still am. . . . You weren't there. Who'll pay.

And I thought, she said and her voice reached me again, about my condition. I'm strong, Ami . . . my life's linked to his life, we loved each other very much. We had some beautiful times, there were bitter moments, you know, but we were happy. Now I'm caring for him, he's sick. . . . Everyone's busy, I'm not accusing, I understand. Maybe I would have behaved differently. When my father died, and my mother remained alone, I sat with her days and nights; but things like that one can't demand. Not everyone's made of the same material.

Mother . . .

No, let me speak. She gripped the espresso cup with trembling hands, a tear perched in her retina, ready to drip, wearing her bridal dress, in a Hungarian café. I have no life of my own, she said, her voice suddenly heavy and dry, but I want you to know that I'm not afraid of death. I don't want to be a burden to

310

anyone.... You're all too busy.... I'm worried only about Father.
I want someone to be responsible for him even if something
happens to me and I go.... I want you to promise me that if
something happens, to me, you'll be ready. He has a pension and
I'm leaving our savings, what we saved from our modest earnings,
in the bank.... That money is solely for Father, Ami. If he gets
better I want him to live in a private home. If you were married
like everyone else and had a house in which people sleep at nights,
I could have asked more of you, but ... I want you to promise
me that you won't abandon Father, that as long as he's in Gedera
—if I'm not here—you'll visit him twice a week. And don't, you
hear, don't, don't dare to take him to one of those terrible institutions. If he can leave Gedera, let him live in a private home. There
are families that for a certain sum will take care of him.... I'll
prepare you a list. . . . Aunt Lifshe knows someone in Hod
HaSharon. I'm asking you to promise me.

I promised her.

And then she said quietly, not looking toward me: I've donated
my body to science.

I drank the rest of the iced coffee and gazed toward the window. Everything seemed still so unjoined. The cemetery. Mother
in her bridal dress seeking to be loved by her mother. Father sick
on my hands. A pension that I'm responsible for and now her
body to science.

My gaze meanders around the café. Women reading magazines. A woman selling her old body to science. The fashions of
Berlin nineteen sixty-seven in the magazines. Recipe, how to
make asparagus soup with sweet cream, bay leaves and ginger.
Waiters with mustaches wiping tables with moist hands. Outside,
the dry hum of a winter heat wave. Cars in Ben Yehuda, the
resurrector of the Hebrew language.

To build a house in Tel Aviv. Who'll build a house in Tel Aviv,
sang the pioneers. And the café proprietor takes money, puts it
in the cash register, which rings. The body from which I came
is being celebrated for the sake of science. Here the liver is filed,
the spleen has to undergo an additional examination, the intes-
tines have expanded in a strange manner, here is death. Where

311

are the memories, and the bitterness. People die of a surfeit of life. Doctors smoke cigarettes beside the body of my dead mother. The assistant is excited. My mother is his first corpse! My mother drinks espresso. She's still alive. But the moment will come when the assistant will cut her open with a knife. With tears, without tears. Here's an interesting blood clot. And the womb . . . See, a woman who gave birth to a boy and her womb is like a virgin's. Where no man has been. Where was Aminadav. Did he come straight from the black spaces, from the antistars? She died old, gave birth to a son, has a granddaughter in America. Her womb is virgin, and the joy in the doctors' chambers is great. And then the head of the department will say with that sorrow that is the lot of rare doctors: Well, apart from this, do you understand everything? Telepathy you understand. The human brain you understand. How Mozart wrote symphonies at the age of five you understand. . . . Where is all the knowledge that was collected in the brain of this woman. She herself didn't know more than a billionth part of what her brain knew. Do you understand everything? A wretched mosquito is born with all the mosquito knowledge that has been acquired by his race since the beginning of the world. Everything that all mosquitoes ever knew every mosquito knows the moment he is born. While we . . . Naked. Without armor. See the bitterness of the muscles. See this sorrow. Inside. An empty womb. What's the meaning of an empty womb. Someone fled it. Or was taken out by force. Or perhaps he wasn't there at all. Perhaps her son returned into the womb and wiped out all traces, like any thief. . . .

But he's a consciencist, the assistant will say.

And the old doctor will laugh toothlessly and speak no more.

Here are the papers, my mother added and handed me a bundle of papers clipped together. I read them. The words leaped from the paper. I couldn't understand. It said there that I was to phone at a certain moment and say to ——— that ———. The words decease and operation recurred many times. And then she said, Whatever happens, I'm not interested, *because I won't be there.*

And there won't be a funeral, she said. That'll save you troubles. Her pathetic voice preserved some trace of strength, as if to gnaw at the separation between us. I wanted to pity her. Didn't she deserve it. If I die, she said, and this time she was irate, no one can harm me anymore.

And thus I felt the hatred of the dead for the living. Like the hatred that bubbles up in the cemetery, bursting from the earth.

My mother *does* want a funeral. She wants an immense funeral. Her embalmed white body, on a wax sheet in the hospital, devoted to science, seeks to tie more and more. A funeral for a lifetime. A funeral one never returns from just as I never returned from Nahum's house after I went out to the dead castor tree standing in the yard, next to Tel Aviv port, and looked inside and his mother was sitting and drinking tea and her eyes wept and she thought of my living image as if I were her son's murderer. To seek forgiveness in a house of mourners.

But then, as in the movies, I got up, and in the sight of waiters and women reading German magazines, I took her hand as they do in the opera and I cried, into her hand, and I kissed the trembling hand of my mother in her bridal dress. I promised to look after Father, and to look after her. I told her how heroic she was. Her dark eyes burned. A hot wind roared outside. Scraps of newspaper to bring news to ravines. I looked like the clown I was in the court of the king of myself in vain. My mother stroked my eyes and I no longer know who played what. Was she playing in Mother and Son or I The Poor Son. Two melodramas from Second Avenue. That we're all in all the time. Irony is only an attempt to prevent surrender to this terrible thing. People walked in the street as if they didn't know. Bialik dead inside his grave. Birds. A man selling peanuts. The El Al Building. A kindergarten teacher singing Passover songs. Soon it'll be spring. We returned to a car with a Hebrew ticket. Ten lira, Mother cried in pain. I took the ticket and threw it at all the plastic shutters.

Soap opera, my mother and I. And that smile. At the traffic lights she warns me to stop.

Mother *I know.*

Some people are color-blind, she said.

I'm not.

She's smiling or crying. The papers for her body are in my

hand. I'll read them the way one reads a holy book. Every morning, the way Stendhal read the Code Napoleon. For precision of style. I wanted to return to the womb on the screen at the Herzlia Studios. The womb that wasn't here. My mother knew. I too, I came from the black spaces. These crazy times, says the man on the radio. And sells Neca 7. A miracle soap. And then someone speaks about the struggle of the metalworkers. There is no death or birth. There is one plane of nothing. A fly buzzed.

```
🁢🁢🁢🁢
```

26

```
🁢🁢🁢🁢
```

Driving to the hospital for incurables in Gedera. Bustanai likes a road between orchards. The sunbeams twinkling among the leaves. He cures the world's diseased through colored lenses. I sit beside a sound man called Uri. Being a gravedigger's a profession too, says the driver, pointing to the Hevra Kadisha hearse passing us in the opposite direction with its driver smoking a cigarette and listening to music on the Light Program. While they carried the equipment into the hospital I went into the waiting room. Two old women sat in the huge room, beside a bookshelf, wearing faded dressing gowns and singing, in two-part harmony, How beautiful are the nights in Canaan, how cool they are, and clear, and the stillness. Their eyes four frightened mice, cleaving to each other, seeking a hold, their arms interlinked. Pure and whispery, crystalline, negatives of what they were once when the nights in Canaan were young. They glance at me bashfully, imprisoned in the song of their salvation. The harmony is rare, they sing together beautifully. I said to them, I've never heard singing as lovely as this. They giggled in embarrassment and instead of answering me went on singing. But now there was something of alarm in the rhythm, which increased somehow. Their voices were thin, like the voices of rare birds. We brought Father to the room and he looked at the two old ladies as if they didn't exist. We took him in the wheelchair. A nurse behind a counter filled small glass saucers with medicines. Behind her was an open cupboard and in it were transparent boxes and in them thousands of capsules and tablets. She carefully placed the medicines in the saucers, her face concentrated, with a nurse's cap on her head. A woman shouted from a room: Nuuuuurse! And a nurse with an alert face and long white socks said, I won't come Malka, don't wet your bed again so soon. People in wheelchairs staring at us, a man walking with a chair in his hands, step after step. We covered Father with a woolen blanket, he wore a black beret and a corduroy jacket. We went outside, circled the hospital, and arrived at a lovely spot Bustanai had found. It was from this precise spot, before this was a hospital, that we, Dr. Neidler and Father and I, had stood planning a German café with white tables facing such a beautiful and idyllic landscape. The purple mountains. From far off appears a red spraying plane doing aerobatics. The poison into this pastoral is exaggerated. Veins of fields in red and purple and green and yellow. Later Ivria said to me that it was cruel. I said to her that my father's wound is me. Look, I said, maybe I love this man.

Bustanai urged me not to photograph. Let's shoot the view from here and leave it at that, he said. Why trouble a sick man, it's as if you were shooting your father's dying. I said to him, It's not as if. I really am shooting my father's dying. We pushed the wheelchair without saying another word to each other.

But Bustanai who had earlier been contemptuous of me photographed with the fervor of a true cameraman. He turned this way and that and found the right angles. He charged the air with his passion to photograph my dying father properly. He sang through colored lenses. He sought the most correct frame and my estimation of him rose beyond measure. My father muttered words by August von Platten. Then he spoke words from a poem by Johann Christian Günther, and suddenly he quoted: "Strong wind strong." The words were strange on the still background. No one was to be seen outside, all the patients were at afternoon tea. The large edifice sat on a landscape and didn't yield to it. The plane hovered without making a noise. My father sat unmoving. He looked like Naomi my daughter when she's sleeping. Mournful and yielding. He raised his hand and tried to grasp mine, as if I were a line in a poem by Günther. Something was fermenting inside him but outwardly he was still as marble. And the words "Strong wind strong" were weak and slack, as if they were trying to explain the irony of life. And then, as if out of the poem, a strong gust of wind began to blow. The bushes rolled and erupted, dust rose like a huge cloud. Everything hazed for a moment and brown dust filled the air and the legendary landscape became a gray-brown opacity. My father bent over, the beret fell off his head, he opened his mouth and shouted, Mamushka! and tried to point with his trembling hand toward the hospital. His eyes seemed torn at the corners. And when Bustanai wanted to come and help me, I filled with rage. Don't stop shooting! It's my money. Shoot, damn you! The wind was awful, everything flew about, the cameras barely stood their ground in the sudden wind. I grabbed the microphone from Uri's hand and placed it next to my father's mouth, and Bustanai, shocked, continued shooting. My father repeated, Mamushka! Mamushka! and didn't stop muttering. The microphone was next to his mouth. The jacket was almost torn off him by the force of the wind. I started pushing the chair toward the hospital and signaled with my hand to Bustanai to come and photograph the flight from in front. I pushed my father's wheelchair and Bustanai photographed. I was glad that the lenses weren't sensitive to sorrow. With my own eyes —while running and pushing my father's wheelchair—I saw my father's tears that I could not weep. He was calling, Mamushka! In the midst of the tumult things come to me, Father and I in an old far-off street. He's angry, why do I ask him about a broken violin, who told you, he asks, annoyed. I eat ice cream and he pays, like a bribe. The dead street of Shabbat morning on the way to the museum to see an exhibition by the painter Reuven. Afterward he stood beside the window. In the window was all the sea and the singer Giulini, father of the excommunicated, sang Aïda. And I said to him, What was the pain, Father? What was it. And he says to me, Sit down Aminadav, reads me Schopenhauer's hatred of women with a restrained laugh on his face, toward the kitchen, where my mother is placing glass beside glass, so that the

317

man who was my father won't shout. I remember a quiet night. I want to paint a Yarkon like the painter Kulyavyansky. I painted trees beside the Yarkon and my father strolled among the trees with a water bottle and a pith helmet and knickerbockers. A stranger stopped, looked at the paintings and asked what the picture was worth and I said to him, It's worth one mil. And the man gave me three mil and there was an excitement on his face. I rejoiced but Father smiled. We walked along Ben Yehuda Street toward our house, through the quiet of Shabbat, from all the windows came Shabbat chants on the radio. I said to him, Father, I'm just a child and I've sold a painting! And he said, It's a scandal (now I remember, seeing his terrified face in the cyclonic wind that comes from the desert and heaps brown dust upon thirty-five-millimeter cameras), painting is evil-heartedness on the map of a world that does not exist, an imagined world! Nature is fatal, said my father, while art is without death and thus has no reality of nothingness, and that's the only reason it's eternal and sickening!

The street was quiet and only the radios brought the cantors from all the windows. Art is the ornamenting of the desert with artificial flowers. So said the man who measured the feelings of artists with a magnifying glass, who lived in everything that was dead. I've sold a picture, for three mil, and that's worth a glass and a half of soda! I said. And he didn't laugh and didn't not laugh. I wanted to know where the name Sussetz came from. For Sussetzes appear for the first time in the eighties of the eighteenth century, after Catherine the Great's victory over the Cossacks. They served as advisers to the hetman Mazepa after the defeat in the battle of Poltava. Afterward they settled in Tarnopol in Galicia, and thus left the Ukraine. Tarnopol is the town of Rabbi Nachman Krochmal, who wrote in the Guide to the Perplexed of the Time: "Pleasure, pride, false position and vain belief are the four sore punishments, corrupters of the spirit of the people. Until they cease from the soul to the flesh of its inwardness and its outwardness, and it will be a nation no more." Sussetzes in the Ukraine, broad vast steppes, Father fleeing from his father's bakery to Goethe. Fifty-four years have passed, damn it, fifty-four years since the day you left the orange-roofed house in the poor little street of a distant *shtetl* with the smile of a scholar of the wise, with a violin in your hand and Spinoza's Ethics in your suitcase. And for fifty-four years you've spoken Hebrew and dreamed German and you didn't speak Polish, and Tarnopol was far away like something dark and forgotten, and your mother a thing dark and oily, and your father with his carved stick. And at my bar mitzvah you laughed: this fake tradition, opium for the masses . . . fallow years instead of morals . . . *kashrut* instead of culture . . . And after all these years now that I'm behind you, and a strong wind is blowing from a German poem of yours, you shout Mamushka! When was the last time you said Mamushka? To push the chair inside. The two old ladies sing like birds. The sky has filled with clouds amazingly quickly, rain comes down in torrents. A nurse will feed him with a spoon. My mortified father is taken to his room. In the genes failure lurks. The advisers of Mazeppa failed, went up in smoke, a violin was smashed, I make a movie. To be born is maybe a moral deception, Mira.

And the next day to develop the film in the heated studio. To sit facing the Steenbeck and examine the contortions of his face the moment he shouted Mamushka in Polish. A dark room, flickerings of light around opacity, Ivria's Broadway cigarettes, the smoke of Aminadav's pipe. Persistent rain scratching against windowpanes. To look at my father's torn face, to see his intelligent eyes, his bright pupils, the whites slightly stained, the contraction of the mucous membrane, the purple of the clouded vision, the eyebrows joined, too deep, eyelids dead on the man's face, the blood membranes shrunken past dignity, the conjunctiva for God's sake, but the tombstone in his eyes, Ivria doesn't see it.

To say to her: Look into the pupils, look into the conjunctiva, into the eyebrows. No, she doesn't see. We tried shortening the shot, to see only the pupil, blown up several times, and she doesn't see. To examine the smile that came before the shout and to discover a jestingness on my father's face, like a lizard, and the disgust of the mouth with its twisted lips. And after the smile the face contorts, the eyes contract, the pupils flash and then the shout Mamushka! We run the film forward and backward. First the clownish smile wrapping sinews over pain and then the shout.

319

And then the other way, first the shout and then the smile. To examine the pain with the pain meter inside me. Ivria measured, from the moment he said "Strong wind strong" until the end of Mamushka, sixty-two seconds. A cosmic passage, a red spraying plane hovering, fields hazing, the camera discovering the cyclone a split second before my father sees it, he says "Strong wind strong" and suddenly the cyclone reaches him and on his face is still the clownish smile, I don't know where it stems from, and then the face contorts with terror and the shout Mamushka!

She cut and spliced and we entered with a superimposition of the cyclone that whirled later on when I was pushing the chair and Bustanai photographed the flight and the pastoral landscape we stuck to later frames and thus received a similar setup, though different, of the happening.

And then, after she'd spliced, again we erased twenty-one seconds and the transition seemed too fast and smooth, I'd even say too elegant. The moment of awakening is Mamushka! And thus a whole scene, my father in a wheelchair, on the screen resembling me a lot, I don't know why, the finger pointing to the hospital, the plane, "Strong wind strong," clownish smile, the plane's steep climb, fields suddenly enveloped by cyclone. My father shocked, the pointing finger, droplets of poison from the plane, two old women singing, their faces white like two frightened mice, and from them to my father's face, the terror begins, the smile vanishes, his eyes stare, in the background, in German, *More light!* The wheelchair being pushed, the powerful wind, trees praying in dread, everything swept and dragged along, the building gray, the wind raising mountains of dust and the shout from the dead eyes, Mamushka! And Ivria doesn't see the tombstone.

We stopped. A still of Father halfway through Mamushka! We stopped at Mamu. . . . A frozen glance, half horror, is it possible to describe in words the meaning of half horror, the middle of the scream. Like a mouth unraveled and frozen. Malice and pain, like a detail from a painting by El Greco, Father's Storm in Toledo. Staring eyes, the hair like a flag gone crazy, the glance of a baby and some trampled old woman. In the expression of my father who resembles me can be seen Naomi losing a dog, as we go to buy The New York Times on a day of snow, wind blowing from the river, a dog who wants to be loved. But what horrifies me is that the half shout of my father to his mother is an expression of serenity on Naomi's face. Are despair and joy simply slight changes of angle? The gleam of a dark tooth in the depths of my father's mouth. In the still everything is clear and frightening, a dark space, the tombstone in his eyes.

Ansberg took off his shoes and socks, which is no pleasure to someone with sensitive nostrils like mine. But this tension in front of Father in the still Mamu . . . And Ansberg has to spread his toes and scratch between them to arrive at some real lucidity. The meticulous checking of his statistics he always does at my place, in the armchair my mother bought me, barefooted, one hand scratching between the spread toes and the other calculating increments in the rate of fornication at Tel Aviv beach.

Strange, he says.

A tombstone? I ask hopefully.

Mockery.

What mockery? Mockery of whom?

And he laughs, with his toes spread out. A true messiah. Listen, he says, what are you looking for? A confession? Love? Aminadav, a man who went to visit the mother of his friend who died in the war to ask for pity and forgiveness instead of giving his own body in exchange deserves to spend the rest of his life in darkness. What do you mean you don't understand.

I didn't say I didn't understand.

You asked what mockery.

Yes, what.

You asked of whom.

Yes, I asked of whom.

Of whom then, Aminadav. You're photographing a dying father. You aim a camera directly at the pain, you make a still of an old man's anguished cry for his mother, an old man who has become again the child he was and is close again to the earth to which he will come, and you ask forgiveness, from him, love, from him?

Not forgiveness, not love, I'm looking for the objective tombstone. What I mean is I want you too to see that in his eyes there is a tombstone which is me. I'm looking for connections, Ansberg, I'm there, the I was supposed to become and didn't become, there's disease in the air, get it?

Everyone has a mother, said Ansberg, every mosquito or cockroach has a mother, Aminadav. Even Ansberg has a mother, says Ansberg.

What was Monsieur Ketzele's real name?

Von Graten.

I laughed. And he wanted to cry, the great lover with his stinking toes spread open.

Did my father, by the very act of smashing his violin, prophesy my life?

Ansberg doesn't know. Prophecy isn't his field, he said. And now I saw that smile on Ivria's face and my heart prophesied something to me and I didn't know what it had prophesied. But I was enthused by the sight of my father in Mamu . . . and I said, Rimbaud wrote a poem in which he prophesied all his future life, the tombstone has to be visible to everyone.

Ansberg calmed down. He put on his socks and shoes. He goes out with Ivria. They'll be back soon. They'll bring me a sandwich, coffee and juice.

From the adjacent editing room a voice roared: The officer said, Follow me. *The officer said follow me* the officer said follow me, and after that came the voice in reverse: em wollof dias reciffo. I was absorbed in a yearning for the tombstone in my father's eyes. Mixing pity with an ancient family from the Ukraine that became uprooted and went to live in Tarnopol. I didn't know the fields and the forests. The village girls and the mushrooms after the rains, the inner life of the ancient memory. Tarnopol. Jews in the marketplace, old men and a *shohet,* an old grandfather weeping texts at night and tormenting himself, mortifying himself for the messiah. Narrow streets between wooden houses. Mamushka was born to me old, I remember her from the day she came to Palestina in '38. But I saw her coming out of a faded painting of a city I was never in. After *badim badim,* Mamushka came, in a ship. My grandfather, dressed like a gentleman, with a very short beard and beautiful white hair, descended into a boat in the new Tel Aviv port and people with sunshades stood gaping at the new immigrants to Eretz Israel. Jewish porters dragged suitcases from an Italian ship. They had arrived a moment before the curtain closed and they brought dried mushrooms strung like necklaces, heavy furniture, lampshades, garlic powder against all diseases, sheets, grandfather clocks, baking utensils. There was a lot of laughter at Purim, I wore a woolen suit, cufflinks and a tie, and my grandfather lent me his gold watch which had Hebrew letters instead of numbers, Aminadav disguised as a man.

Mamushka was a tiny woman, she wore skirts and slammed windows and shutters. People with familiar voices were queer to her. She would hide and count crystals in the brown cupboard, covered in darkness, the smell of naphthalene, the clock chiming Tarnopol hours and everything strange in her house. Tapping she walked the floors of her house with glass feet. In the bakery next door people worked and swore in Yiddish, but the hallahs which they made were marvelous, and the rolls, they'd never tasted the like. Near the Tel Aviv abattoirs, in the far north, among hills, the little house that Father built for them. Today, inside the editing room, I see Mamushka from out of Mamu . . . like a painting by Vermeer, certainly not by Titian, perhaps something by the elder Pasternak, who wanted to paint a Titian in her honor. A sand path led to their house. Past huts of Yemenites. Today they call it Nordau Boulevard, tin shacks and paraffin lamps. Colored washing out to dry, donkeys and foals, fields, and my grandmother with her sunshade hurrying home. At home she sits behind closed shutters and holds a porcelain doll. She spoke only Polish or Yiddish among the shutters and the dolls standing on the cabinet. I said to her, How are you Grandmother, and she said, It's a nice day today, she didn't want to see, the fields were full of demons, people said the Arabs were shooting. There were headlines in the Yiddish newspapers, something full of apprehension—Palestine. Black Jews with mustaches, in undershirts, or bare-chested, with houses rapidly being built opposite her house, with people shouting and yelling. There was no fur shop here. The hostile world around her. With her fine melancholy smile. A barrier fixed. A cardboard queen with gold teeth.

On Shabbat eve I go to see her. Walking among the Yemenite shanties. Seeing Shabbat candles on empty paraffin drums covered with colored tablecloths. They sing chants to Queen Shabbat. The bakery is still. The hallahs with poppy seed, buttered, are laid out in my honor. Grandfather in the bathroom is grooming himself for Shabbat. My grandmother is always ready for Shabbat. Then he comes out and pinches me on the cheek. Nu, Aminke, will we go the synagogue? My father, inside Palestina, doesn't come. He bought them a house. He scoffs. He doesn't admit that there are no hallahs as good as Grandfather's. On Friday night when I go to bed and close my eyes I wait. Five minutes later Father appears in my room, walking on tiptoe. He looks at me for a long while, I hold my breath, he's in his soft slippers and it's hard to hear him. I've learned to see through closed eyelids. The light from the corridor shines on me and he stands there, mute. And then he steals into the kitchen and opens the breadbox and bites into the hallah. The man who screamed Mamushka! thirty years later. But I'm a bastard, Mira, I put on slippers too and like a trained thief slip into the shadow of the passage that leads to the bathroom, and spy on my father. And he chews at the hallah and then at the cookies and his face is aglow, he looks as if he's praying, and then he gathers up the crumbs and leaves the marble beside the sink clean and spotless and puts the hallah and the cookies back in the breadbox and comes back to look at me. And I'm already back in bed, pretending to sleep. I peep at him, as if snoring, but I don't snore. He snores. I'm a child, children don't snore, I snore like a child snores. And he looks at me. He smiles, maybe he doesn't smile, maybe he feels a great remorse and goes back to bed. To Jean Paul or Schiller, and he falls asleep with seven pillows and a high feather bed, with a radio beside the bed to hear the news at five in the morning, to know what has happened in this dead world. But to admit that the cookies are marvelous, that the hallah is beautiful, that he won't do.

My grandfather goes to synagogue with his carved stick, a stick with a silver knob like Bialik's. With a bag for his tallith and a

Shabbat hat. She sits, she doesn't go, mostly she prays at home. She's afraid to go out, Arabs, Yemenites, frightening black people all around. She sits me down in the armchair, gives me sweets and asks:

Tell me about Naftali, what makes he really?

Frames, I say.

Plays not?

No, Grandmother. I've told you a hundred times, he doesn't play.

He played so beautifully. Why plays he not?

I don't know, Grandmother.

Ah, how he played. Whole the street would come to hear.

But he doesn't.

And what makes he?

Frames.

For what?

Pictures.

Of whom?

People. To hang on walls. For the museum too.

And then she'd get up and open a black cabinet on which stood an angel of crystal, which looked as if it had been interrupted in its saccharine flight, and she'd take out a small letter and give it to me: "Naftali mine, my health is so-so, good. Here are hallahs. Love, Mother." Every Shabbat. Three words more than the seven words on the cross by Schütz, Father's great love.

To kiss the mezuzah, she requests, why not, and to walk through fields, with hallahs and cookies and a letter to Father. She had a smell of overseas, something distant of garlic and mushrooms, of forests and mold. With the *shtetl* and Mendele Mocher Sephorim, I'd get home tired, and give Mother the hallahs and the cookies. My mother closes herself in the kitchen, the show is about to begin. Father with Goethe and I with tears. And I fling at him: Why don't you go to your mother's, why don't you visit her. . . . So she has a smell of overseas, so what, she's your mother . . . your mother . . . tears in her eyes all the time . . . she says Naftali with such pain. She just sits there all the time holding a porcelain doll and waiting for you. Father doesn't answer me, and

Mother's in the kitchen, closed in. And then he bursts into the kitchen, the refined man who was my father, and screams at her about the dirt. And there wasn't a crumb in the kitchen, but he found it. And why do they torment him, why do they send Aminadav to his mother so as to come back and bother him. He has done enough for them, he's bought them a house and a bakery, at Rosh Hashana he saw them, he has nothing to say to them, why is the kitchen filthy, why aren't we eating yet, why are the books covered with dust, why why. And I chew at the sweet hallah, Mother drinks tea, waiting for the storm to pass, and it passes. The understanding, startled smile comes. And Father returns to Goethe on the porch, a pleasant breeze blows from the sea, the sea coated with lacquer. Giulini lilts the shofar of Imber and the late Mezuy, or an aria by Puccini. Pikka's father builds blocks out of concrete, I don't know why, Nahum's mother picks guavas, the lemons give out a fragrance, the voice of the turtledove is heard in our land. From the radio comes the voice of the expert on war, when will Hitler die and an end come to all the murder. Songs of Hebrew soldiers on the Italian front. The mother of Nahum the corporal stands on her porch and looks longingly at the sea. Laundry is brought down from the roofs. Basins dry in the setting sun. A donkey leads a caravan of camels on the beach and an Arab sings *Aluma ya aluma* . . . Afterward, dinner on the porch, salad, sour milk, eggs, salt fish. The wonderful hallahs in butter, but Father doesn't taste, he doesn't acknowledge them, he eats bread, he doesn't like hallahs, he says. At night he'll sneak into the kitchen. One day Grandfather took bread out of the oven, and with the baker's shovel in his hand, died. Grandmother came to the funeral in a brown fur, she didn't cry, she stood small and mouselike and waited until they had lowered the body into the grave.

Like an angel of crystal she stood. They filled the grave with earth and came to tear a tear in her clothes. She hadn't brought a shirt for tearing like everyone else, she'd come in the clothes she loved best. She asked them to tear them to pieces. Mother cried, I wanted to cry but the tears got mixed up in me, at a funeral I laugh with embarrassment, I want to cry, and the tears come out in chimes of muted laughter, alarming me. And Mamushka saw Father and smiled at him shyly as if she were a child, with a kind of surrender, she approached him and placed her head on his shoulder and he didn't move. His face was frozen. He looked toward the grave and didn't say a word. Mother caressed Mamushka. Gently Mamushka took down Mother's hand and placed ' Father's arm on her shoulders. He didn't refuse, but he didn't assist. They stood there for a little while and then moved on. She sat in her room and waited for her husband. She wore shrouds, and waited. My aunt came and didn't see the shrouds that Mamushka wore, because she wanted to know what inheritance would remain from the bakery, and how many cupboards she might get. I saw them but no one believed me. My mother sat *shiveh* and didn't see the shrouds, because she saw the absence of Father, who was suddenly forced to become a Civil Defense inspector and to shout: Please turn out the lights. After a week the mourning ceased. And she still in shrouds, knowing that I saw them. She told me how she'd met her husband at a fair in Tarnopol and how handsome he'd been and how the match had been arranged. She died two weeks later, wearing her shrouds. The shutters were closed, the doors locked, everything was ready and she returned to her husband for whom she yearned so. On the table lay a letter, in an envelope, to Father: "Naftali mine, my health is so-so, good. Here are the hallahs. Love, Mother." And beside it were two hallahs and the cookies, fresh. No one knew who had baked them.

Once she opened a window, an Arab passed on a donkey, she quickly slammed the window shut. A Yemenite man stood there, shouting, and she hid. And she played with the doll with frightened hands. Always dressed, she sat and looked like a cardboard princess, from Tarnopol she came and to Tarnopol she returned.

27

I phoned Mrs. Shifhosheth, a friend of my mother's, who said, What? You were a lovely boy, very thin, a dreamer. Once I came to visit, your parents weren't home, and you sat near the door and cried, you said you had a migraine, I thought what's going on children don't have migraines, but I didn't say a thing. Afterward we sat on the steps and you told me, me, who was a friend of your mother's from high school, that your mother was born in Tiberias, that you had a grandmother there who had an Arab friend from Mount Arbel or something, maybe I'm getting it mixed up, and that you have uncles who are hunters and fishermen and that one of them, maybe Avner, the one from Haifa, is a hunter and had killed a lion or had almost killed a lion or a hyena, I don't remember, and that there'd been a nun there who was white or black and wore black or white and didn't speak and maybe you were born in Germany! I really don't remember exactly anymore. Ah, you told me that your grandfather died in Horan, that he'd been a secret adviser to a Bedouin sheik in Trans-Jordan. . . . I told you . . . well, what could I say to you? I bought you some headache pills but they didn't help. Later your mother came and they put you to bed in a dark room and until you fell asleep you moaned with pain. . . . You had the saddest eyes I ever saw, like your grandfather's, Nehemiah of blessed memory who was my teacher

328

at Neveh Tzedek, did you know that all the girls there were in love with him?

I thought he was in love with them, I said.

She laughed and laughed and after that she hung up.

We placed my father, who had just been on the screen, shortened by twenty-one seconds, into a round box, we wrote "Tombstone" on it, placed the box beside all the other round boxes of the movie and left.

We drove down to the esplanade and parked opposite the restaurant. The sea pounded its waves against the esplanade. In the distance Jaffa, the towered castle. And Ivria beside me. After that to the Paris Cinema to see a movie about love, French. Ivria closed her eyes and saw or didn't see the fornications. We were tired from Father on the screen. We walked out and went to the last Tnuva that remained in town and ate an omelet and a vegetable salad, sour milk and fresh bread with sweet butter, and we drank coffee in glasses, the cream of the milk floating on the coffee. We warmed our hands on the glasses. Steam rose from the coffee.

From the small kitchen came the smell of cooked potatoes. A woman wearing an apron came out and took eggs from the refrigerator in which were various salads in nicely arranged plates, and returned to the kitchen. I recalled Gedera. Dr. Neidler eating potatoes with ground parsley and butter. The fresh sour milk of Gedera, in squat glasses. Remembering the porch, with Father in the room and the phonograph playing a *Missa Solemnis.* Father with a score in his hand and Dr. Neidler with a smile. And Lili Neidler collecting the eggs in baskets and sending them to Tnuva. And a boy on a donkey carrying milk to the dairies and a man mounted on a mule riding past the window and behind him acacias and curlicues of bougainvillaea. And a kind of dryness in the air blending with the *Missa Solemnis.* On the wall, pictures by Oppenheimer, Schtrock and Liebermann. The German Jews in Gedera, in Tel Aviv, arrived in '38. How Ben Yehuda Street became Ben Yehudastrasse. Confectionery shops were opened, selling real chocolate wrapped in silver paper. In the groceries the newspapers were replaced by thin, clean wrapping paper. Old scales with weights were discarded for new scales with dials and numbers. White aprons and elegant shops, in German. Heat scorched Berliners and Heidelbergers, in ties, in Ben Yehuda-strasse, coffee with *schlagsahne*. In North Tel Aviv a symphony orchestra was founded in the sands. A line of stubbornly well-dressed people, undaunted elegance, in the sands, to hear Huber-man. And afterward the rain dripped on a tin roof. Everything festive and wretched. I sit between my father and Dr. Neidler. The two women, Mother and Dr. Neidler's wife, beside us. I discovered the sidelong glance of Dr. Neidler on my father. Did Neidler want tears? As if every murder must be repeated again and again. Father listens with severe silence. In the intermission he went to bring us soft drinks.

Ivria fell asleep in the midst of my meditations. I took her to her home. I said, What a pity that Ansberg isn't with us. She said, and her voice was suddenly sad: He's most probably waiting beside some house, so as to love. She pronounced the "to love" with a longing mingled with distress. I left her outside her house. Strong rain fell and she hurried indoors. Rain and windshield wipers and a kind of sour warmth inside the Ford. On the radio they spoke about the recession. It was night and you don't photo-graph at night. Bustanai's asleep at his home. Ivria's reading the *Shulhan Aruk*. Anis, the duty nurse, is very very surprised to see me. I asked her how he is and she said, Fine, he's sleeping. . . . I sat down beside his bed. It was warm in the room. I took off my coat and put it down on a chair. A man snored opposite me, in the bed of the dead. People moaned in their sleep from all the rooms. A nurse read Movie World on the counter and a male nurse poured water into saucers, to be given with the mid-night doses. The powerful light that gleamed in the corridor.

The open doors and the sounds of slow dying. Anis went to bring me a cup of coffee. She sat outside and waited under the neon light and listened to the moans. Maybe she thought I had come because of her. She's from Tunis, she told me, maybe she'd seen too many French movies. I look at my father. I wiped away the sweat that poured down his sleeping face. He turned his head to me with closed eyes and his face was pale and thin. His teeth in a glass, his mouth puckered. He snored and looked like a terrified bird. Nonetheless, he was beautiful in his sleep, and the arch of his cheeks was so gentle above the down of his white and stubbled beard. He looked disarmed, the serenity on his frightened face was strange to him and to me. A woman shouted suddenly in her sleep, *No no,* and a man roared, *All around, there is, all around.* In the dining room two nurses tried to catch a film on television, from Cyprus. Gray ripples ran across the screen.

To sit with Anis and drink brandy. To hear that she lives in Ashdod. Every year she goes to France to buy clothes. We went to see the two old women, who slept in a room painted white in two adjacent beds. On the wall hung a painting by Shor, landscape and a stream and thick-topped trees, a lot of green on a white wall. Holding hands even in their sleep, and on their faces an expression of innocence. Like gentleness domesticated, halved in two, one half to one and one half to the other, both loving the same song, two old women from the Labor Regiment, looking like slaughtered air, whom did they have in the world. Is this a way of cheating the death sitting at the heads of the beds. I kissed Anis over their beds and they didn't move. I thought: Love is love. She took me to a nice enough room, quiet and solid, good for this stormy night. I wanted to be a windshield wiper and to move the storm away for her. In the room she started smiling. She was a boat in a terrible sea, and she was very much there. She didn't look for a thing, she gave as mothers say they give. This was a celebration of orphans, she from Ashdod with sailings to France to buy beautiful things and to clean nightpots, and I with a father on the screen. Afterward she brought me coffee and cookies. We put the coffee cup down on her naked belly, after I'd told her that she had a nice navel, and she'd said that in France they really knew how to cut navels, and was very proud.

She lay spread-eagled on her back, not moving, with the coffee cup on her belly. She tensed a muscle and I drank the coffee without it spilling on her stomach and she was gleeful. I said to her, Come let's try something, in this fucking hospital I want to try to father myself. She laughed and said that that's what she wants to do more than anything. We met again, I inside her and she in me and each of us tried to concentrate on the birth of Aminadav. She said, It's because of the cognac, and she trembled a bit. And I was panicky and maybe I cried out. In this crying, this happy weeping, sometimes we meet. But to father Aminadav so close to my dying father was tasteless. She told me that one night she'd slept with a friend in a hotel in Ashkelon. In the morning she was told that someone had peeped through the keyhole. She'd sat fuming all through breakfast because she didn't know who had peeped. Under us people dreamed and moaned, the heating hums in this building, through the window appeared pale fields in the first light of morning, the rain stopped, the sky was blue to purple, a plane winked its lights toward Tel Nof.

Before leaving I went to him again and kissed him on the mouth. The old women in their room slept, frighteningly restful. Still holding hands. I listened to their breathing and heard How beautiful are the nights in Canaan. And then they woke up as one. Anis stroked their faces. They looked at us and were not frightened now. The night was still in them, the dreams had been about distant things in which were many hidden fears and many hopes. The hope on their faces was bewildering, perhaps they'd woken up aged twenty and only in a minute or two they'd again become frightened mice. I didn't want to see them in their debasement and I approached them. I whispered something to them, I don't remember exactly what. They smiled. Together. And then I said, Sing for me. And they sang in a whisper, in their clear voices, How beautiful are the nights in Canaan. I said to them that I knew Nadiv Israeli and that I'd take them for a tour around the world, Carnegie Hall, Albert Hall, the Olympia in Paris, everywhere, even the Mann Auditorium. The funny smile on their faces before Anis puts their false teeth in their mouths.

Outside, stars. Sky without a cloud. A hundred billion stars in a hundred billion Milky Ways burned with a dim light. I thought: How strange that I'm not at all worried by the fact that every year the earth's orbit around the sun decreases by one second. The billions of distant stars filled me with a powerful joy.

The eye with which I see this immense universe is the same

eye with which the universe sees me. Wherefore the Indian says: Father a son, write a book, plant a tree and die.

The first movie I saw in my life was Stanley and Livingstone with Spencer Tracy, which was shown in the Beit Ha-am in Gedera. On the day I was born, movies started talking. They spoke then too, in Gedera: Dr. Livingstone, I presume, said Tracy. Here, Ivria, you show me in black-and-white that on May second nineteen thirty the famous Mr. Stanley (not Tracy) says to the cotton growers in Britain that "if one day it becomes possible to convince the naked savages of Africa to wear clothes only one day a week, it will be possible to market to Africa three hundred and twenty million yards of cotton from England, and if they learn to wear clothes all the other days of the week too it will be possible to sell them merchandise to the value of twenty-six million pounds sterling a year." And on May second which is Herzl's birthday the newspaper published the testimony of Mr. Yorksteiner who accompanied Dr. Herzl on his mission to the Vatican, and Yorksteiner claims that the Pope said to Herzl that the Holy See would be prepared to support the establishment of a Jewish state in Palestine if all the Jews converted to Catholicism.

Ivria doesn't know what to do with all this.

Explaining to her. Doing. Cutting. Speaking. Photographing fragments. Directing Ansberg as Herzl, as Bialik, Dr. Yorksteiner, Dr. Neidler, Dr. Freund. Who'll sing Sonny Boy. Who'll build a house in Tel Aviv.

Return to innocence. My first day approaches on the screen. We're in bed, Mother, with me inside her. Mother interprets a verse to Dr. Freund. May Day, Communists demonstrating. Women in black jumpers sitting on balconies with bitter smiles to scoff at the demonstrators. Mrs. Persitz, chairman of the cultural department of Tel Aviv municipality, announces in an open letter to the proprietors of the Eden Cinema that she will not attend the gala opening of The Mad Singer with Al Jolson because "the very introduction of sound movies in foreign languages to Eretz Israel is a saddening occurrence . . . which endangers our linguistic achievements in this land and constitutes an obstacle to

333

the resonance of the language." Mr. Abarbanel, the proprietor of the movie house, received the letter with deep sorrow. Walking in his tie and black suit, and a felt hat, this handsome man beside the Hermon Café, a descendant of the house of King David, smelling of perfume, says to my father, Naftali, I'm really sorry about Mrs. Persitz, but when the audience cries, the box office laughs. And my father in the yard hearing Sonny Boy, every two hours a Sonny Boy for Father. We got hold of an old copy of The Jazz Singer. We drank juice and I smoked my pipe. In a moment Sonny Boy. At first Ivria and Ansberg laughed and then they didn't. Even though there was enough to laugh at: Al Jolson, working in Blackie's restaurant, in love with Molly, the lovely waitress, and dedicating songs to her. But Molly dreams of glamour and makes fun of poor Al. One evening who appears, none other than Mr. Marcus, the director of a Broadway theater, with his entourage. Molly is presented to them and is invited to sit at their table. Al stands there, looking on mournfully from the side. A good-hearted ugly waitress suggests to Al that he sing for the guests the new song that he has just composed. He sings a song which he dedicates to Molly who is sitting next to Mr. Marcus and his entourage. Mr. Marcus from Broadway is amazed and hires Al on the spot to sing in his theater but Al sets one condition: He'll sing only if Molly comes too.

They rise to dizzy stardom.

Molly and Al marry. A son is born to them. For their fourth wedding anniversary, Al—the famous star—buys his famous wife an expensive diamond ring. Molly comes to the anniversary party leaning on the shoulder of her lover, the handsome young sportsman, and announces to Al that she's decided to leave him. Al is sad, the baby wakes up, and Al tells him a fairy tale and sings him Sonny Boy.

Al's career is on the downgrade, and with his drunken friends from the old days—before he became a star—he sits sadly when he hears that Molly's star is also on the wane. As luck has it, Mr. Marcus hires him again, and this time in blackface, to sing The Jazz Singer, *Der Meshugana Singer*. And Al succeeds again, a dizzying success, above all expectations, and Al is great! Great!

Molly, however, goes from bad to worse. Now she's at the bottom of the ladder, and she wants to go back to Al, but Al's proud. With terrible pain, with protruding and screaming eyes, he refuses to take her back even though he still loves her. But when he finds out that their son, whom he loved, is fatally ill, the two meet on either side of their dying son's bed, and the boy recognizes his father, reaches out a pain-shriveled hand and Daddy, *Daddy*, takes him in his arms, embraces him and sings to him Sonny Boy, in a foreign language, God save us, and the boy falls asleep with a faint smile dancing around his lips. On the posters in the Eden Cinema the pointed question is put: Will the boy wake up?

When the light goes on I see that the bastards have reddened eyes, both of them. Did they see my eyes? I thought of Naomi, Mira and me standing over the bed of Naomi dying, whom will she reach her hand out to? And Mira will sing her Sonny Boy. And she'll say nursefucker, teacherfucker, kindergartenteacherfucker. And turn her eyes away from me. We drank strong coffee and went back to the editing room. Soon it'll be night on the screen. In another few hours my mother will give birth to me. Sir John Censlore, His Majesty's Government's high commissioner, is selling our nation's fate in his conversations with Sir Simpson, who has come to clarify truths in Eretz Israel after the Hebron riots. The Hapoel Hatzair party has united with Ahdut Ha'avoda, and from now on will be called Mapai. Not every man is born on the day when factions united into a single path on which I will be trampled a million times during all the years to come.

Yeats used to say: "I'm looking for the face I had before the world was made." And Borges writes in the biography of Taddeo Isidoro Cruz: "Any destiny at all, however long and complicated, in reality consists of a single moment."

To phone Mira. What is she doing. The operator asks me to wait, and then her voice comes to me like a message out of that single love which nests in me like a disease. Among other things I asked her if she thinks I'm arrogant. She said that one doesn't make a call from Tel Aviv to New York to find out if one is arrogant or not. I said to her, I love you Mira, and then she said,

Maybe you're arrogant in the declaration of your many failures. . . .

Do you believe in love?

Out of despair, yes.

And then she asks questions about me and I tell her. I'll call Naomi, she says, she doesn't stop asking about you. She's playing downstairs, your letters are really beautiful, Ami.

I said to her, A sinner cannot be arrogant, the knowledge of sin and guilt purifies. Doesn't it?

She didn't answer.

Arrogance is generosity, I said to her, and I envy everyone, Dante, El Greco, Paolo Uccello. The defeated aren't arrogant, Mira. . . . I'm a seaman, searching on the open sea for old wounds, hunting hearts of myself, all the hearts I ever had in a single line. In me. Always. And the crown of them, the celebration of them, their glory! What's the value of anything, of everything? This planet is distant from the black spaces, even its flickerings can't be seen, each insignificant flickering is a life, and in the middle they speak about love and about an apartment with a wall to wall carpet. My tiny pain is just a tiny pain.

A lot, she said.

And then I spoke with Naomi. Daddy Daddy Daddy Daddy Daddy Daddy, she couldn't speak. I told her how much I miss her and that we'd soon see each other. How, where, I didn't know what to say. I have only Mommy, she said to me. And she said Daddy Daddy Daddy. Doesn't she believe me. To Mira I said, Soon I'll be finishing, I'm about to be born, I laughed . . . maybe this week. Maybe we'll be farmers, we'll grow vegetables, fruit . . . we'll milk. We'll be healthy . . . we'll bring to market . . .

The hell with it, we'll build a bridge. I'd give half my life to be able to build a great, beautiful bridge. Like the George Washington Bridge. You remember the Irish cop who said to me that a poem isn't a bridge, I was a painter then. I said to him, I'm a painter, and he said, Same shit, remember. I told you. He was right. A bridge, Mira . . .

28

I sit facing the screen, several hours before my birth, at the edge of my memory. We photographed the projectionist going home, the projectionist of The Jazz Singer. We photographed him from behind and he didn't know. Lilienblum Street, where the Eden Cinema is, empty. Two old men in a small café, opposite it a house with a small tower, like a fairy tale nipped in the bud. A huge truck that has sprouted out of a house with windows sealed by boards. The projectionist totters home. A bottle of *zahlawi* in his pocket. Now they're showing Indian movies at the Eden. Mr. Abarbanel is dead, with all the House of David. A woman laughs in a house surrounded by dead trees. The tapping of footsteps is Oriental music. From the café comes the voice of Um Kultoum. We added shots of Tel Aviv sinking into darkness. It was half-past eleven. Another hour and a half, Mother, and you'll be free of your pains. We finished editing the fragments and I drove home. I parked the Ford. Children played marbles on sand wet from yesterday's rain. A violet peeped out from behind a bush. I looked at the fading light of the day. Opposite, on the third floor, a woman hanging out laundry. A pleasant face on the fading gray background. If I were Ansberg I would come to her. She saw my gaze and didn't blush.

Years ago, I went for a bicycle ride with my father, to Herzliya. There was a dead cat on the road. We rode down some slope and skidded. Both of us fell at once. The fall did something to my father. We sat on the sand. And we laughed, though we'd both been hurt. It was sunny, and there were flowers. We talked about Kirchner. Father said that Kirchner's an honest painter, and I didn't know what an honest painter was. I liked a blue Prussian train by Kirchner that I saw once. Father told me that when he was a boy he went with his father to the cemetery at Tarnopol and saw that Rabbi Nachman Krochmal's grave was hidden by bracken and old leaves. He had cleaned it. He didn't tell me why he had done that. And then he told me that once he had played a violin and had stopped. He said, I had a violin and it broke.

Why didn't you fix it.

I couldn't, he said.

And then he told me a story and the story wasn't true. It was phony. He told me that his mother had seen his father for the first time under the wedding canopy, and that matchmakers had arranged the marriage. She saw her husband and became completely confused, she cried and panicked. Then she got her pain under control and a dull silence remained, a dimness that lasted all the years. His father, my father said, loved his wife and she remained silent, and this silence was terrible. I knew, even then, on the sand, on the road to Herzliya, that my father was telling me a made-up tale. I'm sensitive to made-up tales. After making up biographies all one's life, who wouldn't be. My father laughed and told me, there on the road to Herzliya, why Goethe's meeting with Charlotte in Weimar in Thomas Mann's novel had been so dreadful. He described the prince Goethe had been giving an interview to the beloved of his youth who had become a nightmare for the entire world, while she herself was nothing but a burned-out shadow of a work of art that had become torn out of reality and overwhelmed her. I knew he wouldn't speak anymore about himself. I waited. The night when I kissed him on the mouth I knew that this once was our only closeness since the road to Herzliya. But inside him something intelligent, noble and strong pulsed to me. He wanted to save me the horror of failure. On the day of my birth my father knew who I would be, and wanted to save me the pain of defeat, for he knew, for from him I came.

I poured myself a glass of brandy. And then another and another. The violence of pain arouses tinglings of pleasure. The Bible was written by poets, while the Mishnah and the Talmud were written by sages. From the derangement and the exalted coarseness of the Bible a nation was born, and from the Talmud, exile. The lucidity of the sages is a fascinating thing, but the dread and exaltation of the biblical poets exhilarates. We are cutting into a mountain and I am a small and stricken cutter. I'm not afraid of anyone anymore. Let them come and strike me. If it makes them feel good. I say these things from the inner rhythm of suffering. My father tried to put it in fetters, I toss it around in disorder, like any common gangster, with a pistol and a knife. So that my neighbor can sleep in peace. There are no smart and glittering soap bubbles here, but something with a wound. If they want to, they'll see, if they don't want to, they won't. I'm hidden behind what is visible. All art is a crying which joins with crying and then you cry together and there is happiness. And laughter is there too. Laughter is simply tragedy with perfect timing. I would give half my life at this second (after what I give for building a bridge) to have my father sit and watch my movie and laugh. But how will my father laugh with a brain full of fragments of Goethe. Emerson says that a man is a god in ruins, here is everything at one blow. I'm getting drunk. I saw a projectionist on his way home from Indian movies. The city where I was born, whores shouting in the place where my mother cried. Desolate houses. My city, fallen into neglect. Bialik is waiting and I have to get there for this thing. To see clearly, I had twenty-one Miras on a terra-cotta toilet bowl, wherein did I sin. Frances Elliott, I read in Time this week, is painting Colgate toothpaste tubes and Jerome held an exhibition of his Panamanian flags and Kurt Singer wrote that Jerome has discovered the most lucid astonishability. I try to read Sex in History. And learn that bastards were once highly esteemed because in contrast to the sons of wives they were born in real love. Nuns were whores. I thought of Naomi, of Mira, of the one pain that has no end, but must, must have a beginning. Just as if there is a God He must be at the end of all the roads and not at their beginning. I work and work, photograph and splice, and the pain does not cease. I dialed. Her voice was clear, as if she were speaking from the next room.

Oh, it's you.

It's me. Sleeping?

Not anymore, you woke me, what time is it?

She stretches in her sleep, wakes up, yawns and says, It'd cost you less to live with me in New York and to phone Tel Aviv every night than to live in Tel Aviv and phone New York every night. And in the meantime we could love instead of talking about it.

A silence followed.

And then she said, It doesn't matter. How are you, Ami.

I don't know, I've drunk too much, I see you everywhere I look, you're sitting on the tip of my nose. If you were to meet me today would you be willing to marry me?

No, she said.

I heard her distant breath turning into electrodes, flying to me as electric energy and burning, in the earpiece of the post office director, into the beloved voice of Mira, silksoft and soothing.

I said, There's a tombstone in my father's eye and nobody sees it but me.

That's a pity, she said. But maybe the tombstone's in your eyes. Maybe, I said.

I'm a bit sick, Ami, I've got Asian flu and it's funny that you're calling from Asia, maybe I got it from talking to you on the phone.

You should wear warm underpants, I said, and warm socks.

She laughed.

How's my daughter.

She has an admirer, don't worry, Ami, no wedding or anything like that, he lives on the seventh floor, she goes down to him every day and every evening he comes up here to her and they watch television together. He says that she has lovely eyes. They play, I hope! I'm already talking like my mother. He's very serious, when I come into the room he stands up, shakes hands and says Thank you and Please. But there's something in his eyes that reminds me of you. A kind of hidden madness. If he were grown up, dressed up in five swank suits and a hat, I'd recognize the madman under any façade. . . . He's still little and by the time he grows up we'll get rid of him, I hope. . . . I'm talking too much because I've got a high fever.

You love me?

You're funny, Ami. Soon you'll be a grandfather, and that's what interests you. Of course I . . . I've got a fever, and a running nose, and a sore throat, and a pain in the chest, in my whole body, what love, Naomi can't sleep tonight, she gets engaged every evening, I can't sleep during the day or at night, you call every two days and shake me out of the little peace I have.

Don't phone me, Ami. Decide to come back, or to bring us over to you, or to meet in Majorca or Afghanistan. It's simple, write me. Or send me a cable. But don't phone. I'm lying here feeling I'm dying, swallowing antibiotics and thinking how nice it'll be to die quietly. Why do you ask?

What?

If I love you.

Because.

You show love in a mighty strange way, Ami, and you have a kind of new method. . . . I don't like your new methods. Since I gave birth to a dead baby I've become old-fashioned again. I believe in kisses and in husbands who sleep beside their wives. Listen, I've got a dripping nose, good night or good morning to you, I no longer know what.

回回

The words she said and the words she didn't say. Beloved woman with a dripping nose. How sudden and charming of her. To bring her a clean handkerchief. Or a pack of Kleenex. To buy it for her in a shop. To go down to the flower shop on the corner and bring her flowers. To drink J&B together. To see old movies on television. To enter her with her dripping nose and flu. The distance between me and Mira now, I thought, is like the distance between my father's bed and my mother's bed. Afterward I fell asleep and dreamed. I was on a carrousel, on a path with stuck

341

cars, there were three of us, the other two had made-up names, but I didn't know their real names. Their made-up names were Didi and Tzitzi. I said to them, Somebody here has taken away my foresight, and Didi's self-forming power, for Didi could, I knew, reconstruct himself in any and every moment of his life, whatever had been, or would be, or could be—and they've taken away Tzitzi's talent to externalize form, like painting, or making statues of ice, or drilling imaginary holes in the air and waiting with endless patience for cars to fall into them. We drove in something like cabs. A man sat in a wheelchair and I sat on top of him and he pushed the wheels with his hands. There was a line of cabs, and my innards were shown to a large audience in a movie house. Children ate sunflower seeds and laughed and saw my heart in fluorescent light. I woke and felt a wave of pity for Father, pity over his death, I imagined his death to the last detail and hated myself for thinking these thoughts. I thought that Bustanai would be able to photograph the death and that I would cry, for I knew that despite all this the grief would be true. But I couldn't give up photographing it. Maybe so that I'd be able to live with a certainty of sorts. Mira, why don't I know how to forgive myself.

In the studio we edit sections that Ivria has cut for me. The Ohel-Shem Theater presents Jeremiah. Messaline, a grandiose historical production at the Gan-Rina Cinema. Shelltox kills all kinds of plague. A new book, Spies, about Mata Hari, the dancing courtesan, by H. N. Brendof. Hernia belts, even for the most severe cases . . . twenty-five percent discount for Histadrut members.

In the heavens (David Zakkai's column) two evening planets can be seen: Venus and Jupiter. They're still far from each other, Venus beneath and Jupiter above. Every evening the distance between them gets shorter, and Venus will touch Jupiter.

And on May second a big white star will rise from the northeast, Vega, the brightest star in Lyra.

This year 855 automobiles will be imported into Palestine (Eretz Israel). Profits on tobacco production were 163,049 Eretz Israel lira. Matches for export, in contrast, brought in 6,674 lira.

The hostility of the municipality to the populace of workers is increasing and reaching dangerous proportions. Long live international workers' solidarity. The proletariat will smash its chains! Down with Ziegelbaum! Down with Imperialism! Down with Yitzhak Avinoam Yehieli. Down with Meir Dizengoff. Municipality of exploiters! And Broides writes:

> Where is a plot of earth?
> Here shall we plow, and listen to the sown seed,
> To the echo of sprouting in the villages,
> And the hour will sing, in our hands will shine
> The sheaf of first fruits.

The birth pains have already been going on for thirty-seven and a half hours. To this day no such long period of pains has been registered in Tel Aviv. To enter statistics with your mother's blood, and for nothing. She moans me. A spring night hangs on the tops of the cypresses. The lights of Tel Aviv have gone out one by one. Father has heard Sonny Boy for the last time, and the projectionist as we know has gone home. Two workers with brooms, and the glow of Vega, the brightest star in Lyra. To be born a bright star and not to be, to be born a part of a lyre, to be a sound, like the rhythm of the two old women singing How beautiful are the nights in Canaan, and not to be. To live beside. This is the last moment of happiness. This is the last moment that every insect attains to once in his life. But I am born in absolute forgetfulness, the black spaces are being wiped out. Erased and destroyed. Mathias Grünewald and Ahalibama from the kindergarten of poor Hava remember this happiness. A breeze blows from the sea, C.N. sleeps beside Manya his wife. The fragrance of spring until morning, Dr. Freund sleeps in the room adjacent to ours. My father and a carter drink tea in the yard, from a warm aluminum mug. A poster calling for workers' solidarity flies in the spring breeze. In eleven minutes Mother's pains subsided, for one moment. I took in my hands the end of life and death, was wiped clean of all memories and vanished, curled up, wrapped up in defeat. Frightful arms pressed on me to come out and it was suddenly cold. Frau Doktor Freund woke the doctor and said to my mother, Rivka, put your head back in the pillow and scream! My father's eyes in the corridors glint, the tea still drips from his lips that are cold from the exhilarating spring breeze, I became trapped in a kind of abyss of many days, of millions of years, of unimaginable treasures, and there was a last mute convulsion because my mother herself screamed, our last convulsion together, that awful separation, and she didn't know that there is never any return and no way of bringing back the forgotten, memory shocked out of its squatting, dying on the tip of the tongue, like the straight sides of a sidewalk, a large bubble emerged. Dr. Freund put on his gown and smiled into the pain and the blood, and I emerged.

29

The Independence Day party. Ivria asked Ansberg to go with her.

Bustanai said to me bitterly, I don't know if I'm really all that glad that you were born. I'm sick of it.

I said to him that actually, as far as he was concerned, the movie was finished. Yesterday he had photographed the birth of a baby for me, at the Ein Gedi hospital.

Don't invite me to the screening, he said.

I had no intention of inviting you, Bustanai.

Good, he said. And now let me tell you something. I saw the rushes. . . . They're good. You forced me to photograph a dying man, yesterday I couldn't sit at home, I was restless. I drove to Gedera to visit your father. Your father looked at me with a strange look, as if he was waiting for me to take him out into the yard and photograph him. He said something in German. I asked the old woman in the library and she said it was from Wilhelm Bösch and that it meant A father to become is not hard/A father to be is harder. Your father thought that I was his son. He said to me, *Mein Sohn.* And he never said *Mein Sohn* to you, not once. He looked at me with that strange look and waited for me to photograph. To hell with it. But on the other hand, it's a pity, I've never done a movie like this one, it's savage . . . and Ivria's cutting . . . What am I saying. The cutting, the photography, I'm not only his son to him but to myself too. And she said—

Who?

Anis, the nurse, she said he wouldn't last much longer. . . . She said that you know. That you knew even when we did the photography that his days are numbered. What does a man need with a father on the screen? I asked your father if he had a son called Aminadav and he said *Nein.* I asked, Did you used to make frames, Mr. Sussetz? And he said *Nein.* I asked, Are you happy, and he said *Nein.* Are you unhappy, *Nein.* Do you like Monteverdi's songs, and he said yes. I don't want to see your bloody Mamushka, you hear?

I drank grapefruit juice and heard Ivria asking Ansberg to the Independence Day party.

Everything's turning upside down for me. Two romantics have found each other, they will bring back to the sands the glory of our youth. An end to the order of athletics, they'll fuck with a song in their hearts, give birth to little Ansbergs by lamplight with laughter. He'll coach high school pupils for matriculation examinations in mathematics and she'll cut movies for directors and sit there round and plump until she fills up with little Ansbergs. Television and radio, pseudo-Danish furniture, a square table for afternoon tea, telephone for Mr. Ansberg. Who's calling? A professional rapist. A great lover. The end of the order of queens from behind, through a slit in woolen underpants, in Bograshov Street. Ansberg and Ivria will enter a cage like everyone. With little Ansbergs. We'll visit them on Shabbat afternoons for cake and iced coffee with whipped cream. Ivria's a great laugher, they'll be able to laugh together all the time while they're making little Ansbergs by lamplight.

Before that we were served with a summons on charges of fraud. The date fixed for the trial was the fifth of June nineteen sixty-seven. I phoned all the possible hotels in search of my Dutchwoman, and finally found her in a small hotel in Jerusalem.

She was delighted to hear from me. Ah, what a country, she said, everything's wonderful here, the people, yes. She wants to see me, and she's bought an Arab *kaffiyeh* and a Bedouin dress and looks like a real "sabra." And she has wonderful friends.

I told her I was going to be brought up for trial.

She was shocked. You?

Me.

Why?

I sold a story to two producers at the same time.

You want money? You know I like you. When you get some, you can pay me back. You're the sweetest there is here. Really, I've had lots. You were full of despair and I understood the despair. When do you want the money?

I don't need money, Beatrice, I want to know if I'll really have to face trial. You have contacts, after all, with a fortuneteller everywhere you go. You understand about horoscopes and you can tell me.

She said, Give me your phone number, I'll ring you in another five hours.

Toward evening she called.

Hello, honey mine, I said.

You've been drinking wine.

A little.

That's good. I have good news.

What?

I called Houston Texas.

What did you do?

To my fortuneteller.

And?

There'll be a war.

I know, sweetie, you already told me. This year. But what about my trial.

It won't take place.

Why not.

There'll be a war.

What's the connection.

She didn't say. She just said that there's a connection and you needn't worry.

Thanks.

Don't mention it, sweetie. When will we see each other.

I'll call you in a few days.

You'd better hurry, the day of judgment approacheth. And her voice sounded suddenly strange, as if it were reaching me from inconceivable distances. Or from the eyes of my father on the screen, in the middle of Mamushka. I was frightened. Her voice was thick and raving. She said, Ring soon, and she sounded as if she were speaking from the depths of pits.

Afterward I went home and watered the garden. I ate salad and people hung flags in the windows opposite. In the middle of the neighborhood a platform had been put up and all afternoon they tried out the loudspeakers. Children sang. In the evening I drove to the studio. Nadiv Israeli had invited me to twelve parties. I said I was sick. Masses celebrating, streets thronged with people, children hitting each other with plastic hammers, they yelled and hit my car as it drove past them. I arrived at an empty studio. Trees rustling against its deserted walls. To enter. To see an aging watchman saluting an old photograph of Ben-Gurion. To drink a glass with him to the life of the State of Israel. I phoned my mother.

I said to her, Happy holiday, Mother.

Who's happy? What's happy?

Not me, the holiday, I said.

She paused. She asked me if I could take her to Gedera tomorrow. It would be hard for her to get there on Independence Day. I told her that it'd be nice to drive to Gedera. The three of us, she and Father and I, will be able to celebrate together. She got excited and said, Look, after all, you have a part in this holiday. My white hair, it came from your part in it. You almost died. . . .

Almost isn't anything real, I said.

But you were wounded.

Ten thousand people are wounded in road accidents every year, I told her, and that doesn't give them any rights. There's no holy blood, there's no holy sacrifice. She fumed. You don't understand, Mother. The black screen. The window empty, full of distant people, celebrating, hitting with plastic hammers. Mother, one loves in order to love, one dies because one dies.

My mother cried.

I said to her, I'm not celebrating and you aren't celebrating, what a funny world. She stopped crying and said, You have no respect for anything. Your grandfather arrived in this country in a coffin. We built, we made roads, we brought culture to a forsaken land, we fought a stubborn and terrible war that was forced upon us, the dream and its realization. My father who came to Neveh Tzedek, she said, there were no textbooks so he wrote them himself. I said to her, Look, Mother, you see, we *are* celebrating. We're talking about the State, the dream of two thousand years. And then she asked me how I was and I asked her how she was and she said, How can I be already. I don't sleep at nights, my eyesight is going . . . maybe I have a growth in my head. Apart from that my heartbeat is very weak, but I'm not complaining, she said, I'm alone, at home, after getting back from the hospital, no one comes.

To drink wine. To hang up the phone. To look at the screen that was my father. To see savageness in the genteel face, to know his great distress. To see Ansberg's back walking in the street to father Aminadav. Hava the kindergarten teacher and her little ducks. Looking for Aminadav among the bushes. I dialed again. Somehow my hand dialed of its own accord. The wine in the darkroom. Which hums. Outside there is a distant hubbub coming as if from mists.

My neighbor was surprised to hear my voice. He said, Just a moment, you're looking for . . . His receiver made electronic noises as it knocked against the table, I know that he went to the kitchen to see if I was home, and came back, picked up the phone, and in a trembling voice, still disbelieving, said, If you're at home, why you telephone and not come in.

I'm not at home, I'm a long way from home, I said.

He didn't understand.

A silence ensued and I heard his heart beating. The heart of an old man. Not an ordinary, regular beat, not *a a a a*, but *a aaa a aa a a*. He said, Never are people telephoning to me. Only my sister and my brother-in-law telephone. Sometimes on Tuesday, they are telephoning from electric company and once from one radio program, they was wanting to know if I will be interested to buy one elephant, they was thinking maybe it will make me laugh. It at all did not make me laugh. Never are people telephoning to me, he repeated almost aggressively, as if to say you too, you too never telephone me. Not now and not ever. He was excited. His watch measuring me. Maybe I wanted to convince him that my mother's fate was worse than his. For disorder is worse than injustice. And then I said, Look, I'm calling to wish you a happy holiday.

A happy and joyful holiday to you too, he said. And added, Indeed is this a great holiday, the Independence of Israel, if you were knowing Yiddish I would quote you something from a poem I was writing, but the poem is in Yad Va-Shem. Everything is written, he said, that it may be for the coming generations. Also the martyrs of the camp I mourned, and the mourning was printed in the Morning Journal in America, there were things I was writing that were printed in *Forverts.*

I told him I was sensitive to such things. Once I too found myself mourned.

But you are alive.

I was dead, and someone mourned me. He too wrote the obituary in the international language of mourning, Yiddish.

Who.

A great mourner, I said to him, and there was a hint of a smile in my voice, maybe of jesting, that did not suit this moment.

I said, In Yiddish grief has a deeper ring, I don't know why, it's a scarred and tender language, in the words I sense the creeping death.

Where?

Where what?

Where was you bemourned?

Oh, what difference does it make, I'm alive.

No, it is making much difference, yes, you can be sure and certain it is making a difference, and is very important, if in Yiddish then where?

In New York.

And in Yiddish.

Yes.

And a great mourner?

Very.

Is Mr. Sussetz attempting to hint me that a Yiddish mourner has obituarated him?

Why suddenly the third person?

A great mourner . . . There is only one, Mr. Sussetz. He spoke in a whisper now and I could barely hear. The man was old. . . .

I didn't know if he was asking or telling me, so I said, Yes, he was old. A filed obituary for every event. He was eighty years old, you can't possibly know him, a really strange man. . . .

I don't know. Is Mr. Sussetz saying that Mr. Herzberg Shimon obituarated him?

Yes, I said.

And he was thinking Mr. Herzberg is dead?

Not dead?

How dead, shouted my neighbor in my ear, Mr. Herzberg lives. Only this week I was reading one obituary of him, for Imber . . . dead . . .

For whom?

For whom. Imber. Is he not knowing who is Imber.

Imber the author of *Hatikvah?*

Yes, yes.

The author of The Shofar, I said.

Many songs.

Maybe we can get back to second person singular.

Good. Is you knowing that he was writing many songs and the songs are forgotten.

I said, What are you talking about. Imber died years ago, about . . .

Fifty-eight years ago. So what. He, I mean you, was obituarated and you died not. Imber was died fifty-eight years ago and obituarated this week. What is the difference? An obituary is an obituary and also a judgment. Is you knowing how much death there gives in this life. And the sorrow . . . the shoutings, Independence Day, the day of the dry bones, they should rise from the graves of all the generations for to be hitting with plastic hammers one the other. Ah?

Ah what?

Ah. He was excited. The shouts and whispers alternating. I was writing about this hard bitter things in Yiddish. Who is reading.

351

Herzberg mourns, who is reading. A great language is died, who is crying. What of the smoke that was the folk Israel. How will the smoke be coming to the resurrection of the dead. All the martyrs who became smoke, how will their bones be collected. Will the Messiah be knowing how to collect smoke. Smoke one cannot even say in plural, like sand. Is it not written And a great nation will I make you. And will multiply your seed like the sand upon the seashore. A grain of sand, sands. And who am I? You are telephoning. Happy holiday. Who is telephoning me. Nobody nobody. You are going out in the morning. Tomorrow is Independence Day. And the daughters are not. I am alone. The wife is in the shop. Buying things. Maybe they will be returning. Maybe no. Hershel are driving to Haifa. I worry. I bring chocolate. I am crying, crying, who is hearing. And if I die? But you are telephoning. To say me happy holiday . . .

Good. Who am I. A note on the margin of the page.

I said nothing. He breathed deeply and tried to see us through the receiver. And then he said as if seeing, Imber died long ago and Imber continues to die. He was writing *Hatikvah*. What is *Hatikvah?* As long as is inside the heart a Jewish heart still beating. Where is a Jewish heart still beating? In the smoke . . . But hearing this song. Stupid . . . a Czechish melody! Pardon me, I am speaking too much?

No, no, I said, speak. And I drank a little more wine in the darkroom with Father on the screen, with distant stifled shouts from celebrating streets.

In the camp it was cold at nights, I was lying on how do you call it . . .

A plank bed?

Plank bed. I was lying on. And by me was Dr. Leibel, Polish history, he was a professor . . . maybe the biggest expert in the world he was. Until. He also was writing a book about Mickiewics. Eight editions. Translated in twenty-two languages. In every school they was learning from it. . . . What am I saying, you surely know Dr. Leibel.

Yes, I lied.

What a man he was. And then Dr. Leibel he looked at me and

his eyes suddenly died. And became yellow. He closed his eyes and died. On the plank bed, by me. And I look and see a dead man. A minute before he was living. Suddenly he is dead. And it was cold. I froze. I knew: I also will die. What did I do, legs pinching, body crying with cold, on . . . plank bed. Nazis and Ukrainians outside, by the campfire, drinking schnapps, and I was singing to myself *Hatikvah*. In whisper. To myself. I was not knowing all the words . . . I was not being a Zionist before. I heard my daughters who were being Zionists singing, and I knew words, but not all. Suddenly—are you knowing what happened to me—my back that was broken from blows rose erect of itself. Suddenly was strong and erect and I was proud and it was not cold. Yes . . . On plank bed with Leibel dead by me. Imber died and lives always . . . and he was being, how says Herzberg Shimon, a Jewish vagabond, a Hebrew troubadour. Is you knowing how old is Mr. Herzberg?

I can only guess.

Soon he will be being one hundred.

Maybe the grief of others keeps him young, I said, and was grieved I'd said it. But he didn't respond. He said, What a Yiddish he is writing. The wise words . . . like a melody. There are no more people who write so. The last generation, my neighbor said mournfully. How he is describing the dying of Imber, of this troubadour, with the beautiful eyes, who the girls was falling on his neck. Who an English lord was loving him and he was in the love with the wife of Lord Oliphant. . . . You is knowing about him?

A little, I said. They lived on Mount Carmel. I read about them once, something strange. . . .

What a love, he said. They were pure, they were believing in something, they were praying in the nights. . . .

And here is Imber, in the evening of his days, in the evening of his days, in New York, walking in the city. And snow is falling. And he is tired, hungry, thirsty. . . . And there is being a Zionist meeting. Zionists wearing furs. Steam in windows, what a describing, they are drinking hot tea and talking, and he is standing by the window, alone, freezing, dressing in rags, without shoes without socks without warm underpants, and inside Zionists in furs are singing *Hatikvah*. And he is pressing his face to the cold window. His tears they are being pieces of snow. And the seeing is disturbing the gentlemen and they are going outside and pushing him away. And he is pleading, Give me a little warmth that is in the window, let me steal a little steam from the windowpane. And they are sending him away, because the seeing of him is not suiting a meeting of Zionists in furs. They are saying Home, go home, *shikker iz a yid! Goy!* And he is asking them for a glass of wine. They are laughing at him. And he is saying, I was writing *Hatikvah*, my name is Imber. And, says Herzberg, never have Zionists been laughing so much. Zionists are generally being very serious people. *Hatikvah*, a mournful anthem, but is Eretz Israel being a funny country? A happy country? The earth is mournful, the air, the *khamsins*. . . . They are hitting with plastic hammers, making muscles, and the sufferings are living in the beds. A hard people, there is independence, they are wanting to celebrate. How? How is smoke celebrating, Mr. Sussetz? Is inventing new fire, is killing nations, is making muscles, but is sad. . . . What for an article, Mr. Sussetz, I mean Aminadav . . . soon are coming Hershel. We will go to the center like every year, we will see a sad people making fireworks, nice, no? Tomorrow will be military parade in Jerusalem, we will be seeing on television, you is knowing they are beginning television in Israel, we are having one set. Yes, we are buying. . . . Why? We are old. What else are we having to do. . . . We will be like everybody. Imber will be dying always, and we will be looking at the television. How a sad nation is making muscles . . . After we will be playing cards until morning. I and Hershel and the wife. And we will be going to sleep with these things. If I had daughters, would they be understanding the things I was writing in Yad Va-Shem?

▣▣

Afterward I saw fireworks in the window. Arsalen waiting around the corners. There's no justice. My father in Mamu . . . And I took the fragments and saw Aminadav born and it was sad to be born, and I wasn't proud. I couldn't ring Mira again. It was late, my mother was sleeping, Nadiv Israeli was celebrating with the whole House of Israel and hitting his wife with a plastic hammer, I hummed *Hatikvah* until I fell asleep in the darkroom, and when I woke there were tears of sleep in my eyes. I'd dreamed. I don't know what I'd dreamed, I only knew that in the dream my father and Mr. Herzberg and my neighbor were playing cards on some balcony where my mother waited for me and I didn't come. The Steenbeck was alight and a voice was saying die die die.

30

From the screen Arsalen came back to me. How he stood by the New York Times building and Naomi then two years old. The lights were circling around the building and reporting the news: development of space sciences, the future of flights to distant planets, two old women found strangled in a bathroom on Seventy-second Street. Arsalen wore a dark-blue suit and a tie that was too pink. I saw black under the collar, which reminded me of Naples. His dress marked him as foreign. He passed by me and didn't recognize me. He continued toward the porno movie house on Forty-third Street, I walked after him. Was it possible that he was Arsalen? I knew it was, and to the same extent I knew it wasn't, but he was so familiar to me, and I walked after him. Beside the movie house he sensed he was being followed. He turned his face to me in amazement, his eyes dimmed and filled with dread. He stared and was caught in a sudden beam of light. Then he slipped inside the movie house. I went inside too. I lit match after match, passing from one person to another, all of them muttering and grumbling at me. The hall was half empty. Excited men breathed heavily in the dark. Moving and twisting in the dark, their chairs creaking. They gazed in a kind of trance. Making it with a primeval goddess. The awful silence in that place. Puffing and panting. On the screen a naked woman with a towel over. Embraced from behind by a man with a very protruding thing between his legs. Then the woman's husband came in. All of them got undressed and did things. There was also striptease, some old men in the hall giggled terribly. And stopped all at once. The air smelled of piss and wet extinguished cigarettes. And then I saw Arsalen. When he saw me, he leaped up and ran, I rushed after him, people complained, I ran after him through streets of the immense cold city. I found him beside an apartment nearing collapse on the West Side, Thirty-fifth Street, a street of factories by day and stillness by night. Among houses with fire escapes down their fronts, garbage cans overflowing, a sweet stink and children among the cans throwing stones at cats. He stood there as if crucified against a fence, he spread out his arms in surrender, O.K., you can arrest me.

He spoke a funny English, Arsalen. There will be no peace among Jews and Arabs on the basis of the Balfour Declaration, I heard the echo of his voice from out of a lost childhood. From out of the brain of Nahum smeared over my face, in Jerusalem where crows waited for blood. The lights in the houses went on.

Thank God they've caught me, said Arsalen, as if to himself.

No they, *I've* caught you.

You're them, I know.

I didn't answer. We looked into each other's eyes, he stealing glances at my swollen pocket, a package I'd bought for Mira, Tampax, damn it, should I tell him? He knows that there's a pistol there, I know the eyes of the Arsalens, who know me only with a pistol, or dead, not with Tampax. We were there, far from the battlefield, like wounds torn from the body, meeting in a no man's land. He waited to be arrested, his flush turning pale as paper in the lights shining from the miserable houses. His eyes suddenly revealed him to me, blue showcase eyes, all Arabs have black eyes. . . .

Arsalen, I said.

My name is Mustafa Ishawai, he said. And you people know that.

I didn't know.

From Jaffa, I said.

From Jaffa, he said.

He peered at me, a kind of sweetness in his stealth, a woman ran, a cop and a dog. He said, Palestine is not home anymore, he tried to confuse me with cunning and self-pity. I remained silent and kept my hand in my pocket, the Tampax that would fire at Arsalen.

He said, I have been in all kinds of places. . . . I've had enough. . . . I am glad you have caught me. . . . I have no more strength to keep running. I worked on a Lebanese ship, and I ran away. . . . They laughed at me. But you people know that I ran away from the ship and that I have no papers, but did I have any other chance? Look, see my burns! Every day to be frightened of people, of policemen. I am happy you have found me. Where are the handcuffs?

I said to him, Cats are living beings too!

The Jews threw us out of Jaffa, and I thought: America . . . to forget. To be something.

We stand with our faces to the street and there's nobody around but us. From somewhere came the sound of water being flushed down a toilet. The things you hear at moments when you're sharp as a knife. He wasn't scared anymore. Everything had come to some sort of conclusion, hasty but ordered. As if order was really preferable to justice.

I said to him, Arsalen!

My name is Mustafa Ishawai, he whispered.

I said, *Mustafa min Falstin, Mustafa min Jaffa . . .*

Kill me, he said quietly, kill me. You people are the power.

Don't you want to know where I know you from?

You people are strong, he said. Somebody must have informed on me. I said to him in Arabic, Sixty-six English battleships couldn't get your mustache out of my ass, and he laughed with his arms raised, or spread out alternately, trembling a little, and I spoke quickly: I'm not a cop, I have no pistol, I have Tampax in my pocket. Tampax, for my wife, I have a wife, her name's Mira, look, and I showed it to him and he didn't know what Tampax was, and he didn't laugh and didn't cry. Now come with me, I said, let's have a drink and talk, we have lots to talk about.

358

He said, I wanted to be a cowboy . . . in the West. But now you'll deport me.

I'm not deporting you, I shouted. I'm not we. I'm me. Come and have a drink, maybe I'll even help you, I have contacts in this town.

In a small empty café, a waitress in a mini with fat legs cleaning a table, bored.

He looked at me for a long time. Still full of suspicions. His eyes fixed on the pocket with the Tampax.

And then I told him that I'd lost my memory on the edge of the world. But my memory returned to me in Jaffa, when I was two, I'd lost my mother, I was standing alone in the street, frightened, that was when my memory returned to me, from then on I knew who I am and you were there. You saw me! You were polishing shoes, your eyes were blue and you flung a cigarette butt at a cat that yowled. That was how I came back into the sphere of memories. You were the first man in my life.

He looks at me with panic in his eyes. The world is being cruel to him.

He speaks quickly, cutting me short: From Jaffa we fled to Gaza. From Gaza to Rafa. From Rafa to Amman, and then to Tulkarm. We were lucky. Not a good town, but better than Amman, for me. You're not from Immigration?

No!

There was something with bombs. Once we were six brothers and three sisters. I got wounded. It wasn't much. . . . I was walking in a field and there were Jewish soldiers and they killed me. I didn't die. But my face got burned. After that I went to be a seaman on a Lebanese ship. The sea is no good. For me. Salty and big. Work no good. Suddenly he'd forgotten his English. He started talking to me in translated Arabic. Calmer, or in shock. I don't know. I want to be a cowboy, he said, and his eyes glinted.

And you don't remember the cat?

I don't know what you say. And then he paused for a moment, took out a cigarette, lit it, drew smoke into his lungs noisily, almost demonstratively, and said, You aren't telling me truth!

Only truth, I said to him, I'm Aminadav, from Tel Aviv.

Tel Aviv, he said, and chanted the word as if sweetness could be sucked from it.

Tel Aviv, I said, a big city.

Next to Jaffa, he said.

Jaffa is swallowed up in it, I said.

Yes, he said sadly.

Yes, I said sadly.

We had a shop, he said.

Who?

We.

No you didn't, I told him. You shined shoes in the street.

He gave a start, and stared at the glass. He put out the cigarette. Lit another. I said to him, I've always thought about your blue eyes. Our kindergarten teacher told us that all Arab children have black eyes. I've always thought about your beautiful eyes.

He laughed, confused. He no longer understood a thing. Now that he believed me. He doesn't remember flinging a cigarette. Yes, now he remembers that he used to shine shoes, no, he didn't have parents then. He has no sisters or brothers, he's alone, he's always been alone. I told him that that had been the first cruelty I ever saw and he doesn't remember. Afterward, I told him, Arsalen and I started firing at each other.

I didn't fire, he said. I didn't fight you people. I lived in Amman in the war in '56. Not *fedayeen* . . . But I had to stop him, my war with Arsalen was so deep and desperate that I didn't want to waste it on Mustafa Ishawai.

We went to the office of the lawyer Rothschild. His card was still in my pocket. On the day I arrived in New York he had given it to me, with fifty dollars, and he'd laughed at how I'd almost killed a German with an empty bottle. I remembered him. The card in my wallet, now yellowed with the years, I always carried with me. I remembered him saying that he handled immigration questions. At first he didn't remember, after that he remembered and Mustafa waited outside. An old secretary came in at the push of a button, and he told her in Yiddish about how he'd met me on Forty-second Street. She laughed and brought him cagars. He

360

asked me what was I dealing with an Arab for. I told him that Mustafa was a childhood friend, that his father had saved Jews, and had sold us land, that he was being pursued, and that it would be worthwhile to help him get to the West and be saved. I said very solemnly that the Jewish people owe him a lot. And Mr. Rothschild was convinced. He almost got up and ran to shake the hand of the savior. They signed some papers. They activated something called an Act of Congress, I don't know what they did, a favor for an Israeli, said Rothschild, who didn't want to accept money, not from me, his Israeli. . . . Why haven't you come all these years, you bastard, you've done quite well. When are you going home, or aren't you? Good in America? A pest-ridden country, he said. Violence everywhere, see what a city . . . it's crumbling. You have a new country and you're here. You're cute, killing me Germans on ships with broken bottles. I didn't kill! I said. You almost killed, he said angrily. I was bored and I didn't mean to, I said. Well, it doesn't matter, he said. And thus Mustafa set out for Laramie Wyoming. He became a cowboy, a good cowboy, they said, he found a girl, married her, received citizenship, now his name's John, let him be.

31

Dear Mira,

I'm sitting in the studio. Tonight they're celebrating Independence Day. Ansberg and Ivria went to a party. On the way here I was beaten with plastic hammers. I know you have a cold but I love you very much. You're something special in my life. The glue that joins all the fragments. What O'Neill called the Grace of God. Ansberg and Ivria got back not long ago. At the party no one understood them. I don't have to explain to you how strange it was for Ivria's wealthy and religious friends to meet Ansberg, even though he was nattily dressed. The two of them are sitting in the room and waiting for me to finish writing this letter. Maybe they want me to drive them home. Actually I don't know what they want. Maybe they have nowhere to go. I'll offer them a room in my house, until you come, you and Naomi, but she's religious and she won't agree. Chastity is a nice thing. We started with the thing itself and finished up in love. Others start with kisses and finish with fierce hatred. I think of you. I recall how we drove to Fairfield. We picked those flowers in the field. Beside the lake. And there were sheep there, or deer. The horses grazing in the unending grass. At night, you remember, we slept in Sam Fay's old log cabin. There was a storm and a tree was hit by lightning and fell with a crash. The mad night of the last summer we had without Naomi. I used to listen to her, you remember, inside your stomach. She was born a month and a half later, in September. The air was so fertile. My father on the screen weeps at me. Mira, why can't I forgive. What am I looking for, for God sake. You remember me telling you, there, in Connecticut, that trees burn in a kind of glowing of sparks. And that trees caress. And the rain didn't descend, it fell. Borges calls blood swordwater. . . . Dogs cried to us from the distance. And the lake was rippling with wonder and gleaming. And I said, war, war, and nothing was more innocent or unwarlike. And all the water fell on the house and on the trees. There was a kind of real happening, saturated with water and anguish, trees creaking and deer running to find shelter. And the thundering of horses and their weeping whinnying. That night, when you were like a primeval mother to me and I wanted to marry you again, again and again, like now, on this sad holiday.

And then we spoke about every lover loving only once in his life. And is it really better to be than not to be? And we spoke in the torrentuous rain and the lightning flashes, with Naomi kicking inside your belly, about how love had left everyone and remained between us and had no more owners. And we said that one has to arrive at some sort of harmony with memory, and that one needn't remember. Once I imagined that I was a lone man without Mira and I remember that fear. I walked in the street and saw a shopwindow. I remember that I stood opposite that window and danced to myself, two Aminadavs dancing in the window, I and my image. The dance was slow and solacing, consoling itself, and I spoke to myself, I said, I've killed a man and my lawyer insisted that I ask for an amnesty and I refused, the lawyer came to my jail cell and beat me, I asked for an amnesty and got acquitted. Now the lawyer's rich.

I'm sitting opposite my father, my father is pictures, pictures are frames, I had pictures once. I wanted them to hang at Mr. Dizengoff's, in his small museum. Why does one paint, one paints because one wants to tattoo something, to shout in flowers, and what's the result? It's all the same. Goya's Execution is aesthetics. I'm in love with you and you aren't here. A painting is a machine that annihilates itself, on the screen in the corner is my father's eye, I see the annihilation of the painting. Its heroic and wretched suicide. The god Shiva, says Professor Scharfstein in his illuminating book on Chinese culture, is a painter, who without paint or brush painted all existence on the walls of his own consciousness. Do you understand, my sweet? What remains is to become Shiva. All the other gods have died or betrayed us. The god Shiva who paints all existence on the walls of his own consciousness is the last sanctuary.

The English word author derives from the Latin word *auctor*, which means he who augments or combines. This was the title that Rome bestowed on its generals as payment for the conquest of additional territories for Rome. What remains to the lost? To seek the territories deep deep inside them, and to conquer them. If I were to write a book about the search for the spectacle that I could have been, like any man, I'd call it a journey. I'd say, a bright star in the lyre. And I would go out, extinguished, quiet and alone, and find the happiness we long for in serene and inactive contemplation of life. Without expectations, without any dread or hope and thus without melancholy or gaiety, simply because they pass through me (not beside me) and they're perhaps so lavish, so exalted, and trampled.

Yours, Ami

32

Driving to Gedera on Independence Day. The radio plays old songs of the fifty-year war. I thought of wars and of Nahum my friend. The empty hands and Arsalen. I saw someone firing at me from a concealed position. To be a stone on the mountains. The vultures on the electricity poles and the cemetery in Kiryat Ana-vim with young fighters who didn't even leave pictures behind. Then they sang: If we die, bury us in the mountains of Bab-el-Wad. And now the radio sings Bab-el-Wad, our dead lie along the roadside. A war of boys with dismantled Stens. The trees that saw faceless children. The villages that were cleared on the road to the City of Peace. The road and the war over six meters: the width of the road to Jerusalem. Nahum Alfassi gives an order: Privates retreat, the officers will cover the withdrawal. I stood on top of the Kastel and saw the officers dying. In one hour twenty-three officers were killed, Mira. Young people with a fierceness in them. On the roof of a convent in Katamon, when Beni copped a fragment in the mouth and couldn't speak. He had tried to mount a charge with a two-inch mortar, to conquer a homeland. It all ends in songs. The road to Jerusalem runs between trees and burned-out cars. People make pilgrimages to the divided city. Arsalen and I on either side of Notre Dame. Until when. I embrace his hatred with a kind of avidity to understand him. But I'll fire at him always. My grandfather came to Eretz Israel in a coffin, to an empty land, full of Arsalens. Try and explain to God that swamps are a holy place to the people who live in them. There was no alternative. Not for him, not for me. Everything's mixed up, justice is complete and also divided. My forefathers had twelve tribes and they lived in this land. They went to Rumania and Russia. They invented Marxism, a theory of relativity, modern capitalism, they asked for a pound of flesh in the songs of the bard, they dwelled in ghettoes and traded with each other, and many were defiled. Suddenly my grandfather came in a coffin, without Hebrew textbooks, to teach local lovelies the history of the people of Israel on its land, which is his guilt, which is the wretched home of Arsalen. The land is mine, the land is his. And the war over the Kastel and Nahum Alfassi dying before my eyes at the foot of the slope.

Everyone's looking for answers in a kind of rational freeze. But there's only the solution of the god Shiva. To paint all existence on the walls of consciousness. To stop shooting in another hundred years. My mother hums along with Yaffa Yarkoni, what a cute song about wars. All the crows of song who arise every Independence Day to sing the deaths of others. Who feed on the blood that flowed here with cosmetics and professional smiles. Someone says something about holy blood.

To take Father out into the yard. People sitting in the cool breeze, not seeing the landscape sealed inside themselves. Waiting for some forgiveness from the life that has seeped through their fingers. Laughing nurses lead withered old women into the mazes of an enchanted landscape. Father purses his lips and doesn't say a thing. The wretched celebration of the Sussetz family. I could have had a brother. My mother gave birth to two dead children. The attempts were hopeless. Once I asked her why she thought I'd lived and they hadn't, and she looked at me with an alacrity that was full of love, she wanted to tell me, but she didn't. The answer lay on the tip of her tongue. A person lies in bed and sees things precisely and thinks they're only delusions. There my mother saw answers. But she was afraid to utter them. My brothers were very frightened, they didn't kick inside the womb, they fell as victims before even knowing the disgrace.

Father looked in my eyes, Who am I? He doesn't speak. My mother says, Don't bother him, he simply has nothing to say. I spoke to him about Independence Day, celebrating the State's birthday, you remember the War of Independence, the blood, the bullets, the bombing of Tel Aviv, the first respite, the provisional government sitting in the hall of Dizengoff's museum under pictures that *you had framed.* Ben-Gurion, Shertok, Zigling, others. Did you see only the frames above them or also the fateful decision of the People of Israel vs. Arsalen who was waiting for me with dumdum bullets, with the refined smile of a showcase leader.

We got home tired. It was a wearying day of national songs on the radio.

But he didn't say a word. My mother was sadder than usual. Anis the nurse had hinted what she had hinted, but I am full of an orphanedness inside me and I can't share it with anyone. A stranger to myself in the midst of the celebration. I hear State, and Israel, sung with plastic hammers, and am filled with an inexplicable sadness. Not for myself. My blood is buried somewhere, with a part of my knee bone. Trees grow on the blood. All the forgotten in the divine smile of the altar of life. On a pastoral background, to the strains of popular war songs, they changed Father's catheter. He raised his arm and puckered his lips in anger at the nurse. . . . I said, Leave my father's piss. He didn't respond to this declaration of love and my mother hurriedly arranged matters. Maybe he was waiting for Bustanai to come and photograph. He's dying, says the chief doctor, he's getting worse from day to day. At night he had another minor attack of paralysis. Who knows. There's no improvement, and even the static condition is changing into a dangerous dynamic. We looked at the man who was my father as if we would never see him again. I thought of your body, Mother, on the table of science. Why don't you donate your soul to the investigators of consciousness, to the mystics. Maybe your brain could solve the riddles that science will never solve. But who will listen to these profound and childish words in the most progressive state in the Middle East. A state of Jews with blue numbers building a technology and hitting each other with plastic hammers.

To close myself in the studio. To inspect the mirror in which I am. Ivria comes and goes. She and the Great Fornicator, who has started wearing clothes befitting a proper man and has undergone an immense metamorphosis before my eyes—and I hadn't noticed—are looking for a cage. He will teach and she will go on working. On Shabbat he already dons a skullcap. Goes with Ivria's father to the synagogue, learns rabbinical commentaries so as to argue with his beloved's uncles. My mother phones the studio and Aminadav hides in the darkroom. Slowly editing his birth. Only I see the tombstone in my father's eyes, others don't see a thing. Goya's Execution is nothing but a movie about the birth of a boy in Tel Aviv, almost nostalgia. Ivria tells me that there'll be a war. I remind her that I told her a long time ago that there'll be a war.

Ivria says that I'm talking nonsense.

Why nonsense. I told you, didn't I?

You said something that some Indian woman told you on the ship.

A Dutchwoman. Now there really will be war. I told you then that Nadiv Israeli doesn't know and that the Dutchwoman does know, and that's why I believed her, and you didn't. I told you that the walls of the Garden of Eden are very cracked and that there's a need for thorough repairs. And don't laugh.

I'm not laughing, she said. They're calling up reserves. Nasser has moved troops.

I told her that I'm exempt from service, on account of lameness. That I'm making a movie and generals make wars, and in this way some sort of order exists which it would not be worthwhile to violate. And if a war breaks out let me know who won.

Ansberg has found himself an occupation and has left me. Now that he's about to get married, he has to contribute something to the nation, he said. He'll leave his book of statistics in my care, for he isn't doing any of that anymore. He doesn't even drink iced coffee. And he doesn't look for love in the mornings. His women remain lonely and waiting for love. And even though he has a criminal past they've found him a military occupation. He pulled strings, the studio manager helped, somebody, I don't know who, telephoned somebody else and they called up the harelip and I remain alone with Ivria who, being religious, was never called up and can now pray for Israel's victory. The Dutchwoman had done all my work for me. People tell me awful things: Eshkol spoke, the cabinet discussed, Eban traveled, returned, a million tanks in Sinai. Generals made statements. Moshe Dayan who became defense minister because of women who screamed in the streets goes off to examine the plans and says that there won't be a war and foreign newsmen leave the country and come back too late. They're planning a radio blackout, someone tells me in secret. Everyone knows and they don't know a thing. I'm on the screen, splicing Aminadav piece by piece. Birth and death, birth and death. Potential and failure. Mira Mira. I sat for twenty hours without sleep opposite the screen. I'm marvelously planned, and all the alternatives still exist. In my weariness my eyes closed, I saw, from inside the screen, my life, as if glued together. I saw sights in colors as if I were hallucinating or had taken LSD, but I hadn't taken a thing, I hadn't even drunk brandy or wine. My mother phones and I pretend I'm not there. My neighbor notes down many absences. And I sleep in front of the screen. There are no more men in the city. The studio manager vanished one morning and there isn't even anyone to pay. Only Nadiv phones to report details of the latest developments. Since he discovered that I'd known there'd be a war he's been treating me with too much respect, he's certain that I have contact with secret information and he keeps trying to decipher my hidden connections.

Ivria splices me with Scotch tape. The sights I saw were very defined: the room wasn't an editing room, and a conversation was going on someplace. Someone announced: I met a woman who reminded me of the scents of the Garden of Eden. I said to her: If God dies I won't be to blame for anything anymore. Therefore God can't die. And another voice said: If you reincarnate in a foreign body you cease being foreign, and then added: I am the intelligence of the world—and suddenly I was me, the boy I had been at the beach, eight years old, swimming a long way out, far off I see kites over the Tir Building, the Kita-Dan Hotel, with running water in every room, and houses. And I say to myself, in

my vision: I'm king of the world, because I'm the farthest out—
a powerful moment of courage and clarity, to be cut off and far
out, and then the sight changed: they want to hang me for
something stupid. People are paying to see me hang, and are
bargaining with the hangman, who eats an ice cream. They hang
me. And I fall into a pit. I thought I was Jesus or Himmler. I eat
a tomato, in the background is my father on the screen, I'm glued
to the editing room, Ivria smokes Broadway, they're calling up
reserves. Soon there'll be an explosion in the Garden of Eden and
Moslems will ascend in their thousands to repair it. They say to
me: You're eating a tomato but actually you're eating us, you're
sucking our blood. I went for a walk. Trees blossomed and a thin
rain drizzled. Maybe this was the first rain, there was a fragrance
of perfume in the air. They said to me that I'm an important man,
king of the world, because I swam out the farthest, and I really
did want to be king of the world and I thought that here's the
Garden of Eden, and I knew I was going insane, but like the
madmen who are full of poetry I went insane of my own free
choice.

To win means to lose, a woman said to me once. Maybe
Bernice, with the alabaster face, in a cab heading for Long Island,
when her parents went to Europe and we cooked spaghetti in a
red pan on stones at the beach. To give everything, to be defeated
absolutely. To raise your arms and to reach a victory. I am born
out of the death of my father. The parts are finished. Everything
is edited, spliced. Ansberg, in the reserves, phones Ivria to come
and visit him. My mother phones, my neighbor hoards food,
Beatrice is at the border, the walls of the Garden of Eden are in
a bad way, in the laboratory they will develop my movie. To walk
in a city where there are no men. Nadiv phones and asks for
advice, he drives from place to place, looking for a war, a colonel
in the reserves. The army doesn't need Nadiv. And he must know
that there *isn't going to be a war.* All his cards have got mixed
up. And only I can save him. He sat with nobs and snobs only
a month ago, he sat there and they said that there wouldn't be
a war for the next five years at least. . . . And suddenly along came
Aminadav and brought information from a secret source and now

the Egyptians are crossing the border and blocking straits and the whole country's singing We've returned to you Sharm A al-Sheikh and Nasser's waiting for Rabin. Nadiv has to discover my secret source. I have a friend, he said, an echelon commander, and he'll take care of me. I won't remain idle. And then he added, as if pleading, But there won't be a war, will there? That's what Dayan said only yesterday. I smiled. Yes there will, I told him, because the walls of the Garden of Eden are very cracked. And Nadiv says I'm being derisive.

回回

We drove through the desert. Dust, loess, ruts made by tanks and marker flags of different colors. Armored companies under camouflage nets with flies. Women handing out cakes dripping with cream for our boys. The glint of steel under the beautiful nets. In the eyes of bored soldiers of today (the fourth of June) I saw the eyes of my neighbor. Who closed the notebook that was open and whose hand stopped, for a moment, to write. His face became the face of his daughters. A child strangled in a bunker entered a tank. A million Jews will get up in the morning with my neighbor's face to hit at Himmler wearing the clothes of an Egyptian soldier who didn't know. The things you see in this frightening desert with white mountains and steel skies hanging above and girl soldiers with command cases entering and leaving the camouflaged command tents.

We drove in a jeep through the awesome expanse, Nadiv looking for a war that wouldn't occur. No one needs him today. All the people he'd been giving advice to for ten years. He grinds his teeth in distilled despair. We arrived at a point somewhere near Nitzana. The border's only a few kilometers from here, he said to me proudly. Desert and tank ruts. We eat dust. It's three o'clock in the afternoon, the sun blazing down fiercely on heads, dissolving in clouds of dust. Ants eat an agama. They eat it ruts of blood. Nadiv walks into a headquarters tent, Aminadav walks in the desert. To walk between tank ruts. Hard skies hanging above. The mountains in the east veiled with shadows of an invisible sun. A girl soldier gave me some tepid water to drink

371

from her canteen. My feet sink in the loess and my nostrils are full of dust. Suddenly a man comes out of a hole in the ground, out of the loess and the dust. In a helmet and dusty uniform— a reserve captain—his eyes peeping through his eyelids, twinkling. Sussetz, what the hell are you doing here.

Who?

You.

I know him and I don't know who he is. I told him I'd just seen ants eating an agama. He laughed and looked at me. So familiar! Plump and red as a tomato from the sun and then I understood that this thing that had come out of the hole was the studio manager. He gave me some chocolate. We ate silently, in the dead expanse, among tank ruts. A half-track passed us and we were covered with dust. A soldier asked something and the studio manager yelled: Turn right until the blue flag, and then toward Level C. And the half-track vanished into the immense expanses.

He drank a little water. Then he took a flat flask of Courvoisier out of a pocket and we had a few sips. It descended into us like consolation. I said that Nadiv says that there won't be a war, Nadiv says we've missed out, I said. And the studio manager laughed. Tomorrow morning! And it'd be best if you aren't here. But I saw thousands of soldiers traveling home for leave, I said, and he laughed. At night they'll bring them all back.

We parted. We had never felt closer. The war filled me with a sweet longing mixed with distress. I remembered forgotten things, the smell of sump oil, gunpowder, shells in stacks, bullets in magazines. I wanted a sudden burst of music from behind the meager bushes and then the tanks to charge out in a controlled rush, like in the movies. I knew that I was smelling some immense thing in the air and there's nothing more dreadful and more comical than war. For there's nothing that seems so serious and at the same time childish as war. Officers, like children, seeking lost Gardens of Eden, dressed up as men, with dust, preparing death traps and everything seems so serene and horrifying in its banality. Tomorrow they'll be dead. People will scream from burned tanks, but there's something childish in all this, something that only ecstatic music, marching songs from the movies, can blow some seriousness into.

On the way back I told Nadiv what the studio manager had told me. And he laughed. He said, I'm a colonel in the reserves, I have friends at General Staff, I spoke with the echelon commander, the war's been postponed, Ami, the forecasts have been proved false, don't believe fortunetellers, tomorrow the soldiers will be going home. Did you see all the soldiers heading north? Tomorrow all of them will be getting leave. Shuli Natan on the radio singing Jerusalem of Gold. Nadiv gets very emotional, tears in his eyes. Missing this chance for a war, he declared emotionally, is an irreparable historical loss. He cried over the lost territories— Egypt, Sinai, the Jordan, the Golan. At Gedera I left him. It was late at night. I went upstairs. My mother was crying in a big room. There'll be a war, she said, and we'll all get killed. I'm not afraid, but Father. I went to his room and he was sleeping without his teeth. The two old women in the adjacent room dreamed How beautiful are the nights in Canaan. From outside came the rumbling of convoys. Tanks traveling in all directions. Boats on trucks were taken down to Eilat and driven north for diversion. Planes roared through the sky and set the windows shaking. My mother came up and clung to me. She said, Look after yourself, Ami, and if a war starts go into a shelter! I told her I'd do that and that I wouldn't drink water after eating fruit, that I wouldn't smoke in shelters and I wouldn't fuck without a condom. She made an angry face and went off to the dining room to make hot tea for people. I drove home. Tanks heading south and north. Soldiers sitting silent at the sides of the road and smoking cigarettes. Girl soldiers singing in soft voices. The nation that has been reborn with a clenched fist, with stinking songs. The lights came on again. Jerusalem of Gold became a national anthem overnight. Everybody singing it into the sands. I took a bath and took off a ton of loess. I put on a dressing gown and wanted to read the Bible. Wars do this to Jews: they arouse biblical renaissances in them. I heard a knock on the door. Outside last-minute reserves were being mobilized. Men still half asleep left their homes and got into trucks. Everything was whisper quiet with the tears of women holding children in their arms. With lights on in kitchens all night long. Women sticking adhesive tape crisscross on windowpanes and outside shelters that had been dug only today. My neighbor stood in the doorway. I was the tiredest man in the world and he looked fresh and terrified. He wore khaki clothes, a broad-brimmed cloth hat, and there was a knife in his belt. I wanted to laugh but remembered that all the soldiers under the camouflage nets in the desert had faces like his. I boiled some water and we drank coffee. He was very grave and asked me what I thought.

I said that there'll be a war.

He said, I'm not afraid. We're ready. I have a penknife. Do you have a weapon?

No, I said.

Jews have to have a weapon, he said. A rifle, a pistol, if you haven't got a knife, I'll give you one, I have two. You understand, he said, there are memories, what are memories, they're things that live in the present, not in the past, the past we forget, what remains is a long present. . . .

I understand, I said.

It was chilly at night. The street was quiet. They didn't come for any more reserves. A summer night of mist and dew and breeze. He spoke of cosmic sensor rays, how they learned to live, how they learned not to die, to sense things from afar. He hears the war approaching from afar. He knows, his sensor rays . . .

Suddenly the phone rang. I was startled. I picked up the receiver and heard a very distant voice that seemed to be coming from boundless expanses: This is Ansberg speaking. I only have a minute. Take care, Ami, I'm awfully tired, phone Ivria, tell her everything's all right. She visited me the day before yesterday, thank her, tell her father that everything's all right, I'm hanging up, how are you. And hung up.

My neighbor lit a match and helped my trembling hands to light my pipe. With my sensor rays, he said, I knew all the time what was happening to my wife. On the day my daughters died I knew. Through my rays. I used to speak with my wife across great distances. She was in one camp and I was in another. We sent each other rays of sorrow. I wrote about it for Yad Va-Shem. One day you'll read those things. . . . Aminadav drinks brandy. Tired. Noises from somewhere. Cars stopping with screeching on a distant road. And then he left. I saw him going out armed with his knife, with his melancholy face and a sudden joy I didn't understand. I knew that now he'd get into a tank, strangle a baby, advance on Damascus with an open notebook and a writing hand, and would strike with the angel, until the morning light, against the Lord's enemies.

And the next day there it was. Not a cosmic explosion, but a thin knife. A small fire with a dreadful punch. There was an air-raid siren, the radio went silent except for incomprehensible words about soldiers who had to join their units. They said we had been attacked and that we were taking the war to the enemy. On the BBC Israel was conquered and destroyed.

But my neighbor and I knew what was happening. Through his sensors. The studio manager and Ansberg were smiting them. The sky was empty and this time there was a siren and three shells fell. My consciousness registered it. People were dying and I couldn't help. The strangled baby of my neighbor was leading a people, like Moses' hands, in the Amalekite war, and when he let down his hand. The baby wore pajamas with elephants on them to lead things to their sweet and bitter perdition. In the end the pleasure was small and the joy immense. Sand was mixed with sand. Smoke with smoke. The dead died at one blow with their fathers. The sword inherited from forefathers struck and returned to the grandson's sheaths. My neighbor wept and laughed. He repressed an awful pain and was ashamed to mock the defeated. In his mind's eye he was Mercedeses plowing corpses. He saw smoke with birds of prey in it. His wife hid under the table during the bombardment and ate chocolate with excessive avidity. Hershel arrived in great hubbub and heard the commander of the air force destroying the Nazi air forces. I drove to the Golan Heights looking for Beatrice. I knew that there was only one place where I'd be able to locate her, the final battle of the war of miracles. I saw her in Hurshat Ha-Arbaim, wandering around in jeans and heavily suntanned. A young press liaison officer told me that she was an important journalist. I didn't want to tell him that she was to blame for it all. She knew everyone by their first name and drove up to the Golan in an open jeep with two newsmen from the BBC who were traveling on tranquilizers and said they didn't have strength for any more and they hoped that this was the last front, for they'd been in Sinai, they'd flown to Jerusalem, and now here. At the end of the battle she came back down to me. I wasn't given permission to go up even though I said that I represented some important newspapers and gave them the names of several of them. She came back drained and happy. Now let's go to your place, she said. You'll give me a bath and take all the sand of the world off me. I clutched at her, for she was the last thing that connected me with what had been. The fragments were finished and were being boiled in the laboratory. The war was over. Tomorrow or the next day I'll have to find a place of dishonor in a world that has always been. Ansberg will come back a national hero and will make me best man at his wedding. Ivria phones every day, but she isn't phoning me as much as she's worrying about her harelipped beloved. The Dutchwoman took a bath and the dirt that came off her could have filled an ocean. I watered the garden and heard the screams of pain from the bereaved family opposite. A woman wept in the midst of the great victory and a man struck himself on the chest and wailed. My neighbor returned from Jerusalem with a poem he'd written. Beatrice was generous and let me hang on her breasts in a kind of languor and marvelous lucidity. The glee was restrained. The victory introverted and quiet. And then the Dutchwoman took her suitcase, packed her belongings, and left. And so I remained in Israel alone with heroes living and dead. I knew I had only my neighbor. My mother phones that Father's fatally ill, and she cries and cries and is so estranged from me.

When I started these things I said they were a journey. The Hebrew word for book is the Greek word for journey. With the Dutchwoman's departure the cycle closed. The war ended. Drivers went back to killing each other on the roads. Politeness stopped all at once. Medals of honor and valor were distributed.

People mourned or spoke of the eternity of Israel. They celebrated in open cars. They spoke of a daring victory. People traveled to conquered territories to buy Portuguese sardines and English instant coffee. Hell, how much Alka-Seltzer they bought during the first days of the astounding victory. People carved their names on ancient walls that had stood without a scratch for thousands of years of wilderness. The ancient cities of Eretz Israel turned into a picnic. At Bet-Jallah near Bethlehem I drove toward an attractive woman driving toward me in a sports car. She stopped and I stopped. Her clothes were sumptuous and her hair marvelous. She smiled and said in fluent English, You're driving the wrong way in a one-way street.

I said that I'm a stranger here and I don't know the signs.

You're Israeli, she said, and you're driving the wrong way. But then you're allowed to, she said. I am the wife of the mayor, but you're allowed to, because you have a battered car, but you're a victor and I'm not, you're a conqueror and I'm one of the conquered. She laughed bitterly and lit a cigarette. She was wearing red trousers, and she was too beautiful. A military car appeared with Nadiv Israeli whom I'd lost earlier in Bethlehem at the Church of the Sepulcher and he said: Get this piece of shit out of here, we want to go up top, they say there's a fantastic view from up there. She smiled and drove back and I continued driving the wrong way with Nadiv Israeli and his nobs and snobs behind me. Ansberg came home religious. He wept with Ivria beside the Wall which had waited for him for two thousand years, spoke about Rambam, he reads the Zohar, and believes in the sanctity and uniqueness of the people of Israel. He's willing to admit that it was not he alone who brought the victory. I, he said, deride idolatry, the worship of stones, but Ivria understands that deep inside me are profound religious feelings and like any atheist I fight with fierce belief. I said that I'm not an atheist. I believe in your God, but in contrast to you, I know who he is. She said, I thought you were a Buddhist. So I was. Who prophesied the war, she or a Dutchwoman who believed in stars?

33

(Dear dear Daddy. I cried and I prayed I love you Naomi
When will I see you?)
Aminadav dear,

War's a terrible thing. We saw it on television. I never knew
how much I was tied to that far-off country, until this war began.
Even my father sat glued to the television. He forgot that I was
supposed to give birth to some president of the United States and
not a Jewish prime minister. I tried to get to Israel, but they
wouldn't take me. I lied and said I was a nurse but they refused.
The next day I came and said I was a governess, that Naomi was
the daughter of an Israeli: she'd been left with me and I had to
bring her to him, but they wouldn't listen. For two and a half
weeks Naomi and I sat glued to the television. We ate and lived
beside it. All the lines were busy and I couldn't phone you.

I miss you, my body wants you. I know your fluidity, you need
a hundred women so you can know you exist, but you can love
only one woman. And I will live with this pain, it purifies. But
that isn't why I'm writing. Nor because of the astounding victory.
I'm writing because to this day, for more than ten years, you
haven't asked me how I came to be in your dream, in your
made-up biography. You remember how we met? You came from
a story of the Dead Sea and I from the cave?

When I was in Spain, making occasional trips to Madrid to handle the convent's grain business, I somehow got hold of an old book, a description of a journey to the Holy Land made by an Englishwoman named Miss Hannington Speer. Miss Speer traveled to Palestine in 1874, and wrote a journal. The journal includes photographs taken by Miss Speer's companion, a man named Sir Irving Simpling. A charming Englishman, refined and cool-tempered, courageous and sympathetic, who devoted his last years to a dedicated Platonic love for Miss Speer. He was an amateur photographer and brought photographic plates with him to the Holy Land, which he loaded on a donkey whose name was changed to Haman. His series of photographs of the deserts, Jerusalem, Hebron and Jaffa, the Dead Sea and Jericho, are among the most wonderful I've ever seen.

The photographs are a warm brown sepia in hue and they don't look like photographs at all, but like paintings done by a great artist. There's a picture of trees beside the El-Aksa mosque which looks as if it was painted by Rembrandt and a landscape of Jerusalem which bears a striking resemblance to Toledo in Greco's Storm. I read the book over and over. It enchanted me the way the Japanese tea book enchanted you. Miss Speer describes in a dry and powerful language the desert that she loved, the desert that captivated her, its force, the canyons, the hawks and the eagles. The monasteries in the rockfaces. It's all described with a restrained humor, dry and fine as a knife, evoking the sufferings of a woman at the sight of this cleft and empty wilderness. The sight of the skulls and skeletons in the Marsaba monastery moves her so much that she falls to her knees before the saints who lived there in the cleft ravines, in wadis blasted by sun and wind. She laments the destruction of the Holy Land and the shame of seeing its desolation. Sir Irving, who loved her and respected her precious chastity, photographed each picture with the same love with which his delicate lady saw these things. . . . In a picture at the end of the book she appears as a little woman with an extraordinarily beautiful face, her eyes flashing with the expression of a child who never grew up. The relationship between Sir Irving and Miss Speer which emerged between the lines of the book aroused my imagination no end. I don't know why. To be a nun and a holy woman, to be the beloved whore of God, to love the marvelous secret sight of Him, in the desert. I dreamed I was Miss Speer. I imagined that one day I would meet Sir Irving and he would take me on journeys into the desert lands and would be my master and slave. I wanted someone who would respect the angel in me, the angel that wanted to don a garb of shame. I was bursting with fierce impulses, I dreamed of God as a kind of huge eagle who takes and masters me in a desert. And this huge eagle has the face of a beautiful boy with black eyes. When you told me the story of the Dead Sea I closed my eyes and was the nun you told about. What I'd imagined became real. I had looked for a reality resembling the fiction in my heart and I hadn't found it, I'd returned to New York covered with foulness, and then you appeared and told me love stories and you were a boy with the body of an eagle in a canyon the sight of which I knew in my heart like a sword. I was Miss Speer and you were a boy who had been invented by himself and so you could be Sir Irving even though you weren't. We met for a moment on that threshold where we so much wanted to be and in this we met in truth. You in your dream and I in my dream. You a boy looking for lions and I Miss Speer looking for Sir Irving. So you see people meet, Ami, in an enchanted garden, in a desert, or on Frances Elliott's toilet bowl.

In one of her chapters Miss Speer describes a trip she made to the Dead Sea. It contains a description of a canyon with a monastery quarried into one of its walls. The chapter is a hymn of praise to the stillness reigning over this scarred and cloven place. It tells of nuns who live in silence in the convent in the cliff face. Miss Speer stood on the other side of the canyon, in the same place where you invented yourself, and looked toward the monastery, and I know that this was the same monastery you'd made up in your story. I wanted to be the nun that Miss Speer saw in the entrance to the cave. I imagined myself in the cave quarried out of the rock, loving God, mute for years and years, preserving an eternal youth among the skeletons of saints who had died many years before. I could imagine the cave, the food brought up by a rope from down below, Jericho and its palms. When I returned to New York in my nun's robes with a can of hashish I lost the book, maybe that was symbolic of something. And I found it again the day I met you. Not the book, I never found that again, but the sense of being there, in that monastery, by the Dead Sea.

Two days ago, when they announced that Jerusalem had been captured, and then showed your army speeding through the desert and arriving at Jericho, I thought: My monastery's close and again you'll be able to stand facing its entrance and to see me. I thought: Here's Aminadav going off to the canyon to look for Mira. In a black dress, with a crucifix dancing on her dress, in the savage wilderness. Miss Speer writes that the hyena is a dangerous animal and that its scream resembles the sound of laughter, a scream of horrible laughter, and Sir Irving says (in a footnote) that the hyena hypnotizes people, enchants them, drags them to his cave and kills them, cracks their skulls and feeds off their brains. And then you told me about the hyena skin you'd bought from the Greek. Remember? Everything came full cycle and I knew you there. Every real meeting is unexpected. Love is a matter of chance. No one was destined to meet with the object of his love. Miss Speer and Sir Irving met by chance. One day she was walking in Chapel Street in London, and suddenly she sensed that she didn't know where she was going, she felt that her walking had no direction. So she stopped and didn't budge from the spot. Sir Irving passed then, a man she didn't know at all, wearing a heavy coat and a large hat, and he said to her, May I help you, madam? And she said, No, thank you, and he said, Why are you standing here instead of walking on, and she said, Must one always walk, and he said, The middle of the street, and all that, and she said, That's true, but where should I go? And he asked, Don't you know, and she said, No, no, I don't know.

He took her arm with great care—so she writes—and said to her: Most unique lady, I had a dream last night, I dreamed I was traveling to the Holy Land. I left my house, for I knew that there is no reality in dreams. I was walking along purposelessly and found you standing in the middle of the street, not knowing where you are going. It seems to me that this is no coincidence, don't you think so too, and Miss Speer answered: It *is* strange. I too dreamed last night, I dreamed I went into a Cook's office and asked for two tickets. Then I packed my suitcases and left. I remember traveling to a distant place where there were bald mountains and no water to drink. I don't remember who traveled with me and who it was that photographed me on a background of basalt mountains. Nor do I remember where I traveled to. Now that you've said what you've said, I know where I traveled to: Jerusalem. How strange, they said to each other, and went into a tea shop and had tea. The next day they booked a passage on a ship sailing for Alexandria and from there went by camel caravan to Jerusalem.

Ami, I have to see your movie.

It's mine too. A little.

Every birth of Aminadav on the screen is also a little of Mira. I want to be the servant of your sufferings. To collect your tears for you. To discover the smile. I want dark things. My flesh cries to you in the nights. I keep remembering our marriage ceremonies that never cease. When you used to awake from your sleep and marry me each morning anew. I recall how we both suckled Naomi, who was programmed to be what she was. Could all these things have been had we not met on opposite sides of a made-up canyon, in an arid and primeval desert, which is two fictions that became one reality? Like two negatives making a positive? For according to Miss Speer a monastery like that one exists, and a nun like that one, the reflection of the two dreams. My insensitivity toward your sense of failure stemmed from a moment of dullness. For a moment, that is for a year, I was closed to the thing that matters most to me. I wanted you to be proud, I didn't understand that your sense of defeat is more wonderful than any pride, that you're capable of acting only from defeat and despair. Just as you conquered me by means of a made-up biography, you forced me to enter it and I was in it. For better or worse. Do you remember how I nursed Naomi and you sat beside me and even you suckled her? The milk that flowed from the two of us. Who will understand that? The teacher Peggy? I know things. You were meant to meet with the teacher Peggy, not with me. I am the way through which you must pass with all your sufferings and all your anguishes. All the others are spices. I'm sure of myself because you're engraved in me so deep. I read a beautiful thing about Cézanne. In Paris they said he was not a painter at all or too much of a painter; who paid any attention to him, you know of course. When he was old someone arranged an exhibition of his works in Paris. And he came to Paris leaning on his son's shoulder and saw the pictures hanging at the exhibition, the first exhibition of his life and he already an old man. Do you know what he said to his son? He said, Son, look, *they've put my pictures in frames,* and I felt things for you, for Naftali Sussetz dying before your eyes, the man of frames who struck you with love and pity.

Aminadav, I'm coming to you.

Are you shocked?

So am I.

But I'm coming, even shocked.

I'm sorry.

Actually I'm not. Now I'll tell you about your last painting. You remember, I came back and you were sleeping in the armchair. That was the last Mira on the toilet bowl. I'm sure you remember that Mr. Zwiegel took the painting, that you didn't manage to destroy it. He hung it in the gallery. And Kurt Singer, your friend, wrote an enthusiastic review of the painting, actually he wrote about you. Funny? I'm sending you Kurt's article, read it and laugh. Now he's talking about a new era. Not only he, lots of people are writing the same sort of thing. And you were forsaken and unknown and the world turned a hundred and eighty degrees and now you're in fashion. Isn't it absurd? We won't go into details, they might confuse you and you might think that your failure wasn't as wonderful as you thought it was. Like your corduroy. For twenty years you wore corduroy in winter and it was funny, and now you still wear corduroy, but now it's in fashion. Sussetz's painting, writes some idiot in The New York Times, is the message of the holy aura of hackneyed things. Then come the technical details, the linearity, the shameful formulas. . . . They write that you've found the golden mean between painting as *painting* and the frozen moment, daring colors and all that. The irony of a woman on a toilet bowl of terra cotta. They've even discovered your Sabbattai Zevi from the reject heap. An internalized religiosity. The Panamanian flags are dropping in value. Frances is painting ketchup bottles. Things are changing sharply. They say you've blended exhilarating chaos with the conditioning and deterministic reality of the establishment by putting together a woman cut out of a comic book (that's me) with a toilet bowl which is the symbol of industrial decadence. The picture was bought at quite a high price. And I found more pictures you hadn't managed to destroy (I hid them!). You have a rich wife, Aminadav.

I could have run away, to buy myself a real husband. But I'm coming to you. And you, without knowing it, are paying the expenses. I'm bringing mixers and a refrigerator, a television set and everything I've been told to bring in your consulate. I'm bringing air-conditioned, bourgeois things for a mad husband, I'm bringing a fat checkbook. You feel contempt for me now. Go ahead. Kurt came to visit me and told me to convince you that you *have to paint.* Then he tried to lay me in the wardrobe. I told him that you told me once that he had a glass prick and he laughed. After that he didn't try anymore. He said he was going to the Himalayas to study Zen. He's getting very old. He lives with a new girl, a painter, twenty years old. I told him that he probably needs to connect an atomic turbine to his vibrator now, and he burst out crying, and Naomi had to bring him water and two aspirins. He smokes cannabis, he told me. I said marijuana, and he said, No, African cannabis! That's more impressive, of course. He says that you're a spoiled child who couldn't wait. After all, not everyone attains to immediate recognition. That daring things have a way of their own and it's hard. That Aristotle said that whoever doesn't knock hard on the Muses' door and doesn't struggle to enter doesn't enter. I told him that Frances didn't struggle and he said true, but she'll also be finished fast, and he seemed sad. Maybe he loves you. Maybe his hatred and jealousy stem from something else. Did he want to be Aminadav? It's funny that anyone should want to be you. You with all your wounds. But jealousy is something with laws of its own. One isn't jealous of nice people without scars. It's the scarred who are envied. Now he's sure that Mira on the toilet bowl is an expression of the memory of the womb. I'm not so sure. He says that every artist is the son of a father who smashed a violin. That every artist is an uncertain quest among Kurt Singers, that's exactly what he said. They want to paint like someone and something else comes out. They want to build a palace like the masters and what comes out is blurred and lacking known form. And then they're rejected. Someone who's willing to struggle and mold him a new way, confident, unknown, scarred, comes out a victor, but one needs a long wind. Not everyone. I said to him, The cemeteries are full of people with good intentions. But he's certain that he's right. As usual. He also says that every artist creates biographies for himself, so you're really not all that original. He says that you overdo it in your love of defeat and that you're full of self-pity and that you're too much of a painter or not a painter at all. And that what Hans Hofmann said about you was true, and you should have understood what he said as it was said and not as you thought it was said. It's possible to go insane, to commit suicide, or to invent a different biography. That is, to create out of hostility. Artistic creation, he said, is creation out of hostility, it's war with silk gloves. Every good artist has to lie. Every marvelous sound, every unique word, every true color is a lie with respect to its environment. For they all refer to tomorrow. They're the truth that will come. They're the hiding place from the casualty of bank managers and shopkeepers. He says that it says in the Bible, or in one of the holy books, that the best of the poem is its lie. And what Kurt says also justifies the idea of the consciencist that you wrote me about. You thought that painting is a betrayal of the mission that as it were has been entrusted to you. But you really were a consciencist! You were intended to repair one person. And he who repairs one person is as if he has repaired the whole world. Professional world-changers are irresponsible and very arrogant people. That's a lie which is your truth. Was there really that whore in Naples? I don't think so. I think you made that pain up too. That you make up your life all the time, and not only once, and you haven't stopped even now, that even the defeat and the flight from New York are chapters in a made-up biography and that you discover yourself only in the eyes of others. That's why those women. The whore in Naples was an invention: But what a beautiful invention. And that's your story. The best of the story is its lie. You wanted to be a god. You don't understand that to be a god is to be a lot less than human. You're making a movie so as to meet the forceful blow that descended upon you. A god creates something from nothing. And that's superfluous. You create something from something. You wrote me about the woman who asked, How can I know that is is, and someone answered, Because isn't isn't. Something from something or nothing from nothing. That is man's advantage over a god. The scorpion bites in order to revenge and to die, a god creates nothing from nothing, or, if you like, something from nothing. And therefore he must die. A man creates something from something, and lives. We're arriving on flight one hundred and forty, El Al. Monday, nine-thirty in the evening by your clock. Naomi's leaving school before the end of the school year. The teacher Peggy gave her an excellent report card. She says that Naomi's clever and a good pupil. She sends you her regards. She really is sexy. See you, sweetie.

Love you, Mira

34

The amnesty proclaimed after the war left me with two thousand lira that had been intended for lawyer's fees. I give Ansberg a present so that he can go to his marriage with a dowry. To clean the house. My neighbor with Thermos and coffee, tomorrow he'll be a grandfather, he hangs an engraving of the Wailing Wall on the wall of Naomi's room. Mother rings from Gedera. I tell her I'm preparing a surprise for her.

She sounds alarmed. What kind of a surprise, Ami?

Nothing, a little surprise.

Maybe a big one?

Maybe.

Something bad.

No, something good.

She mulled this over and I heard her brain ticking like a clock, and then she said, What can still be good?

I didn't answer.

I'll cry already.

Maybe this time you'll laugh.

Do I have the muscles to laugh? I laugh? You make me laugh, she said sadly.

See?

What can it be, she asked, a present?

For all of us, I said.

About an hour later she rang to ask if the distress I was about to cause her wouldn't be too great.

I said that everything would be all right, and she asked, You remember Ze'ev Rotman?

Of course, I said. On the day I got back to Israel we saw him standing by the port writing down arrivals and departures of ships, and the driver thought he was a spy.

He's not a spy.

I know, Mother.

He's gone to Sinai, she said, just imagine, at his age. Osnat's husband is an officer! And he took Ze'ev—she's so tied to her father, and her husband really loves him. During the war he found time to write him postcards! The day before yesterday he came along and said, We're off to Sinai, and off they went. They were at Santa Katerina. Ze'ev says that the sight of the destruction is terrible.

I said, All your friends have marvelous children, Mother.

That's true, she said.

And after Sinai?

He came to visit me, and Father. We went walking in Gedera. She was calm, relaxed, and I heard her quiet breathing. We picked flowers, she said, we recalled our youth, we cried about Father, and then we came back and Ze'ev told Father about Santa Katerina.

In Hebrew?

She didn't answer directly, she paused for a moment and then said in a different voice:

Father cried, Ami.

Ivria wants to hang pictures of Israel's generals over Naomi's bed, my neighbor enthuses, I cast a veto. My neighbor filled the house with flowers.

I put on a red shirt. The Ford is still dust-covered from my trip to the Negev. To bring my body among the nobs and the snobs. To park with parking labels. Among chiefs of staff and generals distributing autographs to a crowd of admirers. Rapp arrives for the gala premiere of his sensational movie in a magnificent car. The studio manager is festively dressed and sweating. The photographers, directors and actors shake hands. Ivria's in a distant corner. Ansberg sits in the dress circle. A handsome masculine general mounts the stage to congratulate Rapp. The evening's proceeds were donated to the army. Chiefs of staff smile. The audience cheers. Nadiv Israeli smiles at me from afar, he's squeezed between five generals, I could sense the strength. Somebody says, We've finished them for twenty years. I sit not far from the studio manager. Among nobs and snobs. Women whom I knew as a boy look at me as if I don't exist. Wearing a red shirt, and uncombed.

The movie nauseates Aminadav. To penetrate a life in slippers made of soap bubbles. God sitting up in the balcony. The miracle that was Rapp fucking in a helicopter. The generals grant their patronage with smiles. Somebody speaks about the greatness of the Jewish people. Music by Dov Z. Slaughtered ducks swimming in olive oil. The art of Spartans. Athens is outside crying. In the medley of a summer's night. Among houses close to collapse in a new old city. Large eyes out of mirrors: the mirrors are the eyes of Rapp, the beloved of nobs and snobs. I wanted him to open his pants and show them a sanctified prick. They're already selling Coca-Cola in Israel. And who if not Rapp has brought them the right to destroy their teeth. And the movie that will bring us a Nobel Prize for acrobatics. I can imagine Ansberg crying up in the balcony. Maybe tonight he'll steal into the room of his wife-to-be and mount her from behind with a lamp and laughter. I want to scream while everybody's clapping hands in the excellent conditioned air of Amcor.

To go outside. A line of national flags greets me. The nobs and snobs will be coming out very soon now for gala parties. Chiefs of staff will converse with poets about glorious movies and the conquest of Sinai. They'll shake hands and drink "the president's" champagne. I wanted to go to my grandfather's grave and to send him back in his coffin to Odessa. To Bialik and Ravnitzky, to Buber and Pinsker, all of them now names of streets at the corners of which women wait for Ansberg who isn't coming anymore. The studio manager stands outside glowing. He's waiting for nobs and snobs to come out with clapping hands to shake his hand.

That he'd been in the desert and routed Egyptians. But maybe he has not taken into account the naked Rapp in the helicopter. Mrs. Persitz refused to come to the gala opening of Sonny Boy, while I sit in a red shirt and speak with a handsome silver-haired general about the future of the conquered territories. I'm sorry for Naomi; tomorrow she'll liberate me some territories and she'll go back to Anatot and Shiloh and wait for Arsalen, with a silver platter, conquered in the pincers of the sufferings of the Jewish people. Ansberg smiles from far off. And I'm frightened that he *liked the movie.*

Pressed into a corner of Lod airport. The hubbub of after a war. Everybody comes to see the victory. I was scared I mightn't be able to see Naomi and Mira. From far off I see them. Among sweating backs of shouting people. Whole families, whole masses, stand here to receive their visitors. Trucks that have brought tribes here. They climb on top of each other. Naomi materializes between a crewman and a little woman who moves her hands as in prayer. Her golden hair, her flashing eyes. She's looking for me. And doesn't see me. And then, from the level of the feet of a big man who had pushed a united block of people and had stuck to the windowpane, she discovered me. The big man shouted, Here, Aunt Shura, here! Here! I arr 'ere, I arr yourr cozzen, I arr 'ere, and Mira collects suitcases and the kid's sleepy, frightened, people shout and wave their hands: I arr 'ere Onkel Motke, I arr vaiting in Zimmerrr. Naomi rides to customs on a suitcase trolley pushed by Mira. They come out and we didn't know what to say. Naomi hiding under Mira's coat. Because of the heat Mira took off her coat. Naomi, stupefied, approaches Aminadav, not believing, wondering, stepping back for a better look. And then when we embraced the fear subsided in us. Layers on layers of fears dropped off, we drove in the white Ford to my house enveloped with bougainvillaea.

It was late on a cinnamon night. Marvelous smells rose from somewhere, a plane flew through a quiet sky and Naomi fell asleep in my arms. I laid her down in a new bed and dressed her in pajamas without elephants. Mira stood beside me. Then we played Mozart on the phonograph and drank wine. Through the

390

window was a moon. And a dog barked. Distant cars slowly became still. The land of Israel played its sky for Mira. A night of wine in the air. Naomi sleeps and I look at her. Her naked body gleams in the moonlight dripping into the room. Something is compressed inside me. I stood in the mirror, and she behind me. I saw my eyes, they were my father's eyes. Then they changed and became my grandfather's eyes. Eyes mixed into eyes. Mira laughed and was Lilith and an angel. A city bowing far off. To know or not to know. She received me the way one receives disaster and salvation. Afterward we laughed. Mozart played for us. Bridal lullaby. Naomi woke up and screamed in a dark room. I went to her and calmed her. She asked if she was dreaming and I said, No. She asked if I could sit beside her, and I did. Mira came and brought a glass of water. Naomi sipped from the glass. I wanted to lay my life in front of a movie and let the movie see me, I wanted to return to Mira instead of her to me. Kadar-laomer's found a good home, she said. She wants me to buy her a rabbit, a cat, a dog and a horse. Where will we keep the horse? Afterward I returned to the other bed. Mira came and laughed into me.

For a moment I fell asleep and woke up. And she still beside me smiling.

Naomi jumped out of bed and ran to the corridor, I heard her footsteps, she picked up the phone and yelled, Daddy! Daddy! Daddy! I came to her, embraced her, put the receiver back and brought Naomi to our bed. The three of us fell asleep, wound together in a knot, she in me and I in Mira and she in Mira.

35

The surprise in my mother's eyes beside my father's bed. He's going to his last peace. The anger in her, why hadn't she known. She'd imagined things with a gravity painted black. She cried and scolded at the same time. Mira was alarmingly patient with my mother bewailing the fate of my father, Naomi alarmed, withdrawn into herself, shy. The frightening building. The old women in white gowns. A dead man on a stretcher with a cantor praying. Women waiting for their husbands with catheters. Nurses in white with eyes painted blue, Naomi refuses to kiss my mother and my mother is offended. I explained to my mother that she's still a child and doesn't know her yet.

I'm her grandmother.

Yes, but she doesn't know you, Mother, give her a few hours. . . . She knows that you're her grandmother, but she has to digest the fact.

Father's eyes have died, for several weeks now. There's no more life in them, the flash has gone out. He looked at Naomi a long while and then put out his hand, suddenly, and touched her hair, very very gently. She looked close at my father, bent over him, and kissed him. His face was covered with bristles of beard. And she kissed the bristles of his beard. Two tears rolled down his right cheek, not far, stopping at mouth level. He looked at Naomi with dimmed eyes and said, No contact. Disconnected. In Hebrew, the first thing he had said in Hebrew for many months. But he spread his arms to the sides. He seemed to be covered in a fine film of shame, as if he was trying to become invisible. And then he looked at me and said, There's no point, Hermann. I said to him, I'm Aminadav. And he, perhaps, perhaps not, I'm not sure, tried to smile. For I'm not Dr. Neidler. The last words my father spoke in his life were a few minutes later. He said: This way or that.

And then, on seeing my mother, I was filled with pity for her. Naomi had chosen, of her own free will, to kiss Father. . . . My father nibbled an apple that my mother had peeled for him. She is trying to measure Mira, and Mira is looking at my mother through well-shielded eyelids. Later we went out of the hospital. The sun was about to set, a deep red disk, and from the other side of the world a pale moon rose. For a moment sun and moon hung under the same canopy. Pine trees across from the hospital were full of tenderness. I recalled that in Genesis it says that God created light and divided it from the darkness and only several days later did he create the lights, the moon and the sun. What is that light that God created before there were lights in the world? I knew legends about light for the righteous in the world to come. But within myself I saw the interpretation of the light in the eyes of my father, in the flash of Naomi's eyes, in the fact that there is uncomprehended happiness in this universe. Here I abandon a dying father, tomorrow he will die, maybe the day after, after him I will die, and after me Naomi. And all of us live and die on some single level of energy, all of us flow into each other. Mira into Mother, Mira into Father, Father into me, I into Naomi. The nurses. The medicines. Two old women singing How beautiful are the nights in Canaan. Radiance, of chaos, perhaps that same chaos that King James's men translated as without form and void, perhaps prior to all creation and containing all creation. Naomi drinks a sunset with eyes of gold. Who created whom. Sunset, says Alterman, cows in the field lowed it. Mother scolds, Why are you laughing, your father's dying. I said to her, I'm laughing because suddenly I so loved the man, Mother, and she

393

sent me a baleful and aching glance. Then Naomi approached my mother and said to her in English, You're my grandmother, aren't you?

My mother didn't speak at first and just looked at her. You know I'm your grandmother, she then said angrily, I'll bring you presents and sweets.

Naomi laughed. Her eyes lit up. Her white teeth gleamed. She said, I have everything, but I don't have a horse, a camel and a donkey, a dog and a cat, I had a cat Kadarlaomer, and we found a good home for him.

I'll be your friend, said my mother.

Naomi says sadly, That's not the same thing.

My mother wants a more precise answer.

Naomi said that my mother is very nice but sad. And she'll make her laugh.

My mother said that Naomi's changing the subject.

I tried to intervene but my mother silenced me. She said, Let me try to reach my granddaughter, I have only one granddaughter and she too is turning against me.

Naomi asked what my mother had said. I translated. And my mother said I had a strange nature that I hadn't got from her.

I said to her, Maybe from the milkman?

And she muttered to herself, All these stories about milkmen. I detest stories about milkmen, and I'm entitled to expect of my son, who makes movies about his mother and doesn't invite her to see them, to be more original.

Just a little more, I said, and she continued, raising her voice:

In your childhood we didn't have a milkman. That's one. Two: we bought milk at Feierburg's on the corner of Mendele. It was a little shop and the owner was a crippled veteran of the Crimean War, and almost blind. You went to the shop every morning and bought butter and rolls. And three . . .

Naomi asked what we're talking about. The red sky of twilight. The scent of pine resin and a sadness in the evening that descends and embraces treetops in the sudden stillness. I said that only now my mother had told me about how I used to bring home milk and rolls every morning when I was your age!

394

Naomi said that she wants to bring rolls and milk to Grandmother every morning, and then she approached my mother and without speaking knew things that I will never know and Naomi kissed my mother. Who softened, kissed my daughter, and on a second thought said to me, You told her to kiss me.

And then Naomi kissed my mother again and when my mother, her eyes moist, gave her back a kiss Naomi asked her why she had chewing gum between her teeth.

My mother laughed and said that Naomi has very good eyes, like her father, Nehemiah of blessed memory, had had. And it isn't chewing gum, she said, I'm a very old woman and I've had lots of teeth extracted, and the dentist puts in this material in the place of the missing teeth, until they fix me new ones. And Naomi should brush her teeth regularly twice a day or one day all her teeth will fall out too as will soon happen to Aminadav.

Mira smiled and bent to kiss my mother.

My mother permitted her to. Afterward we drove home and Naomi sang a happy song and the road was suddenly beautiful and the trees, dusty from the first dust of the young summer, were covered with a foliage of splendid and hopeful darkness. I thought of what Erikson had written, that if parents feared death less, children might fear life less.

Two days before he died in the jammed corridor of the hospital (to which he'd been brought from Gedera in a critical condition) my father looked like a child. I looked at him and saw that the hair of his beard was growing. It was frightening to see how the hair wants to continue growing on the life that is going to die. A hard man. Designed like a box, with only the smiles and the strange humor as windows. He was always afraid he might disturb someone with something that surged inside him like fierce lava.

He framed pictures in the city of sands for Mr. Dizengoff. All his days his eyes were sad beside Monteverdi and Palestrina. With the memory of a broken violin. A man of habits, all his life he did the very same things in the same order. Like his God, he believed that non-order is worse than non-justice, he liked things placed in stocks or frames. Like rhymes. Is anything more frightening than a rhyme? It dissolves loneliness and plants belief. Lying dead.

395

That empty face. The birdlike expression. The secrets we will never know. We stand over him. Mother cries. A doctor straightens a curtain. Across the way moan those who have not yet died.

He always sought the formulas in ancient days of laws. He cut his feelings with fury. His love was hard and meticulous. His wisdom was to hide in humility. His hatred for non-order was perfect. That was why he struggled so, all his life, with a kind of stubbornness and rebellion. Rebellion does not go hand in hand with the passion for frames that pulsed in him, so he had no passion for authority, but the torn thing in him cried in secret places we didn't know. He made many errors. But when he was right, he used to hide. He celebrated victories by grinding his teeth. I, to him, was an echo of something distant and dark. I was the wrong child to the right man. He wanted not to want, not to aspire. He told jokes like a man choking himself. We didn't hear the words, he said nothing all his life about what really bubbled and beat in him, and he said what he said through closed teeth. When did he withdraw, never to return? Behind the grave there was sand. I said *kaddish*. My aunt wanted a ritual tearing of clothes, so they tore. Naomi stood and looked at the man who had been her grandfather. Whom she hadn't known. But her kiss descended with him. It was hot and people stood sweating. The cantor said *el male rehamim*. My father entered the eternal cycle of nature. The energy that had been my father penetrated into all of us. I wanted to bring a violin and to play—in his honor— the A minor concerto by Bach. I wanted to be Huberman on a hill. Here, facing Father's grave. Ants beside a fresh grave walked in a long line. Ansberg wore a knitted skullcap and embraced Ivria's shoulders. Farther off I saw the eyes of Bustanai. He was peeping from behind the grave of a known trading-house proprietor. The grave was large and the tombstone magnificent. His eyes that had seen the dying through colored lenses. My mother didn't want to leave the grave. She stood, her eyes turned into the earth being poured into the grave. My aunt in her torn old shirt which she'd brought especially for the ceremony started leaving, supported by her daughters. Her tearful eyes were marvelously ceremonial. My mother hadn't started crying yet.

396

I phoned the studio. The studio manager sounded worried. His voice opaque. He participates in my grief, he'd read in the paper. He hadn't come to the funeral because there had been things to take care of. Nadiv Israeli, who had come, phoned to tell me that the studio manager was in big trouble but he didn't specify. I asked the girl in charge of the developing, When will my film be ready, and she said, Tomorrow or the next day. My mother had changed beyond recognition. Her face was youthful, she had never looked better. Aunt Lifshe and she sitting and looking at old pictures. We had framed pictures of Father with Bialik, with Dizengoff, with the High Commissioner and with David Ben-Gurion. We went through Father's files. He'd kept everything. Every ticket from all the trains he'd traveled in during his life were kept in files. Certificates, letters, income tax receipts from the period of the Mandate, old articles that one could not guess why they'd been kept, locks of hair, sticks, old pens, everything filed. We tried to discover the system but we couldn't. The glue in the drawer had a strong smell. Mira said it was a marvelous smell and my mother said, Would you like some coffee. And they spoke in whispers. They'd found a shared landscape. Mira understands. Mira knows how to live hard and bitter things with a lightness that isn't frivolous. She has a kind of deep understanding of death. She sees it as an understood thing. She soothes my mother who has come back to an empty house. Aunt Lifshe thinks that Mira is too beautiful for me. All my mother's friends have sons who are married to good-looking women, but they're not too beautiful. Aunt Lifshe believes that it's better and surer that way. Women who are too beautiful mean problems. All of Dizengoff Street, she said, is full of boutiques for the beautiful wives of mortgaged men. And Aminadav will finish up in a poorhouse! Mira smiled and said that she'd never bought herself a superfluous thing. Aunt Lifshe laughs with characteristic bitterness. And my mother comes to her defense. I took my mother to the window. It was around noon and there was no one outside. We'd just finished eating the soup. Mira and Naomi had gone out to play in the garden. I embraced my mother and I told her all the awful and hackneyed things: that maybe this way it was better, and that the suffering Father had gone through had been too much. That the last days had been superfluous dying and this way he was better off. And that he didn't even know that he died. And she answered in agreement, without bitterness. There was a joy of new life in her. The old age dropped off her, cross by cross. Her femininity suddenly bubbled up. Her hair was drawn back. Her lovely eyes flashed toward roofs covered with solar water heaters and television antennas like scarecrows. The sun burned between branches. I told her about *badim badim* and about who Ansberg was. She laughed. Behind us was a room empty of Father. The smell of glue was strong and Mira said, What about the shop? She walked in on tiptoe and sniffed the glue. For a moment we didn't know what she meant. The shop? What shop? And then I remembered. For seven months I'd been here and I hadn't gone to the cradle of my childhood.

We drove to the shop and it was still there. Is Monteverdi still played there? We parked and walked. A seller of secondhand books offers books by weight. A woman walks with baskets. A radio screams Arab music. The smell of peppers. Inside the shop we saw two old men. They were framing reproductions from a book. One of them was cutting wood with a sharp knife. Whose is the shop now?

I don't know.

Let's go in, she said.

This smell of glue, maybe this is the place for me, I'll sit and cut jute, Mira will sit behind the counter and sell reproductions of Abel Pan, Van Gogh, Reuven, Murillo, and get fat. Naomi will grow up, go out with boys and raise statistics at the beach. Cars race past. To go in or not. Inside, hit by the smell of turpentine, carpenters' glue, wood cut into thin boards. For a moment I closed my eyes and thought that two smells have accompanied me all my life: the smell of fresh bread from Grandfather's bakery (my grandmother behind her windows could never close it out) and the smell of the shop before closing when Father and I go into the street, into a huge space of lights and shadows. I know everything here: the bucket of gold paint, the jute, the saws, the fine nails, the table for cutting passe-partouts, the strange knives with

398

their sharp blades and contorted forms. One of the old men turned to us and asked if we wanted to buy a picture.

I asked him, Whose is this shop, and he said, A moment, and called to the other old man. The other approached, moved his glasses to his forehead, brought his face close to mine, almost rubbing noses with me, and said, I know you from someplace, aren't you a relative of Goldberg's?

What Goldberg?

From the grocery.

Don't know him, I said.

Strange how alike you are, only the mouth and nose are different, maybe also the lines of the face, but, even so, an amazing resemblance, no, Hirschberg?

Yes, said Hirschberg, only the ears and the nose and the mouth no.

And the lines of the face, added the old man.

Yes, and the lines of the face.

So what's so similar?

Oh, everything, he said.

Yes, everything, the old man repeated.

You understand, there's something in the happening of a face (all this time he's examining me from close up, his nose rubbing against mine), in how the face becomes suddenly sharp. Yes, nu, what do you say, Hirschberg.

Hirschberg says, It's the joy in the face and all that comes with that.

Whose is the shop, I asked.

The old man looked at me, wondering. I see the way his forehead creases, a sight fertile with malice or innocence. I thought: Never let it be said that there was a disaster and I didn't know. Mira plays with the artificial gold for the pseudo-antique frames. He says, A man named Aminodev Sussetz.

And Mira who was standing by the phony gold hears the Hebrew and waits for the name, sensors, antennae recovered, gives a short laugh.

I repeated the name: Sussetz.

He said, Aminodev Sussetz. I too, he continued, thought an

unusual name, but what can you do. In the telephone book there is even one with the name Potz. . . .

And the two old men laughed.

I said, There's nothing funny in the name, it's quite a nice name, maybe, I went on, because I'm Aminadav Sussetz, not Aminodev.

The old man suddenly smiled, not a wicked smile, hiding another, immense smile inside him. Filled with sudden affection, he tried to embrace my shoulders as if he had seen a vision. He said, Ah, they are testing us, Hirschberg . . . and he turned to Mira: I always said that Sussetz was a very Jewish name. . . . Didn't I, Hirschberg?

Hirschberg said, He always said that Sussetz is a Jewish name, and cut a mottled sheet of cardboard with one sweep. I was so entranced by the sharp and precise cutting, the knife so expertly held, that I didn't answer. My eye was fixed on the old man's hand. Hirschberg held the cardboard with a kind of embrace that I knew very well. Father used to stand like that, in the rays of light, at night, when I used to come to the shop (in my heart I used to call the shop a gallery, I always said gallery). There was a kind of power in the familiar embrace and in the other hand which cut the cardboard as if it were cutting butter. What I missed were the strains of Monteverdi and Father's books that always stood on the shelf on which now, as I discovered, stood account books. The figure of Hirschberg cutting cardboard lacked either melancholy or joy. But there was a great strength in it, and I was brought back to some reality from which I had fled a long time ago. My hands trembled. I wanted to hold a paintbrush and paint. To smell the smell of turpentine and linseed oil. The rags and the painting knives.

Aminadav's hands trembled in a terrible desire to get a little dirty, to feel a Rembrandtian green under the fingernails. To sense a color born out of color. To let chance lead you to the border and let the dream lead chance. To delve into the consciousness, on the taut canvas. To lay down sufferings in reds and blues. To put on the canvas things that are banal and exalted. The hand that cut was a hand that made frames. My father had sat here and I had been inside all the frames. As if all the longings of many nights and days can be said in one painting. But I knew that this particular desire would not give birth to any deed. That somewhere inside me I had ceased wanting to be laid out on canvases or engraved on wood, and not because of the reasons that I give myself night and day but because the vision that was in me had died and I no longer want to be a second-rate violinist. And then I understood that Father's Huberman had vanquished me too. Father in his fresh grave smiles now, for I have finally returned to him.

If so then the shop is still ours, I said after a pause of several minutes. The old man smiled. Not ours, yours! It is registered under your name, sir, we only rented.

Who registered, I asked.

Your mother.

When.

Long time ago.

And did she tell you when I'd be coming back to take the shop?

She said that you call it a gallery.

A shop, I said.

Yes, a shop. The old man smiled. And then he added, No, she didn't say when. Look, we make a good living here, both of us are really from "there." We worked in a shop in Jaffa–Tel Aviv Street, I'm sure you know it, next to the monastery that's next to the dogcatcher's, said Hirschberg, and went back to contemplating with great serenity the straight line he had cut just now. He passed his finger along the edge of the cardboard, and his face testified to his complete satisfaction.

Yes, next to the dogcatcher's, said the old man, and then your father, he got sick of it all, and then he became sick. . . . And your mother looked around and found us. . . . And we signed a contract. You know, the lawyer Nahum, what's his name, Hirschberg?

Abramsky.

Abramsky . . . Are you sure, Hirschberg?

Sure I'm sure.

Yes, now I'm sure too. Yes, he's a young man, and already with

401

such a clientele, and he has lovely children, and a villa in Ramat Ha-Sharon, and the contract was written, yes, and then your father fell sick and your mother came and said that she has a son who will come back one day and the gallery is his! And we signed. Whenever you want, it is yours. Now in fact there's lots of work, a good living, after the war. People are buying apartments, there's lots of people with money, they're digging trenches in Sinai. . . . There are apartments and people want pictures, so things are going good. Israelis . . . And there's already a standard, almost like in Poland, you remember, Hirschberg, Rozenzweig's house?

Destroyed in the bombing, said Hirschberg.

Yes, but before. What a collection there was there . . . all originals. Hirschbein, Plotokeni, Abramson, Yitzhok Cavdoini, Holeme Schwend, what painters! But it was all destroyed by the Nazis.

And then he said that my mother had renewed the contract seven months ago.

I translated to Mira.

Allenby Street was noisy and cars packed up at the traffic light. We ate ice cream at Vitman's. I told Mira that for a moment I'd been happy inside my father's shop. The smell, the cardboard, the turpentine.

She said that she understands.

Maybe that's what I was meant to be, I said to her, a frame-maker.

She didn't answer.

I said, Maybe really. Maybe my mother knew things that I didn't know.

All right then, take over the shop and make a melodrama of your life if you want to.

Do I want to?

36

I'm approaching the end. To walk with eyes open toward a disaster, I said, I wanted to go back and I couldn't. At the beginning of things which are a journey because the Hebrew word for book is the Greek for journey. And the other way around. You sit and search for yourself outside. All your life. Suddenly you discover that maybe not. And here you are opposite yourself. Inside yourself. There had been women, things had happened. A daughter had been born. A father had died. An apartment with bougainvillaea. Mira came back and my neighbor became a grandfather. He had strangled a baby and fathered a granddaughter. Tomorrow we'll sit facing the screen, what will we see there? People cry at movies and return to being the hypocrites they were, art doesn't really purify. Aristotle didn't tell the whole truth. A person doesn't become better because of a Guernica by Picasso. The pain of one is the laughter of another, the death of my father is the laughter I laughed this morning with Mira in bed. The rolls that Naomi brought, they're the rolls I brought my father thirty-three years ago. Which of Naomi's granddaughters will know that there once lived a man whose name was Aminadav Sussetz. A tiny corner of Italy, named Toscana, brought to the world Piero della Francesca, Piero di Cosimo, Giotto, Botticelli, Cimabue, Filippo Lippi, Paolo Uccello, Sacchiati, Signorelli, Leonardo da Vinci and Michelangelo. Who can say what was the crucial influence of the

403

development of transistors in Japan on the sociology of Africa. People heard what they heard. They came out of holes. And heard the Voice of America. The Indians, who hate war, invented chess. Ice cream was brought to Europe by the Moslems from China, via India. Howard Johnson isn't such a Yankee. Alcohol, which is forbidden to Moslems, is an Arabic word. The methods of distillation of alcohol used in Ireland and Scotland are derived from the Arab world. Arsalen waits in many corners. *Geshem* is the Hebrew for what in English is rain, but in Chinese it's like this:

雨

At the sight of this sign a Chinese boy recalls the drainpipes of his Tel Aviv. Everything mixes together. Everything's connected. My kindergarten teacher Hava has received many men in her boat. It turns out that Nadiv has been there, and the studio manager too. On the evening of Gav Rapp's gala premiere I had been given hints that another two of the evening's heroes had been in my kindergarten teacher's wonderful boat. We'd met in unexpected places. We'd traveled to different places. We'll arrive at the same place. What will I see in my father's eyes on the screen. I had made the movie for his sake but he isn't here and now Mira will sit in his place. Mother's offended. She hasn't been invited. But I explained to her that to hurt more than is necessary is something I don't want. The studio manager is nice to me. And not because of Hava the kindergarten teacher but because his glorious movie had received bad reviews abroad. And the Foreign Office is alarmed. Overseas they say it's a very poor Levantine film. The festival it was aimed for has refused to accept it for screening. The studio manager's in a dither. He doesn't know what to do. Now he's waiting for me.

What will I see in my movie.

Will I discover.

Have I already discovered.

A journey.

Where to.

From myself to myself.

Waiting for myself, smoking a pipe like Father, I recall a passage from Natan of Gaza: "Tie connections and start into battle, and make a boat that will cross the sea in storm, for we found no provisions for the way. And a great sleep fell upon me." I want to paint, on canvas, on a movie screen, in the camouflage of myself to myself, the impure birds that will kidnap holy souls. And here's a man, and the man uproots a mountain, and the more that he uproots he becomes big and small, and the man is a messiah of one single thought, which is the concealed light for us all, and he climbs to the top of the mountain, and there is a big pit, which reaches to the bottom of the mountain, and the messiah falls into it.

I have been a monk of lies. Everything has been in vain. A moment before the in vain there came a flash of hope. Why live for the in vain. In gematria, Sabbatai Zevi is 814. And this number is also *Mashiah sheker*, false messiah, and also *Yeshua ben Miriam*, Jesus son of Mary. I searched, but always outside, and now what I cry I cry inside. Persecuted. Holy sinners were the delights of my greatest moments. Mira on the toilet bowl. Sabbatai Zevi marrying a whore from Poland. What have I brought. What have we all brought. 814 is also *ruah sheker*, lying spirit.

There's a little poem about me somewhere:

> As I was going up the stair
> I met a man who wasn't there.
> He wasn't there again today.
> I wish to God he'd go away.

An empty chair for my father who isn't there, in the studio. This silence. Air-conditioning and black curtains over the doors. Thirty-five thousand lira for this one evening. Ansberg, Mira, Ivria and I. What I saw on the screen was lacking in importance. I saw a birth and Little Tel Aviv and Ansberg dressed up as my father going to father me. I saw the pleasures of Tel Aviv and Gan-Rina presenting and the Eden Cinema and The Jazz Singer. I saw Aminadav coming into being and being born. One day, one day on which a man is born, on sand, forty-two thousand inhabitants, forty buffalo, *badim badim,* a whore from Naples, in thirty minutes something frightening was spread out, fragments making a painting, I saw a painting living, becoming, going wild. To hold Mira's hands, to think that she's here, with me, to see the sweet gazelles, the harelipped Valentino with his religious girlfriend. To see flashes of life and death. To see a settlement grow into a city, flowers, the lion's jaw, raisins inside the cake, a tombstone inside my father's eyes, horror, and Mamushka.

To see things that are more than things and less than things. Cutting has a grammar of its own. Everything comes to be and negates itself at one and the same time. Dead and living. I and not I. A man wants to understand what's happening to him. This darkness.

Will I burn it. The darkness gives me cover. Goya's Execution.

And there's no knowing if I wanted to or not. I failed at not being born. The isn't isn't. The is—is. I see nothing but pictures, celluloid gleams of light and shade and color and forms and quick transitions and cuts. No more than that.

The lights go on. My father's empty chair is emptier than it was.

I sit with my head between my hands.

I'm ashamed.

I want to die.

What I saw was what was always in me. The total of the things together did not bring any new turn. And Mira came up to me and said that it was beautiful, the most beautiful thing I'd ever created.

Ansberg and Ivria stare. Ivria who'd seen everything hadn't seen a thing, and now she's dazed.

Nothing worked out for me.

I'll return to Mr. Zwiegel. Tomorrow I'll have breakfast with him and we'll hang a movie in his gallery, we'll drink coffee and eat *kuchen.* I want to die.

Why did I die? So I could die again.

The studio manager, from the desert. Goes out and smokes a cigarette butt. To Venice, he shouts, this is a film for the festival!

406

You'll go to Venice for me, you'll bring me back all the money I lost because of that *potz* Kopol, this is a film for prizes, it's beautiful as hell. . . . They don't understand how terrible it is. I want to die. To die.

We'll be rich, said the studio manager.

I want to burn it.

They look at me. Mother and he. A boy and his father. The death of the dying. The eyes of the stubborn silence. The war for life in Goethean formulas. You know how good it is, the studio manager said to me, with five experts repeating it after him. Mr. Sherriff, a well-known critic, asks for details: how much did it cost, how much time, who gave me the idea, did I write the script myself.

I drink wine from a bottle that Ivria had the sense to bring for me. I want to die.

I smoke my father's pipe.

My eyes on Father's empty chair.

Is he laughing in his grave.

There's no laughing in graves.

Mother has atrophied laugh muscles.

Then I closed my eyes. I'd always known that in the heavenly hierarchy there are 7,405,926 demons. But how many angels? Now I saw heaven, and here are all the angels, whose number is beyond measure, and they're gathering to receive those who are to come into the gates of heaven, and Tattiel says to Gabriel, Gabri dear, you said that a man called Aminadav, the son of Naftali and Rivka Sussetz, was arriving, where is he? And Gabriel smiles his mournful angelic smile and says, Tatti dear, he just passed us, but you blinked. And we missed him.

All my life. This movie. My birthday. A blink.

I went outside. Mira with the studio manager and Ivria to consult. They speak of their experiences. I walk in the corridor. I want to die. I want to phone Mother and say to her, Go to the cemetery, tell Father. I go into a small room and pick up a receiver. The operator gives me a line. I ring Marhayim.

Aminadav Sussetz speaking.

How are you.

Everything's fine, Marhayim, how about you?
Living.
Writing music?
Yes.
Ever written for movies?
Yes.
I need music for a film.
How long?
Twenty-eight and a half minutes.
When can I see it?
Tomorrow.
Where?
At the Herzlia Studios.
O.K.
Marhayim?
Yes.
They want to send it to a festival.
O.K.
See you.
Yes.

So close your eyes, to travel into yourself. Not to destroy. Black spaces are a mystery to me. I wrote things about my shame. Every man decorates the tablets of his heart with afflictions, as demons weave tales. Tales. So afflictions become fine and transparent. There is no reality except what appears. How terrible. I want to die. My father placed afflictions in fetters. A smashed violin is my father. Mira, Naomi and I. My mother will cry, and she'll buy a new dress for the festival in Venice. We'll eat pasta. There is morning and sudden rain. The melody of drainpipes sings childhood. Which is no more. In winter the flowering of the citrus. I'll put on a gray suit and a red tie for Venice. It suits me. Mira and Ansberg go outside. The studio manager is looking for me and I come.